Traci Douglass is a *USA TODAY* bestselling romance author with Harlequin/Mills & Boon, Entangled Publishing and Tule Publishing, and has an MFA in Writing Popular Fiction from Seton Hill University. She writes sometimes funny, usually awkward, always emotional stories about strong, quirky, wounded characters overcoming past adversity to find their for ever person. Heartfelt Healing Happily-Ever-Afters. Connect with her through her website: tracidouglassbooks.com.

Deanne Anders was reading romance while her friends were still reading Nancy Drew, and she knew she'd hit the jackpot when she found a shelf of Harlequin Presents in her local library. Years later she discovered the fun of writing her own. Deanne lives in Florida, with her husband and their spoiled Pomeranian. During the day she works as a nursing supervisor. With her love of everything medical and romance, writing for Mills & Boon Medical Romance is a dream come true.

Also by Traci Douglass

Costa Rican Fling with the Doc
Island Reunion with the Single Dad
Their Barcelona Baby Bombshell
A Mistletoe Kiss in Manhattan

Also by Deanne Anders

Sarah and the Single Dad
The Neurosurgeon's Unexpected Family
December Reunion in Central Park
Florida Fling with the Single Dad

Discover more at millsandboon.co.uk.

THE GP'S ROYAL SECRET

TRACI DOUGLASS

PREGNANT WITH THE SECRET PRINCE'S BABIES

DEANNE ANDERS

MILLS & BOON

First published in Great Britain 2022
by Mills & Boon, an imprint of HarperCollins*Publishers* Ltd,
1 London Bridge Street, London, SE1 9GF

www.harpercollins.co.uk

HarperCollins*Publishers*
1st Floor, Watermarque Building,
Ringsend Road, Dublin 4, Ireland

ISBN: 978-0-263-30148-9

12/22

This book is produced from independently certified FSC™ paper
to ensure responsible forest management.
For more information visit: www.harpercollins.co.uk/green.

Printed and Bound in Spain using 100% Renewable Electricity
at CPI Black Print, Barcelona

THE GP'S ROYAL SECRET

TRACI DOUGLASS

MILLS & BOON

CHAPTER ONE

PRINCE DAVIAN MICHAEL JULIAN HENRY CONSTANTINE DE LOROSO had planned all the details of this trip so carefully for his father, the King of Ruclecia, right down to the ports they would visit on their impromptu two-week-long Mediterranean cruise to the selection of crew members. Everything should have been perfect. Unfortunately, it was anything but—starting with the contrary disposition of the chef he'd hired. The chef who was currently arguing vehemently in French with the chief steward, a congenial American named Noah, as Davian intervened. He'd mastered three big *D*'s in his life—diplomacy, determination, and becoming a world-renowned doctor. Davian refused to add defeated to the list because of one irate chef.

"Listen to me," Davian said to François, the chef in question, summoning his most placating tone. The same one that he used to soothe the overblown egos of some surgeons when he taught them cutting-edge techniques to improve their skills. "Please put down the meat cleaver. Let's remain calm."

"Non," François said, pointing to Noah with the cleaver. "Not until he leaves my galley."

The galley in question was on board the *Querencia*, the mega-yacht Davian had hired for this trip. She had recently been refitted with updated technology and security features, as well as amenities, making her the obvious choice for a quick escape from a recently developing threat in their tiny island nation. Normally on yachts, even the mega ones, the kitchen facilities could be smaller and cramped. But not so with the *Querencia.* At one hundred and eighty feet, the *Querencia* was bigger and better than anything else on the sea and that went for her galley too. Sparkling tile floors, sparkling top-tier stainless-steel appliances, sparkling utensils and equipment. No expense had been spared. Nothing but the best for the royal family of Ruclecia.

At least those in line for the throne. As the spare to the heir, Davian had been regulated to second-tier status, like a built-in advisor and assistant to his family rather than a titled prince, obligated to do his duty but not overshadow those above him in the line of succession. Even so, he'd managed to carve out a life he loved for himself. He'd never wanted the power, and the headaches that came with it. He was more than content to follow his own ambitions and dreams, to help those who needed his skills as a doctor and surgeon and make the world a better place. And today, that started with keeping the peace of his well-chosen crew.

"Chef François, put down the cleaver and please explain what our chief steward said to upset you so," Davian tried again. "Was it about your menu?"

"He said my *fines ravioles potagères au consommé ambré* looked like *vomi anémique*!"

A long stream of invectives hurled in rapid-fire French followed. Davian closed his eyes and took a deep breath. Even if Davian hadn't spoken six languages, the fact that each curse was punctuated by a slam of the cleaver into the wooden carving board made it abundantly clear his highly regarded, three-starred Michelin chef was deeply offended by what was probably an off-hand comment by the chief stew.

Davian had gone to medical school in America and done most of his residency there, so he understood their humor. François, on the other hand, obviously did not. Heat from the galley prickled Davian's face and neck. It had to be close to triple digits in there, with all the cooking and shouting happening. And even all the port-holes being open didn't help. Most likely because they'd set off from Gibraltar earlier that morning and August in the Mediterranean had been the hottest month of the year so far.

"That's not what I said," Noah said from behind Davian. "I said perhaps they needed a bit more color before we served them to the King and Queen."

"Bâtard! Tu mens!"

"Stop!" Davian said, giving each man a stern stare. Both men had been hired because of their impeccable résumés and skills. He didn't want to fire either. Just keep them from killing each other for the duration of this cruise. Davian looked down at the plates of food ready to be delivered upon his parents' arrival and sighed. They did look a bit…bland, but then bland was what his father's health required at present. After a major heart attack and quadruple bypass surgery the previous year, King Phillipe was on a strict diet for the foreseeable future to keep his risk factors for another cardiac event low. Another reason they were on this impromptu cruise. Whispers of assassination threats tended to raise one's blood pressure considerably. Especially when the Ruclecian royal family had already lost one member to a bullet. Davian sometimes still dreamed about the day his beloved grandfather had been shot…

Another whack of the cleaver into the cutting board jarred Davian out of his memories and back to the present situation.

"Right. Well, I think these dishes look *très bien*," he told François. "And since I am your employer, my opinion is the only one that matters."

That seemed to appease the chef, since François slowly lowered the cleaver back down to the counter, where Davian quickly claimed it. Used to handling scalpels, he found the cleaver's weight was a bit unsettling. Still, there was no way he was letting François get his hands on the thing again. Not right now, anyway.

"*Merci*, Chef," Davian said to François then turned to Noah, who still stood behind him, his expression stoic with an undercurrent of antipathy. The relationship between a chef and a chief stew was always fraught with a bit of that, Davian had learned from his years on board his father's yachts.

Almost like siblings, he thought.

Heaven knew Davian and his older brother, Arthur, had their share of issues with each other.

And while Davian had been sent to the same schools and traveled to the same places over the years as his older brother, it was always made clear that they were different. Arthur would one day become King. Davian would only ascend if something awful happened to his father and his brother, and any male children his brother might have. The royal guard and Ruclecian security forces worked day and night to make sure that never happened. Not that Davian wasn't important in the system though. He had other uses. Like playing travel agent, or diplomat, or even fiancé, when needed, only to be quickly shoved aside when the need no longer existed.

As an accomplished man with goals and dreams of his own, he was sick of it.

He'd disrupted his own life more times than he could count for his family and enough was enough. After this cruise was over and the assassination threat had passed, Davian planned to sit down with his parents and tell them he was done. No more neglecting his life and his medical career for the sake of his royal duties. He'd been through a lifetime of putting his family needs and obligations ahead of his own and now he was done. He just had to get through this last cruise first.

"Noah, once my parents and their guests have arrived and settled in, please have your staff take these plates up to them in the main dining room," Davian said in the voice he used in his operating rooms, the precise one that brooked no argument. Then he turned back to the chef. "And François, carry on with dinner preparations. No more comments from either of you on the other's performance. Understood?"

"Yes, sir," Noah grumbled, stepping forward to grab three plates while his second stew did the same.

"Oui," mumbled François.

"Good." Davian then started out of the galley in the opposite direction, toward the stairs leading up to the private cabins, where he'd been headed when this whole debacle started. He made it up two steps when an announcement crackled over the yacht's PA system from the captain.

"All medical personnel to the bridge stat. All medical personnel to the bridge for an emergency."

With a curse, Davian changed directions and sprinted back through the galley and up a different set of stairs to the bridge, adrenaline pumping again. Seemed his work was never done on this cruise.

* * *

"Mommy, what's that?"

Dr. Cate Neves gazed over at the huge limestone promontory near the southernmost tip of the Iberian Peninsula and smiled. "That, Adella, is the Rock of Gibraltar."

The five-year-old frowned, scrunching her nose up. "It's really big."

"Yes, it is." Cate chuckled then crouched beside her daughter on the deck of the *Querencia*, the luxury megayacht she'd been hired to act as assistant physician on for this voyage. She then turned her daughter around to face the opposite shoreline again, resting her chin on the little girl's shoulder while keeping an arm around her waist to hold her close as the wind blew around them. "See that land there? That's Morocco." Then Cate turned with Adella in her arm to face the opposite direction. "In Africa. We're currently between two continents."

"What's a continent?" Adella asked. She was full of questions these days. Same as Cate had been at that age. "And where are we going?"

"A continent is a large landmass." Cate straightened and took her daughter's hand. They'd be on board this yacht for the next two weeks and she intended to make the most of it, showing her daughter all the amazing things you could see and experience while traveling. "And we're sailing the Mediterranean for Mommy's work, remember?"

"Who do you work for, Mommy? And why do you work on a boat?" Adella tugged free and ran over to sit on one of the outdoor sofas on the *Querencia*'s uppermost deck with her new favorite stuffed animal, a monkey named Fred. She was at that age where everything was an endless stream of "why" questions.

"Well, on this cruise I work for Dr. Will." With a sigh, Cate walked over and joined her daughter, sinking into the plush royal blue cushions and staring out at the horizon. It was around noon now and the mist was finally burning off. The Spanish locals here called it *levanta* and it was common most days, what with the water and air temperatures between the colder Atlantic and the warmer Mediterranean. The sun and wind would drive it off soon enough.

Cate had learned a lot about sailing over the past five years, first by working on board cruise ships as a doctor and now in locum tenses support positions on private vessels like the *Querencia*. This was the first time, however, she'd signed on without knowing anything about the primary clients on board. They'd made her sign all sorts of nondisclosure agreements and privacy clauses. A formality, Dr. William Bryant had said. Nothing more. And the pay for this voyage was incredible, so she couldn't say no. Not if she wanted to start her own practice once she got back to the States after this last cruise. She'd been squirreling away funds since she'd graduated from Stanford medical school five years ago to make her dream come true and now it was finally so close she could taste it. And the fact that this whole job had appeared basically out of the blue… Well, it seemed like fate.

So, with just a general reassurance from Will that this cruise was above board and did not involve any mafia or oligarchs or anything, plus with the agreement that she could bring her daughter, Adella, with her, Cate had signed on the dotted line. Still, Cate couldn't help wondering who could afford to charter a ship like this, plus pay all the crew and expenses that went along with running it.

"Mommy? Do we have to go back downstairs again? I like it up here."

"I like it up here too, sweetie." She ran her fingers through her daughter's long black hair, left loose today to hang down her back in a riot of curls and clipped on the side with two rainbow barrettes. "But Mommy needs to finish stocking her clinic and you need to have some lunch, so yes. We must go back downstairs soon."

She'd taken a quick break and come up and seen the Port of Gibraltar from the uppermost deck. It was one of her favorite things since she'd first started sailing. So pretty and peaceful. Except when the wind picked up and the water got choppy, like now.

After they'd restocked supplies and fuel here at Gibraltar and the rest of the guests arrived, they'd continue into the Mediterranean, stopping in Marseille, and Monaco, before finishing in Sicily. A short, relaxing trip. And after the past five years, struggling to survive as a single mother, Cate deserved this hopefully relaxing break. Not that she wasn't working. She was. But most of the time, the worst she dealt with on these luxury trips were the occasional stomach ailment or migraine. Every so often, there'd be something more serious though, like heatstroke or cardiac issues—like the primary guest on this cruise had, according to the brief overview she'd been given by Will earlier—but hopefully, this trip would fall more on the easier side.

After one long, last glance at the gorgeous scenery, Cate stood and smoothed a hand down the front of her white shirt and pants, standard medical uniform on board the *Querencia*, before reaching for her daughter's hand. "C'mon, sweetie. Time to go."

The little girl sighed, then slid down off her seat, staring up at Cate with the same blue eyes as her father. A man she hadn't seen in five years. By choice, since he'd lied to her about who he was and left her when she'd need him most. Cate had grown up with a father like that already and didn't want or need more of that in her life now. "Can we visit that big rock while we're here, Mommy? I'd like to climb it."

Cate smiled as they started downstairs toward the crew cafeteria. "Not this time, sweetie. But maybe we can come back someday, just you and I, and spend some time here. What do you say?"

"I'd like that." Adella grinned, making Cate's heart pinch. That grin she remembered too. In fact, she remembered everything about the man who'd deceived her about everything. But then if it wasn't for him, Cate wouldn't have her daughter, so she couldn't regret it entirely.

Adella whispered something to her stuffed monkey then said, "Fred likes it here too. And he's hungry. Can I have fruit for lunch, Mommy?"

"We'll see what the chef put out today." The yacht not only had all the amenities for its passengers, but they also had a great setup for the crew as well with the chef-prepared buffets for each meal for them. And between the stewards and the deckhands, she always had someone to watch Adella for her when Cate couldn't. She knew most of them from working together on previous cruises and considered them friends. After getting fruit for her daughter and eggs and a cup of much-needed coffee for herself from the buffet, they settled at a table near the wall to eat quickly. Cate had just sat down when the call came over the PA system.

"All medical personnel to the bridge stat. All medical personnel to the bridge for an emergency."

Cate was on her feet and signaling for one of her

crewmates, a third stew named Andy. She and Cate had quickly become close friends on the *Querencia.* Andy had joined the crew to help her recover after the loss of her wife to leukemia. They'd been together for almost twenty years. Loving and losing left scars. Cate knew that from experience. Her own father had walked out on her and her mother when Cate was just ten. "Andy's going to watch you until I get back, okay? Mommy needs to go."

Cate ran down the hall to the clinic and grabbed her medic bag then raced up the stairs to the bridge. She had no idea what she'd encounter once she got there, but she'd seen plenty of emergencies during her residency in California and her work since. So much so that she'd even considered doing that as her specialty rather than general practice at one point. But life intervened and she'd needed the steady work hours being a GP provided to be there for Adella. Now, as she raced toward who knew what, her blood pumped and her heart raced and she relished the urgency.

"Dr. Cate Neves," she announced as she burst onto the bridge and weaved through the people gathered there, without really looking at them. Her complete focus was on the female crew member on the floor, apparently unconscious. She pulled out her stethoscope to check the woman's vitals. "What happened here?"

"They were cleaning the artifacts in the case over there," Captain Stan said. "She'd put on gloves to remove one of the statues and had this reaction. She's cleaned them many times before, so we thought it was fine."

Another crew member held up the box and Cate gave a curt nod.

Classic latex allergy. They often developed after repeated exposures and in some cases could become life-threatening, as appeared to be the case here. You never knew when someone might have a bad reaction, which was why Cate never used latex gloves in her practice. But she'd never lost a patient before and wasn't about to start now.

She focused on the patient again, as she dug into her bag for the EpiPen she always kept stashed there for emergencies. A quick dose of epinephrine into an anaphylactic patient helped them recover much faster. "Someone please call 112 and have an ambulance ready to take this crew member to the hospital in Gibraltar. And does anyone else here have basic medical training to assist me?"

"I do," a man said, the voice deep and oddly familiar. "I'm a doctor as well."

He weaved through the crowd on the bridge and knelt opposite Cate. She hazarded a glance up at the new arrival and…

Oh, God! No. It couldn't be.

And yet, it was. The man who'd disappeared from her life five years ago. Adella's father.

David Laurence.

At least that was the name he'd gone by during residency.

The name of the man she'd studied with, fallen in love with.

Except it was all a lie. Everything about him had been a lie.

If she hadn't been so well trained in emergency situations, Cate might have frozen. As it was, her surprise paralysis only lasted a few seconds before she snapped out of it and continued working on her patient. The woman's breathing had become more labored, and a nasty allergic rash now spread up her arms and neck. Time for the EpiPen. Cate pinched the woman's thigh and jammed the needle in to administer the lifesaving drug, then checked the woman's pulse and respirations again. Most times the results were dramatic, stopping the anaphylaxis in its tracks.

"Is the ambulance on the way?" Cate asked one of the crew standing by as she noticed the patient's breathing had become deeper and more regular already. The rash was going down too. Good signs.

Her gaze flicked up to the man across from her who was taking the patient's pulse and Cate's own heart stumbled once more. What in the hell was Adella's father, the man who'd walked out of Cate's life five years ago, doing on board the *Querencia*?

"Ambulance is here, doc," the crew member said, jarring Cate back to the present. "The medics are bringing in a gurney."

"Thank you." Cate glanced up at her ex again to find him scowling in concentration, an expression she recognized from their years of working together. He looked nearly the same as the last time she'd seen him—still tanned, toned and gorgeous. Short dark hair and cerulean blue eyes. Her chest squeezed and she looked away fast as the patient groaned, the woman's eyelids fluttering as she came around.

"Alice?" Cate patted the crew member's cheek lightly. "It's Dr. Neves. Do you remember what happened?"

The patient tried to sit up, but Cate placed a hand on the woman's chest to keep her from moving.

"N-no," Alice said, her white ship's uniform rumpled from the collapse. "Wh-where am I? Why is everyone staring at me?"

"You had an allergic reaction to the latex gloves you

were wearing. Has that ever happened to you before, Alice?" Cate pulled an IV kit out of her medical bag and began swabbing the woman's arm while she waited for an answer.

"N-no. I don't have any allergies, that I'm aware of."

"Well, now you do." Cate tossed the alcohol pad she'd used into the trash then opened the IV kit. Best to put it in now so the medics could give Alice fluids on the way to the hospital. "I'll be sure to fill the medics in on what happened here so your doctor at the hospital can go over it all with you. I'm going to put another needle into your arm, Alice. You'll feel a quick stick and that's it. Okay?"

Alice nodded and Cate hit the vein on her first try then taped the cannula into place. "All done."

"Wh-why can't I remember anything?" The woman blinked up at Cate, tears forming in her eyes. "Wh-what's happening to me?"

"Disorientation is normal after an episode like yours. Don't worry, Alice. Rest now. You just had a bad reaction to the latex gloves you were wearing, but I've given you a shot of epinephrine and you should make a full recovery. We've got an ambulance here now to take you to the hospital for an all clear, just to be on the safe side."

Behind Cate, the medics arrived and brought the gurney in. She moved out of the way, giving the medics the rundown of the incident and the patient's current vitals as they got Alice started on IV fluids then prepared to take her out to the ambulance. David stayed by Cate's side, his arm occasionally brushing hers in the crowded bridge area, making a rush of unwanted awareness shimmer through her nervous system. It had always been like that between them.

Instant connection. Prolonged hurt.

Alice groaned again. "Where are they taking me?"

"To the local medical center in Gibraltar, ma'am," one of the medics said. "We'll take good care of you, I promise."

"Pulse is back in normal range and so is her b/p," the other paramedic said. "Good response to the EpiPen. Dr. Neves." The man's gaze flicked to David and widened slightly before he bowed. "And you, Your Highness."

Cate's hackles rose and she forced her tense shoulders to relax. Yes, her ex, David Laurence, had turned out to be none other than Prince Davian de Loroso of the tiny, wealthy European island nation of Ruclecia. Just one of the things he'd lied to her about when they'd been together in college, making Cate believe he was only a young, ambitious medical student like herself, working his way through school to follow his dreams. None of it was true, of course, but she'd been so naive and in love, she'd bought it hook, line and sinker, until it was too late. Even now, anger buzzed inside her, mainly at herself. Seeing what her own mother had gone through, raising Cate on her own and dealing with the heartbreak of being left behind, Cate had sworn to never be taken in like that again. It was the main reason she'd stayed on her own so long. If you didn't put yourself out there, you didn't get hurt.

"Stay calm, Alice. You're doing great. Once you get those IV fluids in your system, you'll feel a lot better and be back on board before you know it." Cate patted the woman's hand in sympathy, noting the rash on Alice's arms was nearly gone now too.

"I'll go with her to the hospital," another crew member said, stepping forward. "To make sure she makes it back before we leave port."

* * *

She waited until the patient was gone before she stooped to repack her medical bag. Davian crouched beside her to help.

"We should talk, Cate," he said, his blue gaze locked on Cate's green eyes. A myriad of emotions flitted there—shock, confusion, hurt, hesitation—though he kept his stoic facade in place the same as Cate. But it was still unsettling to find the same blue eyes her daughter Adella had inherited staring back at her now after all these years. "I… I never expected to see you today."

"That makes two of us," Cate hissed, keeping her voice low to avoid the other crew on the bridge hearing. She shoved the last items into her bag and zipped it up before straightening. "I need to get back to my clinic now."

Cate turned and left without waiting for a response from Davian. As far as she was concerned, the fact he'd vanished into thin air five years ago without even a goodbye said more than enough already.

CHAPTER TWO

AFTER THE EMERGENCY on the bridge, Davian stood at the railing of the ship, overlooking the Port of Gibraltar, enjoying a few quiet moments alone and replaying the moment he'd seen the last person he'd ever thought he'd see again—Cate Neves. It was still hard to fathom that she was on board the ship. Of all the medical clinics in all the world…

Then again, fate had thrown them together before, so he probably shouldn't be so surprised it was doing so again. Especially considering he'd hired one of their old professors from Stanford, Dr. Will Bryant, to be chief medical officer on board this cruise, and given him full authority to fill out his staff as he saw fit. Especially since Dr. Bryant had been one of the few people who'd known Davian's true identity back then…

Cate had looked as effortlessly gorgeous as he remembered. Long honey-blond hair, streaked with platinum, secured back in an efficient ponytail, her wide green eyes reminding Davian of the emerald hills of Ruclecia, and her body…the same body that had filled his fantasies for the past five years.

Cate was the one who got away.

No. More precisely, Cate was the one he'd let go. Because he'd had no choice.

Stop it.

Imagining what might have been did him no good now. For all his pragmatism and acumen, sometimes Davian's daydreams turned his own stomach. He had his duties, his career. The life he'd built for himself. He needed to be content with that. Cate had moved on, obviously, and they were different people now than they had been back in college.

Davian did wonder about her serving on a luxury yacht though. Back in residency, Cate had been focused on serving underprivileged communities and finding solutions to health disparities in underserved patient populations. Big difference between that and serving the rich and famous on yachts. Had she given up on her dreams? Changed her mind?

That didn't strike true. Cate had never been a person who gave up easily.

Most likely she'd seen the headlines of his engagement. What a joke that whole debacle had been. Arranged when Davian had barely been out of diapers to the daughter of an advantageous political ally, he'd had no say and even less choice in the matter. It had been revealed to the world when it suited his family's royal agenda. Just one more example of him being used as a pawn in a bigger game of power and PR his family participated in with the wider world. The worst thing was, Davian understood why they did it. It made sense. As the ruling family of Ruclecia, a country whose main economic engine was tourism, they needed to project a certain appearance of wealth and prestige to the rest of the world to keep people coming in. And perhaps even more importantly, he loved his family. They were good people. But they also had duties to uphold. And from the time he'd been old enough to understand such things, Davian had been taught that duty came before all else in life.

Until now, he'd believed it, lived by it.

But things had changed and his time with Cate in college had been a part of that. For the first time, he'd had a taste of what life might have been like if he'd not been royal, if he'd had the opportunity to live as others did—with freedom. Yet just when he'd thought perhaps he and Cate might have a life together after medical school, reality had landed hard on him once more. His father had fallen ill because of heart issues and Davian had been forced to flee back to Ruclecia like a thief in the night. He'd always intended to return to Cate as soon as possible, but again, his duty interceded. To throw the press off the story of his father's illness, and against Davian's will, the palace PR team had leaked news of his engagement to the press, and Davian had been forced to go through the motions of a sham engagement to Namina, his childhood arranged bride. She'd not wanted to marry him any more than he had her, but by the time his father had recovered and the engagement had been called off, it was too late. The damage had been done. He'd felt betrayed and furious. Heartbroken when he'd returned to Stanford only to find that Cate was gone. She'd graduated and moved on without him. He'd spent about a month in California, sorting through all his emotions and deciding what to do from there. He'd tried to call her, tried to make contact, but had never heard anything back from Cate. In the end, he'd finished his last few courses and graduated himself, then returned to Ruclecia alone to start over and begin his career there. For the past five years, he'd lived quietly, doing what was best for the people of his country and practicing medicine, always dreaming about the day he could walk away from the royal life when his brother became King and Davian could then immerse himself full-time in his medical career and his hospital.

He sighed and leaned his forearms on the railing, inhaling deep the sea breeze blowing in his face.

His mind still couldn't quite believe Cate was here, now, after all these years. Seeing her had been…

They'd lost so much time. There was so much water under the bridge.

Not that he could blame her for moving on from him, not after the way he'd left. Not after how he'd deceived her about his true identity. Again, that had been his father's doing, not Davian's. He'd insisted Davian attended Stanford under a false name for security reasons and Davian had agreed because he would have done anything to pursue his dreams. But still, it was no excuse for how he'd handled things with Cate. At the time, he'd thought it was for the best, but now…

Dammit.

Dredging all this up again was worthless. It was all done. Over. He needed to let it go and stay focused on the work in front of him. This cruise, his family, the upcoming talk with his parents.

Except once again, more images of Cate on the bridge filled his stubborn mind.

He pictured her as she'd knelt across from him as they locked eyes again for the first time, all the emotions flickering through her lovely eyes—surprise, hurt, anger, anxiety. How those walls of hers had slammed down again as she'd walked away from him this time. Part of him had wanted to run after her, to beg her to allow him to explain why he'd left all those years ago, but what was the point? At best, they'd have fourteen days to get reacquainted, then go their separate ways again.

No. It was better to leave things as they were. Simpler.

Since when have you ever been simple?

With a sigh, Davian straightened and fiddled with his aqua silk tie then buttoned his suit jacket. It was way too hot here to be so formal, but his parents would expect him in a suit and right now it was easier to appease than to argue about it. He glanced over at the dock as their injured crew member returned to the yacht by taxi, then saw the deckhands begin working the large mechanical metal spools to bring up the anchor so they could finally set sail. How had Cate ended up working on a yacht? Did she enjoy it? Remembering her carefree nature back in college, he suspected she would.

Making his way back toward his stateroom, he thought about working with her to help the patient on the bridge. The same awareness shimmering through his bloodstream despite the circumstances, how it had always been like that between them from the first time they'd met.

CHAPTER THREE

CATE WAS JUST finishing up restocking the supply cabinet in the yacht's small medical clinic. It was one of the guest cabins they'd quickly renovated for this charter. In her experience, most super-yachts didn't have medical personnel aboard unless the primary guests brought their own, but this trip was different. In more ways than one.

Adella was with chef François in the galley, helping him clean vegetables for dinner tonight. All the crew loved having Cate's daughter on board and everyone took turns spending days with her whenever Cate had other duties to attend to. Talk about a village to raise a child. It was one of the things Cate would miss when she left after this charter. The sense of family and close friends aboard. Even when she'd worked on the larger cruise ships when she'd first started out, that camaraderie had been there, though it was more close-knit with a smaller yacht crew. Back home in Boston, it was usually just her and Adella at the apartment, or sometimes Cate's mother too, when she came over to babysit or spend the weekend with them. Her mom and Adella were close and Cate loved seeing her mother tell Adella some of the same family stories she'd told Cate growing up or teaching her how to make some of the recipes that had been passed down for generations.

She'd just completed her daily check of the medicine cabinet and logged her results with Carrie, the clinic's receptionist, when the crew member from earlier, the one with the allergic reaction arrived.

"Hey, doc," Alice said from the doorway of the clinic. She was still a bit pale and her expression sheepish, but otherwise a thousand times better than when she'd left that morning. "Got the all clear to return."

Cate took the discharge papers the woman handed her and glanced over them. "Good. Everything looks fine on here, though I'd advise you take it easy the rest of the day, just to be sure. And stay away from anything latex from here on out, yeah?"

"Will do, doc," Alice said, tucking the papers Cate handed her back into the pocket of her uniform pants. "So weird that it hit me out of nowhere. Never had that happen before."

"Not uncommon for them to build up over time until one day it becomes life-threatening. I've seen it happen with nuts and beestings before too."

"Wow." Before Alice could say anything more, the walkie-talkie on her belt crackled to life and Captain Stan's voice issued forth.

"Captain to Alice. Captain to Alice. Report to the bridge ASAP."

Alice exhaled and shrugged. "Guess it's back to duty for me."

"Guess so," Cate said, smiling. "Don't work too hard."

"I won't, doc." Alice waved before walking away. "See you later."

"Always."

Cate returned to cleaning the clinic and getting it ready for the new set of guests who'd be boarding soon. She didn't know anything about their identities other than their basic medical histories. Both were in their sixties. The woman was healthy with only the normal hypertension and arthritis issues typically seen in patients that age. The man, however, had serious cardiac problems post–quadruple bypass surgery the previous year. He was on a variety of medications and was regularly checked by a top-notch cardiologist. Cate was anxious to meet her patients and get to know the people she'd be caring for this charter. Or at least she had been until David had shown up.

Not David. Davian.

Why did he have to appear after all these years? After she and Adella had made a life for themselves, independent of him and everything that had happened in the past. Seeing him there on the bridge had been like a sucker punch, stealing her breath and freezing her mind. Luckily, she'd snapped out of it quickly and been able to save the patient.

With Davian's help…

She sighed and hung her head. He'd always been an excellent physician, regardless of what happened between them, and she probably ought to apologize to him for walking away like she had. Five years had passed, so she should be over it by now, right?

Except how exactly did you get over something like that?

In her case, you didn't.

But now she was worried because if Davian was here, aboard the *Querencia*, did that mean he was sailing with them too? Over the years, Cate had worried about the implications of royalty after she'd discovered Davian's true identity. What she knew about how all that worked could fill a thimble, but some internet research did show that as the child of a second son, and the fact that Davian's older brother was married and had two children of his own, it was highly unlikely that Adella would ever be heir of Ruclecia. Still, Davian had been swept back to his country in the middle of the night and engaged within a week—not to mention all the deception and secrecy surrounding his identity and his security—and Cate wanted no part of that for her daughter. So, she'd kept all that from Adella, not really telling her anything about her father. Up until now, it hadn't been a problem, since Cate had doubted she'd ever see Davian again. Except as Adella got older, she'd started asking more questions about who her father was and where he was. And now Davian had appeared in Cate's life again out of the blue and…

What a mess.

Cate had become a shipboard doctor to get away from her past and start fresh, but now she was trapped out at sea with her past for the next two weeks. She sighed and stared up at the ceiling as more memories flooded back.

She'd been so sick those first few weeks of her pregnancy that searching for David had taken everything she'd had. When she'd seen his face splashed all over the news with the story of his upcoming nuptials, her heart had shattered. How could he do that to her? They'd been friends and work colleagues before they'd ever been lovers. They'd talked together, studied together. Cate had felt closer to Davian than anyone else in her life besides her mother. He'd told her he felt the same. So how in the world could he have made love to her, taken their relationship to the next level, knowing he was engaged to another woman? Her heart still ached over that, even five years on. She'd thought David was different, not like her father. Honorable and true. But apparently that wasn't the case at all. Cate had allowed desire and passion to cloud her logic. She'd vowed never to make that mistake again.

By the end of her third trimester, Cate had felt more like herself and accepted the fact David was gone for good. He'd lied about his royal status and the fact she'd been turned away like so much trash told her exactly what she needed to know—that even if he'd told her the truth about who he was, she wasn't good enough to be part of his world. Fine. She'd been independent her whole life and she'd continue to make it on her own. Leaving California behind and making the decision to take to the sea once she'd had Adella had been the best choice Cate had ever made. The money was good, and she got to travel all over the world and show her daughter around all the exotic places they visited. She wouldn't have traded it for anything. That kind of education was priceless.

She didn't need David anymore. She had worked hard the past five years to build the life she'd planned for her and Adella and after this charter she would finally reach her goal of opening her own family practice outside Boston. She'd saved enough money to put a down payment on property and had already researched all the equipment and staff she'd need. Luxury cruises were nice, but her dream had always been to help those most in need and now she could do that full-time. No way would she let Davian derail her again. Even if he still made her pulse trip the same way it always had around him.

"Hey," a voice said from the doorway and Cate looked back to see Noah there with Adella. "Someone's looking for their mom."

"Mommy!" Adella said, running over to jump into Cate's arms and hug her tight around the neck as Cate picked her up and buried her face in her daughter's hair, inhaling the good smell of baby shampoo and sea. "I got to hold a parsnip!"

"Really?" Cate leaned back and grinned at the little girl, then glanced over to Noah. "Thanks for bringing her back."

"No problem. Cap says we need to be on deck in our whites to greet the new guests in five minutes."

"Thanks." Cate carried Adella out into the hall and down a set of spiral stairs to the crew deck and put her in their cabin. Most crew members shared cabins, with bunk beds in each and a small bathroom. But because Cate was traveling with her daughter, they put them in their own cabin. She got Adella settled on the bottom bunk and turned the small TV on for her. "You okay here until Mommy gets done?"

"Yep," Adella said, already occupied with changing one of her doll's outfits. "All good."

"Great." Cate checked her appearance in the mirror. Thankfully, she'd already dressed in her whites this morning in preparation for the guests' arrival. She walked out of the head and kissed the top of her daughter's head before exiting the cabin and hurrying up to the main deck just in time to see a small convoy of three black SUVs with black tinted windows arrive at the dock. Two men got out of the first truck dressed in black suits and sunglasses, clearly bodyguards. They spoke into devices in their ears as they checked the area then were joined by four more men in black from the third SUV. All six men formed a perimeter around the middle SUV as the driver got out and opened the doors to reveal an older couple.

The crew of the *Querencia* had been trained not to gawk at their sometimes famous guests but it was difficult when those guests turned out to be none other than the King and Queen of Ruclecia.

Oh, boy.

Cate's stomach lurched and her mind raced. Davian's parents were here. Which explained why he was on board. But she would have thought that they would have owned a private yacht of their own. That would seem the most secure choice. She obviously wasn't the only one thinking this as a low murmur passed through the crew. Her second thoughts were of Adella. Having the King and Queen aboard meant more chance of someone recognizing her striking resemblance to Davian. Cate felt a bit light-headed at the ramifications. She had some money saved, but not nearly enough to wage a custody fight with royalty.

An urge to grab her daughter and run away was stopped by the approach of the royal couple on the red carpet spread on the dock leading to the ship. Davian stepped out on the main deck and joined his parents on the passerelle to escort them aboard. Cate's heart sank to her toes.

This was not going to go well.

As the party made their way down the receiving line of crew members, Cate hazarded a glance at Davian and found him staring stoically ahead at the wall of the yacht in front of him. He looked about as miserable as Cate felt.

"And this is the ship's physician, Dr. Cate Neves," Davian said as he and his parents reached her. Having watched the other crew members before her, Cate bent into an awkward curtsy.

"Your Majesties," she said.

When she straightened, Cate locked gazes with Davian and her mouth dried. Blood pounding in her ears and, her knees wobbly, she kept her smile in place through sheer force of will until the King and Queen moved on to Noah beside her.

The rest of the day passed in a bit of a blur, and Cate thought perhaps she could get through this by just keeping her head down and concentrating on her work and Adella. But when she fell asleep that night, her dreams were tangled. She was lost and alone. She could see Davian in the distance, but he wasn't looking at her. She couldn't get his attention, couldn't call out for help.

She woke early, tears on her cheeks. She got up and got dressed then got Adella ready. Despite sleeping, she felt exhausted. Sunshine spilled in through the porthole in their cabin and she could hear the deck crew outside as they secured the yacht to the dock in Marseille. They'd traveled through the night to arrive at their first port of call. The *Querencia* creaked and strained against her moorings.

She wondered about Davian's homeland of Ruclecia. From the research she'd done on the place when trying to contact Davian about Adella years ago, it was a gorgeous island nation, filled with green farmland and rugged cliffs dropping off into the Baltic Sea below. Cate had spent hours online clicking through pictures of their coastlines and beautiful medieval architecture. Ruclecians spoke German, English and a smattering of Italian and French. And apparently, their royal family was far more famous than Cate had realized.

The nation had been founded centuries ago as a stronghold for spices and teas from China and their monarchy had become incredibly wealthy because of it. Now the majority of the island nation's GDP came from tourism, along with fishing, farming and clean energy. There were also casinos and horse racing, like they had in Monaco, and Ruclecia was now another tax haven for the world's wealthy.

Which again begged the question: Why were they here?

She sighed as she led Adella down to the galley for breakfast. The simplest thing to do would be to ask Davian, but that would mean talking to him again and Cate wanted to avoid that as much as possible. She had no interest in talking to him—at least for now. Bad enough she had to deal with his parents this cruise, but that was her job. She was paid to do that. Deal with the man who'd broken her heart? Not so much. Yes, eventually, she'd have to confront him and tell him the truth about Adella, but she wanted to wait. Take a little more time to get her own head on straight about it all before she said anything to him.

"Noah!" Adella called and pulled free of Cate's hand as they entered the crew mess and ran over to the chief stew. "I put a new outfit on Jenny! Do you like it?"

Adella held her doll up so the man could see and Noah gushed over the mismatched pink-and-orange ensemble appropriately before catching Cate's eye and winking.

"Stunning!" he said, placing a hand over his heart. "She'll be going to the Met Gala before you know it."

"Met Gala?" Adella scrunched her nose. "What's that?"

As Noah explained the elaborate fundraising party for the New York art museum, Cate went over to get food for her and her daughter, her mind still stuck in the past. She could still remember the day she'd decided to try being a cruise ship physician. Her mother had suggested it after seeing how unhappy Cate was stuck in Boston after Adella was born. Trying to work and be a parent was tough enough and then doing it all with a broken heart had been eating her alive inside. So, Cate's mom had shown her an ad for yacht crew training coming up in Connecticut. At first, she'd been skeptical, but then she'd called about it on a whim and soon she was enrolled. After graduation, she met with two different big cruise lines and was hired the same day. Good pay, no living expenses, free travel, and she'd been able to either take Adella with her or leave her back with her mother. Back then there'd been no downside.

Now though, after four years, Cate was ready to put down roots again. And follow her dreams.

She loaded a tray up with coffee and toast for herself and cereal and milk for Adella then went back to the table. The fact was Davian and his family were there, and she couldn't do anything about that. But she could do something about how she handled it. She'd remain professional but distant and hopefully get through this with as little turbulence as possible. And with all the usual activities and tours the interior crew normally planned for guests on these charters, it was likely she and Davian would see very little of each other. She could keep Adella out of the guest areas and with her down in the clinic. And with Davian's father's medical conditions well controlled already, it seemed unlikely he'd require her services much during the trip.

Once they docked back in Gibraltar, she'd be home free. It was good this was her last charter. Now all she had to do was figure out when, during the next two weeks, she'd sit down with Davian and tell him the truth about his daughter.

Davian woke that morning with purpose. First on his list of priorities, talk to Cate and explain his abrupt disappearance five years ago. He'd asked the captain about the clinic hours last night after dinner and wanted to get there early before Cate got busy and found another reason to avoid him.

He reached the lower deck and headed toward the door at the end of the hall. The yacht must've been recently refitted because everything looked and smelled brand-new—plush carpets, gleaming hardwood paneling, recessed lighting, gold fixtures. He'd just about reached the door to the clinic when it opened suddenly. Cate appeared. Her eyes widened slightly, and her expression fell. Before she could disappear back inside the clinic, Davian rushed forward to stop her. "Cate. Please wait. I just want to talk."

"I'm busy," she mumbled, trying to shut him out, but he wedged his foot in the door, preventing her from closing it on him. He wasn't usually aggressive like this where women were concerned, but it felt like fate that they'd been thrown together like this after all this time, and he didn't want to waste his chance. "You'll have to make an appointment."

"Why? So you can cancel it?" he asked.

He heard her curse under her breath from the other side of the door, then she whispered something to someone else. That gave Davian pause. Did she really have a patient in there? Oh, God. Now he felt awful. He'd not meant to disrupt her life—he just wanted to talk to her, put their past to rest.

Then Cate came out and closed the clinic door behind her, herding him back down the hall to the stairs. They climbed back up and Davian asked, "Where are we going?"

"Sundeck," she said, her tone as clipped as her steps. Yep, she was pissed. Davian couldn't blame her. Even more reason to have this conversation now and clear the air since they'd be stuck on this charter together for the next two weeks. No sense making it any more awkward than it had to be. Besides, he missed her. He always had. Cate led him across the bright, deserted space and over to the railings at the front of the deck. Her hair was secured back in a bun at the base of her neck this morning, but a few strands had come loose to blow in the breeze. She slipped on a pair of mirrored aviator sunglasses, masking her eyes from him, and stared out to sea. "Why are you here? You're a prince. You probably own twenty yachts of your own. So why did you rent one, Your Highness?"

The title had never set well with him and made him grit his teeth. "We don't need to be formal, Cate."

"Oh, I think we do," she said, glancing his way, reflecting his determined expression back to him. "Because if I call you what I want to, you wouldn't like that any better. Trust me."

He deserved that. Davian exhaled slowly. This was not going how he'd wanted at all. He tried again. "I want you to know how sorry I am about how things ended between us back in residency. I'd like to explain why I left the way I did after—"

"I don't care." Her tone slammed down like a wall between them. "It doesn't matter now anyway."

"It matters to me."

Cate gave a derisive snort. "I'm glad something does."

He managed to suppress a wince, barely, as her barb hit its mark. He'd lived with the guilt over leaving her that night without any word or warning, not even a goodbye, for the past five years. But he'd had no choice. Back then he'd been at the mercy of his parents and after the close call with his brother's life they'd feared the worst.

Now Davian was thirty-six and his own man. He was through ripping his life apart for the benefit of others.

"I need to get back to my clinic," Cate said then, turning to walk away. "Enjoy the rest of your trip, Prince Davian."

"Cate, please," he said, rushing after her to block her path down the stairs. "Let's get all this out in the open. I don't want to let it fester anymore." When she crossed her arms and didn't budge, he added, "Please. It won't take long. I just would like a chance to apologize and explain myself, then I'll let you be."

A beat passed. Two. Three. So long that Davian feared they might still be standing there two weeks later. Even though he couldn't see her eyes, he felt that penetrating green gaze burning a hole through him anyway.

Finally, she huffed out a breath and threw her hands up. "Fine. Let's get this over with. I'm busy."

She turned on her heel and headed back to the railing while Davian bit back a smile. Regardless of the tension between them, damn it was good to see Cate again. He'd missed her. Hadn't realized how much until now. They'd been more than lovers. They'd been best friends. She'd understood him as no one else had and he'd lost a part of himself when he'd lost her. Now he'd found that piece again and he'd do whatever he could to make amends. He followed her to the railing and leaned his forearms on it, facing the Mediterranean as she was. Seemed easier that way, dulling the sharp ache of the past a bit.

Davian took a deep breath for courage and opened his mouth to start, but never got the chance.

"Mommy! Noah took me down on the dock and I made a new friend on the dock. This is Paulo. Can we play up here with you?"

CHAPTER FOUR

CATE DID HER best to hide her alarm at Adella appearing at possibly the worst possible time, but feared she'd not done a good job of it, if the curious look on Davian's face was any indication. "Uh, yes. That's fine, honey." She hurried over to where the children were playing on the deck and crouched down, all too aware of Davian's gaze tracking her every movement. "And hello, Paulo. You must be Juan's son."

"Sí," the little boy said, grinning up at her and showing his missing two front teeth. Juan was one of the mechanics who worked in the engine room. He was from Spain and had custody of Paulo for the summer. Since accommodations had been made for Cate to bring Adella on, the captain did the same for Juan and his son. They shared a cabin just down the hall from Cate's.

She smiled and straightened, walking back over to where Davian still stood at the railing, watching the kids closely. His azure gaze quickly returned to her though, full of questions.

Tell him.

But she wasn't ready. Not yet. Not after everything she'd been through the past five years raising a child on her own. So, instead, she said, "Things change, as you know."

A flicker of hurt crossed his handsome face. Cate regretted her words instantly, but it was too late. They were already out there. She sighed and looked away, gentling her tone. "Your life has changed too. Wife, family of your own."

"I'm not married."

Oh.

Honestly, after the whole nightmare early in her pregnancy of trying to contact him then finding out about his engagement through the tabloids, Cate had steered very clear of any news related to the royals. Much less painful that way. She'd assumed he'd gotten married, had a family of his own now, was happy with his life. But based on his solemn expression and his blunt statement, that wasn't the case.

"I'm sorry," she said, meaning it. The kids' giggles as they chased each other around the circular hot tub in the middle of the deck was at odds with their serious conversation. "How long have you been divorced?"

"I'm not divorced either."

Now Cate felt terrible. "I'm so sorry for your loss. I had no idea."

Davian cursed under his breath then looked over at her. "I was never married, Cate. Namina and I called off the engagement shortly after it was announced. I figured you knew, since it was all over the press, but..." His voice trailed off and he looked away, raking a hand through his already messy hair. Her heart pinched at the sight of it, same as it always used to back in college. Cate quickly pushed it aside though. Now wasn't the time to get nostalgic over what might have been. He took a deep breath and focused on her again. "It's obvious to me now that you didn't know." Davian shook his head. "I should have called you right away, Cate. I know that now. But back then everything was so turbulent and then too much time had passed, and I didn't think I had the right. Plus, the last thing I wanted to do was bring you into all my family drama. I thought time would make it better. But time only caused more chaos between us, it seems."

He was right. Time had not been their friend. And while she still felt woefully unprepared for this conversation, it seemed like a now-or-never-type deal. She nodded. "Fine. Let's sit down over here and you can tell me your side of things. We can—"

Before they took a step though, a scream tore through the air and both Cate and Davian sprang into action without a second thought. Heart pounding, she made a beeline toward the children, panic squeezing her throat tight. If anything happened to Adella…

They rounded the hot tub and found poor Paulo on the wooden deck, pale and seemingly unconscious, a small puddle of blood near his head.

"What happened?" Cate asked, kneeling in front of her daughter, and pulling the shaking, crying little girl into her arms. "Are you okay?"

"We were playing tag and I was trying to get away. The deck was slick because of the water, and he slipped and hit his head. Mommy, is he okay?" Adella buried her face in Cate's neck and cried hard.

Footsteps pounded up the stairs and soon several other crew members stood around them, looking stricken as Davian assessed the boy's condition.

"Pulse is steady, and breathing is normal," Davian said. "We need an ambulance, please. And someone get his father."

One of the deck crew raced back down the stairs to get Juan from the engine room while Cate passed Adella off to Noah so she could assist Davian. She glanced at her watch then carefully helped him turn the boy onto his back. "From the time we heard the scream, he's been out three minutes."

Davian patted the boy's cheek. "Paulo. Paulo, can you hear me? I need you to wake up."

"Santo Christo!" Juan gasped as he ran up the stairs and knelt next to his son. "What's happened to him?"

"He and Adella were playing tag and he slipped on the wet deck around the hot tub and hit his head," Cate said, fresh guilt welling up inside her. Already Davian had become a distraction again. One she didn't need.

Thankfully, the boy began to stir, his eyelids fluttering before opening. Paulo groaned and squinted up at Cate.

"Paulo, *mi hijo*." Juan hugged Paulo's hand to his heart. Paulo tried to sit up, but Davian placed a hand on his chest, keeping him lying flat on the deck.

"My head..." Paulo started to say.

"You slipped," Davian said, checking the boy's pulse again. "Do you remember, Paulo?"

"No." Paulo frowned. Tears welled in his eyes and his breath caught.

Juan leaned in to kiss his son's cheek and whispered something in Spanish to him that seemed to calm him down as the ambulance arrived and once again the EMTs boarded the *Querencia*. Twice in two days. Cate thought that had to be a record.

Davian didn't miss a beat, suggesting he'd kept up his medical training as Cate had, after leaving Stanford. He gave them the rundown quickly and efficiently. "We have a..." He glanced at Juan. "How old is your son?"

"Seven."

"We have a seven-year-old boy who slipped and fell

on the deck, hitting his head against the side of the hot tub here, and lost consciousness for about three minutes. Pulse is strong bilaterally and respirations normal."

One of the EMTs moved in to help Cate continue to examine Paulo while Davian monitored the boy's vitals. That fact that it could so easily have been Adella lying there made Cate shudder.

I should've been watching them more closely. I shouldn't have let myself get distracted by Davian and all the drama between us.

"Can you tell me if anything hurts, Paulo? Besides your head?" Cate asked.

The little boy shook his head. "I want my papa."

"He's right here," she said. "And he'll be with you when we take you to the hospital too, okay?"

Paulo's bottom lip quivered but he didn't start crying again. Brave boy. He gave a little nod as Cate began palpating his neck. "How about here? Does this hurt?"

"Ow!" Paulo scowled. "*Sí.* That hurt."

"Okay." Cate began examining the little boy's head, no easy feat considering the thick dark hair obscuring Paulo's scalp. "Looks like we have a two-centimeter laceration over the right parietal skull area. No evidence of fracture at this point but they'll probably want to do a CT to confirm."

"Can you open your mouth for me?" Davian asked the boy, and Paulo did so. "Very good. There's good maxillary stability." He continued palpating over the boy's shoulders and down his arms. "Any pain here?"

"I can't feel my arm," Paulo said, his dark brows knitting.

Davian and Cate exchanged curt nods then Cate looked back over her shoulder at Juan. "That's normal with these types of injuries. Usually a temporary pinched nerve. Should go away in a little while, but the hospital will check, just in case."

Juan made the sign of the cross and Davian coaxed a little smile from Paulo by telling him a knock-knock joke as he slipped a neck brace into place around the boy's neck. He'd always had great bedside manner with patients, especially children, Cate remembered.

"Okay." Cate and Davian moved aside to let the EMTs in with a body board they'd brought on board to transport little Paulo. "These men are going to lift you up onto this so we can get you off the boat, okay, Paulo? You just stay still."

The boy closed his eyes again. "I'm dizzy."

"I know," Cate said, her voice low and soothing. "But we're almost done here and then we'll get you all fixed up and you'll feel lots better."

"I'm going with him," Juan said, his expression anxious as he watched the EMTs carefully lift his son onto the board then secure him for transport. "Papa's right here, *mi hijo*."

Then, as quickly as the emergency began, it cleared, leaving only the EMT's voice as he radioed into the hospital echoing behind them as they moved Paulo off the boat and the rest of the crew returned to their stations. Soon, it was just Cate and Adella and Davian alone again on the sundeck. She picked up her daughter and walked over to one of the bench seats near the railing and sat down, holding her close.

"Is Paulo gonna die?" Adella asked between sniffles.

"What?" Cate blinked away tears of her own, smiling. "No, sweetie. He'll be fine. They just need to take him to the hospital to patch him up. That's all."

"I was scared, Mommy," Adella said, burying her face in Cate's chest.

Cate rested her chin atop her daughter's head, her heart aching with the sweetness. "I know, sweetie. I was scared too. Life is like that sometimes. But we get through it by doing the hard things and having courage to keep moving anyway. And you were so brave right now. Paulo too."

Adella didn't respond, just held on to Cate tighter.

Davian came over and sat next to them. He hadn't said a word since the EMTs had left, though Cate knew from his pensive expression that the wheels were turning in his head. She just hoped they weren't turning in the direction of Adella and how much she looked like him.

To forestall any questions, she said, "You did good work there with him. You're still practicing then?"

"Thank you," he said, his tone quiet. "And yes. I run a teaching hospital in Ruclecia now, training the next generation of internists and helping all the patients I can."

"That's great." She adjusted her daughter on her lap and leaned back. "Hopefully poor Paulo won't be away long."

"I don't think he'll have any lasting issues," Davian said, scrubbing a hand over his face, his gaze on Adella now. Cate's heart fell. "You have a child."

Vocal cords tight with tension, she responded, "Yes."

"Congratulations. I know you always wanted kids. What's her name?"

"Adella."

"Lovely name for a lovely girl." He smiled and Cate's chest pinched with bittersweet memories. That crooked little grin of his always had made her knees go weak. "How old is she?"

Cate hesitated. If she told him the truth, it would be easy enough for Davian to work out the dates. But she couldn't lie to him either. She took a deep breath then answered. "Five."

"Hmm," he said, not seeming to register it at first. Then, slowly, his smile faltered, and his dark brows knitted. "I see." He looked away at last, his features tight. "You moved on quickly after I left."

Easier to seize on her anger then, Cate held Adella tighter. "After you disappeared, you mean. What was I supposed to do? Pine for you forever?"

He exhaled slow and hung his head. "No, Cate. Of course not. I didn't mean it that way. I just..." Davian shook his head. "We missed so much, you and me. So much time, so many possibilities for the future. All because of my family and my duty."

"Why didn't you just tell me who you were? Why did you lie to me? Lead me on like that when you were never available to begin with? I thought you cared about me, Davian. I thought you were my friend."

At first, Davian just blinked at her. The edge of hurt in her tone cut deeper than any scalpel ever could because it was true. They had been friends. More than friends. And he had cared for her. Still did, truth be told, even if he'd never act on that now. Too much time had passed. They were different people now, despite the lingering thread of connection between them.

But the time had finally come for him to tell her the truth. He took a deep breath and began.

"I did try to contact you, Cate. After my engagement ended and my father's health cleared. But as I said, things in my world were chaotic and I didn't want to bring all that drama into your life—especially after disrupting it so much already..." He sighed and stared out at the horizon. "I should have done better. And I'm sorry. About all of it. Lying was never my idea and I'm so sorry you were hurt because of it, Cate. That was never my intention." When she just stared at him, holding her daughter closer, he continued. She wasn't going to make this easy and that was her prerogative. Time to put it all out there for her, at last. "The whole charade started when I wanted to go to medical school in the States. Ruclecia has some fine institutions, but all the cutting-edge medicine was happening in America back then. I wanted to be part of that, wanted to learn everything I could there and bring it back home to Ruclecia to help my homeland." He gave a sad little snort. "My father, of course, hated the idea. Not that I'm all that important in the scheme of the royal family at home, but I am the stand-in."

"Stand-in?" Cate scowled. "I don't understand."

"I'm the spare to the heir. Insurance, in case something happens to my brother, Crown Prince Arthur. But since both my father and my brother—and any heirs my brother might have—need to be taken out before the throne would fall to me, most of my time is spent waiting."

"Waiting?"

"Yes. Waiting for something that's never going to happen, waiting for orders about what they want me to do, where I'm needed next, what mess it's become my job to clean up. But after I got into Stanford, I was through with waiting. I wanted to do something more with my life than just wait around for catastrophe or averting the next calamity to befall my family at the hands of the tabloids. I wanted to help people, make a real difference. So, I went to my father and we struck a deal. He'd let me go to America to school if I took security with me and used a false name so no one would know my true identity. Well, other than a few school officials who needed that information for my credentialing. At that time, I jumped on it."

Cate kissed the top of her daughter's head then exhaled a long breath. "Okay. So, you took a fake name and came to the US. Still doesn't explain why you didn't tell me the truth, Davian. I thought you trusted me. I trusted you. We..." Her voice trailed off as she made a vague gesture between them. "We were as close as two people could be. We spent all that time together. Working, studying, other...things."

"I know." He inhaled deep and ran a hand through his wind-tousled dark hair. "And I would have told you, Cate. I swear. In fact, I was planning to the next morning after we..." *Made love.* The words stuck in his throat, still tender after all these years. Because if he was honest with himself, he had loved Cate, more than anyone else he'd ever met. But duty had called, and he couldn't refuse back then. Today, however, the only duty he had was to the woman beside him, to explain his past actions as best he could. "I got a call, Cate. Or rather Grigorio got a call."

"Wait." Her brows knit. "You mean Greg, your roommate?"

Davian gave a curt nod. "His real name is Grigorio. He's been my valet since we were both boys. We grew up together."

"So, he works for you?"

"Did, yes," Davian said. "He's since left royal service to start his own company. Anyway, Grigorio received a call in the middle of the night from my mother telling him that I needed to return to Ruclecia. My father had had a massive heart attack and his life hung in the balance. My brother was already being prepared to ascend the throne, if needed, and I was to rush home to deal with fallout of that situation and assist with the transition of power, as was my duty. I tried to get them to allow me to stay until at least the morning so I could explain to you what was happening, but there was no time to waste. Grigorio and I packed quickly and were whisked away by the security team to a private jet and flown home all within the span of a few hours. When I left the apartment, you were still asleep. I thought I'd get to phone you the next day and talk to you, but then when I arrived in Ruclecia it was chaos. Between my family working 24/7 to keep the news out of the press and my father's condition being touch-and-go, there was barely time eat and sleep, let alone have a much-needed conversation."

A beat passed, then two. Finally, Cate asked, "And what about your engagement?"

Davian gave a harsh chuckle. "It was a publicity stunt. Namina never wanted to marry me any more than I wanted to marry her. It was all arranged when we were both toddlers. We barely knew each other. The only reason that juicy little false tidbit was leaked to the press—without my permission—was to throw the spotlight off my father's illness. My mother thought that a royal wedding was just the thing to keep the public distracted. And if it screwed up my life and plans? Well, that was too bad but all in service to the almighty crown. We de Lorosos have a long history of throwing the press off our scent. Probably started with my grandfather's assassination."

Cate looked stunned. "I'm sorry. I had no idea."

"It happened a long time ago," he said, exhaling slowly. "I was only five when it happened. Some fringe political group planned it around a story in the press about my grandfather attending the opening of a new government building in our country's capital. They shot him on national television, in front of everyone. It was awful."

"Oh, Davian." Cate reached over and placed her hand atop his, her skin warm and soft. "How terrible."

"I just remember the whole country being sad and everyone wearing black armbands in honor of him. But after that, new rules were put in place. The press was no longer a close ally and members of the royal family never travel together in the same contingent." Cate frowned and he smiled. "Well, almost never. This is a special case," Davian said, connecting the dots for her. "The fringe political group I mentioned in regard to my grandfather never went entirely away, just underground for decades. They recently resurfaced, making new threats against us. With my father's recent health crisis and rumors of him stepping down and allowing my brother to take over the throne, the palace security team decided it might be best to get them out of Ruclecia for a while. Normally, we would have used one of the royal yachts for such a trip, but they wanted to make doubly sure that this trip was conducted as incognito as possible, so we rented the *Querencia* instead. We hope to make it the whole trip before our ruse is discovered."

Cate sat back, her shoulders relaxing a tad. "Well, at least I have a better understanding about all the secrets and false names now."

Davian leaned into the cushions beside her, their shoulders brushing slightly and sending a fresh wave of awareness through his system before he tamped it down. "It's still no excuse for how I left things back in college, Cate, and there aren't enough apologies in the world to cover it. But yes. It was all a sham, Cate. The engagement, the wedding preparations. All of it. Namina never loved me, and I never loved her. As I said, we broke things off amicably as soon as my father recovered. It was all done to throw the press off the story of my father's health. I mean, I've grown up with it and I still feel manipulated by the palace press machine and all the duties to king and country I'm expected to put before my own wants and needs. I can't imagine what someone from the outside must think of us."

"Hmm," she said, a touch of wariness lingering in her tone. Davian couldn't blame her. Maybe after some time to absorb it all she would come to see that he too had been nothing but a pawn in his family's royal games and be able to at least understand why he'd done what he'd done, even if she couldn't forgive him. "That explains a lot, actually. About you, I mean."

Now it was his turn to frown. "How so?"

One side of her pink lips quirked up into a smile and he couldn't stop his gaze from flicking there before returning to her eyes. Memories of how those lips had felt beneath his flooded his mind before he forced them away, swallowing hard.

Stop it.

"Well, you never really sounded like any of the other med students I knew," Cate said, shrugging. "You always had a kind of...*formal* speech pattern."

"Formal?"

"Yeah. Like someone whacked you upside the head with a dictionary or something."

Davian chuckled. "I've heard that before."

They sat there in silence for a few moments, just the warm breeze and the call of seagulls around them. He'd said his piece and thought that would lessen the tension in the air, but there still seemed to be so much lingering, so much left to discuss.

"I—" he started at the same time Cate said, "We need—"

"Sorry," Davian said. "Go ahead."

"No, no. You go."

Cate adjusted her daughter again, the girl now sound asleep. Adella. Such a pretty name for a pretty girl. Long, curly hair and dark lashes fanned atop her tiny cheeks. There seemed something familiar about her features that Davian couldn't quite place, though he supposed that was to be expected with Cate being her mother and all.

When neither of them spoke, the awkwardness grew stronger, until Cate finally asked, "So, you're cruising with your family now?"

"Yes." Davian stared out at the passing coastline. "I'm here to cater to my parents' every whim."

"And act as hero," Cate added. When Davian glanced sideways at her, she smiled, genuine this time, and warmth flooded his bloodstream, making his pulse trip. Man, he'd missed that smile. "You've intervened twice now in medical emergencies, Dr. de Loroso. Thank you for your help."

"My pleasure, Dr. Neves." He grinned back and it was like the years fell away and they were back in medical school again. During both emergencies, they'd fell right back into their old routines, working like a synchronous, harmonious team. So good. So right. His chest ached with yearning to continue that easy partnership. It was rare enough in the workplace, let alone in one's personal life. Yet he and Cate had fallen into that naturally. Like they were meant to be together.

Until you weren't.

Those last words acted like a bucket of cold water on his fond memories, jarring him back to reality.

After checking his watch, Davian got up to peer over

the railing and down to the bow of the ship where the deckhands were preparing for docking at their next destination, Mallorca. "I, uh, I should get back to the salon and check on my parents. Make sure everything is all right with them." He turned back to Cate. "Thank you for talking to me and letting me explain what happened. I appreciate it."

He'd hoped for a quick escape, time to ponder his thoughts and figure out where to go from here, but it was short-lived as Cate stopped him before he reached the stairs.

"Wait, Davian." She remained on the bench seat and beckoned him back. "There's something I need to tell you too."

He walked back over and sat down again. He owed her this much, considering she'd listened to him before. And given that he'd vanished out of her life without a word, there wasn't much she could say to him to shock him at this point. Cate had always been the most honest, straightforward person he'd ever known. Whatever she had to say, he knew he could trust her.

She inhaled deep, staring down at her daughter instead of looking at him, uncharacteristically nervous. "I'm not sure how to say this, honestly."

Davian laughed congenially. "From someone who has experience saying difficult things, getting it out there quickly and decisively is the best course of action."

Cate looked at him a long moment, her lovely green eyes wide and bright, then she said, "It's about Adella." She swallowed and took another breath. "She's yours, Davian. Adella is your daughter."

He sat there, the words not really registering at first as his mind raced. Funny, it sounded like she'd said the little girl was his daughter too. But that couldn't be correct. They'd only had the one night together and they'd been careful. Cate had told him she was on the pill, and he'd used a condom as well, so…

Neither is one hundred percent effective, his medical brain supplied.

But…no. That couldn't be right. His gaze dropped to the little girl's sleeping face again, the dark hair that was so like his own. Like his father's and brother's too. And that jawline… Images of his brother when they'd been younger flashed into Davian's mind. Pictures of himself too.

You recognize it because you recognize yourself in her.

Those words stole all the breath from his lungs and his chest tightened.

Oh, God.

Davian gaped, first at Cate, then Adella, then Cate again. "I don't… I… How? Why?"

He sounded ridiculous, he knew, but he couldn't seem to wrap his mind around the fact that he had a child. With Cate.

My daughter.

Never once did he doubt Cate's statement. He knew her too well to think her a liar and the timeline worked with what she'd told him earlier about Adella's age. He just… "Why didn't you tell me sooner?"

"I tried to, Davian. I did. As soon as I found out. I got the first positive test a few weeks after you'd left. By then I'd seen the tabloid stories about your engagement and knew the truth of who you were, but I still thought you should know." She sighed and hugged Adella tighter. "I tried to get hold of you, but the school wouldn't give me any of your information. So, I went to the Ruclecian embassy next and explained to them who I was and why

I needed to speak with you." Cate snorted. "Looking back now, I can see why they brushed me off as a kook. You must get tons of people claiming to know you, but back then, I was desperate. I even managed to get all the way to one of your security people, but they refused to let me speak with you. Finally, I gave up."

"Cate, I…" For once in his life, Davian was speechless. What could he say to that? He absolutely believed what she said about trying to contact him. And she was right. The tabloids paid big money to people who claimed they knew the royal family of Ruclecia. And kooks abounded, lying about dating the princes or having their babies. Those rules about contacting a member of the royal family were there for a reason. But not for Cate. If there was anyone he'd wanted to talk to back then, it had been her. He'd been too wrapped up in all the scandal and the stress of his father's illness and his fake engagement and he'd never thought…never known…

Davian hung his head, hating how much time they'd lost, how much they'd hurt themselves and each other over the past five years with their estrangement. Then Adella stirred in her mother's arms and blinked her eyes open. Blue. Just like Davian's. And his heart melted completely.

I have a daughter. Adella. My daughter.

Adella sat up and rubbed her eyes, her little mouth pursed. She blinked up at Cate, then over at Davian, her frown increasing. "Who are you? Are you a doctor like Mommy?"

He'd been trained to speak in front of multitudes, to speak with kings and queens and billionaires. But one question from this little girl left him tongue-tied and twisted. Davian stared bug-eyed at his daughter as the gravity of the situation settled in.

Thankfully, Cate intervened by standing, hoisting Adella higher in her arms. "This is Mommy's friend." Davian didn't miss the slight edge on that word. "His name is Dr. de Loroso and you can meet him later, after your nap."

"But I don't want to take a nap, Mommy." Adella's bottom lip trembled. "I want to stay up here with you and Dr. de Loroso. Please?"

Cate took the whining in stride. "I bet by the time you wake up, François will have the lunch buffet out, and I heard he's going to have fresh pineapple today. That's your favorite, right?"

Adella nodded, still staring over the top of her doll's head at Davian. "Do you like pineapple, Dr. de Loroso?"

Davian swallowed hard against his sandpaper throat and managed to croak out, "Yes. I do."

"Good." Adella grinned and it felt like the sun coming out from behind the clouds to Davian. "We can have pineapple together at lunch then. Right, Mommy?"

Cate looked from their daughter to Davian then back again, wariness still lurking in the shadows of her green eyes. She'd told him the truth about their daughter, but she still didn't trust him with Adella, that much was clear.

Davian didn't know if he trusted himself with Adella. He treated kids in his practice and loved being around them, but he'd never had one of his own. To care for, to raise, to be responsible for. Most days he felt like he barely had enough energy to care for himself and his patients. How was he supposed to ensure the survival of this adorable little girl as well?

But before panic could set in, an odd sense of peace and purpose took over.

Adella is mine. My daughter.

His chest warmed with dedication and determination.

He would do it. Take care of Adella, take care of Cate too. They were his responsibility, and he would not fail. Not now. Not ever.

"Yes," Davian said, pushing to his feet and walking over to them at the top of the stairs. "We'll have pineapple, Adella. I'll make sure of it. Now, go take your nap. I'll see you soon."

To Cate he whispered, "Can we talk more after you put her down?"

She gave a short nod then headed toward the stairs, leaving Davian to watch after them, still coming to grips with the fact that within a matter of minutes he'd gone from a bachelor to a family man with a child and all that implied.

CHAPTER FIVE

BY THE TIME Cate got Adella down for her nap, it was after ten. She carefully closed the cabin door then sagged against the gleaming wood-paneled wall in the hallway and took a deep breath, eyes closed.

What in the world was I thinking, telling Davian about Adella so soon?

Yes, he deserved to know and yes, she'd kept it from him for long enough. But now that the truth was out there, she'd created a whole other boatload of problems. Once she'd discovered he was on board the *Querencia*, she'd planned to observe, see how he was, how things had changed, then ease into the topic when the time was right.

But then there'd been the emergency with Paulo and Davian diving right into why he'd left, and she'd felt vulnerable and open and so why not tell him then. Get it all out in the open.

Except now she was due to meet him in the library, Cate felt oddly protective of her life with Adella. For five years, it had been just them. Now she had no idea what Davian might ask of her in regard to their daughter and she wasn't sure how to adjust to that.

But if not now, when?

Never one to back down from hard things, Cate

steeled herself and pushed away from the wall, and headed upstairs to the library. She'd figure it out. Just like she'd figured out everything else up until now. She entered the yacht's deserted library two minutes later and closed the door behind her. No one usually came here, which was why Cate had suggested this spot for their talk.

Today though, her stomach was full of butterflies and a tremor of adrenaline shook through her bloodstream, keeping her pacing the area instead of settling on one of the comfy seats. She was just about to start straightening the shelves, just to have something to do, when the door opened and in walked Davian.

Lord, he looked good. Nearly the same as he had back in residency. Well, except for the slight hints of silver in the dark hair at his temples. He still had on his black suit, though he'd loosened his tie, she noticed, revealing a tiny vee of tanned throat. She felt a crazy urge to kiss that spot before she clenched her fists at her sides.

Davian closed the door behind him then ran a hand through his wind-tousled hair, those intense blue eyes searching the room before landing on her in the corner. She'd noticed outside, with everything else going on, but shadows marred the skin beneath his eyes, as if he hadn't been sleeping. Cate knew the feeling. She'd tossed and turned most of the night last night after seeing him again. She found herself wanting to walk over and pull Davian into her arms, let him rest against her for a little while.

Or something.

No. Stop it.

That was the fatigue talking. Back in residency, she'd been used to long hours and little sleep. But years on cruise ships had reset her internal clock. She'd moved past weary some time ago, and if she'd been wise, Cate would've taken a nap right alongside Adella instead of standing here now. But unfortunately, on top of this drama in her personal life, she was also on call today for any medical emergencies that might come up for the clinic, so no rest for her anytime soon. Given that it was just Davian and his parents aboard, they weren't likely to need her, but the crew might. Like poor Juan and Paulo. She made a note to call and check in on him as soon as she and Davian were done talking.

"Hello," Davian said, walking over to take a seat on the sofa. "Am I late?"

"Uh, no. No. You're right on time. Not that this is a formal meeting or anything, I just meant…"

Stop babbling.

Cate started toward the chair across from Davian then halted halfway there, uncertain where to go. Finally, she slipped into the chair across from him and exhaled slowly. "So."

"So."

They watched each other from across the span of the coffee table, but it could've been the Grand Canyon for all the distance between them. The odd intimacy that had surrounded them upstairs on the sundeck earlier had evaporated like the morning fog, leaving nothing but tension in its wake.

"I'm sorry," Davian finally said, frowning down at his hands folded in his lap. "I guess I'm still trying to wrap my head around what you told me earlier. I should be better prepared for this discussion, I suppose, I just…" He threw his hands up. "It's not every day you find out you're a father."

"No, it's not." She almost felt sorry for him. Almost. But she couldn't let herself go there because communication worked both ways and even though she hadn't been able to reach him about the pregnancy, he'd never once tried to check up on her either. Just to make sure she was doing okay, even if he didn't know about the baby. They slept together. That meant something to Cate. But apparently not Davian. So, no. She refused to feel sorry for him now, shoving the traitorous pinch in her chest aside. Summoning her courage, she added, "I don't expect anything from you."

He blinked at her, frowning. "What?"

"For Adella, I mean," Cate clarified. "I only told you about her upstairs because I thought you should know. But I don't need your money or anything. We're doing fine on our own."

Davian shook his head. "I'm sure you are. It's obvious that you're a great mother, Cate. And you're the strongest person I've ever met. I've no doubt you and Adella are doing fine."

"But?"

"But what?"

"You're sure we're doing fine, but..." Cate inhaled deep. "I'm sure there's more to it than that, Davian. You never could leave well enough alone. I remember you running all those extra tests back in residency just to make sure all your i's were dotted and your t's crossed. Even when it drew the ire of our attending. I can't believe you'd do less now when you've just discovered your daughter."

Urgh. *This isn't going well.* Unfortunately, although she did manage to put a halt to her babbling, she couldn't seem to pull her gaze away from Davian and the way he'd unbuttoned his suit coat to show the white shirt beneath. The soft cotton material pulling tighter across his torso to reveal the muscles beneath. Five years might have passed, but if she closed her eyes Cate could still remember the feel of those muscles beneath her fingertips, the warmth of his skin, the scent of soap and spice that clung to his neck, the catch in his breath when her fingers slipped down his abdomen to the waistband of his pants then lower still… She was only human, after all, and it had been so long, too long since she'd been with anyone else. In fact, if she was honest, there hadn't been anyone for her after Davian. What with the pregnancy and her busy work schedule, then later taking care of Adella, there'd been no time for relationships or romance.

"What's she like?" Davian asked quietly, jarring Cate out of her heated thoughts. "What's Adella's favorite color? Her favorite food? When's her birthday? Does she like seafood? Does she have any allergies?" He sat back and shook his head. "I feel like I've missed so much of her life already. I have so much catching up to do." He met Cate's gaze then. "Does she know about me? I mean, about who I am, really?"

Cate bit back a small smile. Davian always did jump in headfirst with things. "She's a typical five-year-old. She constantly asks questions about everything. Her favorite color is pink. Her favorite food is French fries. And pineapple. As you learned earlier. Her birthday is August twelfth. She likes shrimp, crab and lobster, but not so much fish. And no allergies. That I know of yet, anyway." Cate tilted her head slightly. "And no. She only knows you from this morning. I didn't want to say anything to her until an occasion arose when I needed to, like seeing you again. So far, she's never pushed too much for answers about a father, but I suspect that will change soon, what with her starting school when we get back to the States."

"You're going back to the States?" Davian sat forward again.

"Yes, after this charter. It's time we settled down so Adella can get some roots and grow up in one spot." Cate realized this was the first time she'd talked to anyone about her plans, other than Dr. Bryant and her mother back in Boston. "And I've saved up enough now to start my own practice, so that's what I'm going to do."

"Wow, congratulations." Davian's tone held a bit of awe. "I wondered what happened to your old dreams."

"Still alive and well, thanks." She hesitated a moment, wondering how much to share with him, then thought what the hell. Might as well put it all on the table now. Save time later. "I have the property picked out and everything. All I need to do is make a down payment and hire the construction company."

"In Boston, then? Where you grew up?"

"No. California." She brushed nonexistent lint from the front of her shirt. "Near Salinas. There's a huge migrant population in that area and I want to help them get affordable medical care."

Davian smiled then and Cate's pulse stumbled like a drunken sailor. "Always the idealist, eh?"

"Always." She ignored the thrill of having his full attention on her again and switched the spotlight back to him. "What about you? You said you run a hospital in Ruclecia? Wouldn't have taken you for an administrator. You always loved surgery so much."

"Still do," he said, his face lighting up as he talked shop with her. "I've hired people to help with the administrative aspects. You're right. I don't like that part. Too much paperwork and red tape. I do the hands-on work. And I teach. I've been giving seminars on new advancements in lasers for general surgery for the last year or so. Patients are still my top priority."

"Well, it sounds like we both got what we wanted then," Cate said.

"Not everything, no."

The flicker of hurt and loneliness in his eyes made her chest squeeze tight. If Cate was honest, she'd not gotten everything she wanted either. The one thing that had gotten away sat across from her now, as far out of her reach as he'd ever been, single or not. She'd opened up to him, told him things she'd never told anyone else—about her past, about her father, about her dreams for the future. She'd felt closer to him than anyone else on earth. She'd thought they'd find happily ever after together and ride off into the sunset. But then his lies had been revealed. He wasn't who he'd pretended to be. He wasn't trustworthy. He'd trampled on her heart just like her father had done. Even worse, he was royalty. He was wealthy and worldly and had duties and responsibilities far beyond what Cate would ever know. There was no way they could be together now, even with a daughter between them.

Not that she was thinking of being with Davian again. She wasn't. It was the tiredness talking.

That was the excuse she was going with anyway.

Nothing but fantasies about what might have been. That was normal, right? Wishing and wondering.

They stared at each other again, until Davian shifted his weight in his seat and crossed his legs to mirror hers. "Look, do you think we could start over, Cate?" he asked. "We kind of got off on the wrong foot yesterday, I think."

"That might be because you disappeared five years ago into thin air," Cate said pointedly.

His gaze darted to the other side of the room. "Yes, there is that I suppose."

It was still odd to hear him admit it so freely, even after their conversation on the sundeck. But he'd told her the details of his hasty departure and it was all in the past now anyway. No way to change it. Still, she wanted to make sure it wouldn't happen again, with Adella. "Look, you haven't said what your intentions are regarding Adella, or even if you intend to tell her that you're her father, but I feel I must set some ground rules for you, as her mother. And I want to be clear up front. If you're planning to disappear again without a word, then I think it's best if we just leave things as they are right now. She can learn more about you and her heritage later when she'll understand better."

For a moment, it looked like Davian would argue. But then he sighed and gave a curt nod. "Agreed. But for the record, I do not plan to disappear again. I never meant to disappear at all. But my duties demanded—"

"If we tell Adella who you are, then you have a duty to her as well," Cate said, not budging an inch. "Better she has no father at all than to have one that vanishes from her life without a trace. I know what that feels like, and I won't put my daughter through that ever."

"I'll be there for her, Cate. I promise." He sighed and hung his head. "I know how difficult this is for you. After what you went through with your own father. And I know that I went and did the same..." He threw up his hands and looked away. "I'm sorrier about that than I can ever say. I screwed up and I know it. And all I can do now is beg your forgiveness and say that no matter what else happens, I will never disappear on you and Adella again."

She wanted to believe him, so much her heart ached,

but she couldn't. Not yet. Not until he'd proven himself worthy. She'd trusted him once and it had nearly broken her. She uncrossed then recrossed her legs the opposite direction, wincing at the needle pricks through her nerve endings as the blood began to circulate to her lower extremities again.

"Perhaps you could come to dinner one night," Davian said, sounding exhausted. "Here on the yacht. My parents would be there..."

"No," she said, meeting his gaze again. "Not until we've talked to Adella and worked out how all of this will work. I don't want to confuse her by having her meet grandparents."

"Okay." He nodded. "I get that. Maybe we could go ashore at our next stop. Spend a day together, get to know each other then maybe we can tell her the truth about who I am." Davian cleared his throat. "I mean, if it feels right and all."

Cate wasn't sure what she'd expected of this conversation, but this wasn't it. The fact Davian was being so gracious and accepting of it all set her warning bells on high alert. She wasn't used to things going so smoothly. Even Cate had to admit though that his excursion plan sounded like a good idea. "Okay," she said at last. "But I'll need to check my schedule at the clinic and make sure I have the day off. I'll let you know."

There was still one question though that lingered in her mind.

"Why haven't you asked for paternity tests?" Cate asked bluntly.

Davian chuckled. "Because I know that once my parents find out, all of that will be done. Royal succession and all. But for now, it's only you and I that know, and I trust you, Cate. I always have."

Now it was her turn to be speechless. For all the faults and foibles they'd had back in residency, trust wasn't one of them. At least until he'd left her high and dry, that was. The fact he still trusted her now though…well, that was something, wasn't it?

"Right." Davian stood then and walked to the door. "I need to get back to my parents. They've been raving about some tour of Monte Carlo they want to take when we get to Monaco, and I need to make sure everything is set up properly and security is in place for them."

Cate stood too and followed him out of the library. "Don't you have people for that?"

He snorted. "I'm the spare to the heir, Cate. I'm all the 'people' they need."

The twinge of resignation in his voice made her sympathize for him, despite her wishes. "I'm sorry. It must be hard to be treated like a servant in your own household."

"I'm used to it," he said. "It's been that way since I was a boy, so I've learned to work within it. And really, I don't have it so hard. I'm privileged and I know it. No reason to feel sorry for myself. A lot of other people have it much, much worse and I know it. So, I've made it my mission in life to help them as much as I can, through my medical work and through the charities I support. Hopefully, I'm doing so."

Back in residency, Cate had been drawn to him because of their shared vision and ideals, and the pull was no less strong now, even all these years later. As she turned to head back to the clinic as he went the opposite way down the hall to go above decks, Cate said, "I think you are, from what you've told me." Their gazes held for a beat or two, until the warmth of awareness sizzling between them grew too hot to ignore. Rather than deal with that though, Cate inched back down the hall toward the safety of her clinic. "I'll let you know my schedule for Monaco."

"Cate?" Davian called just as she reached the clinic door. He waited until she turned back to him to say, "Thank you."

A long moment passed after he was gone before Cate moved again, an odd mix of anticipation and apprehension bubbling inside her. She'd just made either the best or worst decision of her life. Only time would tell.

CHAPTER SIX

ONCE THE SHOCK of knowing he had a daughter wore off for Davian, he began to realize that keeping Adella sheltered from the truth of her heritage might not be so simple after all. Especially with his nosy parents watching him like a hawk every second of the cruise. God. What an absolute mess he'd made of all this. And whether that had been his decision or intention or not, it was up to him to clean it up now and deal with the consequences of his actions back then.

A daughter. I have a daughter.

Those words still filled him with an odd mix of elation and apprehension. He'd always wanted children, a family of his own, but had thought he'd have more time to plan and prepare. The last thing he wanted to do was bring a child of his into the turmoil of royalty, but the reality was he didn't have much choice in the matter now. Adella was his and as such he would protect her with his own life against any foe, even his own family, if necessary. They'd already cost him too much in his life. A relationship with his own daughter would not be another casualty of his duties. He refused to let that happen.

"What is wrong with you, my son?" Davian's father, King Phillipe, said the next morning over breakfast.

"You seem distracted. And your expression is as fierce as a tiger."

"I'm fine," Davian mumbled, sipping more of his coffee and scowling.

The crew of the *Querencia* had laid out a fine feast for the first meal of the day, but Davian didn't have much appetite. The same did not seem to be an issue for his parents and their guests. Besides King Phillipe and Davian's mother, Queen Arabella, they'd invited a small cohort of their most trusted friends and advisors to come along on this trip, both as a reward for years of loyal service and to keep his parents from getting bored while sailing between destinations, and allowing Davian time to do other things besides entertaining them. At first, he'd figured he'd spend most of the time in his cabin, preparing notes and lecture materials for another medical conference coming up the following month where Davian was presenting on a new medical technology in the operating room to three-dimensionally print implants to perfectly match the patient's needs at the time of surgery. Normally, he'd be doing all of this at home, in his private villa. But he and his older brother had discussed the rising threats against his parents and decided it was best to separate the current King from the Crown Prince for a while, and because Davian's work was more portable, he'd gotten the job of babysitting his parents on this cruise. He took a deep breath and stared down at his notes again. It was all incredibly fascinating and state-of-the-art medicine that Davian hoped to bring to his teaching hospital and the people of Ruclecia soon. But for now, instead, he was torn between preparations for his presentation and spending more time with Cate and Adella.

"Are you hungry, sweetheart?" his mother asked from

beside Davian at the table. "You should eat a little something at least. Keep your strength up."

Davian gave his mother a small smile and served himself up some fresh fruit from the nearby platter in front of him, then also took a freshly made croissant, still warm from the oven, and added it to his plate.

"Have you planned out our agenda yet for Monte Carlo?" his mother asked. "Please don't forget to coordinate with Marco at the hotel. He knows exactly what we want to see on our tour this week."

"Yes." King Phillipe sat back with a sigh. "It's too bad your brother couldn't be here as well. He loves Monte Carlo so."

The reason he's not here is to keep you safe, Davian wanted to say, but bit back the response. Fighting with his father over an issue that had long since been settled would do him no good. Best to just let it slide off him and get on with his day. He had more important things to think about now.

Like Cate and his daughter.

Adella.

While he'd never cared for the wealth and privileges his royal status provided, his daughter deserved to at least have access to those benefits until she was old enough to choose on her own. Davian could provide that for her, once all the paternity tests were completed and the results confirmed. Not that there'd been a second when he'd doubted Cate's word about Adella. He believed Cate. Trusted her. He always had. But once Adella's identity was confirmed, then a whole new set of issues would arise. He worried she would also become a target for the extremist threats. Having Cate and their daughter back in his life meant they would be involved now too. And that was why he couldn't let his feelings get the better of him. He had to remain rational, logical, as he figured all this out.

Davian exhaled slowly and scrubbed a hand over his face, sinking back into the cushions of the sofa he sat on. It was all so complex and complicated.

He walked up to the upper sundeck and stared out over the turquoise waters of the Mediterranean. It was about nine thirty now and the sun was rising. Blue skies above as far as the eye could see and already the sea was busy. Smaller vessels sailed alongside huge cargo ships, delivering goods from all over the globe. A slight breeze blew as they cut through the water, their captain steering them deftly through the traffic and out into the less crowded areas. Perhaps, if he'd not become a doctor, Davian would've joined the royal Ruclecian navy. He loved the water and loved sailing.

From somewhere down below, he heard a familiar chuckle dancing through the air like wind chimes and a sizzle of awareness went through him once more, same as it always did when she was close to him.

Cate.

Even after all these years, the attraction was still there, stronger than ever. Even more so now that he knew what she'd gone through without him. Carrying his baby, alone. Completing residency without him as he'd completed his own back in Ruclecia. Making a life for herself and Adella, on her own, as he'd taken over the hospital in his homeland and begun to build it into the powerhouse, world-renowned medical center it was today.

She'd been through so much already, before they'd met, then he'd put her through so much more. Not intentionally, but that meant little now. Cate's life had been totally disrupted after he'd left. And while she'd managed to bounce back from it all admirably, he still wanted to take care of Cate too. For all they once meant to each other and because she was Adella's mother.

The only trouble was, he would need to keep all of it—and them—out of the public eye. Not because he was embarrassed by them, but for their own protection. They had no idea what he and his family went through daily, hounded by the paparazzi whenever they went out. Not to mention the threats and security scares that had driven them to take this cruise now. Davian wanted none of that sordidness to touch Cate and Adella.

What they had, his past with Cate, and his future with Adella, was all too personal, too precious to him, especially now he'd just rediscovered Cate and found out for the first time about Adella. Davian never wanted them to be in danger because of who he was or what he had.

He stood there for a long time, staring out to sea and thinking. His chest ached at the thought of the press hounding his little girl as they'd done to Davian his whole life. The constant sting of feeling vulnerable, of being used and hurt and betrayed by those closest to you for their own devices were wounds he'd carried with him daily and Davian vowed now to do what he must to protect Cate and their daughter from the speculation, the rumors, the constant threats—especially if he wasn't there to protect them personally.

Dammit.

He removed his sunglasses and scrubbed a hand over his face, before replacing his shades. He needed to concentrate on the security for his parents' upcoming tour of Monte Carlo and his presentation, not Cate. And yet, he couldn't seem to stop himself. He glanced at his watch and realized he'd been up here fifteen minutes now and he needed to get a move on.

He had phone calls to make, a man named Marco

to locate and speak with about his parents' "special" tours, then security staff to brief on the agenda. He also needed to make sure all the paperwork and IDs were in place for customs ahead of time to make sure his parents would not be stopped or detained in any way. A day of leisure for the royals made possible by Davian's day of hard work and frustration. If things went as they were supposed to.

If...

And yet more proof that Davian was more of a highly decorated secretary than a prince.

He missed his patients and his hospital. Yet here he was, fulfilling his duties again instead of fulfilling his passions in life. He'd stuck with his family this long out of a sense of obligation, a sense of loyalty. He'd admired his grandfather, loved his parents and brother too—even if he didn't always understand or agree with their motivations. And after the debacle with Cate, he'd honestly not had much else going on with his life other than his work, thinking he'd throw himself into medicine and let the rest play out without him. But then the threats had increased and he'd been called into service for king and crown again.

When he and his brother had originally planned this impromptu trip for the King and Queen, it was meant to be a quiet recuperation period for their father and mother, a way to keep them safe and out of the public eye until the would-be assassins were captured. But with their father loving the spotlight and pomp his position afforded, keeping King Phillipe from his adoring public was like trying to keep sand from slipping through your fingers. Davian sighed and stared out at the horizon, rocky cliffs dotted with pastel houses and white umbrellas. Sometimes it felt like even with all his careful planning and work, they were all doomed.

Davian quickly shoved aside those thoughts though. Feeling sorry for himself was not his nature. Action was, and he had plenty of work to keep him busy. He went back downstairs to his stateroom and began preparing for the Monte Carlo visit. He talked to the infamous Marco and was assured the tour was taken care of. Then he'd sat down and gone through all the tabloids he'd asked Chief Stew Noah to deliver to him earlier. Thankfully, there was no sign of any stories about their trip aboard the *Querencia.* After going through the papers and the websites on the internet, he called his hospital back in Ruclecia to check on his patients. So far, so good.

By the time he was done with his calls and his work, it was late afternoon. Davian went back up on deck to stretch his legs and get some fresh air. He walked to the aft deck and stood watching the waves made by the *Querencia*'s powerful engines as she sliced through the sea, pushing them onward toward Monaco and the future. He turned to rest his elbows on the shiny metal railing when he spotted Cate, standing on the forward starboard bow, her blond hair blowing in the breeze and her eyes closed, as if she were making a wish or dreaming. She wasn't wearing her medical uniform today. Instead, she was in a white polo shirt and shorts, her long tan legs and bare feet making his throat constrict with sudden want. He remembered those legs, how soft and smooth they'd felt beneath his hands, how strong they were wrapped around his waist as he'd driven them both to the edge of ecstasy inside her…

Adella wasn't around, that he could see, and Davian found himself wanting to walk up there, to pull her into his arms and kiss her, run his hands through her silky hair and tangle his fingers in it as he tipped her head back to lick the pulse point at the base of her neck, the one that made her gasp and whimper when he nipped it gently just so.

His body tightened and Davian suddenly felt way too overdressed in his cream linen suit and ivory dress shirt, the aqua silk tie he'd chosen in homage to the sea. He wanted to strip then and there. Put on comfortable clothes like hers and…

Cate turned slightly then and saw him down the length of the ship. Davian took an involuntary step forward and Cate took one back. Of their own accord, his feet led him toward her. But the nearer Davian drew to Cate, the farther away she seemed to move, until she backed herself right into the railing behind her.

"How are you this morning?" Davian asked past his tight vocal cords, doing his best to sound casual as he came to a halt beside Cate. "You look lovely today."

Alone with Cate, a bit of awkwardness kicked in again. He'd called her lovely, but it paled in comparison to her true beauty. She was the loveliest person, inside and out, he'd ever seen, but that wasn't something you just walked up and said to a person, right? Especially after five years apart and the history they'd had.

Still, Cate blushed under his words and gripped the railing more tightly, lowering her head. He couldn't see her eyes behind those dark sunglasses she wore, but Davian got the sense—as he always had—that Cate was uncomfortable with praise, simple or not. As if she was unused to receiving it. She'd talked to him briefly back in residency about her childhood, being raised by a single mother after her father left them when Cate was ten. At the time, she'd brushed over it so swiftly that

Davian had assumed she'd bounced back from the pain of it quickly and resiliently. But now, considering what he knew about her and what he was observing today, he had to wonder if that experience hadn't left deeper scars that were still affecting Cate today. Especially since her demeanor suggested she had no idea how to react to receiving a compliment.

"Uh, thanks," Cate said, still looking downward, her tone edged with discomfort. "When we're not working aboard ship, we dress down in our casual uniforms. They're supplied by the yacht owners, so we don't have much choice in color or style," Cate hastened to add.

The fact she was babbling, as if nervous, helped lessen the tension inside Davian. He wasn't the only one scared of messing this up then. That was reassuring. Because given how much he wanted this reunion with Cate to go well, it felt like all his years of elocution training had gone right out the window and he might start babbling himself soon too.

Instead, he cleared his throat and took a deep breath before saying, "No, can't go wrong there."

They stood staring out to sea again, shoulder to shoulder at the railing. Every so often, Davian's arm would brush against Cate's and a frisson of need would race through him like a Formula 1 car, prompting new images of Cate in a tiny bikini and nothing else to flash in his mind. His traitorous body went into overdrive again—heart racing, blood thumping in his ears, chest constricted, and pants suddenly too tight for comfort. Thank goodness for his suit coat to cover his reactions or he'd embarrass himself. Davian squeezed his eyes shut and battled for control. He wasn't some schoolboy virgin. He had years of experience with beautiful women. He shouldn't be this way just standing next to

Cate—fumbling and frustrated and fantastically turned on—and yet, he was.

God help me.

"So, I checked the clinic schedule for our arrival in Monaco in a couple days' time," Cate said. "And I should be able to go into Monte Carlo during the day, as Dr. Bryant is on call then. But I'll need to be back that night to take over from him."

"Great," Davian said, wondering when the temperature here had gotten so hot.

They stood side by side again in silence. Davian didn't know about Cate's nervousness, but his own was still there, just beneath the surface, ready to trickle out and ruin any cool confidence he might have projected up to this point, so he kept quiet again.

"Anyway," Cate said after a while. "I told Adella that we'd be going ashore, and she was super excited. She was asking me all about Monaco and I told her as much as I could, but I'm hoping you'll know more about it, being—" she waved a hand over him "—a prince and all." Her cheeks pinked adorably again. "I mean, not that you spend all your time there or anything. Obviously, you don't. Or you didn't, because you went to medical school and everything, so that was four years right there. Then residency, which was another four years. And a fellowship that took another three. So, eleven years you spent not going to Monaco."

Davian let her finish, biting back a smile. "Yes. Thanks for the rundown of my schooling thus far."

Even with the sunglasses in place, he could imagine those green eyes of hers widening with mortification. Cate cursed under her breath then shook her head. "Sorry. I don't know why I'm so nervous. It's not like we haven't talked before or anything. Hell, we did a lot more than talk—" She stopped abruptly. "Sorry. God, just stop talking already, Cate."

Davian did smile then, shoving his hands in his pockets to keep from reaching for her. She looked so adorably ruffled he just wanted to hug her and tell her everything would be fine, even if it wouldn't. "It's okay. I understand, Cate. I do. And you make me nervous too. I think maybe it's just been a while and we're both trying to be careful not to screw this up, yeah?"

She inhaled deep and grinned back at him and his world went supernova bright, like the difference between regular color and Technicolor brilliance. "Yeah. You're right. Maybe we're putting too much pressure on ourselves."

"Maybe we are." Davian rocked back on his heels, searching for a new, safer topic of conversation. "Have you gotten any updates on Paulo?"

"Yes," Cate said, shifting her weight to lean a hip against the railing. "He's doing much better. I spoke to his father, and he said they should be releasing his son later today. He had a concussion, but no fracture, thank goodness. They should be rejoining us on board the *Querencia* in Monaco."

"Excellent."

"What about your parents?" Cate asked, tilting her head slightly. "Aren't they going into Monte Carlo too? I heard Noah talking to the crew about it this morning in the cafeteria. They're making plans for a big picnic lunch and everything for the guests."

"Yes, they're going ashore too. Not with us though," Davian added. "I spent the better part of my day today making sure everything was set and security would be in place for their visit."

She studied him for along moment, then frowned. "You don't look happy about it."

"I'm just concerned, that's all."

"About their safety?"

"Yes. There've been threats back in Ruclecia."

"Threats?" Cate's frown deepened. "What kind of threats?"

"Of assassination. Like what happened to my grandfather." Davian leaned his elbows on the railing then, glad for the cool sea breeze on his heated face. He hung his head and took a deep breath as the old grief dissolved. "The original group of fringe radicals responsible for my grandfather's death were locked away for life years ago. But now a new group has resurfaced and are demanding an end to the monarchy in my country. They're a small but vocal minority. My father, King Phillipe, has done well though for the people of Ruclecia and most of our citizens want my family to remain in power. Of course, my father's recent heart attack didn't help, nor did his quadruple bypass surgery. He's in his late sixties now and ready to step down. He wants to turn things over to my older brother, Crown Prince Arthur, and let him lead Ruclecia into the future, but it's risky at present with all these new threats and his health concerns. The last thing we want is to start a revolution or damage the people's faith in our monarchy. So, my brother and I decided, along with our security team, that the best thing at this point was to get our parents out of the country for a while. Let him rest and recuperate while Arthur takes the reins temporarily to prove he can do it. Let the anger and outrage of the fringe calm a bit. Then we'll go back home and see where things stand."

"Wow." The sun disappeared behind a cloud and Cate lifted her sunglasses, allowing him to see her gorgeous green eyes. Davian did the same with his own glasses, letting them rest atop his head.

They watched each other for a beat or two, before Cate crossed her arms and stared down at her bare toes on the deck. Her toenails were painted pink, Davian noticed. His mind then imagined him kissing each of her cute toes and making her giggle then gasp with need, which wasn't helpful at all.

Oh, boy.

Cate must've been able to read his thoughts because her gaze flicked down to his lips, her own mouth going a little slack as her green eyes darkened slightly. His pulse tripped at the idea that maybe he wasn't the only one struggling to keep his reactions hidden. The atmosphere between them seemed to crackle with energy and if he leaned in, just a few inches, he could kiss her. See for himself if it was as wonderful as he remembered. See if she tasted as sweet as she had five years ago or…

Stop. Focus.

"So, Monaco," Cate said a short while later, her voice a tad breathless as he turned to face the sea again and slid her sunglasses back into place and the sun blazed once more.

"Yes, Monaco," he responded, for lack of anything better. "It's nice there. Have you been before?"

Now it was her turn to snort. "God, no. Telegraph Hill, Boston," Cate said, laying on her accent thick. "I'm a Southie through and through. Never imagined Monaco in my future."

Davian understood that, though in a slightly different way. Growing up in the palace in Ruclecia, he'd never imagined having the chance to go to live in America, to attend medical school there, to meet a woman as wonderful as Cate. But even back then, he'd dreamed of getting out, of living a real life, a true life, helping people. Part of that had to do with his grandfather's assassination, as he'd told her, but the other part was just born into him, he supposed. The need for more than just an existence of pampered perfection where life was kept a safe distance away and nothing ever changed. Maybe that was what Cate had felt growing up too. Not the pampered perfection part, obviously, but the need to forge a new path, to escape the monotony, to create your own destiny.

"Was it terrible, growing up where you did?" Davian asked.

"No. Not terrible. Just not…" Cate shrugged. "Not what I wanted. So, I left home and struck out on my own."

"When you went to medical school?"

"Yep. Not that I went far. Just across town. I got a cheap apartment with three other girls off campus, and we all worked waitress jobs to pay the bills while we were in school. My financial aid covered classes and books and stuff, but not room and board."

"And you still graduated top of your class."

"Damn straight I did." Cate grinned. She lifted her face to the sun and Davian couldn't help tracking the line of her long, tanned throat before he forced his gaze elsewhere. When she finally looked at him again, Cate asked him, "What about you? You must love being home in Ruclecia again."

"Hmm." He did love his homeland. Always would. But lately, he couldn't help feeling there was something missing. Or more precisely, someone. Someone to share his life with, someone to make a home with. "Ruclecia is very beautiful, but so was California. I guess I'm still searching for my true home. The place where I fit in the most. I feel that at work, at my hospital. I know I'm doing good there."

"But not at the palace," she said, turning to mimic his stance, leaning her elbows on the railing beside his.

"No, not at the palace."

Cate nodded. "I'm glad you know about Adella now. But if you hurt her, Davian, you will have to deal with me. Understand?"

"I won't hurt her," he said. "I swear." At Cate's raised brow, he added, "I swear I'll do my very best never to hurt her. There are no guarantees in life, but I promise, on my honor, to never intentionally do anything to cause her pain in any way. All right?"

"All right." Cate gave a curt nod then straightened. "I should probably get back to the clinic. Lots of stocking to do."

Davian straightened as well. "I'll keep planning our day in Monaco. It's your first time and I want it to be special. For you and for Adella."

"Sounds good."

As Davian watched Cate walk away down the stairs, a strange sense of gravity came over him. This moment felt huge, even though it was such a small thing. A conversation between two people, and yet, he'd never felt anything quite like it in his life. So full of potential and promise and possibilities. This day would be important, in ways he could only imagine, and he doubted he'd ever get another chance like it again, so he wanted to make the most of the opportunity and make their day in Monaco as a family as amazing as he could for all of them.

Cate went back downstairs to the clinic and began helping Carrie, the clinic's second crew member and receptionist, restock the supply cabinets. After the first two days of the charter, there hadn't been much for them to do on board, though with the King's heart condition Davian wanted a trained physician on call 24/7, so…

Davian. David.

No matter what name he went by, her body would still recognize him a mile away.

Hard to believe that even after all that had happened between them, that same awareness, that same heightened attraction was still there. At least for her. And after catching Davian looking at her like he wanted to devour her whole, Cate thought it was for him too.

Not that they'd act on it.

Been there, done that. Had the scars to prove it.

But still, a girl could dream.

And speaking of dreams…

"And did you see the pictures of their palace in the latest issue of *Royal Life*?" Carrie asked as she stuffed another handful of alcohol wipes into a bin on the shelf. "Talk about opulence. I think one rug alone in that place costs more than the entire house I grew up in."

Cate wasn't really paying attention though, her mind focused on the man upstairs, who'd told her about his past and seeing his grandfather assassinated before his eyes and how that made him want to be a doctor. She could see that now, in how dedicated he was to his patients, in his need to give back and help others. In his desire to serve instead of being served. Another reason, she supposed, why he'd put up with all the royal intrigue and disruptions to his life thus far. His innate sense of needing to be helpful. A trait he'd shown her so many times during their residency together.

When Davian had walked out of her life five years ago, Cate had convinced herself that all the stories and rumors of the playboy prince who only cared for himself were true. Given how angry and betrayed she'd felt because of his lies, hearing about all his awful deeds confirmed she didn't need him in her life. That him leaving was the best thing that could have happened to her.

Then she'd found out she was pregnant, and the world had dropped out from under her.

And the fact he hadn't responded when she tried to reach out, well that was more than enough reason for Cate to go it alone.

But now, she was exhausted. Raising a child with limited support and crazy doctor's hours was far more difficult than she'd realized. Her mother helped some, when she could, but Cate needed more.

Davian could give you more.

And she had to think of Adella's future too. Ruclecia and its royal family were a part of her birthright. She deserved to know them and what she'd be giving up, but not until she was older and could make her own choice. Which left Cate in charge until then.

"Okay. Let's do the tongue depressors next," Carrie said, walking over to grab another box from the stack against the wall. They brought aboard fresh provisions at their last stop at Marseille last night, so there was quite a bit of stuff to put away. Carrie opened the top of the box and set it between her and Cate on the counter before grabbing a clear glass jar from the row of them against the wall on the countertop and began to fill it with the wooden sticks. "So, what do you think of Prince Davian? Pretty hot, huh?"

Cate scowled, feeling oddly protective of him. "How would you know?"

"I met him yesterday," Carrie said, grinning. "When he came to the clinic looking for you. Lucky girl. How did you meet him?"

Not sure how to answer that without getting into a whole thing, Cate grabbed a huge handful of tongue depressors and shoved them into the jar, then got up and went over to look through the other boxes, still aware of Carrie's stare following her around the room.

"Oh, uh..." Cate grabbed a box of paper gowns and bent to fill the drawer below the exam table. "We met in passing at a medical conference one year in California. Barely know the guy. Not sure why he'd come looking for me now."

"Really?" Rather than taking the hint of Cate's less than enthusiastic tone that she didn't want to discuss this anymore, Carrie straightened and gave Cate an inquiring look. "That's weird, because I swear I overheard Dr. Bryant talking to him like you two were old friends."

"What?" Cate tensed up then forced herself to relax. "Seriously. I've no idea what Dr. Bryant was talking about." Then just to drive home her point, Cate looked up at her coworker over the exam table with a pointed stare.

The assistant sighed and turned back around to shove the rest of the tongue depressors into the jar. Thankfully, they worked in companionable silence after that, getting everything ready in case the guests needed medical attention while aboard the yacht.

So, what do you think of Prince Davian? Pretty hot, huh?

Still, Carrie's question kept looping around in Cate's mind. Yes, Davian was hot, regardless of how much she might want to pretend otherwise. In fact, spending time with him up on deck earlier had been nice. Better than nice if she was honest. It reminded her of the easy camaraderie they'd always shared working together back in residency. They seemed to know each other's thoughts and actions before they even knew themselves. Weird, that.

And then there'd been that look.

The one there when they'd been at the railing, where Davian's blue eyes had lit with fire and hunger as he'd stared at her mouth, making her lips tingle even if he'd never kissed her today. Made her remember what it had been like all those years ago between them. She'd had to grip the railing tight just to keep from reaching for him then, to keep from throwing him down on the deck and having her wicked way with him over and over again.

Which made no sense. They were different people now than they'd been five years ago, and she doubted that even with a child between them she'd be the kind of woman Davian wanted or needed in his life. She was too busy, too focused on her work and her and Adella's futures.

Davian, even though he didn't really claim the title, was still a prince. The son of a king. An accomplished doctor and surgeon in his own right. He could rent boats like the *Querencia* to just sail around on for two weeks. He could jet off to the other side of the world on a private jet whenever he liked. Why would he want a plain old GP like Cate Neves who planned to set up a neighborhood clinic when she was done with this charter and leave her yachting life behind for their daughter's schooling?

It made no sense. And yes, there was Adella, but couples coparented all the time now and lived in different countries while doing it. There was no reason they had to spend time together after this charter. And yet, a deep ache of loneliness inside her said that Cate still wanted him to want that, the same as she did.

Silly, but still there regardless.

And going into Monaco with him in a couple of days won't make that any easier to deny...

True. But it was too late to back out now. In fact, not going would probably look even more conspicuous than going, so yeah. Cate was stuck with that decision. She could do it. She'd be fine. And they'd have Adella there as a buffer. Adella, who never stopped asking questions about everything could carry a conversation all by herself if Cate let her. No need to worry about those awkward silences between her and Davian. Nope. Or those steamy stares that made her heart race and her body throb. Hard to get your groove on with a talkative, nosy kid around all day.

Maybe it wouldn't be so bad after all. Cate was excited to see Monte Carlo, so…

Besides, Davian hadn't once done anything earlier to back up those heated glances of his, so maybe she'd been mistaken about his intentions, or made it up entirely in her own head.

Then she pictured him up on deck, sunlight bathing him, windblown and way too handsome for his own good in his suit and tie. Cate chuckled. Only Davian could get away with wearing a suit and tie at sea and not look like a pompous ass. She hadn't missed the fact that the shade of his blue tie had perfectly matched his eyes either. For an odd second, Cate remembered that Grace Kelly had become Princess of Monaco and wondered what it might be like to marry a man like Davian.

Then she quickly snapped out of it. This wasn't some Hollywood fairy tale and Davian wasn't her Prince Charming to sweep Cate and Adella away to his castle to live happily ever after. At best, they'd have one full day together, to get to know one another better and build a bond that would have to last them for years or longer.

Because once Adella was in school, Cate didn't want to move her around too much, so if Davian wanted to see her, he'd have to travel to America. Or maybe she and Adella could go see him in Ruclecia during the summer break. But then Cate would have her clinic and it might be difficult to get away then too and…

"Cate?" Carrie asked. "Did you hear me?"

Nope. She hadn't. Heat prickled her cheeks as Cate glanced over at the young receptionist. "Sorry. I didn't."

"Everything okay?"

"Fine. Thanks." She swiped the back of her hand over her forehead. "Just tired. Sorry. What was your question again?"

"No question." Carrie gave her a curious look. "Just said my shift's over now. I'll see you tomorrow."

"Yes, see you tomorrow," Cate said. "I have the day off after that but I'll be back on Thursday."

"That's right." Carrie grinned and pointed to the calendar on her desk out front. "See you tomorrow then."

"Thanks. Enjoy your night."

Once she was alone, Cate finished with the last few boxes of supplies and broke down the boxes for recycling, then locked up the clinic for the night. She made sure the yacht's walkie-talkie was still clipped to the back waistband of her shorts in case there was an emergency, then checked her watch. Almost dinnertime. If she hurried, she might be able to grab a plate of food to take out on the deck by the anchors to watch the sunset with Noah and Adella.

Francois had outdone himself again with the galley fare for the crew. There was grilled shrimp and roasted veggies. Rice and homemade French fries. Even some leftover crab and lobster tails from the lunch buffet for the royals. She loaded up a plate with enough food for all three of them to enjoy, then headed upstairs to the front of the ship. They were sailing west, and the sky was clear, so the view of the sunset should be spectacular tonight.

Except when she got close to the bow, the male voice she heard with Adella wasn't the one she expected.

Davian. What the—?

She hurried to the bow and stopped short at the sight of Davian and their daughter. He was pointing out different spots on the shoreline and Adella seemed completely enraptured in his voice. For a brief second, panic welled inside her because she realized everything was changing. Then she quickly got herself back under control, forcing her feelings down deep where they belonged.

Of course he should spend time with Adella. She was his daughter. No need to worry.

Nope.

Cate still worried deep inside. Rather than voicing that though, she asked instead, "Where's Noah?"

Davian looked up, his cheeks pink from the wind and damn if Cate's heart didn't melt a little more. His smile, even and white in his tanned face, didn't help either. "He went inside to change."

"And eat," Adella added, looking over at Cate for the first time. Or rather, the plate of food in her hand. "Is that for me, Mommy? I'm starving."

"Yes," Cate said, her gaze still locked with Davian's. "I mean, yes. It's dinner. I brought enough for you and I and Noah, but if he's not here then—"

"I guess I'll just have to take his place," Davian volunteered, eyeing the lobster tails on the plate Cate held. "The seafood on board is excellent."

Flustered, Cate set the food and napkins on a small table Noah had set up earlier, then pulled out the bottles of water she'd stuck in her shorts pockets to carry them up here. "Uh, yeah. They catch it all locally. The seafood, I mean. The chef buys it right off the boats each morning. Can't get any fresher than that."

She helped Adella into one of the seats and got her situated with a bottle of water, a napkin tucked into the collar of her shirt like a bib, and some shrimp and fries. Then she picked up a lobster tail and perched atop one of the shiny silver windlasses used to raise and lower the anchors, since there were only two chairs to sit on to eat. Davian picked up a lobster tail as well and took a huge bite of the meat before looking up and catching her watching him with amusement. Butter slicked his mouth and he looked like a guilty schoolboy caught with his hand in the cookie jar. So, basically adorable. And handsome. And sexy. And enticing. And…

"Should you be sitting on that?" Davian asked, indicating the windlass with his non-lobster-holding hand.

"He's right, Mommy. Noah told me to never touch those things," Adella added.

"Oh, well." Cate stood and moved over to the table again. "I think he meant that kids shouldn't touch them, but adults are okay."

"I want to be an adult," Adella said, pouting. "You guys get to do all the fun stuff."

Cate and Davian locked eyes, both obviously fighting smiles, before Davian reached over to ruffle his daughter's hair. "Don't rush it, kid. Take your time. Enjoy being a kid."

"That's what everyone always says." Adella sighed, then brightened as she looked up at Cate. "Mommy, do you know Davian? He's my new friend. He knows all about the g'ography here."

"Uh, yes. I met Davian before," she said, giving him a warning look. "And I think you mean geography. That's the study of land."

"That's what I said." Adella giggled, then tried to feed her stuffed monkey a chip. "Are we going to watch the sunset, Mommy?"

"That's the plan." Cate took another bite of lobster. Sweet and salty goodness.

"Mind if I join you?" Davian asked quietly, probably to avoid Adella hearing him.

Unfortunately, what he wasn't familiar with was a five-year-old's bat-like sonar. When it was something she cared about, Adella could hear things a whole ship-length away. Now, if she was trying to ignore you, then it was another story.

"Oh, Mommy!" Adella said, bouncing excitedly in her chair. "Can he, Mommy? Can Davian watch the sunset with us?"

Between Davian's startled look and Adella's sly grin, Cate couldn't help laughing. "Fine. It's a free ship. Watch if you want."

Not exactly a romantic invitation, but Cate hadn't intended it to be.

They continued eating, Adella chattering away about what she and Davian had seen before Cate's arrival. Every so often Cate hazarded a glance up to find Davian watching their daughter, a look of pure captivation on his face. It would've been amazing if the rest of their situation hadn't been such a mess.

Finally, Adella finished her meal and asked if she could go play with the rest of her toys near the wall of the boat. Cate let her, keeping an eye on her daughter from the table. She and Davian sat across from each other now as the sun crept lower toward the horizon.

"Cate?"

His voice interrupted her thoughts and she looked over to find him watching her expectantly. Crap. Once again, she'd let herself get distracted and missed what someone was saying. So frustrating. This wasn't her, dammit. But the second her eyes met Davian's she wished they hadn't because suddenly he was too close and yes, too hot, for her to handle.

"You've got some butter on your face," he said, holding out a napkin.

"Oh." She took the napkin and wiped her mouth where he'd indicated. "Gone?"

"No."

She tried again. "How about now?"

He squinted over at her. "Still there. Let me try."

Davian snatched the napkin back from her before she could stop him, then stood to lean over the table toward her, lifting her chin gently with one hand while he brushed the napkin lightly over the corner of her mouth with the other. Her eyelids fluttered closed against her will as intoxicating sensation flooded her system. It had been so long, too long since someone had touched her the way Davian did. With such care and kindness and…

Time slowed as their gazes locked and the air between them sizzled. His eyes flicked to her mouth then back again, and Cate swallowed hard, fresh warmth tingling through her midsection. The same desire swarming inside her filled Davian's blue eyes as well, heating them. His gaze seemed to go darker then, still locked on Cate's face, his entire expression changing from intense concern to intense need. Davian leaned in a few inches more, so close that Cate could feel his breath on her cheeks. The napkin fell to the table, only to be replaced by Davian's hand cupping her cheek. They shouldn't be doing this. It was craziness. And Adella was right there, playing with her toys and ignoring them completely, but still.

This wasn't good. Not because she didn't want Davian too. In truth, she'd never really stopped wanting him, even after five years. But because right then, she wanted him too much. Anything that might happen between them on this charter couldn't last. He was going back to his country and his hospital, and she was going back to Boston to start her clinic. They'd keep in touch for Adella, but that was about it. This was just a remembrance of old feelings, an old life, making them imagine things that weren't there. There was no future in this. None. Not beyond a short-lived explosion of heat flaring hot and heavy between them, that would soon fizzle to nothing when they went their separate ways. Same as before.

But no matter how many times her logical mind shouted those things, Cate couldn't seem to make herself move away. He stayed where he was, watching, waiting, until finally, Davian leaned all the way in and kissed her, sending her blood racing and her heart pounding and man, oh, man… It was good.

Sweet and soft and so very sexy.

At least until…

"Mommy! Look at the sunset!" Adella yelled, running up to tug on the leg of Cate's shorts. "There's so many different colors."

A bit flummoxed by passion, Cate blinked at Davian for a few seconds before backing off and picking up her daughter, doing her best to concentrate on the moment, and not the man still standing behind her, looking as discombobulated as Cate felt.

Wow. That kiss had been everything she'd remember with Davian and more.

Which meant she couldn't let it happen again.

CHAPTER SEVEN

THEY WERE AT sea the next day. Not because they had a long voyage to reach their next destination, but because some of the members of the King's entourage wanted to play with the water toys. Jet Skis, a Jetlev, water skis, wakeboards, floats, hydrofoils, paddleboards, Seabobs, even a huge inflatable slide hung from the uppermost deck of the yacht down to the water—it had all been put out by the deck crew for their guests' entertainment. The sun was out, the water was relatively warm and it looked to be a great day of sun and fun.

For everyone except Davian, that was. He was still too focused on the almost-kiss last night with Cate to think of anything other than her and the fact that even after all these years his feelings for her were still just as strong. Even now, when he closed his eyes, he swore he could feel her breath on his face, see the tiny shudder that ran through her when his fingertips traced her cheek, the catch of her breath when he'd leaned in close, closer, so close that his lips nearly met hers and…

"Look out below!" Maybrook, one of his father's friends and an earl, yelled before barreling down the water slide and splashing into the water. Raucous laughter followed from the others already in the sea below.

They'd all been drinking for a while now, even though it was just barely noon.

Davian sighed and shook his head before returning his attention to the article he'd been reading. Of course, he could have been staring at a page full of cartoons for all his heart was in it right then. Normally, he loved reading all the technical aspects of new procedures, committing them to memory for later trial. But each time his thoughts started to drift, it was not to the OR where he performed his procedures, but to Cate.

Always Cate.

Or more precisely, at that point, why she continually changed the subject or refused to delve deeper into the issues surrounding their daughter, Adella.

Their daughter.

My daughter.

It still shocked him to say those words, despite repeating them in his head over and over and knowing in his heart it was true. Adella was his. She could have been his twin at that age. No denying it. But accepting it and feeling one hundred percent comfortable with the idea were two different things. Davian loved children. Always had. He'd just not expected to find out he had one out of the blue like this. And the fact that Cate still seemed wary of him didn't help matters. Yes, he'd hurt her. Yes, he was sorry for it. Sorrier than she could ever know. But if they were going to make this work, somehow, they had to get past that and move forward.

And speaking of moving forward…

"Let's try this again," Maybrook said, slurring his words slightly as he walked over to the inflatable slide once more. Puddles formed around his wet footprints on the wooden deck and his steps swayed a bit as he approached the area where two deckhands were positioned to help the guests up the steps to the top of the slide. "Can't let Shorington show me up, eh, Davie?"

Davian raised one hand in brief acknowledgment but didn't look up from his journal. He hated the nickname Davie and had told Maybrook on several occasions, to no avail. Still, the man was one of his father's oldest and dearest friends so there wasn't much he could do about it now.

"Gonna climb back up here like this..." Maybrook said from behind Davian.

"Sir, please wait a moment while we straighten the slide. The last wind gust— Sir!" one of the deckhands shouted.

The next thing Davian heard was a loud thud and a woman's scream. He was up and out of his chair in a second, his journal tossed aside without another thought in the face of a possible emergency. "What's wrong?" he said, hurrying over to where the two ashen-faced deckhands were staring down at the deck below theirs. "What's happened?"

"We told him to wait, sir," the one deckhand said. "The wind gust had twisted the slide and we were trying to straighten it, but he climbed up anyway and..."

One glance over the railing at the still body of Lord Maybrook on the deck below had adrenaline flooding Davian's system. He switched into surgeon mode immediately. "Call emergency. We need a medevac here ASAP."

Then he was jogging down the stairs to the lower deck, heart pounding in his ears in time with his steps. It had to be at least a fifteen-foot fall from the uppermost sundeck where they'd been down to here. And the teakwood decking was hard. Not good. Not good at all.

He ran over to where the man lay prone, his chest barely rising and falling.

"Maybrook," Davian said, palpating his head and neck, searching for injuries. "Maybrook, can you hear me?"

"What's happened?" Cate asked, running over to kneel on the other side of the patient.

Davian filled her in on the slide incident then took her stethoscope to listen to the man's lungs. "Shallow respirations. So far, he's remained unconscious and unresponsive."

"Sir! Sir!" Cate patted the man's cheeks again. "Sir, this is Dr. Neves. Can you answer me?"

Maybrook moaned a little then began flailing his arms and legs, nearly knocking Cate over. Davian moved fast to pin them down so Maybrook wouldn't hurt himself or them. The man's eyes flickered open, dazed and confused.

"Maybrook," Davian said, staring down into the older man's face. "It's Davian. You've had a fall and you're hurt. We're trying to help you. Please stay still."

"Medevac is on the way," one of the deckhands said, keeping the other guests off to the side, including Maybrook's sobbing wife. "Should be here in five minutes."

"Sir, can you tell me where it hurts?" Cate asked opening the man's life vest to palpate his chest. "Here? Or what about here?"

"Yes! There! Dammit, that hurts. Ouch!" Maybrook yelled, the scent of alcohol heavy on his breath. They could talk to the crew later about the hazards of letting guests under the influence use the water toys, not that Maybrook would have listened. But right now everything had to be about saving their patient's life.

"Abdomen tender," Cate noted. "Also swollen. I'm

guessing we've got some internal bleeding going on in there too."

"Do you have a catheter in that medical pack?" Davian asked, hiking his chin toward the black bag near Cate's feet.

"I do."

"Okay." Davian glanced over to where a small crowd had gathered on the deck. "Can you please move everyone away? We need to perform a procedure on the patient to assess his internal injuries."

The deckhands quickly herded the others away from the scene, Maybrook's wife still crying softly into Davian's mother's shoulder.

"We need to get a catheter in him and see if there's blood in his urine," Davian said, moving to the medical kit for the necessary supplies. Once he'd gloved up and gotten the equipment, he moved back to Maybrook and inserted the catheter. It was no sooner in than bright red blood filled the tube. "We have blood. I'm guessing a liver laceration and probably kidney injury as well."

"Dammit. Okay." Cate continued her steady, thorough exam of the man's torso. "Sir, where else does it hurt?"

"My back!" Maybrook said. "My back is killing me. Can I turn onto my side?"

"No." Davian positioned himself over the man's torso to prevent him from moving again. "Maybrook, listen to me. You've had a fall. A pretty bad one. You can't move until the medics get here or you could risk hurting yourself even more. Just lay still, all right?"

Cate finished her assessment then sat back, catching Davian's eye. They both had their game faces on because of the emergency. Even during the most difficult cases, the physician had to keep control, otherwise the patient's chances of making it were almost nil. But he could see in her eyes the seriousness of Maybrook's condition. They'd already confirmed internal bleeding, which meant they had perhaps a fifteen- to twenty-minute window to get him to a medical facility and into surgery or he could bleed out and die.

Cate took the stethoscope back from Davian and checked Maybrook's blood pressure. "It's low. Eighty over sixty. From the internal bleeding most likely."

"I need to get up," Maybrook said, struggling against Davian. "I don't want my wife to see me like this. I have an image to protect."

Davian opened his mouth to tell the man that when your life was falling apart, image meant nothing. He should know. But before he could, the whomp-whomp-whomp of the approaching medevac helicopter stopped him. Soon, the chopper landed on the aft deck helipad a short distance away and two medics raced up to where Cate and Davian were working on Maybrook. He filled them in on what he knew.

"Sixty-two-year-old male fell from a height of about fifteen feet and landed on his back. Exam shows suspected internal bleeding, possibly liver and kidney, and there is blood in his urine. He complains of back pain also. Loss of consciousness and some combativeness and disorientation."

"What's happening with my husband?" Maybrook's wife cried out, a brightly colored beach towel wrapped around her still-wet, bathing suit–clad body. She had on flip-flops and a sun hat, about as far away from courtly glitz and glamour as a person could be. In the end, they were all just people, doing the best they could to get by, Davian realized. Same as him. He moved aside as the medics got Maybrook carefully loaded onto a body board and started an IV in his arm then trundled him off to the waiting chopper.

"Wait!" Maybrook's wife called. "I want to go with him."

The medics hurried her aboard the helicopter alongside her husband then quickly took off for the shore and an awaiting surgical team at the hospital there who'd been briefed on the situation.

Afterward, Davian and Cate stood with the others, watching the chopper recede into the distance, the air oddly silent except for the caw of seagulls and the whistle of the wind.

Davian didn't realize until someone bumped his arm that his father was standing beside him, looking gruff and visibly shaken. He turned and guided his father to a nearby chair to sit in. "You should rest. That was quite a nasty ordeal."

"Will he be all right?" the King asked, seemingly having aged ten years in the past ten minutes.

"I don't know," Davian said, honestly, crouching beside his father. "But he's in good hands with the surgeons. I'll call later and get an update on him."

His father nodded gravely. "Thank God you were here, son."

"It's my job," Davian said.

"It's your calling," his father said. And for the first time, Davian felt seen. Medicine was his calling. Always had been, but he'd never imagined his father recognizing that and acknowledging it. Then as quickly as the moment had arrived, it disappeared, and his father visibly withdrew again behind his walls of kingly distance. The King cleared his throat and stood, gripping the chair back. "Make sure this never leaks into the press."

Davian rocked back on his heels and hung his head.

There it was again. The press. Always the press. His father's good friend had been badly injured and still, all his father was worried about was if the story would be leaked. Enough. This was exactly why Davian wanted no more of the royal life. Putting image above all else. And it nudged him one step closer to renouncing it all for good.

"Well, that was not how I pictured my lunch hour going," Cate said as she cleaned up the medical supplies strewn on the deck from the emergency. "How about you?"

Davian had withdrawn again, closing himself off behind those walls of his, after talking to his father. Her heart ached for him a little that they didn't get along, but then at least he had his father there. It was more than she'd had growing up.

"Hmm." He walked back over to help her. "You did good work there, Doctor."

"As did you." She smiled. If she was being truthful, she'd always loved working with Davian because they made each other better. They had a healthy competition that kept them both performing at the top of their games. "Good call with the catheter."

"Thanks."

"Is your father okay?" she asked as she zipped up an outside pocket on the med pack.

"He'll be fine." Davian frowned then straightened, holding out a hand to help Cate up. "Got to project that strong image, you know."

There was a brittleness to his tone that pricked her heart. "Must be exhausting, always being strong like that."

"It is," he said, following her back down to the clinic belowdecks.

Having him there, in her space was…odd. Obviously,

with the whole Adella issue out there now, they'd be spending more time together this charter, but still. Cate had been on her own a long time and having Davian there now felt strange. Not bad necessarily, but different. Plus, she was still having a hard time dealing with all the ramifications of telling him about his daughter. It was too late now, but perhaps she shouldn't have told him. Or should have chosen her moment better. But then, when would exactly the right time be to tell a man that he had a five-year-old daughter he never knew about?

Ugh. Those thoughts had kept Cate tossing and turning all last night and still had her tied in knots today. She unlocked the clinic door and pushed inside, flipping the lights on and setting the med pack down on the floor near the supply closet for refilling, as Davian followed her inside then closed the door behind them. Dr. Bryant had the day off and Carrie was on break so that left just Cate to man the clinic at present. Probably a good thing, since her heart was racing, and it had nothing to do with the trek down here and everything to do with the man across from her who seemed to suck up all the oxygen in the room.

"It makes you think, doesn't it?" Davian said, sinking down into one of the chairs near the door in their makeshift waiting room. "An accident like that."

"How do you mean?" she asked, pulling a couple bottles of water out of a small fridge behind the reception desk. Cate handed one to Davian then took a seat in the chair beside his.

"Just how things can change so quickly, out of the blue."

She nodded and sipped her water. "That's certainly true in our case."

"Yes, it is."

They sat in silence a moment, Davian leaning forward to rest his forearms atop his thighs, his hands between his knees. He took a deep breath then looked back at her over his shoulder. "How are you coping with it all?"

"Us, you mean?" She shrugged. "Okay, I guess. It's a lot. How about you?"

He bit his lower lip then sat back, his arm brushing hers as he did so, sending shocks of unwanted awareness through her body. Coping with the mental reality of having Davian back in her life was enough at present. She didn't need the physical and emotional realities jamming up her circuits too. Except, her body seemed to have other ideas. Davian ran a hand through his dark hair then stared up at the ceiling. "I don't know, Cate. I really don't. I'd like to say that I'm overjoyed by the news of Adella, but that would be a lie."

Cate's posture stiffened. "You said you were happy."

"I am happy. I'm also just…confused. Torn." He shook his head and closed his eyes. "I'm trying to stay present here for this. To keep you in the loop with what I'm feeling and thinking. Figure that's the least I can do after shutting you out all those years ago. But it's hard."

"I know." She fiddled with the label on her bottle, picking at one corner.

"You do?"

He was looking at her now. Even though she was staring at her bottle she could feel his gaze, burning into her temple.

She sighed and looked over at him. It would be so easy, to let him in again, to talk to him. Davian had always been such a good listener, despite how things had ended with them. But no. She couldn't trust him again, certainly not so quickly. Still, he was watching her with such concern in his eyes that she felt like she should give him something, so she said, "I do. I mean, growing up an only child of a single mom, you learn to keep things in."

Not a lie. Not the complete truth either.

He blinked at her a few times, then nodded. "I can see that. I remember you talking about her back in residency. How is your mom?"

"Good. Still living in Boston. She keeps an eye on my house for me while we're away."

"That's convenient."

"Yep."

Another awkward silence ensued, all the things that hadn't been said hanging heavy between them like an overfilled clothesline. Finally, Davian blurted out, "I'm going to talk to my parents before this trip is over and tell them that I'm leaving royal life."

Cate looked over at him, her brows knit. "What? Why?"

"Because it's the right decision for me. I've felt it for quite some time, but now with Adella, I know it's what I must do. I don't want to expose her to all the horrible things that happened to me growing up in that life." He sighed and shook his head. "The deception, the unfair duty, the false bravado. I just want to practice medicine and have a normal life. And I want Adella to have a normal life too."

Her alarm bells went off before she could stop them. Hearing Davian talk so passionately about a future with their daughter brought out her mama bear side again and Cate pushed to her feet, her tone cool. "Well, just remember that I'm the one who sets the ground rules here. I decide what does and does not happen in Adella's future, whether you remain a prince or not. And I'll still be the one deciding when we tell her about you. Understood?"

Davian narrowed his gaze on her and for a moment,

Cate worried she'd pushed too far. But then he sighed and stood as well, his small smile conciliatory. "Yes, Cate. I understand. But you should also know that I plan to be so charming and indispensable that you and Adella won't be able to live without me."

Cate watched as he opened the door and walked out, still staring after him as he retreated down the hallway.

Unfortunately, not being able to live without him was exactly what she feared most.

CHAPTER EIGHT

THE NEXT MORNING, bright and early, Davian was up and ready to go ashore. But first he needed to see his parents off with their security team. Unfortunately, though, when he arrived on deck for breakfast, Noah was waiting for him. He'd gotten word from the hospital onshore that Lord Maybrook had come through surgery well and his condition had improved, which was an encouraging sign.

"Where are the King and Queen?" Davian asked, frowning.

"Still abed. Your father says he's not up to traipsing around Monaco today and wishes to stay on board the ship instead. Your mother agrees. After everything that happened yesterday, they don't feel up to leaving."

"Are you sure?" Concern edged Davian's tone. When he'd talked to his father the night before, they'd still been excited to go into Monte Carlo and Davian had worked hard to arrange everything they wanted to do, including having lunch with old friends they'd not seen in years at a private villa. "Is everything all right? My father is feeling all right?"

"The King said yes, Your Highness," Noah said. "Just that they wished to stay on the ship instead. They said not to change your plans at all, and they would see you at dinner tonight."

And now Davian's concern deepened to worry. His father loved to travel and his mother loved to shop. Both were possible today, so them deciding not to go was a huge red flag. Between his father's health issues and the assassination threats, stress levels were through the roof for his family. Questioning the chief steward about it though wouldn't get him any further, so Davian decided to go straight to the source.

"Thank you, Noah. If Dr. Neves and her daughter arrive, please tell them to wait. I'll be right back."

"Yes, Your Highness."

Davian hurried downstairs to the master suite and knocked on the door. "Mother, Father? It's Davian. May I come in?"

The door opened slightly a moment later to his mother, still in her silk dressing gown, looking up at him through the crack. "Yes, dear. What is it?"

"I was told you won't be going ashore today. Is everything all right?"

"Yes, dear," his mother said, not moving to allow the door to open wider. "We're fine. Just want to stay here and relax a bit. Enjoy the sunshine."

On the surface, it sounded plausible enough, but Davian was still wary. "What about your friends? They were so excited to see you both today and went to a lot of trouble to get the villa ready for your visit."

"I've called them already to explain. They're going to come to the yacht for lunch instead, dear. All taken care of."

"Oh." Davian didn't have a response for that. He tried to lean around his mother to see his father in the room but couldn't. "What about Father? Is he feeling well?"

"Fine, son," came a deep voice echoing out of the suite. "Just catching up on some business emails while

I'm resting," his father said. "Let the boy in, Arabella. You know how he worries."

His mother moved aside then and opened the door so Davian could see his father stretched out atop the huge king-size bed. Pillows were stacked up behind him, propping him up so he could work on his tablet comfortably. He too had a silk dressing gown on over black silk pants, and glasses so he could see the screen better. He appeared healthy and hearty, despite Davian's concerns.

Okay. Maybe he was projecting some of his own nerves about the day ahead with Cate and Adella onto a situation where they weren't warranted. Being a doctor was sometimes a double-edged sword. You sometimes saw emergencies where there were none, especially with those closest to you. It seemed that was what was happening here.

Davian took a deep breath then raked a hand through his hair. "Okay. Sorry. Sounds like you two have things all squared away then. But please call me if you need anything, yes? I'll have my phone with me all day."

"Thank you, dear," his mother said, looking him up and down with a smile. He'd dressed casually today in a loose-fitting Hawaiian-style shirt and cargo shorts, sandals on his feet. "Good to see you having some fun for a change. Enjoy yourself."

"Thanks. I hope to," Davian said, turning to leave.

"Son, come here." His father's voice stopped him. "I have some questions."

He exhaled slowly then walked into the master cabin to stand by the side of the bed. "Yes, Father?"

"This woman you're going with, Dr. Neves. You knew her in college?" his father asked.

"Yes. We did our residency together at Stanford." *Or*

most of it, anyway, until you called me home abruptly. Davian left that last part out. "She's a friend. Why?"

"Just be careful, son," his father said, looking up at Davian over the rim of his glasses. "The last thing we need right now is a scandal."

It took most of his effort to bite back his response to that. The only scandals Davian had ever been involved in at the palace had been ones of his father's PR team's invention. Anger burned in his gut before he extinguished it. The cruise would be over in a few days, then they could get back to their normal lives again and Davian could keep more distance between himself and his royal duty. Until then, it was best to just grin and bear it. "Today will be scandal free, I promise. She'll have her five-year-old daughter there. Hard to be scandalous with kids around."

"Hmm," his father said, sounding thoroughly unconvinced, which rubbed Davian wrong, but nothing to do for it except leave. "Bring her to dinner tonight. I want to meet her myself."

"Uh, okay. I'll do that," Davian said, kissing his mother briefly on the cheek before heading upstairs again to find Cate and Adella waiting for him near the passerelle. They were wearing matching white tops and jean shorts, with white sneakers. Davian had a hard time looking away from Cate's long, bare legs, but forced himself to, smiling as he approached. "Good morning, ladies. Are we ready for an adventure?"

"Yes, please," Adella said, letting go of Cate's hand to clap. "I want an adventure, Davian!"

"Then you shall have one, Princess!" He laughed and swooped her up in his arms as she giggled and held on to him tight. His chest squeezed at the sweetness of holding his daughter for the first time. Then he glanced at

Cate and saw the flicker of wariness in her green eyes and vowed to do whatever he must to make that disappear by the end of the day. His gaze dropped to her pink lips for a second, remembering their kiss from the night before—hot, electric and far too brief—then he shoved that aside too. If things went to plan, there'd be no time for kissing today. Besides, with Adella there and the fact that there were still so many unknowns between him and Cate, no kissing was probably a good idea, regardless of how his heart raced at the thought. She smiled and gestured toward the passerelle extending to the concrete dock on the other side. "Shall we go?"

The principality of Monaco was not big, but what it lacked in size, it made up for in style. One of the most affluent spots in the world, with its palace and grand casino, it was also rich in nature. Today, Davian had designed a private tour for them to see it all.

They started at the Palais du Prince, the residence of the royal family of Monaco. While Davian had grown up in his own family's smaller and more rugged castle back in Ruclecia, this palace was much older and much more ornate than any in his homeland. Built in the thirteenth century as a Genoese fortress, the Palais du Prince overlooked the whole of Monaco from its lofty perch, allowing for great views of the city of Monte Carlo and the sea below. As they walked through the gilded halls and the lush Blue Room, Cate whispered and pointed out things to Adella, who seemed enthralled with it all. But it wasn't until they reached the throne room, with its huge gold and red velvet throne at the front, that Adella said, "Is that where you sit, Davian?"

Eyes wide, he looked over at Cate, who seemed as shocked as he was that Adella knew his status. He crouched beside her and said, "No, I don't sit on a throne like that, Princess. My father does. And how did you know that?"

"Noah told me about you," Adella said, sounding very forthright. "He said you're nobility."

"Ah." Davian straightened. "Right," he said, leading them out of the throne room toward the exit. "Where should we go next? How about the aquarium?"

"Is that where they have all the fish?" Adella asked, taking hold of Davian's hand, so she was between both him and Cate. "I want to see a shark. Do they have a shark, Mommy?"

"I don't know, sweetie. I guess we'll find out."

Not only did they have sharks, but they also had a huge cylindrical tank filled with jellyfish, an extensive coral exhibit, a rehab center for injured sea turtles, and a gorgeous observation deck with incredible views of the Mediterranean. There were also numerous exhibits about the north and south poles and climate change, something Davian and his older brother were passionate about as well. It was all very well done and informative and gave Davian lots of ideas to talk to his brother about when he got back to Ruclecia—things they could do similarly in their own country to bring in more tourists while also helping the planet. By the time they were done there and heading to lunch, they were all starving.

"Mommy!" Adella said in the private chauffeured van Davian had rented for their use for the day. "Did you see me walking on those whale skeletons? That was so cool!"

"I did, sweetie." Cate laughed and kissed the top of Adella's head. "It's amazing what they can do with those lights now."

"Isn't it?" Davian said, his arm draped along the back of the seat, his fingers grazing Cate's shoulder as Adella sat between them. It felt so natural and normal and right, them being together like this. Almost like a real family. He hadn't realized how much he craved that until now. "Have you seen the Van Gogh immersive exhibition that uses the same technology?"

"Yes. My mom and I went when it came to Boston and it was incredible. Adella was still too young to remember it, but she was there too."

"Where was I, Mommy?" Adella asked, frowning as she looked up from playing with her stuffed toys. In addition to her monkey, now she also had a stuffed octopus that Davian had bought for her at the aquarium. "And who's Van Gogh?"

"He's a famous artist, sweetie," Cate said, stroking Adella's hair back from her face. It was pulled back into a ponytail, but some strands had come loose. "And you were with Grandmom and me at the exhibit of his work when you were just a baby."

"Oh. I don't remember that." Adella fiddled with her toys again before adding, "Davian should come with us next time too. You'll come too, won't you, Davian?"

"I... Uh..." He looked from Adella to Cate then back again. "We'll see, Princess."

The little girl sighed. "I don't have a daddy, you know."

Talk about a sucker punch to the gut. All the air huffed out of Davian's lungs as he struggled with how to handle that. Part of him wanted to scoop his daughter up and say, *Yes, you do have a father. Me. Right here. And I'll never leave you again.* But the other part of him, the part trained for years to look out for the family first, held him back. Once that secret was out of the box, it couldn't be put back in again. For the moment, only he and Cate knew, and Davian wanted to keep it that way until they'd worked out all the details of handling it going forward. Only then did he plan to tell Adella, followed by his parents and brother, then finally the rest of the world.

So, instead of answering her question, Davian changed subjects by asking one of his own. "Okay. Who's hungry?"

The relief on Cate's face mirrored his own when Adella quickly raised her hand, her former melancholy apparently forgotten. "Me! I'm so hungry!"

"Great." Davian leaned closer to the driver to whisper something to him then sat back again. "We should be there shortly."

A few minutes later, they pulled up in front of a long, narrow alleyway packed on both sides with shops and vendors. They got out and walked through the crowds, stopping every so often to look at items on sale or to window-shop. Finally, they went around a slight bend and the smells of garlic and fresh baked bread made Davian's stomach rumble.

"Oh, that smells good!" Cate said, inhaling deep. "Where are we going?"

"Just to the best pizza place in all of Monaco!" He took Adella's hand and they walked the little girl between them up to a doorway with a white awning over the top reading La Tavernetta. The hostess inside recognized Davian from his last trip there a few years earlier with this brother and rushed over to give him a hug. They were an old Italian family who'd run the little restaurant for years. Not many tourists knew about it, but all the locals did, which meant the food was excellent. They were shown to a quiet table in the corner, near the windows, where they could people watch while they ate.

They ordered drinks and pizza, then chatted while they waited for their food.

"How did you know about this place?" Cate asked between sips of her water.

"This is one of my favorite places in Monaco," Davian said, smiling. "My brother and I discovered it while visiting here with our parents years ago and I've kept coming back since. It's a good spot to just sit and wonder about things." He sighed. "And when my life fell apart during residency, I'd come here alone for privacy. It was my sanctuary."

"It's good that you had a place of your own to go to," Cate said. "And that you had your brother to hang out with. Are you two still close?"

"Not as much as we were back then," Davian said, his chest squeezing a bit with nostalgia. "When we were kids, it was like us against the world. But as we grew older, he was put on track to become King and I was left more to my own devices." He snorted. "Well, at least until they needed me to quell an emergency in the PR department."

Cate reached over and took his hand, frowning. "And your brother was okay with that? Them using you, I mean?"

"No. Of course not." He took a deep breath and put his head back, closing his eyes. "But as Crown Prince, Arthur had about as much power to stop the royal press machine as I did back then. He tried to be as supportive as possible, telling me that we'd fix whatever had broken once the crisis was over, but then he'd be taken away to do a diplomacy visit or give a speech or visit some dignitary and I'd still have a mess on my hands." Her fingers tightened around his gently in a show of support. "Anyway, I'm sure that's part of the reason why I acted out in my teens, partied so much. Just to forget it all for a while."

"I'm so sorry, Davian. I had no idea you went through all that. You deserved better."

His breath caught at the tender conviction in her tone, and he wanted nothing more than to pull her into his arms and hold her close but didn't dare. Not yet.

Her gaze flicked from his to scan the interior, the plain white walls, the curved ceiling, the simple, local paintings hanging around the space, and she smiled. She looked even more beautiful today, if that were possible, relaxed and enjoying herself—at least until his little confession—and Davian's heart squeezed. He wanted to get the spotlight off himself and learn more about her. To know everything there was to know about Cate Neves. "It must be hard, traveling so much with charters. Do you miss your mother?"

"Sometimes." Cate looked at him, blinking for a second like it took her that moment to register what he'd said. Then her cheeks flushed pink, and her gaze darted away again. "I talk to her at least once a week on the phone, so that helps."

Davian wished she'd let him in, reveal more about herself, but he didn't want to push. As much as he was press-phobic, he knew trust was an issue for her and stressing her out about it would only make it worse. She'd tell him more when she was ready.

"And here we are," their server said, setting a tray full of food on a stand nearby. The man set out plates and silverware, then a large stone-fired margherita pizza and a fresh salad.

Hungry, they all dug into their food, not taking much time to converse until out of the blue Adella said,

"Where do the baby whales we saw in the aquarium come from?"

He nearly choked on a bite of pizza, coughing into his napkin then taking a big swig of soda to cover it. "Uh…"

"Finish your food, sweetie," Cate intervened, giving Davian a little wink. "We can have crème brûlée for dessert."

"Creamy what?" Adella scrunched her nose.

"Crème brûlée," Cate repeated, her soft pink lips forming all sorts of interesting shapes that had Davian looking away fast to avoid embarrassing himself again. "It's like vanilla custard, but with a crunchy layer of toasted sugar on top."

"Oh, yes! I want to try that, Mommy!"

To prove it, Adella shoved a large bite of pizza into her mouth and chewed fast, making both Cate and Davian laugh. "A girl after my own heart," he said, reaching over to ruffle Adella's hair. There was a slight curl to it, just like his. One more way they were alike.

After they finished lunch, Davian paid the bill, then they went back out to the rental van again to head to their afternoon destination, Les Jardins Saint Martin. The lovely gardens were located right next to the aquarium, but Davian had thought it might be too much to do all at once with little Adella, and he'd been right. Before they even reached their last destination, Adella fell asleep in the van, her toys clutched to her chest to keep them safe. When they got to the gardens, which stretched along the coastline near Le Rocher and featured stunning views of the Mediterranean, Davian hired a stroller to carry Adella in to save his and Cate's arms. Their daughter didn't even wake up when they transferred her, showing how tired out she was.

Strolling the quiet, peaceful paths was the perfect

ending to a lovely day. Sun-dappled trails hugging the Rock of Monaco led them through the gardens themselves, past statues, fountains, Aleppo pines, yellow agave and even the famed Monaco Cathedral. Cate had had her phone out all day, snapping pictures for posterity. Normally, Davian shied away from cameras, but he trusted Cate and knew they were for her own memories, nothing more.

They stopped to gaze out over the sea near the statue of Prince Albert as a sailor near the center of the gardens and took a seat on a bench to rest a while before heading back to the van.

Cate stared out to sea, the breeze gently ruffling her hair, and if circumstances had been different, Davian would've pulled her into his side and inhaled her scent. Soap and lemons. As it was, they sat side by side with silence stretching between them like a sail.

Finally, she said, "Thank you, Davian. For bringing us here today. It was wonderful."

"I'm glad you liked it." He exhaled slowly, his shoulders slumping as he thought about returning to the yacht. "I'm worried about my father."

She looked over at him, frowning behind her sunglasses. "Why? What happened?"

"They didn't go on their tour today. The one I spent days planning for them. I don't care about the tour, but it's not like them to cancel plans with friends." He shook his head and looked out over the blue waters that stretched to the horizon, sunlight sparkling atop them. "I told you about his heart attack and bypass and I'm concerned he's having problems again."

"Did you ask him about it?"

"Yes. This morning before we left. Both he and my mother said he was fine, but…"

"You don't believe them?"

"No, I don't." Davian looked away. "It wouldn't be the first time they kept me out of the loop on things."

"No, I guess it wouldn't." Cate watched him a moment, then said, "I'm sorry about how they treated you in residency. That wasn't right."

"No, it wasn't." He took a deep breath then reached for her hand on the bench, glad when she didn't pull away. "And I'm sorry for everything I've put you through, Cate. None of this was ever my intention. I hope you know that now."

She gave a small nod, staring down at their entwined fingers on the white stone bench. "I never told you back in residency, but after my father walked out on us, I still remember seeing him with his new family sometimes, so happy and carefree, so different from how he was with us." She gave a mirthless laugh. "You know, he never once told me he was sorry. Sorry about walking away, sorry about lying to us. Just goodbye and that was that. He threw us away like we were trash, Davian. Like we didn't matter at all. I never want Adella to go through feeling that way. That's why I'm so careful with her." She took a deep breath then released it. "That's why I have such a hard time trusting people."

He didn't respond, just stroked his thumb over her wrist and squeezed her fingers, letting her know he was there to support her, if needed.

"I've done well raising Adella on my own, so it's not easy for me to let someone into our lives now. Especially you…after what happened." She inhaled and looked up at him, his face reflected in her sunglass lenses. "But after talking with you, hearing your side of things…"

"Davian?" Adella's little voice, still groggy with sleep, said from the stroller. "Can we go look at those flowers? The pretty pink ones by the wall?" She squirmed in her seat, the restraints keeping her from getting out by herself. "Pink's my favorite color."

He swallowed hard and looked to Cate for guidance or permission or both. She gave a subtle nod and Davian smiled. He wasn't sure how they'd navigate this new path going forward, but he did want to try. With every bone in his body. "Sure, Princess. Let me just get you out of this stroller and we'll go look at them."

Cate stayed back on the bench with the stroller watching her daughter and Davian whispering to each other about the flowers and Adella listening raptly to Davian as he explained to her about the bees and pollination. It would be obvious to anyone who saw the two together that they were related—same eyes, same coloring, same intense expression when they were consumed with a topic that interested them—but Cate couldn't bring herself to care about the risks that might cause. Not then. Not when joy bubbled in her bloodstream to see Adella so happy with her father.

Until that moment, the idea that her daughter might be missing out on important life lessons because she was without her father had been more of a nebulous thing, something to deal with down the road. But now it was plain as day. Davian had a way of relating to Adella that was different than Cate, but just as important. More as a teacher, a confidant, a friend. And while Cate hoped that her daughter saw her as all those things too, it was unique with Davian.

Even more impressive to her was the fact of how available Davian made himself to Adella. Never balking at her constant questions, never hesitating to do whatever Adella asked of him, no matter how silly. The fact that a prince of Ruclecia was currently sitting on the ground talking to a bumblebee for his daughter's amusement was proof enough of that. He was there. Present. In ways Cate's own father had never been for her. And perhaps it was that fact, more than anything else, that finally made something click inside her. Finally pushed her suspicions and skepticism aside and made Cate realize that telling Adella that Davian was her father was the right thing to do.

She inhaled deep, expecting the same rush of tension that usually accompanied that thought to course through her, but it never came. Huh. Cate exhaled through her nose, still watching Adella and Davian move on to a different set of flowers, these white and yellow and purple. Davian seemed to know the names of all of them and shared little tidbits of information about the plants with Adella, delighting her and keeping her in a state of amazed curiosity. No small feat with a five-year-old.

No. Telling their daughter the truth was the right thing to do. After all, Cate had shared more with Davian today about her own father and the pain that seeing him with a new family, a different family, had caused her. As if Cate and her mother were a mistake and his new family was a do-over. But she'd wanted him to know, wanted Davian to have all the facts about her and her past before he made a decision about his future with Adella. Because for Cate, there was no in between. Davian had to be all in or all out. No hesitation. No second-guessing afterward. She'd been through that searing, scalding shame, that feeling of utter, gut-wrenching abandonment, and she would never, ever put her precious Adella through that.

When Adella and Davian returned to her at last and they got their daughter secured back in the stroller, they started back down toward the yacht. More people had arrived, it seemed, and the footpaths were more crowded, forcing her and Davian to walk closer together, their shoulders brushing with each step. Adella was chattering away to herself about the flowers and the bees and a comfortable silence settled between them.

At least until Cate said the words she needed to say. "Davian, I've been thinking."

He chuckled and smiled over at her. "Uh-oh."

"I'm serious." She gave him a playful swat on the arm then lowered her voice to make sure Adella wouldn't hear. "I have no idea how this will work, with us half a world apart, but Adella likes you and I think she should have a father in her life. You two are good together. I think we should tell her. About you being her father. If that's what you want too."

Davian's eyes widened and he stopped in the middle of the footpath, to the discontent of the people behind them. They moved over to the side, near a small flowering bush out of the flow of traffic and into a small private alcove in the shade. He looked astonished. A tad apprehensive too. But also excited. "Yes," he said. "I'd like that too."

"Good."

"Good."

They were closer here, closer than Cate had realized initially. And with all the extra people around now, they had to wait a moment for a break in traffic to ease back onto the footpath. Still, Cate didn't mind. Neither did Davian apparently, since his gaze was still locked on hers, bluer than any sea she'd ever imagined. Time seemed to slow in their little paradise as he leaned in, his eyes flicking down to her lips, which were tingling as if she'd been stung. Then his mouth was on hers, soft and slow and lingering. Sweet and sinful and so very good all at the same time.

Davian pulled back a little. “Cate, I…”

Before he could finish she grabbed him by the front of his shirt and pulled him back to her to kiss him again, a bit harder this time.

When they parted this time, they were both breathless and grinning, their foreheads together.

Cate felt lighter than she had in days, years even, despite everything that had happened on this charter. Having Davian in her life again felt good, right. And she wasn’t ready to give that up yet. “We should probably keep going,” she said after a moment, smoothing his shirt back into place. “Wouldn’t want you to be late for dinner.”

“My parents want you to join us,” he blurted out with less finesse than usual.

“What? Really?” Now it was Cate’s turn to be astonished, her brows rising. “We’ve never dined with royalty. What if I pull a *Pretty Woman* and send a snail flying up against the wall?”

“I doubt that will happen.” Davian leaned in to sneak one last, quick kiss then grinned. “From what I remember at Stanford, we attended several highbrow conferences together and you always had perfect table manners.”

“Yeah, but this is with a king and queen.”

“They’re just my family, at the end of the day. Don’t worry. My mom is great, and she can keep my dad reined in just fine.”

“I hope so.”

I hope so too.

“Mommy? Davian? Why are we stopped?” Adella asked, her tone starting to turn a tad whiny.

Yep. Definitely time to get back to the boat.

They left the alcove and returned to the footpath while Adella waved goodbye to all the flowers and bushes and bees on the way back to the park entrance. By the time the shuttle van arrived to take them to the dock, their daughter was snoozing. Davian took Cate's hand in his to help her into the van, then kept ahold of it, and Cate couldn't remember a time she'd felt more at peace.

CHAPTER NINE

CATE GAVE HERSELF a pep talk in the shower that night and as she got dressed, building her confidence for dining with a king and queen, but it all faltered when she entered the formal dining room on the main deck of the *Querencia*. Davian had told her eight sharp for dinner and she was right on time, but the rest of them were already there and seated at her arrival.

She was used to walking into exam rooms and boardrooms full of men and holding her head high and proving her point. But tonight felt more important than any procedure or treatment she'd ever performed in her life. And while she'd never been overly fixated on her appearance, she'd spent at least an hour going back and forth over what to wear and had ended up settling on the only thing that was appropriate for such an event, her standard little black dress. It wasn't anything spectacular, hitting just above her knees, with three-quarter-length sleeves and a boatneck that showed off her neck and collarbones. But the fabric was good and so was the cut. She'd spent way too much money buying it at a fancy designer boutique in Boston before working on her first cruise ship at the insistence of her mother, who'd said she'd need something nice to wear to dinners at the captain's table. At the time, Cate had thought the suggestion silly, but now she was grateful for all those reruns of *The Love Boat* her mother had watched while Cate was growing up.

The whole day had felt like a magical dream. And in the gardens, it felt like things had changed between her and Davian, that they'd taken a major step forward. Not just in regard to telling Adella about her father, but also between Cate and Davian. They weren't lovers, but she felt closer to him now than she ever had before. Probably because for the first time, they saw each other. The real people, flaws and all. Not the polished, perfected facades they presented to the world. It left Cate feeling unsettled and unexpectedly energized to see what happened next. She wasn't a risk-taker by nature, but Davian seemed to bring out her boldness.

Stomach as tight as her smile, Cate dropped into a tiny curtsy at the top of the stairs and prayed for grace. "Good evening, Your Majesties."

Davian stood and grinned, warm and genuine, holding out a hand to her. "Ah, here's Dr. Neves now." When Cate drew nearer, he whispered in her ear, "You look lovely tonight."

Heat prickled her cheeks at the rush of warmth in her system, bringing back thoughts of their kisses earlier. She quickly pushed those away though as her gaze remained fixed on Davian's parents sitting directly across from them at the long table.

It was apparent that Davian had taken after his father in build and bone structure as King Phillipe stood, his attention zeroed in on Cate. "Dr. Neves. Nice to finally meet you," he said, his voice deeper and more accented than Davian's. He wore a plain black suit, white shirt, and dark tie emblazoned with tiny embroidered Ruclecian flags. "My son has told us so much about you."

Unsure how to greet royalty, Cate dipped into an awkward curtsy. “Thank you, Your Majesty. I’m honored to dine with you tonight.”

“Oh, my dear,” Davian’s mother, Queen Arabella, said, her voice sweet and warm like honey. “No need to be so formal here. We’re on vacation, after all.” She stood as well and reached across the table to shake Cate’s hand. She wore a pale blue sleeveless sheath dress that was deceptively simple but had to cost a lot of money, based on the perfect fit and how the color perfectly matched her eyes. The same shade as Davian’s and Adella’s. “You’re as lovely as Davian said. Please do sit down.”

Once they were all settled again and their drinks had been served, Cate hazarded a nervous smile at Davian beside her. “Adella couldn’t stop talking about the trip today. She had a fabulous time, Davian. We both did. Thank you for showing us around Monaco.”

“My pleasure.”

Beneath the table, Davian reached over and took her hand, giving it a reassuring squeeze. Before today, Cate would’ve pulled away. But tonight, she could use all the support she could get, especially when King Phillipe began questioning her.

“Adella is your daughter, Dr. Neves?” he asked.

“Yes, Your Majesty,” she replied. “And please, call me Cate.”

Davian’s father blinked at her, his expression unreadable. “And how old is your child?”

“She’s five. A friend on the crew is watching her for me tonight.”

“I see.” The King sat back as the first course of their dinner was served, fine vegetable ravioli with amber consommé and spring herbs. He glanced over at his son and shook his head. "I may turn into a rabbit soon."

Davian chuckled. "Try it, Father. It's very good. And vegetables are healthier for you." In a lower voice he said to Cate, "He's on a strict diet now because of his heart. He'll get used to it."

"It's delicious," Queen Arabella said, nodding to Noah, who stood near the wall to serve them as needed throughout the meal. "So fresh and well seasoned."

King Phillipe ate his two raviolis then sat back so Noah could clear his plate. "More meals like that and I'll waste away to nothing."

"I don't believe we need to worry," the Queen said loftily. "There's plenty of you to go around."

Even with the banter, Cate could hear the affection between the two and she couldn't help smiling. She hoped to find that for herself one day, the comfort of knowing you were loved and supported and that your person would always be there for you, no matter what.

As if reading her thoughts, Davian squeezed her hand again, his blue eyes glowing with encouragement. Once upon a time, she'd thought Davian was her person. Then he'd disappeared. Now that he was back again, she was fighting to remember not to trust him, but after the past few days it was getting harder and harder to remember exactly why she shouldn't.

"Where is your daughter's father, Dr. Neves?" the King asked out of the blue, knocking Cate right out of her fuzzy warm thoughts regarding Davian and straight back to reality.

"Oh. Uh..." She swallowed the last bite of her first course and kept her eyes down as Noah cleared her plate. The last thing she wanted was for the crew to get ideas about her and Davian and start spreading that around.

Bad enough Carrie in the clinic pored over those stupid tabloid rags about the royals. Cate took a sip of water, considering her answer carefully. "He's not part of the picture at present."

Not a total lie. Not the complete truth either.

Beside her, Cate felt Davian tense and he pushed his plate away half-finished.

"Perhaps, Father," Davian said, his voice edged sharply, "we could discuss something other than Cate's personal life."

"Why?" King Phillipe countered. "When that is the elephant in the room?"

"Father!" Davian said at the same time his mother said, "Phillipe!"

"What?" The King shrugged. "I just like to get things out in the open is all."

Oh, God.

Cate looked at Davian, blood pounding in her ears. They'd talked about this. They'd decided together that they wouldn't tell anyone about Adella being his daughter yet. Not until they'd worked out all the logistics of coparenting. But what if he'd gone ahead and told his parents anyway? What if…

This was exactly why Cate didn't trust people. This was exactly why—

"Out in the open?" Davian's voice went cold as ice. "I think you mean cover things up, don't you? That's what you always used me for, isn't it? To deflect attention away from the things you'd rather not have seen or discussed, Father? That is in no way getting things out in the open." His mother gasped, and Cate held his hand tighter, trying to get him to stop and sit down. This wasn't the time or place to have an argument. But it seemed that Davian took after his father in more ways than looks, because the next thing Cate knew, both men had stood and were facing off across the table, while the two women looked on, wide-eyed and horrified. "So do not speak to me of openness and truth, Father. And what elephant is it you speak of here?"

"I'm trying to protect our family's reputation, son," his father said, not backing down an inch. "That's all I've ever tried to do. Protect this family. And look at what it's gotten me. A bad heart, death threats and our names splashed over every cheap newspaper in the world." His dark, intense gaze moved from Davian to Cate. "So, Dr. Neves. I ask you point-blank. What is your interest in my son? Are you being paid to get information from him? It seems rather convenient that you'd reappear in his life on board this ship so suddenly after five years. And what a coincidence that that's the exact age of your daughter as well. Are you trying to blackmail him? How can you possibly trust this woman, Davian? I taught you better than that."

Stunned speechless, Cate looked from the King to the Queen, to Davian, to finally Noah, who still stood near the wall, his face impassive even though he must've heard the fight going on. How could he not, with the King bellowing?

This was her worst nightmare come true. Her personal business, the thing she'd worked so hard to get past in her life, rising to consume her now. She should have never taken this charter in the first place. She should have gone back to Boston and continued with her plans to open her clinic. That would've been the smart choice. The safe choice.

But then I'd never have seen Davian again...

And much as she wanted to deny it, she'd missed him. More than she ever thought possible. The brief time they'd spent together aboard the *Querencia* the past week, and today in Monaco, it was like they'd taken up right where they'd left off five years ago. Easy. Comfortable. Right. Like two halves of one whole. And Adella adored him too. How could she have missed that?

Before she could say anything though, Davian squared his broad shoulders beneath his expensive tailored charcoal-gray suit and rode to her defense, just like the white knight in a fairy tale, his face tight and his gaze bright with suppressed emotion. "First of all, Father, I trust Cate implicitly. She has been steadfast and supportive and always there when I needed her, no matter the situation. She is an excellent physician and a good friend. She has never once betrayed me, even after I did so to her. There is no one on earth I trust more." He inhaled deep through his nose, ignoring the King's disgruntled snort. "Second, I'm tired of living my life on a maybe. Maybe this person is bad. Maybe this person is lying. Maybe this person will hurt me. Who knows? Maybe they will. But you can't go through life expecting the worst. And I refuse to do it anymore. Not for you, not for the family, not for anyone."

"Now, see here, son—" his father started, but Davian cut him off.

"No, you see here, Father." Davian tugged on Cate's hand until she stood beside him. He looked over at her and whispered, "Trust me?"

Despite the past, despite the tiny alarms going off in the back of her head, right then and there—tonight—she did trust him. Cate nodded, heart pounding and throat dry as bone.

Davian gave a small nod then turned back to his parents. His father had moved closer to his mother now, his hand on her shoulder, as if for support. Davian looked between the two of them then said, "Cate and I were involved back in college. Romantically. The night you called me home to Ruclecia, we made love for the first time. We've rekindled our relationship now. And plan to continue doing so, regardless of your objections."

Oh, boy.

She waited for him to drop the rest of the bombshell. This was not how Cate had intended for them to find out about Adella, but now that he seemed intent on going there, she had no way of pulling Davian back. Thankfully, Davian had slid his arm around her waist because her knees were wobbling so much Cate thought she might collapse otherwise. She'd worked through life-threatening medical emergencies that were less stressful than this.

Except…he said instead, "Adella is a wonderful little girl. Smart, funny, kind, inquisitive. Any father would be proud to have her as his child and any family would be lucky to have her. Please do not ever let me hear you disparage her or her mother again. I've missed five years with Cate, and I don't intend to miss any more while I'm here. There are no ulterior motives behind Cate and Adella's appearance now. They are close friends of mine and therefore have my protection. Is that understood?"

"But what about the tabloids?" the King blustered. "What about the threats in Ruclecia?"

"What about them?" Davian stood firm. "I'm aware of the dangers we face, Father. But I refuse to let them rule my life any longer. We have the best security team available, both back home and here on the yacht, and there's nothing more we could ask for. I'm not the Crown Prince. My brother has trained his whole life for that position, and he will rule Ruclecia well. Please allow me to live the life that I've trained for as a doctor and stop using me as a pawn in your royal games."

The two men eyed each other across the table, the air taut with tension, until finally Davian's mother cleared her throat delicately.

"Perhaps we should continue dinner now? Two raviolis, no matter how delicious, won't keep me from starving tonight."

Her touch of humor broke the intense bubble they found themselves in and everyone could breathe again. Davian helped Cate back into her seat before taking his own once more. The King sat also, his cheeks a bit ruddier from the exchange with his son, but he let his line of questioning go, staying mainly silent the rest of the meal, while Cate and Davian and his mother discussed their day in Monaco and the weather on the cruise.

Noah, being the excellent steward he was, never showed any sign of hearing a word of the argument that had happened in front of him, just continued to serve the chef's amazing dinner. For the second course, they had flowery spring sushi with Alentejo olive oil, followed by a spring fricassee with Ciflorette strawberries, broad beans, Selma fennel and gourmet peas for the third course, white asparagus from Laigné-en-Belin browned in salted butter for the fourth, and spring cabbage stuffed with fresh garlic Thermidrome with Parmigiano-Reggiano for the fifth. For the sixth main course, the chef made aiguillette of midnight blue lobster with Côtes du Jura and fondant potatoes and finished it all up with a final trio of sweets—profiteroles glazed with verbena, all-flower honey soufflé, and crispy millefeuille.

"Ah, such a wonderful dinner," the Queen said to

Noah as he cleared her plates. "Please give the chef our sincere thanks for his skills tonight."

"Of course, Your Majesty," Noah said, bowing. "I'm so glad you enjoyed it."

Once the table had been cleared, Noah and another steward came around with coffees and champagne. Davian's parents, however, declined both.

"We're going back to our cabin," the King said. "Please excuse us."

"Father, I—" Davian started.

"No, son. You made yourself quite clear earlier. No need to say any more." The King met Cate's gaze and gave a curt nod. "Glad to have finally met you, Dr. Neves."

"Same, Your Majesty," she said, dropping one more awkward curtsy.

"Don't worry about him," the Queen said, coming around the table to hug and kiss Davian. "He'll adjust, as he always does. Just give him time."

Then she moved to hug and kiss Cate as well. She was so astonished, she stood like a statue as the Queen embraced her. "It really was lovely to meet you, dear. I can tell how happy you make my youngest son and he deserves that so much. I'm glad you're here."

The royal couple then glided away back downstairs to the master suite in a swirl of lilac-scented perfume and pomp, leaving Cate feeling both bewildered and bewitched by it all.

"Wow. That was…" she mumbled.

"Yes, it was," Davian agreed. "I'm sorry about my father. He goes over the top sometimes."

"He cares about you and wants you to be safe, that's all," Cate said, being diplomatic.

"Right." Davian grabbed two champagne flutes off

the table and handed one to Cate, then led her upstairs to the top deck to sit and relax. Once they settled on the comfy, oversize love seat, Cate toed off her shoes and tucked her feet under her. Davian took off his suit jacket and draped it over the back of the seat, then took off his shoes as well. He took a long swig of champagne and stared out into the night, his handsome face carved in moonlight. "What my father cares about most is maintaining the family reputation. The royal destiny."

"How so? If you're talking about the tabloids, well, that's been going on for years..."

"No. More than that. He's very old-school. Always has been. To him, it's all about the succession of the crown. I mean, my parents love me. I know that. And I never lacked for anything in my life, but I also knew that I was lower on the list of importance, title-wise."

"Because your brother is the Crown Prince."

"Yes, exactly."

Cate frowned. "Do you resent him for that?"

"No, not at all!" Davian sounded adamant. "I love Arthur and I meant what I said earlier to my father. He's trained hard to be King and will make an excellent ruler someday. But that doesn't mean that I don't have my own goals and dreams outside of the royal family as well."

"Of course." Cate sipped her champagne. The bubbles tickled her nose and on top of the wine she'd had at dinner, the alcohol was creating a nice little buzz inside her. "That's why you went to medical school."

"Exactly." He looked over at her now, smiling, and the effect was devastatingly sexy. Their knees brushed on the love seat and awareness shimmered through her bloodstream. "And that's why I started my charity and my hospital. To make a name for myself outside of my title and my family. To make a real mark on the world outside of money and privilege. To give back." He sighed and closed his eyes. "But my father has a restricted view of what royals should and should not do and be. He doesn't feel I need a career outside of the family business, and he worries about the threats made against us as well. It took years of convincing for him to let me go to America for medical school, and even then I had a full security detail and Grigorio with me to report back to my father regularly. All that pressure, all that responsibility. It's been like a cage around me my whole life. Trapping me inside."

"I'm sorry," Cate said, placing her hand on his leg to comfort him. "That must be very hard for you."

Davian put his hand over hers on his knee and entwined their fingers, then downed the rest of his champagne with one gulp.

"Well," she said, finishing her own champagne then setting the glass aside on the floor next to his. "I enjoyed meeting them tonight anyway. You probably don't want to hear this, but you look a lot like your father." Davian groaned and she laughed. "But you have your mother's eyes. And she is a sweetheart."

"She really is." He had an elbow on the back of the love seat and rested his cheek in his hand, grinning. Then he let go of Cate's other hand and placed his palm on her bare calf, slowly massaging the muscle there, relaxing her even more. "And so are you. You handled them both brilliantly tonight. Especially my father. When I saw him interrogating you like that, Cate, I wanted to dive across the table at him."

"I can handle myself," she said, moving her legs slightly so her toes brushed the side of his thigh. "But I appreciate your support. And I also appreciate you not telling them everything about Adella too. For a moment there, I was scared. Wasn't sure I could trust you."

"Hmm." Davian moved closer on the love seat, pulling Cate's legs across his lap, and causing the skirt of her dress to ride higher, exposing more of her tanned skin to him. His fingers traced higher up her leg, to the outside of her thigh, making her shiver in the warm night. Stars twinkled above them, and it all felt magical. "You can, you know."

"What?" she asked, frowning, her mind moving a bit slower from the champagne and wine.

"Trust me," he said, scooting closer still, his hand on her hip now. "I never wanted to hurt you, Cate. I hope you can believe me now."

Cate narrowed her gaze in the moonlight, reaching out her hand to trace her fingers down his cheek and neck to the top of his tie, loosening it then undoing the button beneath. None of this felt real, yet every nerve in her body felt hyperaware of him. She wasn't sure where life would take them after this charter, or what would happen with them and Adella, but she was sure of one thing. She wanted Davian. And tonight, she'd have him.

Before he could react, she tugged him to her by his tie and kissed him soundly. Davian groaned low in his throat, his fingers digging into her hip through her dress, moving her closer still, as his other hand slid into her hair, keeping her mouth on his as he pulled her completely onto his lap to straddle him.

It felt like a switch had been flipped inside Cate then and she couldn't get enough.

Eventually, Davian pulled away slightly, both of them breathless as he met her gaze in the moonlight. "Come to my cabin, Cate. Please. I don't want this night to end. Not yet."

She watched him a long moment, her whole being pulsing for his, then raised a hand to trace her fingers down his cheek, making him shiver. An answering yearning lit his eyes, making her pulse notch higher and her blood sing. "I don't want it to end either, Davian. Let's go."

They kissed as he picked her up and carried her down the stairs. For a quick second, Cate worried about the crew seeing them like this, since she still had to work with them for the rest of the charter, but they didn't encounter anyone on the way belowdecks, thankfully. And once Davian began nuzzling her neck and she had her legs wrapped around his waist, she stopped caring about everything but him anyway.

They made their way down the hall to his stateroom, still not breaking the kiss. Once inside, they discarded their clothes in a fast flurry, then fell naked onto his bed, neither able to stop touching and stroking and tasting the other, bolder now than the first time they'd been together, but then they were five years older now too. Back then it had been more tentative, all about exploring, getting to know what the other liked. Now it was hot and intense, making every touch, every sigh more meaningful.

Davian kissed his way down to her breasts, cupping them in his palms then taking one taut nipple into his mouth. Cate arched into him, crying out, her need for him shooting like lightning straight between her legs. She pulled him closer, needing more, and Davian gave her everything, putting all his emotions into his caresses. This was more than sex for her. Way more. It always had been with Davian. To Cate, they were making love in every sense of the word.

* * *

Davian thought he'd died and gone to heaven when Cate turned the tables on him, kissing her way down his body to his abdomen, then lower still, tracing her tongue over the tip of his erection. While Davian was an experienced man, being with Cate was different from any lover he'd had before. Always had been. Even that first time together, all those years ago. But before, he'd felt heated and rushed and inquisitive, still learning how to please her. Now he knew Cate better and it seemed to shed a new light on their lovemaking. He knew what she liked, knew how to make her comfortable and happy and satisfied before he took his own pleasure. When the attention of her lips and tongue on his most sensitive flesh grew to be too much for him to bear much longer, he pulled her away to kiss her before turning them over, so Cate was on her back beneath him. Then he kissed and nuzzled his way down her body, wanting to return the favor for her, to make love to her with his hands and mouth until she tumbled over the brink into orgasm, unable to keep from whispering his name over and over as the waves of ecstasy rocked her entire being.

At last, he rose above her, reaching into his nightstand drawer for a condom. They gazes met as he put it on, then positioned himself at her wet entrance. Then she reached down between them again, encircling his hard length, stroking him until Davian pulled her hand away and kissed her palm. "Too much of that, darling, and I won't last."

In answer, Cate drew him down for an open-mouthed kiss, pressing her body to his. "Please, my prince. I need you..."

Hearing his title on her lips nearly drove him over the edge again. But Davian summoned his willpower and held his weight on his forearms, the tip of his hard length poised to enter her. He wanted tonight to last. To be so hot and so good, it was seared into both their memories for eternity. A beat passed, then two, before he finally entered her in one long stroke, then held still, allowing Cate's body to adjust to his. When he did move at last, they both moaned deeply, and he began a rhythm that had them teetering on the brink in no time at all.

"Davian, I..." Cate cried out as she climaxed once more, her words lost as the pleasure overtook her. Davian was close behind. Maybe it was finding each other again after all this time. Maybe it was the moonlight. Maybe it was how they were still so in sync, even after all this time, that set Davian's nerve endings on fire and rocked his foundations. Whatever it was, being inside her felt like a live wire, sparking and shimmering with pleasure. He drove into her once, twice more, wanting it to last forever, but knowing it would be over too soon. Then his body tightened, and he came hard inside Cate, his face buried in her neck and her name on his lips, murmuring sweet nothings into the side of her neck.

Afterward, they lay in the darkness, listening to the sound of the waves outside, gently lapping against the side of the yacht, his head resting in the valley between her breasts, over Cate's heart, and her fingers in his hair, tracing lazy circles against his scalp. Davian felt sated and relaxed for the first time in recent memory and he had his Cate to thank for that as well. "That... Wow," he said, his voice quiet in the shadows. "I don't know what this is between us, but it's still there. And I'm not ready to let it go yet."

"Agreed."

He moved to look up at her, but couldn't really see her face in the shadows, but the vulnerability in her tone made his heart clench. He wanted to explore the possibilities, try to find a workable way to be together as a family, even if it scared them. Davian rolled over onto his back and pulled Cate into his side, her leg sprawling across his and her head on his chest as he pulled the covers up over them and gathered her close. "You know, I came on this yacht to protect my parents, but it seems we're continuing our own journey now. History is repeating itself." He sighed, hesitated. "I only ever wanted to protect you, Cate. And now Adella too. To have a family of my own. A life of my own. Perhaps we can make that together, you and I."

"Perhaps," she whispered, her tone bittersweet, and Davian's chest tightened.

He knew this was tender territory for her, after what happened with her father. He knew she didn't trust easily. Neither did he. But he was willing to try, for Cate. For their daughter. Still, he didn't want to ruin this moment, this one perfect evening together, so he kept that to himself. They'd have plenty of time to talk about it tomorrow.

"Let's get some sleep," he said, his words buried in her hair, warm and deep as he nestled Cate's head under his chin, and she snuggled closer into his heat. "Sweet dreams, Cate."

"Sweet dreams, my prince," Cate said, kissing his chest before they both drifted off to slumber.

CHAPTER TEN

EARLY THE NEXT MORNING, Cate was back in the clinic, still reeling a bit from her night with Davian. Her body ached in interesting ways when she moved around the exam room and her heart felt full. She'd awakened before dawn and left a sleeping Davian in bed, giving him a soft kiss on the cheek before sneaking back to her own cabin for a shower and change of clothes. Then she'd picked up Adella at Carrie's cabin and taken her daughter to breakfast in the crew cafeteria before work.

"Did you have a sleepover last night, Mommy?" Adella asked, milk from her cereal dripping down her chin. "You won't let me have sleepovers."

Cate grabbed a napkin to clean up Adella's chin, her face prickling with embarrassment. "That's because you're five."

"So, when I'm older, I can have sleepovers like you?"

"No," Cate said quickly, frowning down at her plate of toast. "I mean, yes. I mean, Mommy didn't have a sleepover, sweetie. I was just up late talking to a friend, that's all."

"Uh-huh," Noah said, coming over to sit at their table. "Is that what they're calling it now?"

Great. Just when she thought she'd escaped the prying eyes of her cocrew. She should've known better. The life of a yachtie didn't exactly lend itself to privacy. Cate picked up her coffee and scowled over the rim at her friend. Noah grinned, ignoring her pointed suggestion for him to change subjects. "So, how was dinner with the Prince last night?"

"You ate with the King and Queen!" Adella clapped her hands. "Did you get to wear a crown too?"

"No." Cate set her mug down and pushed her toast away. Any appetite she'd had was now gone under the realization that yep, she'd slept with Davian again last night. Not that she hadn't been a willing and enthusiastic participant at the time, but now in the light of day, the ramifications of that were starting to sink in.

I only ever wanted to protect you, Cate. And now Adella too. To have a family of my own. A life of my own. Perhaps we can make that together, you and me...

Together.

You and me.

Oh, Lord.

Cate realized her daughter and Noah were both looking at her expectantly, so she added, "No crowns. Just fancy food and conversation."

"Mmm. More like interrogation," Noah said.

He wasn't wrong. Cate had expected his parents to be curious about her, but she hadn't expected the third degree. It had been a bit unsettling, on top of the stress of meeting royalty, and had set her back a step. Thankfully, Davian had been there to support her. That was nice, knowing someone had her back. He'd been that way in residency too, and she'd missed that about him. Among other things.

Okay, fine. She'd missed pretty much everything about him.

Which was a serious problem.

Cate didn't want to miss him. Didn't want to need anyone. Because people let you down.

"Mommy, isn't that your face?" Adella asked, pointing at the newspaper another crew member was reading at the table.

Cate glanced behind her to see what her daughter was pointing at and nearly fell out of her chair.

"Oh, my God!" Noah gasped. "That is you."

He got up and walked over the table and asked to see the paper then brought it back to Cate. It was one of the local gossip sheets the crew member had picked up in Monaco before they'd left port early that morning. Noah sat back down and held up the front page.

The headline made Cate's stomach knot. "Passionate Prince Hooks Up with Ship Doc."

Adella had abandoned her soggy cereal and was gawking at the selfie Cate had taken near the Albert statue of her and Davian before they sat down to rest. And kiss. And, oh, my God indeed! She swallowed hard and grabbed the paper away from Noah and stared down at it, her own smiling face mocking her from the tabloid. "How in the world did they get this shot? I took it on my personal phone."

"Paparazzi?" Noah suggested, squinting at the picture. "You look cute though. Both of you. And look at Adella, sleeping in the stroller like a baby. So cute!"

"I'm not a baby!" Adella said, crossing her arms and pouting. "Mommy, tell him I'm not a baby!"

"She's not a baby," Cate murmured without really paying much attention. This was bad. She felt violated, taken advantage of by some unknown photographer. But no. Looking closer at the picture, there was no way someone else had taken this shot. It was identical to the one on her phone. So how in the world... Then she read the article and it went from bad to worse. The reporter, if you could call them that, cited an anonymous source who remarked on how much Adella resembled Davian. The hair, the eyes, even her little expressions sometimes. All Davian, through and through.

Cate stood quickly, nearly knocking over her chair in her haste. "I need to go. Noah, can you watch Adella for me for a bit, please?"

"Uh, yeah. Sure." He frowned at her. "Everything okay?"

"No, it really isn't," she said. "Be good, sweetie. Mommy loves you."

Cate rushed out of the cafeteria and headed up toward the guest staterooms intent on talking to Davian about the article immediately. But when he answered her knock on his door, he was already on the phone with someone, and from his tight expression, the conversation wasn't going well.

He waved her inside then closed the door and held up a finger for her to wait.

"Hang on, Arthur. What are you saying? How is that possible?"

Her mind kept whirling, her old fears creeping up again. There were only the two of them in Monaco yesterday. If she didn't send those photos to the press then who did? Davian? His family?

She didn't want to believe that, but he'd told her himself how devious his family had been in manipulating the press to their whims. Would they try to use Cate and Adella as their pawns now? To throw the press off the King's health issues?

Cate hated to believe that, but with only the two of them there, it was hard to find another explanation for the leak.

No. Stop.

Maybe this was just another coping mechanism. Another way to keep herself guarded because she was falling for Davian all over again. She didn't want to get hurt. Didn't want to open her heart to him and be vulnerable when their future was so uncertain.

Unfortunately, Cate was confused and confounded and feared it wouldn't get better any time soon.

"I'm telling you what I'm seeing, brother," the Crown Prince said into the phone. "It's all over the tabloids here in Ruclecia. Which means it's all over everywhere else too."

Dammit.

Davian had thought he'd been so careful yesterday, so careful with this charter, but apparently not. He looked over at Cate and spotted the paper under her arm. His stomach dropped to his toes. Yep, she'd seen it too. He walked over and held out his hand for the paper and she gave it to him.

In bold, bright colors across the front page were their faces, happy and smiling in Monaco. Given that they'd been about to kiss, it could've been worse, though he wasn't in a forgiving mood now.

"I need to go, Arthur," Davian said. "I'll call you back."

"Wait!" his brother shouted. "Be careful with telling Father. You know how upset he gets."

"I know. And I will."

He ended the call then stalked over to Cate, skimming the article on the way. Nothing too detailed, thank goodness, though there were speculations made about Adella and her resemblance to Davian. His chest burned hotter. It was one thing for the press to go after him. It was another to involve an innocent child.

My innocent child.

"I'm afraid they're going to connect the dots between all of this, Davian," Cate said, looking pale and fraught. "This is exactly what I didn't want to happen. Not until we've figured things out ourselves. Told Adella."

"Same." He slumped down onto the sofa and scrubbed a hand over his face. He'd showered but hadn't had a chance to shave yet. Hell, he still only had on a towel around his waist. Still, he was glad Cate was there so they could get to the bottom of this. "How did they get this photo?"

"That's what I can't figure out." Cate took the paper back from him to stare at the photo again. "At first, I thought it was paparazzi, but this is a selfie from my phone, Davian. Which means someone must've hacked into it."

"But how?" He scowled. "It is password-protected and encrypted, yes?"

"Yes." She sighed and sat back. "I've no idea how they do any of that, but I do know they get better at breaking into things every day. Oh, God." Cate closed her eyes and tipped her head back. "What are we going to do? I mean, I don't care so much for myself, but I don't want Adella involved. And what about your father?"

Davian took her hand and exhaled slow. "My brother said the picture and article are already making the news circuit, but hopefully being at sea today will keep my father from finding out until I can decide how best to tell him."

"Well, at least it wasn't too scandalous. He knew we were going into Monaco, so it's not totally out of the realm of possibility that someone might see us and snap a photo."

"True." Davian shook his head. "But he will be upset and blame me anyway, because that's what he does."

"I'm sorry." She leaned her head on his shoulder then straightened fast. "And please know I had nothing to do with this, Davian. I swear to you."

"I believe you." He kissed her cheek then rested his cheek against the top of her head as she relaxed it on his shoulder again. "We'll figure it out. But let me finish getting dressed first."

While he did that, Cate scrolled through her phone, checking emails, and searching for any more information about their visit that had been released to the press. By the time Davian was done getting ready and was back by her side on the sofa, she'd found a dozen articles—all speculating about their relationship and about Adella's parentage.

"Davian, what are we going to do? According to the number of search engine hits this has, the story is going viral."

"Let me make some calls."

Davian stood and paced his stateroom as he talked with the IT security team back in Ruclecia. They took all the information from him and from Cate's phone to try to track how the photo had been hacked. He next talked to the palace PR team and put them on disaster mode, having them arrange a different departure point for the private jet that would take his parents back to Ruclecia so they wouldn't be mobbed at their arrival at the island of Corsica. They had originally planned to sail on to Sicily before ending their charter, but with all this nonsense, it was probably better to return early.

Once that was finished, he returned to Cate. "We

should go up and speak to my father before he finds out about this elsewhere. Come."

He took her hand and helped her up then led her to the door. As soon as Davian opened it though, his father stood there, red-faced and fuming angry, glaring at them.

"I told you this would happen," his father spat out, pointing at Cate. "I told you not to trust her."

Davian thrust Cate behind him, keeping himself between her and his father. He was used to these outbursts. Cate was not. "This is not her fault, Father. Her phone was hacked."

"Hacked? Is that what she told you?"

"Yes. And I believe her."

His father sputtered a moment and Davian feared he might have another coronary right there in the hall.

"Please, Father. Calm down. I've already got the palace on alert and the IT security team is looking into it. It's all handled. And Arthur called me first thing. We've got this under control."

"These insidious rumors are never under control once they start, Davian. You know that."

"Then we will deal with the fires as they come up." Davian had felt Cate tense behind him and wanted to shield her as best he could from his father's anger. Lord knew he'd been the brunt of it enough growing up and it could be brutal. "Please, Father. Let's go upstairs and have a nice breakfast. Forget about this nonsense. I've contacted the jet pilot and have arranged for them to pick us up the day after tomorrow in Corsica. All is well, I promise. Don't concern yourself over this."

"Don't concern myself?" he continued to bluster as Davian herded the King down the hall toward the stairs. "How exactly am I supposed to do that when the press is speculating that this woman's child is yours, Davian? I can't have people running around calling every bastard on the planet part of my family. How much did they pay you for the pictures? I hope it was worth it."

"Hey!" Cate shouted sternly from behind Davian. "My daughter is not a bastard. Don't you ever call her that again. You'd be lucky to have her in your family. And for your information, I—"

"Father, stop," Davian commanded, cutting her off, for what little good it did. His father continued grumbling and climbing up to the deck anyway. "Don't say things you'll regret."

They stepped out into the sunshine when his father rounded on Davian, his dark eyes hard. "The only thing I regret, Davian, is that you can't be more like your brother. At least he does his duty for this family."

Only years of swallowing his emotions kept Davian from lashing out then. He squeezed his fists tight, so tight that Cate gasped and pulled free of him. Still, something of his outrage must've shown on his face because his father took a step back, apparently knowing he'd gone too far. Lips tight, Davian managed to grind out, "My whole life, all I've ever been about is duty to this family, Father."

The King took another step back, the color draining from his face before he turned and walked away.

CHAPTER ELEVEN

INSTEAD OF IMPROVING, Davian's frustrations only worsened.

The palace IT security team had spent the better part of the day investigating the leaked photos from Cate's phone and had traced their sending back to the yacht itself, meaning someone on board the *Querencia* had sent them to the press. And not just any crew either. The transmission signal for the email could be tracked to the area where the medical clinic was located.

A black hole had opened in Davian's gut at that news. He left the abominably hot galley and went back upstairs to the top deck from some fresh air. In his heart of hearts, he never wanted to believe that Cate had been involved in the leak at all. It was ridiculous. Absurd. She had absolutely nothing to gain by having those photos appear in the press and everything to lose.

Except money...

No. He shook off the sound of his father's voice in his head. Cate did not need money. Having seen the budget himself for this charter, he knew all the crew were well compensated for their work here. And if there was anything she needed, Cate knew all she had to do was ask him, right? She was starting her own clinic, which wasn't cheap, but she was also smart and resourceful and had told him she'd been planning for the project for a while now, so that meant she had funding secured, didn't it?

How much did they pay you for the pictures? I hope it was worth it.

Cursing under his breath, Davian leaned on the railing and stared out over the turquoise water of the Mediterranean. They'd started this trip with so much hope, and yesterday in Monaco had been so delightful, but now the bright sunshine seemed to mock him. Davian was tired, so very tired of cleaning up other people's messes, of always being on guard, of the constant scrutiny, of never measuring up in his father's eyes, despite his best efforts. He wanted to just live his life, run his hospital, help people, cure diseases, be happy, start a family of his own, be a good father to Adella and support Cate in whatever way she'd let him.

Cate.

He hung his head and closed his eyes behind his sunglasses. The winds were stronger today, blowing the linen shirt he wore around his torso and tousling his hair. The scent of salt and sea and suspicions surrounded him, churning his emotions into a tangled mess.

There were only three people in the clinic for this charter. Dr. Bryant, who'd been a trusted mentor to Davian for years and was above reproach in this whole situation. Hell, given the man's age and the fact he'd never even seen him use a cell phone, Davian wasn't even sure the man owned one, let alone had the technical skills to leak photos to someone without getting caught. Which left Cate and the receptionist, Carrie.

He doubted the receptionist would have done it, given that she was in her cabin the whole night watching Adella while he and Cate had dinner with his parents then went back to Davian's stateroom afterward. And the IT team had specifically traced the signal to the clinic area of the ship. It made no sense. The tension in his gut tightened. Thinking logically, if the receptionist had been eliminated, then the potential for it to be Cate increased and…

No. Absolutely not.

Davian refused to believe Cate had anything to do with this. She'd vehemently denied it at the time and had been as shocked as he was about the leak. She'd taken measures from the time she'd discovered Davian was on board the *Querencia* to shield their daughter from any hint of scandal. It made no sense for her to blow all that up for a few thousand dollars, or whatever amount the paparazzi were paying for photos of the Ruclecian royals these days.

Maybe it's payback...

Payback? He wasn't sure where that had come from, but it had him sitting down as his knees buckled. They'd had this conversation. She'd accepted his explanation about why he'd left so quickly back in residency. She'd said she understood his reasons and forgave him. And she'd been keeping a huge secret of her own from him. They were both guilty there. Cate would never use that against him. She knew that would gut him. She knew how he felt about her, how he'd always felt about her. She was the only person he'd ever loved, ever allowed inside, ever been truly vulnerable with.

He couldn't, wouldn't accept that it was Cate behind all this.

But if not her, who?

Enough. Enough guessing and speculation. Time to have the difficult conversation and get it all out there.

Only then would he know the truth. Davian stood and headed back downstairs to the clinic to find Cate.

"I just can't figure out how that picture got from my phone to the press," Cate said, as she sorted files in the clinic. "I had my phone with me all day. It's not like I left it somewhere and a stranger accessed it or anything."

"It is weird," Carrie said from the reception desk, where she was looking at said photo online. "But it's not the end of the world, right? And you all look amazing in the picture, so there's that."

Cate gave the younger woman a look. "Seriously? That's the last thing I care about here. My privacy was invaded, Carrie. I didn't show those photos to anyone. The only reason I took them was to have memories of our day yesterday to look back on once I'm in Boston again." Cate shuddered and closed the file cabinet drawer. "To think someone close enough to me to take my phone did that to me. I feel so violated."

Carrie turned away to continue reading the article while Cate continued to stew to herself. "I mean, who would do that? It's awful, taking advantage of people like that. I can understand why now Davian's family detests the paparazzi so much. And poor Adella. She's just an innocent child in all this. It was my duty to protect her, and I failed as a mother." She covered her face with her hands and sighed. "I've failed her all around here. I'm a failure."

"Mommy?" Adella said from where she was playing with her toys in a corner of the clinic. "What's a failure?"

Me, Cate wanted to say, but held back. She took a deep breath and walked over to crouch beside Adella. "It's when someone doesn't get the outcome they wanted, or things don't end up the way you wanted them, sweetie. It's a part of life, but it can hurt sometimes."

"I'm sorry, Mommy," Adella said, reaching up to pat Cate's cheek. "But I still love you."

"I love you too, sweetie." She pulled her little girl into a hug. "More than I can every say."

They were still like that when Davian arrived at the clinic. He walked in and headed straight to Carrie's desk, apparently not seeing Cate and Adella off to the side.

Carrie looked up then did a double take, nearly falling out of her chair to get up and curtsy before Davian. "Your Highness, good morning. How can the clinic help you today?"

"I need to see Dr. Neves," he said. "It's urgent."

"I'm here," Cate said, pulling back from Adella. She straightened and pointed to Dr. Bryant's office. "We can go in here for privacy. He's not working today."

They went into the office and Cate closed the door behind them before Davian took her into his arms and held her tight. He whispered into her temple, "How are you holding up?"

"Okay." She shrugged and leaned back to meet his gaze. He looked about as rumpled and unsettled as she felt, his shirt and shorts wrinkled and his hair disheveled. Davian had probably been up on deck since he carried the scent of warm sun and salt on his skin. "Just still trying to figure out how all this happened." Cate smoothed a hand down the front of her white medical uniform pants then leaned her hips back against Dr. Bryant's desk. "Have you heard anything from your IT team at the palace?"

He gave a curt nod, staring down at his phone screen and not at her. "They were able to trace the email transmission to on board the ship."

"Oh, wow." Cate frowned and straightened, walking over to peer at his phone too. "Any more details than that?"

"Yes." Davian shut off his phone before she could get a good look at the information there and shoved it into his pocket. "Apparently, it was sent from right here in the clinic."

"What?" She took a step back, as if she'd been struck. "But that can't be right. I was never here last night, Davian. I went right to my cabin after we returned to the *Querencia.* You know that because you walked me here. Then I showered and changed and took Adella to Carrie for her to babysit last night. I was running late so I hurried from there up to the main salon for dinner. And you and I were together after that, so..."

"I know," he said, exhaling slowly and shaking his head as she walked over to sit in one of the chairs before the desk. "That's what makes no sense to me." He scowled and looked up at her. "And you're sure you had your phone with you the entire time?"

"Of course!" Cate crossed her arms, a sudden chill running through her. "I was on call, so I had to have it in case of an emergency. You know that."

"Hmm."

"'Hmm'?" She didn't mean to be snippy, but the stress was getting to her now and she didn't like the direction this conversation was headed. "What does that mean?"

"I don't know, Cate. All I'm certain of is that the evidence doesn't lie. And the evidence says that your phone was here last night to send that photo to the press."

Her breath whooshed out of her in astonishment. "Wait. You think it was me who did this now?"

"I didn't say that," Davian started.

"That's what you're implying!" Hurt and horror quickly bubbled over into outrage, making her words froth over like a too-full boiling pot. "We were literally together last night from dinner on, Davian. When exactly did I supposedly have time to send this email?"

"Calm down, Cate. Please. I'm not accusing you of anything. And fighting with me won't help anything."

"It certainly will because you're wrong! I had nothing to do with this. Why would I send that, huh? It goes against everything I want for myself, everything I want for my daughter."

A small muscle ticked in his cheek as he looked away, his voice tight with tension, "Money, perhaps?"

"Money." Cate's eyes widened as realization hit home. He wasn't kidding here. He really thought she'd done this. Searing self-recriminations stabbed her in the chest, making it hard to speak past the constriction in her throat. "You think I did this? Sold you out? Betrayed you for money?"

"No." He began pacing again, his gestures agitated. "I don't know. I just… I'm trying to make sense of this and that's the only reason I can come up with, Cate. You said you were going to open your own clinic after this and that takes funds. I thought you—"

"What? That I'd sell you and your family out for a couple of extra bucks? Well, screw you, Davian. I don't need any extra bucks and I certainly don't need to stand here and take this from you!"

She started toward the door, her eyes burning from unshed tears, but she sure as hell refused to let him see her cry. Not after what he'd put her through back in residency and certainly not now, after the awful things he'd just accused her of. Cate made it as far as the door before Davian took her arm, stopping her.

"Cate, please," he said, his grip gentle but firm. "Don't go like this. Let's talk this out."

"Oh, no. I think you've said more than enough already." She rounded on him then, determined to say her piece before she couldn't anymore. "You made me believe you, Davian. You made me open up and start to trust you again. You made me love you again and then you turn around and accuse me of being nothing but a gold digger, looking for an easy paycheck?" Her face felt hotter than the sun then and her vision blurred with the tears she couldn't hold back any longer. "How dare you!" She angrily swiped the back of her hand over her wet cheeks. "How dare you walk back into my life, into Adella's life, like some white knight on your horse and act like you care about us and like you want to have a future with us, then drop us like a hot potato at the first sign of trouble? We are not playthings, and this is not a game, Davian. I told you that from the start. If you want to be Adella's father, you need to be there through it all—the good, the bad and everything in between. I won't take less, and she deserves nothing less than that." Dammit, this was going off the rails now and her heart ached like it would die and she just wanted to get out of there and take Adella back to their cabin, where she could keep her safe from the world and Davian and all this mess. But first, she wanted to break down his walls a little too, make him hurt like he'd hurt her, make him see that he wasn't above accusation either. Petty? Maybe, but she didn't care at this point. Cate sniffled and raised her chin, meeting Davian's cold blue gaze directly. "And for your information, how do I know it wasn't you who leaked that photo?"

"Me?" Now it was his turn to sound outraged. "How the hell would I do that?"

"No idea. But you were there with me all night. You had access to my phone. And it wouldn't be the first time that a royal leaked information to get what they wanted, would it? You said yourself, Davian, that your family was expert at that. Maybe you decided that you could use this scandal to blackmail your own father to get him to allow you to live the life you want, eh?" She squared her shoulders, taking refuge in her old doubts and fears. Trust had always been her Achilles' heel and now she could see a very good reason why. People always let you down in the end. First her father, now Davian. She was done with letting people hurt her or her daughter like this ever again. Cate could tell her barb had struck deep when Davian paled beneath his tan and the corners of his mouth tightened. Time to go. Cate tugged free and grabbed the door handle, the cool metal a shock against her heated palm. "Goodbye, Davian. I doubt we'll see each other again."

But the scene she opened the door to was a chaotic surprise. Four of the royal guards filled the waiting room, two at the entrance, one standing watch over Adella and the fourth one handcuffing Carrie.

"What's going on?" Cate asked, rushing over to sweep her daughter into her arms.

"Mommy? I'm scared," Adella said, burying her face in Cate's chest.

"Explain yourselves," Davian demanded, stalking out into the room. "Why are you arresting this woman?"

"I'm sorry, Your Highness," Carrie said, tears streaming down her face now. "I never meant to cause any problems."

"Speak!" Davian said to the guard holding on to the receptionist. "Tell me what's going on."

"The head of IT called us, Your Highness," the guard said. "They got more information on the leaked photo.

Apparently, it wasn't Dr. Neves's phone that sent the picture, but another device with a very similar IMEI number. IT said since the devices were the same make and model, it was possible that the photo could've been copied wirelessly if the two phones were in close proximity, without Dr. Neves even knowing."

"Oh, my God!" Cate stared at Carrie, still trying to take that in. "Is that what happened? Did you copy my photo, Carrie? When?"

Carrie huffed out a breath, her body trembling slightly as she stared down at the floor. "I didn't think it would be a big deal. I never meant to hurt you or anyone else," she said, between sobs. "The paper contacted me before we sailed. They said they'd pay me well for any pictures or juicy tidbits I might hear while we were on charter. I didn't know that you and Prince Davian would get involved, Dr. Neves. I never thought…" She sighed. "I'm so sorry."

"Why didn't you just tell them no?" Cate asked, walking over with Adella to stand beside Davian.

"By the time I had the pictures, I couldn't. I'd already spent the money they'd paid me on bills back home and I had no way of paying it back." Carrie started crying. "I never meant for any of this to happen, Cate. I swear. You're my friend. I just needed the money and thought this would be an easy way to get it."

"Take her away," Davian said to the guard, and they led Carrie away in handcuffs.

Cate stood and watched, oddly numb. Her life had gone from heavenly to hellish in the span of twenty-four hours and she had no clue what to do about that. The only thing she was certain of at that point was that things between her and Davian had been broken and she wasn't sure they could ever be fixed again.

Davian turned to her, his expression unreadable. "Cate, I'm…"

"No." She started for the door, Adella clutched tight to her like a shield. "I think we've said everything we need to today, Davian. This is exactly what I wanted to avoid, exactly what I feared the most getting involved with you again, knowing who and what you were." She inhaled deep, her lungs tight with sorrow. "I can't live like this. And I won't put my daughter through it either. The constant hounding by the press, the lack of privacy, no personal life. I can't." Her voice broke and she swallowed hard. "I love you, Davian. I always have. But maybe that isn't enough anymore. I must think of Adella. And if you don't trust me, then…"

"I do trust you, Cate. And I'm thinking of Adella too," he said, striding over to her, his blue gaze shining with earnestness. "I want what's best for all of us. And I love you too." He took a deep breath and looked away. "But I agree. Maybe you should take her away, keep her safe. I obviously can't do it."

"Davian, you—" she started, then stopped because what was the point? His words and actions didn't match. "You say you trust me now, but you don't. What you did in that office showed me that. And without trust, we have nothing, Davian. Not love, not a future. Nothing. None of it will work. I'm sorry."

And with that, she walked away from him, back to her cabin, back to her old life and fears, where she should've stayed to begin with. Perhaps then she would've saved herself a lifetime of pain and heartache over the man she'd loved and lost.

CHAPTER TWELVE

FOR THE REST of the day and evening, Davian steered clear of everyone, needing to work through all the complications in his life and future alone. His whole life had been spent in duty to others. First to his family, then to his patients, and now to Cate and Adella. But now he feared he was at a breaking point, a crossroads, and decisions had to be made.

He had to choose who he wanted to be and who he would protect and cherish above all others going forward—his family, his career, or Cate and Adella. Until now, the first had always taken precedence, but deep inside, Davian knew that wasn't what he wanted for his future. He loved his work as well, but not as much as he loved Cate and Adella.

His family would be fine without him. His brother was strong and ready to ascend to the throne of their country. Yes, he wouldn't have Davian to advise him or to take the fall if things went sideways, but Arthur was smart and compassionate, and he had a wife and children of his own. He'd find a way through just fine. Davian's parents? That was more concerning. He knew they loved him, in their own ways. His mother was affectionate and kind, if a bit distracted. And his father, well, the man was used to getting his own way. Sometimes it felt as if he saw both of his sons as pawns in a chess game he played to win. But deep down, Davian believed that his father did care for them, even if he didn't show it in the ways Davian wished he would.

The conversation he needed to have with his parents would be difficult, but necessary. They would make their choice about what part Davian would play in their future after he told them his plans, but his own choice was made. He was done with royal life.

His parents were in the main salon when he found them. The King was reading the day's papers and the Queen was doing a crossword puzzle. They both looked up when he walked in, still dressed casually in his shirt and shorts.

"We need to talk," Davian said, taking a seat at the formal dining table.

His father peered at him over the top of his newspaper. "You've handled the photo scandal, I see. Good work, son."

Davian gave him a curt nod, biting back an I-told-you-so where Cate was concerned. What troubled him most though was the fact he'd let his father convince him that maybe he was right. Maybe Cate had betrayed him, just as he'd feared she would. But that wasn't the case. Cate had been true to him, and he'd doubted her for no other reason than his father's accusations. He refused to ever let that occur again.

Once his parents were seated across from him, Davian came out with it, crisp and clear. "I wanted to tell you today that I'm retiring from royal life, effective immediately."

"What?" the King blustered. "That's unacceptable. I refuse to accept."

"Dear, what's this all about?" his mother asked, her tone concerned. "Is it the doctor? Cate?"

"Yes, she's a part of it, but it's much more than that. This had been building for years."

"Of all the ungrateful…" His father's face grew redder by the second. "This family has done everything for you. Supported you, educated you, fed and clothed you."

"As families are supposed to do."

"Stop this impertinence!" His father pounded a fist on the table, his booming voice reverberating around the room. "I will not hear of any withdrawal or retirement or whatever else you call it from this family, do you understand?"

"What I understand is that I've been used and deceived by this family one too many times, Father." Davian remained calm, his tone low and measured. "For too many occasions, I've been a pawn in a larger game to protect the family and serve my duty to you. I've had my life uprooted and my future jeopardized to deflect attention from whatever scandal or crisis rules the day. But I'm done with that. I have a life of my own now. I have work that I enjoy and people that I love and want to spend my future with. And I do not want any of that to be threatened anymore because of my family ties. So, I hereby withdraw from all titles and duties associated with the House of De Loroso and wish to move forward being a full-time doctor and humanitarian, and perhaps one day, if I'm lucky, a husband and father. Also, you should know that Adella Neves is my child. Cate and I had an affair back in residency and there was a baby born, shortly after I was called back to Ruclecia. Cate tried to contact me, but the palace security turned her away. One more reason I want to leave this life behind. I refuse to ever be separated from my daughter again."

"Oh, my!" His mother gasped, trembling. "Davian, is this true? You have a child? I have a granddaughter?"

His father, the King, took the opposite stance. "How do you know this child is yours? Have you had DNA testing done? If she is a member of the family, that will be required for her to take her rightful place in the lineage. I demand to see the results, proof that what you say is true, Davian. You cannot just—"

At that point, having said what he'd intended to say, Davian rose and pushed he chair in. "Actually, I can, Father. Adella is mine. I love her and Cate. I hope to spend the rest of my life with them if they'll have me. You can choose to accept that, accept them and my decisions, or I can walk out of here and out of your lives forever. I've made my choice. Now you must make yours."

The King and Queen spoke quietly to each other, Davian's mother crying softly and his father's color slowly returning to normal as he comforted his wife. Finally, they turned back to Davian and said in unison, "We accept."

For the first time in a very long time, Davian felt a weight being lifted off him. Things weren't perfect, not yet, but perhaps they would be someday. He smiled at his parents. "Good. Thank you. Now, if you'll excuse me, there's someone I need to speak with."

CHAPTER THIRTEEN

CATE WAS IN her cabin packing up her and Adella's stuff. They had a flight home scheduled for the next day and were staying in a hotel on Corsica that night after debarking the yacht. While Cate filled their suitcases and carry-ons, Adella played with her toys on the bed with Paulo, who was back to his old self again following his head injury scare. The boy still had a couple of stitches that would need to come out in a week or so, but otherwise had made a full recovery. Lord Maybrook was also doing better, though his recovery would take longer due to the severity of his injuries and his age.

All they had left to do now was have the crew line up as the charter guests left the yacht and then it would all be over.

Over.

So much had changed in the span of just a couple of weeks that Cate was still trying to wrap her head around it all. Seeing Davian again. Telling him about Adella. Meeting his family. Falling for him all over again.

That last one still scared her, but she kept reminding herself that nothing had been decided and as of right now, things were proceeding as planned. She'd go back to Boston and begin preparations to open her clinic, spend some time with her mother, get Adella scheduled and registered for school in the fall. Try to get on with life without knowing when or if Davian might be a part of their future going forward. Of course, he could be a part of Adella's life if he chose, but he either needed to be all in or all out.

She shook her head.

Silly, really. All of it. Two weeks ago, she'd been fine going it alone. She'd be fine now doing the same. Except deep inside her, she wondered if she still wanted to…

"Attention all crew members, please be on deck in five minutes in dress uniform to say goodbye to our guests."

"Yes, Captain," Cate said into the comm unit clipped to the belt of her white uniform pants, then closed the last suitcase she'd been working on. "Okay, kiddos. We need to go up on deck. Put your toys away and let's go."

Both Adella and Paulo, used to this routine by now, did as she asked, waiting for Cate by the door, where she ushered them out of the cabin and up the stairs to the main deck where the other crew were lining up to receive the Ruclecian royals.

After Cate left Adella and Paulo in a corner to sit quietly while she worked, she took her place in line and waited for the King and Queen to come through. She couldn't help wondering how Davian's talk with them had gone. Considering he'd not found her afterward to let her know suggested not as well as he'd planned.

"Dr. Neves," Queen Arabella said as she stopped before Cate. "Thank you for helping to make our cruise such a pleasure. We hope to see more of both of you in the future."

"Thank you, Your Majesty." Cate curtsied, more smoothly this time, then was surprised when the Queen embraced her.

"Our son told us about you and Adella, and I'm so glad he did," Queen Arabella whispered for Cate's ears only. "We've missed so much time with you and Adella. Please come visit us soon at the palace so we can get to know you both properly and welcome you to the family."

Stunned, Cate blinked at the woman once they pulled apart. "Uh, I… I guess we'll need to discuss that."

"Yes. There is much to discuss in that situation," the King said, looking the opposite of his wife's joyful demeanor. In fact, there was a slight grayish pallor to his complexion that Cate didn't like one bit. If he'd been one of her patients, she'd have ordered him admitted for testing. Still, given all the stress they were all under now, and the fact he wasn't her patient, she let it pass. He would be on a plane home within the hour and would be back under his own physician's care soon. Davian's father hardly needed her intercession at this point. The King stood before her, his posture rigid, and his gaze incisive. "I blame you for what my son is doing. Before we came on this trip, he had his head on straight. He knew his duty and was committed to it. Now he's full of fanciful ideas and ridiculous dreams."

"Phillipe!" Queen Arabella gasped, glancing up at her husband. "This is not the place."

"Father," Davian said, coming up behind the King and giving Cate a conciliatory look. "Mother's right. I'm sure Dr. Neves has things to get done before her departure. We can continue our discussion later by phone or video conference."

An angry vein pulsed near the King's temple and his complexion grew mottled. "Do not dare to tell me my place, either of you. I am the King of Ruclecia, and I will—"

The older man froze in place, his face going ashen

before he collapsed onto the deck amid surprised cries and calls from the crew.

Cate and Davian immediately sprang into action as another crew member ran downstairs for the emergency kit and portable ECG and defibrillator.

She moved to the King's head to assess his airway, while Davian checked for a pulse.

"Thready and uneven," he said, scowling down at his father's chest as he opened the man's suit jacket and shirt to expose his chest. "Airway?"

"No discernable breaths. Someone call an ambulance to the dock!"

While another crew member ran to report the emergency, Davian began CPR chest compressions on his father while Cate established a clear and open airway, then asked another crew member to administer oxygen to the King using a bag and mask while she moved to the King's other side to place the patches for the defibrillator machine and turn on the monitor. "Davian, can you stop chest compressions to see what kind of rhythm we have?"

They both stared at the screen.

"Definite defib," Davian said, glancing behind him to where Noah waited to take over CPR when Davian tired. "Okay, let's defibrillate at one hundred and fifty joules, please, and we'll change compressors afterward, yes?"

Noah nodded. "Yes."

"Stand clear," Cate said, turning the dial on the machine to the requested amount then hitting the button. The King's body jerked from the electric jolt. "Shock delivered."

"Okay. Let's continue compressions," Davian said, his voice flat and stoic.

Cate ached for him. This was why doctors never

worked on their own family members. Emergencies were high-emotion, high-stress incidents anyway. Add in all the other dynamics and it was far too difficult to be objective about the treatment and the outcome.

Davian took up the oxygen delivery once Noah took over on the CPR. "We can handle this. You should see about your mother."

"No. She's fine." He glanced over to where the captain was comforting the Queen. "I need to do this. It's my fault this happened."

"This isn't your fault," Cate said. "You said yourself your father's been in poor health. He recently had bypass surgery and has a history of cardiac problems. None of this now is your fault."

"I shouldn't have talked to him about leaving my royal duties. I should have waited until we were home," he said, his gaze locked on his father's grayish face. "I should have—"

"Stop." Cate kept her tone firm but quiet. "Second-guessing yourself now doesn't do anyone any good. If you'd waited, then something else would've come up, preventing you from telling him again. You did what you did because you had to, Davian. Living a lie hurts everyone involved. Believe me, I know." She drew up one milligram of epinephrine into a syringe then injected it into a vein in the King's arm. "Administering meds now."

After Cate disposed of the used syringe, Davian looked up at the monitor again. "Still in defib."

"Ambulance on the way," the crew member said, returning.

"Good." Cate checked her watch again. "Okay. It's been two minutes since the last shock. Let's stop compressions and reassess his rhythm again."

Noah lifted his hands away from the King's chest.

"Still in defib," Cate said. "Let's deliver another one hundred and fifty joules, then change compressors again. Oxygen clear?"

"Clear," Davian said, removing the mask from the King's face and stepping back.

"Clear." Cate pressed the button on the machine and the King's body jerked again. "Shock given. Resume compressions."

Davian and Noah switched places and the cycle began again as sirens approached from the dock.

Soon, the EMTs boarded and took over, continuing the CPR and getting a rundown from Cate while hooking up an IV with saline and glucose and giving the King a dose of amiodarone as well. Cate stepped back to allow them to intubate the King then watched as they loaded him onto a gurney and raced him off the yacht to take him to the nearby hospital.

"Cate, I'm sorry I—"

"Don't worry about me. Go!" she said, helping his mother over so Davian could take her hand and lead her off the ship. "I'll check in with you later to see how he's doing."

Even though Davian was a highly trained physician himself, everything changed when it was your loved one on the table. Cate had seen it many times before and she empathized with him. But the King was in the best hands now and they would do what they could to save him.

"Mommy?" Adella asked, coming up beside Cate as she and Noah cleaned up the mess they'd made during the resuscitation. "Will the King be all right?"

"I don't know, sweetie," she said, honestly. They'd caught his cardiac arrest early, but given his medical history, that might not have been enough. For the first time since the emergency had started, her emotions began to surface, and her chest tightened with unshed tears. For Davian and his family and what they were going through now. She blinked hard to keep them at bay, scowling down at the supplies she was gathering up and putting away. Against her wishes and against all odds, Davian had gotten into her heart again. She loved him. But even that might not be enough. "Whatever happens, sweetie, you and I will be there for Davian and the Queen."

Adella hugged her around the neck, the sweetness of it making Cate tear up even more. "I miss Davian."

"I do too, sweetie."

She needed to tell Adella the truth.

Not right then because everything was too crazy. But soon.

First though, they had to get off the yacht and catch their flight home to Boston.

The next several hours were touch and go for the King.

Davian stayed by his father's bedside, holding his mother's hand, and trying to make sense of it all. The day had not gone as he'd planned at all. After the difficult talk with his parents, he'd felt buoyant, like any untethered balloon finally able to fly into the sky. But now, that familiar weight of guilt and responsibility was back.

Worse, he missed Cate and Adella something awful. But he'd had no right to ask them to stay. And his place was here at present, at least until his father's condition had improved or…

Either way, this was where he was needed right now and so he sat there, waiting for news on his father's prognosis. They'd gotten him stabilized at least, and had run numerous tests, with little information as to why his heart had stopped. Some of the cardiologists speculated it had been a stent they'd put in during his bypass.

Others thought perhaps a medication issue or chemical imbalance brought on by stress.

Whatever the reason, Davian had been on the phone to the palace and his brother in Ruclecia, alerting them to the situation. Even now, his brother was taking steps to become the interim leader of the country in his father's stead, until the King recovered.

If my father recovers...

It was just the previous year they'd been through all this before, with his heart surgery. Davian had thought that would buy his father at least another decade of good health, but apparently not. His poor mother looked wan and worried and rightfully so. Davian knew from his own medical experience that of cardiac arrest patients whose arrests were witnessed, only 50 percent ever left the hospital again. And with his father's medical history, the odds were significantly worse.

Still, if money could buy anything, it was the best medical care possible, and Davian still had hope. They'd extubated him and the King was breathing on his own now, just still unconscious. His father was strong, despite his age and his medical setbacks. Otherwise healthy and stubborn as a mule. He and Davian went round and round over subjects they both cared about and had different ideas about the monarchy and their place in it, but in the end, they loved each other. He wanted his father to get well, not just for himself, but for his dear mother too. They'd been married over forty years.

Davian couldn't imagine losing a partner after that long. What if that had been Cate lying there…

My Cate...

"Your Highness?" One of the cardiologists gestured from the private hospital room's doorway to Davian. "May I speak with you a moment, please?"

He kissed his mother on the cheek and released her hand, then walked out of the room to the nurse's station with the other physician. "How is he doing?"

"Remarkably well, actually, given his age and his history," the cardiologist said. "His heart is pumping normally again, which is good, and his breathing is regular. We'll need to do more tests once he wakes up, but I'd say your father is a very lucky man."

Relief washed over Davian like rain. "Thank you, Doctor. What's his prognosis then?"

"Well, as I said, there are more tests to run and I'm sure his royal doctors back home will want to watch him like a hawk for the next few months to make sure this doesn't happen again, but as for now, he should be fine to leave in the next few days, once he wakes up. I'll have a better idea of exactly when that will be once he's conscious again."

"Okay. Anything he should avoid until he gets home?"

"Stress, mainly. And that goes for even after he's back in Ruclecia," the cardiologist said. "Your father is nearly seventy now. It's time for him to consider pulling back, delegating some of his royal duties to the next generation."

"Agreed." Davian gave a curt nod. This was the moment his brother had trained for his whole life. "Thank you again, Doctor."

"My pleasure." The cardiologist smiled. "I'm sure we'll speak again before the King is discharged."

Davian returned to the hospital room to tell his mother about what the cardiologist had said.

"I'd told him for years he needs to relax and let Arthur take over." The Queen sniffled and squeezed the King's hand through the bars on the side of the hospital bed. "Perhaps now he'll listen to me."

"Perhaps so."

"Oh!" The Queen gasped. "He squeezed my hand back!"

"Did he? Do it again." Davian watched while his mother held his father's hand tighter and sure enough, his father squeezed her hand back. "That's excellent. Means he's waking up."

The Queen leaned in to kiss the King's fingers and smiled. "Come back to me, my love."

Davian's chest tightened. Speaking of love…

"Excuse me for a moment, Mother." He went back out of the room again and down the hall to a small private waiting area for the ICU guests. There, he pulled out his phone and sent Cate a text, updating her on his father's condition, then asking her a very important question.

Will you and Adella come visit me in Ruclecia?

CHAPTER FOURTEEN

CATE DIDN'T GET the message until they arrived back in Boston, what with all the chaos of connecting flights and keeping Adella occupied and happy. It was early the next morning, and they were in a cab on the way to her mother's house in Medford, northwest of downtown Boston. Adella was asleep in her lap, and when Cate pulled out her phone and unlocked the screen, it took several moments for her tired eyes to adjust to the tiny text and read what it said.

Davian's father had made it and was expected to make a full recovery. That was wonderful. Cate scrolled down farther, stopping at the last line of the message as her own heart skipped a beat.

Will you and Adella come visit me in Ruclecia?

The way they'd left things between them was still very much up in the air.

They still had so much to talk about, so much to decide—about their relationship, about Adella's future. Cate still needed to talk to Adella about who Davian really was. More than anything though, she needed to get out of her own head about it and talk to her mom about it all.

If anyone could give her perspective on things, it would be her mom.

Maya Neves, Cate's mom, was waiting for them when they arrived. She welcomed them home with hugs and a pot of fresh coffee for Cate and hot cocoa for little Adella. They had toast and waffles in the kitchen, then Cate took Adella upstairs for a nap before returning for a private talk with her mother.

She told her about seeing Davian again and them reconnecting, about Cate telling Davian that Adella was his, and the King's cardiac arrest before they left the yacht.

"He invited Adella and me to visit him in Ruclecia," Cate said, staring down into her coffee mug.

"Are you going to go?" Her mother raised a brow at her. At sixty-two, her mother still looked fifteen years younger than that, with a bright, infectious smile and green eyes the same shade as her daughter's. Her mom's hair had gone silver though, giving her a bit of an ethereal look these days. "I mean, he is still a prince, even if it's only by blood. Could be fun to see his palace."

Cate chuckled. "I'm sure it's a very grand palace. I remember seeing pictures of it back in residency when I was trying to get ahold of him about my pregnancy."

The reminder of everything they'd been through put a bit of a damper on Cate's good humor. "I don't know, Mom. It's been a lot happening in a short period of time. And when you're on the yacht, it's like its own little universe. Everything feels heightened there. But now that we're home, what if things have changed?"

"Doesn't sound like it has for him, since he invited you to visit him halfway around the world."

She sighed. "I know. But what if it was just residual adrenaline from the emergency with his father? I'm sure Davian is exhausted from that and dealing with his mother and his family business in the aftermath. He probably needs a good night's sleep and time to think. I know I do."

"Hmm." Her mom sat back, mug cupped in her hands and expression thoughtful. "Well, just don't think too much, Cate. I know you. And you'll think yourself right out of it."

Cate frowned but couldn't deny her mom might be right. She was a first-class overthinker. Always had been. "I just… I'm scared, okay? I got burned once before with him and I survived. Not sure I want to take that chance again. And it's not just me now I must worry about. It's Adella too. I haven't told her anything about Davian yet, so please don't bring it up in front of her until I give you the all clear."

"I won't say anything to her about him yet."

They sat there for a while, the only sound the ticking of the old clock on the wall, until finally her mother asked, "Do you love him?"

"Yes. But I'm not sure that's enough."

"It's a lot." Her mom sat forward again. "Look, honey. I hope this isn't about me and your dad."

She looked up from the table to her mother. "A little, maybe. He walked out on us without a word. He left us to fend for ourselves."

"True, but I wouldn't have had it any other way."

"What?"

"Why would I want a man to be here, in our lives, if he wasn't committed to us? If we weren't the top priority in his life?"

"But you struggled so much, raising me alone. He could've helped with bills and food and—"

"If I'd needed help with that, I could've gotten food

stamps. And I did a few times. But financial security is no reason for a marriage." At Cate's dubious look, her mom snorted. "Fine. Not the most important reason. Your father and I loved each other once upon a time, but not the way we needed to for things to work. Sometimes you must let that go to get what you really need and want and deserve in life. You need a man in your life, a father for Adella, who is all in, Cate. Someone who will be there for you through thick and thin. Perhaps your Davian could be that someone for you."

"I don't know, Mom," Cate said, shaking her head. "I'm scared. I don't want to get hurt again."

"I get that, honey. But you'll never find out if you don't give him a chance."

Cate sighed. "You're right. It's just so hard. Letting him close again, after everything that happened between us."

"I don't want to tell you what to do one way or another," her mother said, leaning her hips back against the edge of the counter and crossing her arms. "Lord knows I made enough mistakes in my own life. But please, honey. Don't let your father's actions in the past dictate your choices going forward. The day I broke free of those chains was the best day of my life. I pray it's the same for you, Cate."

"But what about companionship? You've been alone ever since. Don't you get lonely, Mom?"

"Yes, sometimes. But then I have you and Adella and all my friends in the neighborhood. You are only alone if you choose to be. And that's a fine choice to make if it's the right one for you. I did fine on my own, with you. We were two warriors against the world, you and me. And I think we were closer for it. But that doesn't mean the same choice is right for you." Her mother reached across the table and took Cate's hand. "Now, I've never met your prince, and I only know what you've told me about him, but he sounds like a good man. Devoted, dedicated, caring, supportive, loyal. And it seems to me that those qualities extend from his family to you and Adella now too. Your father was none of those things for us, but please don't think he and Davian are anything alike. If you love him as you say you do, I think you need to at least go and see him. If you don't, you'll regret it the rest of your life."

Cate took that it and turned it over in her mind as she had everything else over the last whirlwind two weeks, until finally exhaustion took over and she yawned. "I think I need a nap before I decide."

Her mom smiled. "There's my smart girl. A nap is always a good decision."

"Thanks." She got up and rinsed her cup in the sink then kissed her mom's cheek as she passed her on the way to the door. But when she got up to her room, instead of going to bed right away, Cate pulled out her phone and sent a text back to Davian before she lost her nerve. For better or worse, her mother was right. She needed to go and see Davian once more to see if this thing between them was real or not. And Adella deserved to see her family's homeland.

Tell me when and where and we'll be there. Glad your father's doing better. Cate.

"So, can I call him Daddy?" Adella asked two weeks later when she and Cate were sitting on a plane in Athelas, the capital city of Ruclecia, waiting to disembark. "Or do I have to call him Prince?"

"Well, I think Daddy would be fine, but that's something you two should decide together once we get to the palace," Cate said, undoing her seat belt then reaching over do the same to her daughter's. "But first, we need to get our luggage and find the car they've sent for us."

The captain announced that first-class passengers could exit the plane first, so Cate stood and grabbed their carry-ons from the overhead bin then took Adella's hand to lead her off the plane. She rarely splurged for such luxury travel herself, but Davian had handled all the arrangements for them, so Cate had had little say in the matter. Though she did appreciate the extra legroom and amenities first class offered, especially when Adella was treated to warm cookies and a set of golden wings from the pilot.

They thanked the crew and walked down the gangway to the terminal. Cate hoped she'd be able to find the driver without too much trouble, but it turned out her fears were unnecessary. As soon as they walked out into the gate waiting area, a man in a chauffeur's uniform rushed up to them and quickly guided them through customs, then down the corridor to the baggage claim area. Good thing too, since apparently the paparazzi had been alerted to their arrival as well and were bustling around them, snapping photos and calling out questions. Cate held Adella's hand tighter and quickened her steps.

"Just ignore them, sweetie."

"But Mommy? Why are they following us?" Adella asked, her nose scrunched. "And they keep calling me Princess. You told me I shouldn't call myself that back home."

"That's true," Cate said, pointing to their bags on the carousel so the driver could grab them. "But here in Ruclecia, it's a bit different."

"So, I am a princess here?"

"You're always a princess to me, sweetie." Rather than risk tiring her daughter out so soon, Cate bent and swept the little girl up into her arms and followed the driver out a nearby revolving door to where a black Bentley waited near the curb. The driver stowed their luggage in the trunk and held the door for Cate and Adella to get in the back seat then hurried around to slide behind the wheel. All in all, Cate thought it was probably the fastest trip through an airport she'd ever had. Guess there was something to say for being royal after all. Or at least royal-adjacent.

The drive to the palace took them through the glittering downtown of Athelas then out into the suburbs and finally into the lush green countryside of Ruclecia. There were mountains in the distance and a grayish mist near the ground, reminding her somewhat the Scottish Highlands or Switzerland. Every so often they'd pass a farm or a quaint cottage.

"Look at the cows, Mommy!" Adella pointed them out, her nose plastered to the window to catch all the scenery rushing by them.

It had taken a while for the idea of visiting Davian here to settle in with her, even though Cate had accepted his invitation right away. But in the end, she couldn't bear the thought of never seeing him again, even if he didn't feel the same way about her or want a future together. And the fact was, Adella needed a father. Cate hadn't given up entirely on her plans to start a GP practice either, but now she had widened her scope. Nothing was set in stone, but depending on how this visit went, she might choose to move to Ruclecia instead. Start a practice here, perhaps work in conjunction with Davian's hospital, if he was amenable to that.

They'd texted back and forth a lot the past few weeks

as her and Adella's trip neared, discussing plans and arrival times and such. Davian had been busy catching up with his patients and his work as administrator of the hospital. Add to that the fact that his father had recovered enough to finally make the decision to step down and turn the throne over to his son, Crown Prince Arthur. Davian had decided to have their visit coincide with the announcement so that it would hopefully overshadow the news of Adella being Davian's daughter. They'd both decided a more gradual introduction to royal life would be the best for their little girl and hopefully coming now, with so much else going on, would distract from Cate and Adella's presence.

The crowd of press at the airport, however, made her think twice on that subject.

Nervous butterflies took flight inside Cate, but as they rounded a turn in the highway, and the onion-domed cupolas, tea caddy tower and pointed spires of the royal palace came into view in the distance, she knew it was too late to turn around and run. They weren't in Boston anymore, that was for sure.

"Mommy! Look!" Adella gasped. "It's just like my playhouse at Grandma's!"

"Yes, it is," Cate said, smiling. Built on the site of an original castle from the 900s, this version of the royal palace was done in the Romantic historicism style by one of Davian's ancestors in the mid-1800s. And soon, they'd be staying there. Unbelievable. "Are you excited, sweetie?"

"I am!" Adella clapped. "Do you think I can sleep in one of those towers?"

Cate laughed. "Sweetie, I think anything is possible at this point."

CHAPTER FIFTEEN

THAT NIGHT, AS his father came to the end of his speech, Davian stood near the edge of the dais and gazed out at the assembled crowd. It was filled with various politicians and celebrities, as well as the usual glitterati of Ruclecian society. However, he'd yet to spot the two people he wanted to see most in the world. Cate and Adella. He'd been told by staff that they'd arrived safely at the palace earlier that afternoon, and if his schedule hadn't been completely crazy and overpacked with important appointments and patient visits, he would've gone to see them before the reception tonight. As it was though, he'd barely made it here on time himself, only finishing with his last responsibilities about fifteen minutes before his father took the stage.

"And so, it is with great nostalgia and hope for the future of our great nation that I humbly resign as your monarch and turn the throne over to my eldest son, Crown Prince Arthur. Thank you."

His father took a short bow toward the crowd that had erupted into applause and shouts of "God save the King." King Phillipe was looking much better these days. And while the cane he used to walk with now would probably be a lifelong companion after the nerve damage suffered to his leg following the cardiac arrest on the yacht, his color was good, as were his lab results. In fact, if he kept going on with his healthy habits, he might well outlive them all.

The King made his way offstage as Crown Prince Arthur took over the mic to give his acceptance speech, and Davian was there to help his father down the short set of stairs. Their relationship, while certainly better than how they'd left things on the *Querencia*, still held a bit of tension and chill to it. Davian hoped one day they could resolve their issues with one another and, if not accept their differences wholeheartedly, then at least get back to the friendly relationship they'd had prior to the cruise. But honestly, if this was how it had to be for Davian to have his freedom, he could live with it.

"Thank you, dear," his mother said, kissing Davian's cheek. "You are so wonderful, always looking out for us."

His father grumbled and straightened, pulling free of Davian's helpful grip. Still stubborn, as always. "I am not an invalid, son. I can walk by myself."

"Of course, Father," Davian said.

"And where are these guests of yours?" his father asked, giving his youngest son an arch stare, trying to goad Davian into another argument. "The doctor and her daughter."

But tonight, he wasn't taking the bait. "I think you mean Cate, the woman I love, and *our* daughter, Adella. And the answer is, I'm not sure. I was told they arrived safely, but I haven't had time to see them yet." Davian searched the crowd around them again, without success. "In fact, if you don't require me, I think I'll go and find them."

"Run along, dear," his mother said. "Go find your

lady love and bring her back here. I've so much to talk to her about."

"And I want to get a look at this granddaughter of mine," his father added, surprisingly Davian.

"Be back," Davian said, kissing his mother once more on the cheek before weaving into the spectators to try to find Cate. He found them near the back wall, Adella playing with the stuffed octopus he'd bought for her at the aquarium. He couldn't fight the wide grin blossoming on his face and didn't try. Damn, it was good to see them again. For the first time in weeks, he felt like he could breathe again.

"There you are!" He walked over and without waiting, pulled Cate into a hug. She felt wonderful in his arms, warm and strong and real. "How was your trip in?"

"Great," Cate said, pulling back to run a hand down the skirt of the ball gown she wore. Everyone was dressed formally for the occasion—Davian in a tux, like the rest of the male guests, while his father and brother were dressed in their finest military regalia. The shimmery seafoam green color of Cate's gown set off her eyes and blond hair to perfection, also highlighting her tanned skin. She went to say more but was interrupted by a tug on her hand.

"Mommy?" Adella asked, in a whisper loud enough for Davian to hear with no problems. "Can I say it now?"

Cate took a deep breath, glancing from Adella to Davian then back again. She nodded and Adella squared her little shoulders, then dropped into a cute little curtsy. "Hello, Daddy."

Davian feared his heart would trip right out of his chest and land in a puddle of goo at his daughter's feet. It was the first time Adella had called him that and he wanted to remember the moment forever. He bowed to her, then crouched, putting them at eye level. "Hello, Princess. I'm very glad you're here."

"Me too." She smiled at him, clutching her octopus tight. "Can I call you Daddy? Or should I say Prince? I asked Mommy, but she said I had to talk to you about it first."

"Well..." Davian swallowed hard against the sudden lump of emotion in his throat. "I think Daddy has a really nice ring to it."

"Yay!" With that, Adella launched herself into his arms and hugged him tight around the neck, her stuffed toy squashed between them as he stood with his daughter in his arms. "I've always wanted a daddy and now I have one and you're a prince too and I'm so excited to show you all my toys and maybe we can play together and then you can read me a story at bedtime. Do you like stories, Daddy? I love them and..."

He caught Cate's eye over the top of Adella's head and saw her fighting hard not to laugh at his astonishment. He'd dreamed of this moment going well, but never imagined Adella taking to him so quickly or so enthusiastically.

Cate stepped closer to whisper, "She's been eagerly awaiting seeing you since I told her the truth a few weeks ago. She always liked you, even on the yacht, so when she found out you're her daddy, it was icing on the cake. Good luck!"

"Thanks." He chuckled.

"So," his father's voice said from behind him, causing Davian's pulse to stumble. Their little family might be new, but Davian already vowed to fight anyone, friend or foe, who tried to take it from him. Including his father. He turned slowly, Adella still chattering on obliviously in his arms, to find his father, scowling over at them from a few feet away. "We meet at last."

"Phillipe," his mother said, coming up to take his father's arm. "Perhaps we should wait..."

"I've waited long enough," the old King said, stepping closer with his cane to squint at Adella, who was now staring back at him too, wide-eyed and curious. The King's bushy gray eyebrows knitted. "What do you have to say for yourself, young lady?"

Adella squeaked and Cate stepped closer, apparently feeling as protective as Davian at that moment. Then their daughter cocked her head and squinted right back at the former King of Ruclecia. "My name's Adella Neves and I'm a princess. And you look like King Lars!"

Davian's father blinked at the little girl a moment then glanced at Cate. "I am unfamiliar with this ruler."

Cate bit her lips again. "He's on her favorite TV show, *Elena of Avelor*. It's a cartoon."

"Oh." The King seemed puzzled by that for a moment, then looked at Adella again. "He must be very handsome and kind and wise then."

"He is," Adella said, seriously. "But it's more about your fancy medals."

Davian and his mother and Cate all stared at each other a moment then burst into laughter simultaneously while his father straightened, and Adella held on to her octopus tighter. Then, finally, his father cracked a smile and, even more surprisingly, began to laugh as well. Big, full belly laughs that Davian hadn't heard from the man in years, decades even. It was refreshing and went a good way toward mending bridges between them.

Then his mother moved forward to smile at Adella. "You look just like your father at that age. You're five, aren't you?"

Adella, now shy, nodded, chewing on a stuffed tentacle.

"Well, I'm your grandmother, Arabella," his mother said. "May I hold you?"

Adella's expression turned wary. "I already have a grandma. Her name is Maya."

"You can have more than one, sweetie," Cate said, stepping in beside Davian to rub Adella's back. "We talked about this. Queen Arabella is your grandmother too. And King Phillipe is your grandfather."

"Really?" Adella looked between the two older people suspiciously.

"Really," Davian's parents said in unison.

"Oh." Then, just as suddenly as she'd taken to Davian, his daughter wanted down to go over to his parents. "In that case, can you show me the stage up front, please?"

His mother looked at Cate, who nodded. "Just don't let her talk you into eating all the sweets at the refreshment table. She's already had enough for one night."

They watched his parents walk away, Adella holding their hands between them.

"So," Davian said, after a moment. "Would you take a walk with me?"

She nodded and they went out a side entrance to the main ballroom to a small private balcony overlooking the royal gardens below. When Davian had been a boy, this was one of his favorite spots to sit and think by himself. Few people came out here, and he wanted to share it with Cate now. Especially since he had something very important to ask her.

"It's lovely out here," she said, leaning over the granite railing. The air had turned colder this November but was still refreshing after the stuffy ballroom.

Davian couldn't get enough of seeing her tonight. The slight blush in her cheeks, visible in the light from the sconces on the wall. The softness of her green eyes. The sweet floral scent of her perfume. Cate looked up and caught him staring and Davian looked away fast, heat prickling his neck from beneath the collar of his starched white tuxedo shirt.

"How was your trip in?" he asked, flustered by her nearness in a way he'd never been before.

She laughed softly, the sound wafting around him on the slight breeze. "You asked me that already, Davian. What's got you so on edge?"

"I..." His hand brushed against the small box-shaped lump in his pocket and his pulse tripped. This wasn't like him. He was always cool, collected, calm under pressure. But whenever he was around Cate, all that went right out the window. *Just do it. Just ask her.* He took her hand and brought it to his lips to brush a kiss across the back of it. "I need to ask you a question."

Cate turned to face him, her expression quizzical. "Okay."

Davian took a deep breath for courage and reached into his pocket for the little velvet box he'd stashed there earlier, creaking it open to reveal the sparkling emerald cut diamond engagement ring inside.

"What are you..." Cate frowned, her free hand trembling as she covered her lips with her fingers. "Davian."

Now that he'd started, he couldn't stop. Not until he heard her answer. "I love you, Cate. I always have. From the first time we met back in residency until tonight, you've knocked me off my feet in the best way. I lost you once, and nearly lost you again after the yacht charter. I don't ever want to lose you again. Will you do me the supreme honor of becoming my wife, Cate Neves?"

With that, he got down on one knee and held the ring up to her.

Cate's breath caught and her lovely green eyes filled with tears as she smiled. "I love you too, Davian. Even when you were David. I'll always love you."

Then Davian was standing and slipping his ring onto her finger, and they were kissing, soft and sweet, a promise of more—much more—to come. When he pulled back, resting his forehead against hers, they were both grinning. "That's a yes, right?"

She giggled and nodded then kissed him again. "Of course, it's a yes."

Three months later...

Cate and Adella were back in Ruclecia, permanently this time, and Davian couldn't have been happier. They were all at the grand cathedral in Athelas for his brother's official coronation as King of Ruclecia. His parents were there too, as was Cate's mother and his brother's wife and children, the soon-to-be Queen and Crown Prince and Princess of Ruclecia. Outside of the royal family, the pews were filled with friends and well-wishers, international guests and celebrities and all the major news outlets.

His brother had struck a bargain with the tabloids. The palace would provide regular updates and selected photos for their use in exchange for privacy outside of that. For now, the agreement seemed to be holding and for that, Davian was glad.

Even more encouraging was the fact that the palace security team had managed to capture and arrest all the members of the radical group behind the assassination threats made against the royal family. They would still be cautious because they'd all lived that way so long it was hard to break the habit, but a huge weight had been lifted off Davian and his brother. All of them were expected to be convicted based on the overwhelming evidence that had been compiled against them.

All was well in Ruclecia again.

"Mommy?" Adella whispered, squirming in her seat between her mother and father. "Will I have a fancy dress like that in June?"

Cate tracked where her daughter was pointing to Arianna, Arthur's daughter and Adella's royal cousin. She smiled. "If you want, sweetie. You're going to be the prettiest flower girl regardless."

"Cool!"

Davian bent to kiss his daughter's head, then Cate. They were planning their wedding, and while Davian no longer participated in official royal duties around the country, the people still loved him and all he did to help keep the people of Ruclecia healthy, and they demanded a large spectacle of a ceremony.

"And what kind of dress is your mommy going to have?" he asked, slipping his arm around Cate's shoulders and pulling both her and Adella closer.

"Whatever kind of dress fits by then," Cate said, laughing as she placed a hand over her small baby bump. They were expecting another child, though they were keeping it a secret for now. "Your mother, the Queen, said she still had her old wedding dress, so we might try to work that in somehow. She'd like that, I think."

"I'm sure she would," Davian said, leaning in to kiss his soon-to-be wife's cheek again.

Adella slipped out from between them and leaned over to glance down the pew to where her grandparents were all sitting together. She'd adjusted well to their recent move and life in Ruclecia and was currently being spoiled rotten by all her grandparents. "Can I go sit with them, Mommy?"

Cate sighed, then nodded. "Fine. But hurry. And be quiet so you don't disturb the ceremony."

Adella hurried off, leaving Davian and Cate alone. He snuggled her closer, more content than he could ever remember being. They were working together at the hospital and building a new life together at home. What more could a man ask for? "Happy, darling?"

Cate tucked her head into the crook of his neck and gave a happy sigh. "Beyond happy, my love."

* * * * *

PREGNANT WITH THE SECRET PRINCE'S BABIES

DEANNE ANDERS

MILLS & BOON

This book is dedicated to Jacob, Abigail, Josie, Roman and Molly, who are always eager to share with their teachers that their nana is an author, even though they aren't allowed to read her books until they get older.

CHAPTER ONE

"THE KING IS not happy."

Though thousands of miles away, his brother's booming voice ricocheted inside his pounding head like it was a pinball machine.

After spending over twelve hours on a plane, Dr. Alex Leonelli had finally made it home to Key West, leaving behind his life as Alexandro Michael Leonelli, best friend and secret half brother of Crown Prince Nicholas of Soura. The last thing he wanted was to listen to his brother try to lay a guilt trip on him. He'd more than done his duty for his brother. It was only right for Nicholas to get stuck with their father's bad temper after all the trouble he'd been the last five months.

He punched in the code on the front door to HeliCare's headquarters. He was glad they hadn't changed the code. He was even luckier that he still had a job.

"Sounds like a personal problem," Alex said as he looked up at the clear sky overhead. The moon and stars were still putting on an early morning show for all the tourists who'd soon be heading home after their night of partying in downtown Key West.

It was so good to be back. He'd missed everything about the small island. Because while the palm trees reminded him of where he had grown up in California and the local beaches reminded him of the Mediterranean ones of his father's small country, Key West was his home. Here he was just Dr. Alex, ER doc and medical chief of Heli-Care's local medevac unit. He liked who he was able to be here.

"You stole out in the middle of the night like you were some common thief," his brother said.

"And whose fault is that? Every time I mentioned heading home you suddenly had a supposed relapse. And don't get me started on all the ways our father tried to keep me there." He didn't have time for this. He only had a few hours before jet lag brought him to a crashing halt. He'd been away for too long and he was ready to get back to work. It was his friend Dylan's hard work covering for him that had helped him keep his job and he knew his crew had been in good hands. But Dylan now had a new wife and needed to get on with his own life. Just like Alex needed to get on with his.

Which was why he'd headed to Heli-Care's base, instead of heading home, or at least that was what he was telling himself. It had absolutely nothing to do with the petite blond registered nurse who, according to the crew schedule, was on an overnight shift right now.

Summer. What was going on with her? With them? And how was he going to fix it?

"It's that girl, isn't it?" his brother said, as if he had just read Alex's mind.

"Just because you bounce between one woman to another doesn't mean that everyone is happy with that life." Alex had never understood his brother's insistence on playing the bad-boy crown prince when he could do so much more with his life.

"You could be if you'd let yourself. And I think she made it pretty clear that she has moved on even if you haven't. How many times does a woman have to refuse your calls for you to get a hint?"

"Shouldn't you be working on your rehab instead of worrying about my love life?" His brother was right, but Alex wasn't ready to admit it. Not yet. Summer had cut all contact between them the moment he had left Key West. When she'd refused his calls and hadn't returned any of his texts, he'd been surprised. Summer wasn't someone who liked a lot of drama in her life. If she was angry, she told you. Her not returning his calls didn't make sense. But he'd had to put aside all of that until his brother's life was out of danger.

"I just hope she's worth making our father angry. You have to know that he's looking for a reason to out you."

"What?" Alex's hand froze on the door handle.

"He wants to acknowledge you as his son, Alex." His brother's voice gave no hint about how he personally felt about his father's plan.

"Isn't it a little late for that? I've played the game of hiding who I am too long to change my life now." And he didn't want to change. Living in Key West as a simple doctor was the life he had dreamed of. No cameras, no reporters, no paparazzi. No one wanting to highlight and criticize everything he did. It was the perfect life for him.

"Besides, we both know the scandal would be bad for all of us," Alex said. If he could only get his brother on his side, maybe they could get his father to see reason.

"Maybe for our father and your mother. But for us? I'd say the benefits will balance out the burden of the media attention," his brother said with his usual nonchalance.

"And what benefit would that be?" His father and brother had never understood his life. Bringing media attention into his life would have direct consequences for his job. How could he work out in the open if he constantly had to be worrying about the paparazzi showing up?

He stepped into the building and entered the multiuse room, where he'd spent many an hour with his crew watching movies and gaming. It was empty—not surprising at this time of the morning. The overnight crew would be catching some downtime before being dispatched to the next call, or the morning crew came in.

The thought of giving up this place, these people, was impossible to consider.

This was where he belonged. Not stashed in some palace with his only patient being a grouchy royal. He rubbed his temples as the aching in his head seemed to magnify with that thought. Leaving the palace when he had had been the right thing for him. He would have lost his mind if he'd stayed another day.

And his timing was perfect. He would have enough time to catch up on some emails before shift change. Then he could see his staff and let them know he was back.

And then there was Summer. He needed her to see that he had returned, just like he'd promised all those months ago. He could only hope that her seeing he had kept his promise to return would help make things right between them.

And if she wanted the details on why he had been gone so long? How would he answer her questions? He'd wanted to tell her about his other life for months before he'd left, but he'd always hesitated, afraid that it would change things between them.

"It's time, Alex," his brother said, startling him. The pounding in his head doubled.

"For what exactly?" He couldn't keep the irritation

out of his voice. All of this was his brother's fault. The Crown Prince of Soura should have been taking care of his royal duties instead of chasing his latest daring thrill.

Which was why he had ended up in a critical-care unit with half of his ribs broken, a punctured lung and both his femurs fractured, and as a result, Alex had left Key West without any notice. His lack of explanation meant that Summer had cut all communication between the two of them.

Alex couldn't blame his father for calling him and demanding that he come to his tiny Mediterranean kingdom of Soura immediately. His brother had needed him.

But so had Summer.

And he didn't understand that. Not really. Summer had always been so independent and so understanding about his job and the crazy hours he worked. He couldn't understand why she had reacted so differently that day. His father's phone call had left no doubt of how urgent it was for him to get to his brother. He'd had no choice. Jeopardizing his job and running out on his crew was not something that he would have ever dreamed of doing. She'd known that. Just like she'd had to have known that he wouldn't have left her if it hadn't been urgent. If he'd only had more time to figure out what had been going on with her. But he'd panicked. He could see that now. After working in an emergency room and with a flight crew, he'd imagined the worst. And he'd been right to.

While the public knew that Nicholas had been involved in an accident, the king had left out the details. Only the medical staff and Alex's father knew that it was touch and go right after the accident.

But that would all end soon. As soon as the crew got up, Summer would be able to see with her own eyes that he had returned just like he had promised her. Then he could explain everything to her, and they could get back to their normal lives together.

After months of living in a palace, he craved his normal life. He needed his normal life.

A dramatic sigh reminded him that his brother was still on the phone. It made Alex want to roll his eyes like a teenager as he made his way down the hall to his office. Both his brother and his father had a flair for drama. "You know the local media has been asking questions about our friendship for years," Nicholas said. "And that little man from the local tabloid, the one that ran all the old headlines about your mother and my father—security caught him sneaking around the service entrance yesterday questioning the staff."

Alex knew the man he was talking about. He'd tried to corner Alex more than once. But Soura and the journalist were far away now. No one would have followed him back to Key West.

"How's the new nurse?" Alex asked. They'd both said everything there was to say on the subject of the king claiming him as his son. They would never agree.

And they didn't need to. It was Alex's life, something he had reminded his father and brother a thousand times in the last few months.

"The woman is a tyrant. Telling me what to eat. When to sleep," Nicholas complained. "Did you really give her an order that I couldn't stay up past midnight?"

"No. I told her you were to get plenty of sleep while you recuperated. I left the rest up to her." Alex had known the moment he'd met the woman that she would be capable of keeping Nicholas in line with the regimen that was needed for his full recovery.

His phone went off with an alert. The crew was being activated.

"Tell the king that I will call soon and don't give Ellie a hard time." Alex could still hear his brother grumbling as he ended the call and took his seat behind his desk only a second before people began to emerge from the sleep rooms that opened into the hallway.

"Boss, you finally found your way home. It's about time," Casey, the first to see him, said, giving him a big smile and wave before he hurried off down the hall.

It was then that he saw her. Standing in the hallway, Summer went from half-asleep to fully awake in a nanosecond. Her eyes met his for only a second before she turned away from him. In that brief moment, he'd seen none of the pleasure he'd hoped for. Instead, there'd been nothing. Not even anger. He could deal with anger. They could talk their way through that. But nothing? He would rather she had yelled at him.

Of course, she was working. It wasn't like she would want to get into things here at work. Especially before she went on a call.

He rubbed his aching head again. He needed sleep, but he needed to talk to Summer more. He turned on his computer and opened up his emails. He might as well get some work done while he waited for her to return.

She'd run. She'd run like a little kid caught with a hand in the cookie jar.

No. More like a scared, embarrassed teenager caught stealing a prom dress at the local department store. Her face heated with the memory.

"You know you're going to have to talk to him at some point," Casey said as they buckled into their seats as their pilot, Roy, started the helicopter rotors. Her queasy stomach did a small somersault as they rose into the air and headed for their small island hospital.

Choosing to ignore him, Summer opened the respiratory supply box. All the adult-size emergency equipment needed to be changed to pediatric size for the little girl they would be transporting to the children's hospital in Miami. "Can you hand me a pediatric IV start kit?"

Casey pulled open the drawer holding the intravenous supplies. "You can't put it off. It's not like he's not going to notice. He's not blind. The two of you just need to talk it out."

She wanted to tell the man that he was not one to give love advice, since he couldn't see what was right in front of his own eyes. But that would mean betraying her friend Jo's confidence and she wouldn't do that, though it was a big temptation. She knew Casey wasn't going to quit dogging her about Alex.

"ETA, two minutes," Roy's voice said over their headphones.

"I'm just saying, Alex will do the right thing," Casey said, handing the supplies over to her.

The right thing? The right thing like her father had done by marrying her mother when he'd found out she was pregnant with her? Would he be doing "the right thing" like her father had done when he'd then left her mother when things got hard? She didn't need anyone else to do the right thing for her. She'd learned at an early age that the only person she could count on was herself. She'd forgotten that for a short period of time while she'd been with Alex. She wouldn't forget it again.

Her hand went protectively to her stomach. No, she wasn't going to let history repeat itself with her. The only thing she needed was to finish this shift and get home before she had to confront Alex at the office. That wasn't the place, and today, when she was worn out from working, wasn't the time.

Casey was right. They would have to talk, but she knew she needed to prepare herself. Just that one look at Alex had made her want to forget the last five months. But that sounded just like something her mother would have done.

She had never been like her mother and she wouldn't let herself become like her. Summer was responsible for more than just herself now. She would continue her relationship with Alex, but it would be with her in the lead. Alex could choose to follow or not. That was up to him.

Today, she had a job to do, and that job was what she needed to concentrate on, not the fact that Alex had finally returned.

Upon arrival, the trauma room they were directed to was buzzing with activity as nurses and the emergency doctor surrounded their patient. Casey moved to talk to the respiratory tech, who was standing by the ventilator that the small child had been attached to.

"What happened?" Summer asked the charge nurse, who was busy filling out the transport paperwork.

"It appears to have been a freak accident. The Fraziers..." The woman motioned to a corner, where a woman and man stood staring at the small, still body of the little girl lying on the oversize trauma stretcher. It was clear that the two of them were in shock. "The Fraziers," she began again, "just arrived from Texas last night. They're staying at a small bungalow with a loft, which is where Emma was sleeping. They think she was trying to get down the stairs and tripped on one of the steps. They called 911 as soon as it happened."

"How bad is it?" Summer asked, having no doubt that the injury had to be more than a broken arm or leg, since Emma had been intubated and needed to be flown off the island.

"Head bleed, fractured skull with a subdural hematoma. Dr. Wade has spoken with a pediatric neurologist in Miami and it was suggested that we go ahead and intubate her before transport. You'll be taking her to the emergency room before she heads to surgery."

Summer saw that Casey and the staff were about to transfer the child to their own transport stretcher, so she thanked the nurse and moved over to the child's parents.

"My name is Summer, and that," she said, pointing to her blond coworker, "is Casey. We'll be transporting Emma to the emergency room of the children's hospital in Miami. The staff here will give you directions and provide the address. If you give me your number, I'll call you as soon as we arrive and I'll pass your number to the emergency-room staff. Do you have any questions for me?"

"I… W-we don't…" the girl's mother stammered. Her husband wrapped his arm around the woman, who had begun to shake.

"We'll find our way," he said, then pulled a business card out of his wallet, "but if you could please keep us informed?"

Summer nodded, took the card and then stuck it into one of the many pockets of her flight suit. A small hand grabbed her sleeve.

"Please—please take care of my baby," Emma's mother begged as her eyes filled with tears. "And if she wakes up, please tell her Mommy and Daddy love her."

Summer stared into the heartbroken woman's eyes. She couldn't imagine a parent entrusting their child, their world, into the care of someone else. Summer covered the woman's hand with her own and held it tight. "I promise, we'll take the best of care of your daughter."

Summer grabbed the back of the stretcher and followed Casey out of the emergency room, never taking her eyes off the little girl until she was loaded, and the doors were closed.

"Roy, let's make this a fast one," Summer told their pilot, though she knew he always made their trips to Miami as fast and safe as possible.

"Vital signs stable," Casey said as he removed the Ambu bag he'd been using to help the little girl breathe and changed her to their portable in-flight ventilator. "Cute kid."

Summer applied monitor pads and checked the little girl's heart rhythm. "She's still in a sinus rhythm."

"The parents looked freaked out. I hope they make it to the hospital okay," Casey said as he picked up the computer pad to record the events of the transfer.

"Emma's father seems to have a cool head. He'll get them there." The man had impressed her as someone who would do whatever it took to take care of his family.

"It really sucks that something like this happened when they're so far away from home, where they don't know anyone." Casey said.

"It does," Summer agreed as she carefully brushed the little girl's dark hair from her face. She'd spent most of her own life not having anyone she could depend on to help her when she needed someone. "I'll see what we can do to help when I call them from the hospital."

"That sounds like a good plan. I know some of the staff at the hospital will want to help, too. If you can find out the address where they were staying, I can work on getting their things packed up and sent to the hospital.

They're not going to leave the hospital long enough to drive back to Key West," Casey said.

"I'll check with them, but I'm sure you're right," Summer said. Casey might be an interfering busybody, but Summer had never met anyone more willing to help someone out when they were down.

"ETA, five minutes," Roy called over the radio.

As Casey used the radio system to call his report into the Miami hospital, Summer checked all the monitors. Emma's vital signs had remained stable throughout the transfer. It was a good sign.

As the helicopter started descending, Summer bent down to the little girl and whispered into her ear, "It's going to be okay, Emma. You're a very lucky girl who has a mommy and daddy that love you very much, and when you wake up, they're going to be right there waiting for you. You just hang on."

The sun was up by the time they made the return trip to the island and a fresh-looking crew met them at the door. Summer was glad to see that Alex's office door was shut when she grabbed her bag from the sleep room.

She was too tired and confused to process all the emotions that Alex's return had brought. Relief? Fear? Pain? Excitement?

No. It wasn't excitement. It was just that she was anxious now that she knew she'd have to face him. She needed to rest and think about exactly what she wanted to do next. There was a time when she would have been happy just to empty out everything she was feeling on Alex. How angry she was. How much he had hurt her. Everything. But that was before. Now her life with Alex would always be divided into two parts. The old part of their life, before he'd left, and the new part of their life, when he had returned. Right now, she wasn't up to dealing with either one. All she wanted to do was go home and climb into her bed.

And if she shed a few tears for that old part of their life, at least there wouldn't be anyone there to see them. Just like there hadn't been anyone to see them the day her worse nightmare had come true. How a day could take you from hope to despair so quickly, she had never understood.

She'd been so excited that morning. Scared, yes, but still excited. She'd known something was wrong for a few weeks. She'd had queasy mornings and her appetite had been off, but she'd blamed it on a stomach bug and gone on with her busy life. It wasn't until she'd begun counting out weeks on her calendar that she'd realized it could be something a lot more serious. One home pregnancy test later and her life had changed.

She'd started to panic. Pregnancy had not been in her plans. Not yet. And Alex? They'd never discussed having children. Only the knowledge that she wouldn't be alone, that Alex would be there with her, had helped calm her fears and bring her hope.

She'd rushed over to Alex's house to tell him, wanting to share the news with him, praying that he would be just as excited as she was, only to find him packing to leave.

"I have to go. A friend needs me," he'd said when she'd questioned him, trying to understand what was happening.

But she could still remember the way he'd pushed past her as he'd headed to his front door, still refusing to explain where or why he had to leave that very minute. Even when she'd known there was something wrong with his excuses, she'd tried to tell him her news. Their news. But he wouldn't stop. He couldn't even give her a moment of his time.

"It's going to be okay. I'll call once I get settled. You can tell me whatever it is then," he'd said, brushing her off as a car horn honked in the driveway. He'd turned and walked away from her carrying a lone duffel bag, leaving her alone and confused.

Until that day she had thought the pain of her father walking away from her had been the worst moment of her life. She'd been wrong.

Alex watched as Summer's car pulled from the parking lot. He'd stayed at the office so that he could see her, and she'd still managed to slip away.

"You know we'll do everything here that we can do. We're family here. This is our home. We have a great relationship with this community. I'm sure the county board will take that into consideration." Over the phone, the voice of his boss droned on about the importance of Alex's crew at Key West keeping their contract as the door to the office opened.

"I'll send out an email to all the staff," Alex said as he nodded to Casey to come in and take a seat. "Let me know if there is anything I can do to help from here. I'd be happy to meet with the board and answer any questions."

Finally, the phone call ended. If the pain in Alex's head got any worse, he was sure his skull would explode like a volcano erupting. He'd not made a dent in his emails before his phone rang with the call from his boss. This was really turning out to be some welcome-home party.

"What's up?" Casey asked.

Alex pushed away from the desk, stood and walked

over to where a picture of their crew, all dressed in their flight suits, hung. They were a great group of caring and hard-working professionals that helped save lives daily. And now they would have to depend on some corporate suits to negotiate to keep their jobs.

"I might as well tell you—I'll be sending out an email today informing everyone that another company is vying for the county emergency-services contract, which will include emergency-helicopter services," Alex said.

Alex's eyes rested on the woman standing beside him in the picture. Standing just barely past his shoulders, her bluc eyes sparkled, and her smile shone brightly as she'd posed with the crew for the picture. It hadn't been long after it was taken that he had finally gotten up the nerve to ask her out. Never would he have imagined that things between the two of them could have become this broken.

He'd planned on talking to her the moment she had returned from Miami, but it seemed like phone calls were always coming between the two of them.

First, it had been the call he'd received from his father. Then there'd been those phone calls that Summer had refused to answer. And now, when he had finally made it home, he'd been stopped from speaking to her by another phone call.

"Do you know where Summer was rushing off to?" he asked, hoping maybe she'd said something to Casey concerning her plans.

"I'm pretty sure she was headed home. She worked extra this week and was tired," Casey said. "Should we be worried about this contract business?"

Alex turned away from the picture. He needed to concentrate on his job, not his relationship with Summer. They'd work things out now that he was back.

"Heli-Care was the first medevac company here in the Florida Keys and we have a great relationship with the community, but the corporate office is taking it seriously. That's their job. We just need to keep giving the best care possible. That's our job."

"And we do it well," Casey said as he stood. "It's a good thing you came back when you did."

"She's pretty mad, I guess?" Alex asked as they both stared at the picture.

"It'll be okay. You both just need to talk," Casey said as he moved toward the door. "I've got faith in you. Just be yourself. You'll know what to do."

Be himself? If only people knew how hard that was for him.

As soon as Casey exited, Alex pulled out his phone and called Summer. If he was lucky, he'd be able to catch her before she went to bed. When the call went to voice mail, he left the same message he'd left for the past five months. "Hey, Summer. Please call me back. We need to talk."

He'd give her some time—she'd had a busy shift and she would need to recover—but eventually she would have to stop avoiding him. They would talk and it would be soon.

CHAPTER TWO

HER HANDS TIGHTENED on the steering wheel as the large gates leading to Alex's driveway slowly swung open. Though very impressive, with their swirling scrolls of wrought iron, she'd never understood why Alex had had the security gates installed when he'd had the house built. This was Key West, not Hollywood. Of course, she couldn't imagine the lifestyle Alex had lived with his mother in California, where people like them often had to live their lives behind fences.

Maybe that had been one of their problems. They'd come from such different backgrounds. He'd grown up the son of one of the nation's most popular actresses, while she'd grown up in poverty in a small town in Texas.

Why had she ever thought that what the two of them had was more than a fling? People that came from Alex's background didn't mix, for long, with people like her.

No. That wasn't fair. She couldn't compare him to the people in her hometown. Alex had never acted like she didn't belong here. He treated every one of their crew members equally. It was one of the things about him that had first gotten her attention. Well, that and the fact that just looking at him had made her knees go weak.

* * *

She had punched the numbers into the gate's keypad, surprised that she remembered the code to get inside the property, though Alex might change it now that they were just… What were they supposed to be now? They'd been friends. Then lovers. And now? Well, that was what she was here to figure out, wasn't it?

She eased her small compact down the crushed-rock driveway with a speed that a conch snail could match. There was no getting around this. She had to face him eventually.

And it had to be on her terms. It all had to be on her terms. It was her life. Her family. She'd lay out everything for him and then explain how things were going to be.

She hit the brakes. She wasn't ready for this. It had sounded so simple in her mind before she had left her apartment, but just the one look at the man yesterday had sent her into a tailspin. His dark brown eyes so intense as they met hers, that day-old stubble that had once scratched her cheek as he'd held her, the dark brown hair that she'd clung to as he'd driven into her body… It had all been too much. Her mind had been filled with memories and her body had turned traitor. She hadn't been able to handle a confrontation with him. Not then. Not when her chest had ached with the same pain that had consumed her the moment he'd told her he was leaving with only the lame excuse of an unknown friend needing him.

It had to have been all her hormone changes. That had been the problem. Just stupid hormones that made her heart race and her eyes water.

There was no way that she still had feelings for him. Letting a man waltz in and out of one's life was an emotional suicide that she'd witnessed too many times in her childhood.

She wouldn't let herself turn into her mother.

She took a moment to shore up her tattered courage. Then, with her back straight and her chin up, she continued down the drive. She parked under the royal poinciana tree, which was full of red blooms, that stood beside the front porch.

The two-story yellow-sided house would be the perfect vacation home anywhere else, but in Key West it was just a way of life. *Sun*, *sand* and *party* were everyone's favorite words here. But Alex had always treated his home as more of a refuge than a party house, only inviting his closest friends into this part of his life. She'd once been part of that group, part of his life. Now, both of their lives were about to change.

As she stepped out of her car, she tried to imagine how they would go on from here. The last few months of separation had proved that Alex didn't need her in his life like she had thought he had. No matter what happened today, they could never go back to the way things had been before. Not that she wanted to. She'd made the mistake of letting someone control her happiness. She wouldn't do it again.

After ringing the doorbell and not receiving an answer, Summer started to leave. His black Jeep was sitting in the driveway, so she was sure he was home. Was he sleeping? The alarm at the front gate should have woken him. Did he know it was her and didn't want to see her?

That thought reminded her of the last time she'd been there when he hadn't had time for her. Well, that was just too bad. He'd just have to make the time to see her now.

Trying the door, she wasn't surprised to find it locked. Alex was never one to take chances. He'd told her once of a fan of his mother's who'd broken into their home just so that she could sit at their dining room table and pretend to be Melanie Leonelli.

She'd wondered at the time what he would think if she'd told him she'd never even had a dining room. The small, rusted trailer she'd grown up in had only a small bar with two mismatched barstools and she couldn't remember a time when both her and her mother had sat there together.

Deciding to check the locks on the French doors that led out to the patio, she walked around the side of the house.

And there he was. With water dripping from every bare inch of his body, Alex strode out of his pool like the Greek god he had always reminded her of. Her eyes followed a stream of water as it ran down his body. Her knees went weak. Once more Alex sent her heart racing, and this time she couldn't even blame it on her hormones. No, not hormones, at least not the pregnancy kind. No, it was the memories that had her body overheating even as a soft breeze blew against her skin. Memories of his strong arms wrapped around her. Memories of his bare skin sliding over her. Memories of his body hard and hot as it moved against hers.

Her breath caught and she took a step toward him even as her brain told her to turn and run.

Alex's intuition kicked in the minute someone stepped into his backyard. His first instinct was to confront them, but he knew he'd be able to handle the interloper better if he was dressed. After grabbing the towel he'd thrown over a chair, he wrapped it around his waist before turning around. Only, it wasn't a stranger he found standing behind him. It was Summer.

The smile that had begun to spread across his face froze. Something wasn't right. There was something different about her. Something very different. Her beautiful suntanned face was pale. Her bright blue eyes had shadows. But it was her new curvy body, the one with the unmistakable baby bump, that immediately got his attention. And held it.

"I don't understand…" he began, as the wheels in his befuddled brain tried to turn. This didn't make sense. How could this be possible?

Well, he knew how. He even knew the answer to when. But why? He'd used protection. They both had. None of this made any sense.

But that didn't matter at this moment. What mattered was that Summer looked as if she was about to drop.

"You need to sit down," Alex said as he crossed the grass to where she was standing, took her arm and led her to a chair. "We both need to sit down."

He took a seat beside her. He'd known that there was something wrong when Summer had become more adamant about knowing where he was going and when he was returning, but he had never imagined this.

"Why didn't you tell me?" he asked. Hadn't she known he'd have returned the minute he'd gotten the news that she was pregnant? Or did she not tell him because…? "Is it mine?"

He wanted to take back the words the moment they'd left his mouth.

"I can't believe you'd ask me that!" The hurt in her voice was quickly replaced by anger. "If that makes you feel better, then sure, I'll tell you that you're not the father and you can go on disappearing whenever it suits you."

She stood, her face as hard as stone, but this stone looked like it was about to crumble any second.

"Wait," he said before she could walk away. "I'm sorry, I know it's mine. I do. It's just a shock."

"It wouldn't have been a shock if you had been here," Summer said as she eased back into her seat, though she still looked like she could bolt at any moment.

"You cut all contact with me. You wouldn't take my calls, wouldn't return my texts, and all the time you were pregnant with my child? Why, Summer? Why did you do that?"

"Why should I have told you I was pregnant when for all I knew you had run off to another woman?" Summer said, the color now returning to her face. "And quit staring at my stomach."

"Sorry, it's just..." Alex, a man who had seen every type of trauma, every type of illness and injury, suddenly found himself fascinated with the round bump. A baby. Summer was having his baby.

"As far as me running away with someone, you know that isn't true." At least he hoped she did. They'd never discussed their relationship being monogamous. There had been no reason to. Going from friends to lovers had seemed so natural for the two of them, as if it was meant to be. But this change in their relationship didn't feel natural at all.

"You were gone five months, Alex. I didn't know where you were or why it had been necessary for you to leave. I didn't even know if you were coming back. You just abandoned your life here, so that you could do... what? Help a friend? It only made sense that this 'friend' was someone you cared for more than...the crew."

She didn't say it. Didn't have to. He knew what she thought. She thought he had cared more for his "friend" than he cared for her. And why shouldn't she have? He'd never expressed how he felt about her. He'd never felt the need to. He'd been taking things slow between the two of them because that's what he did. He didn't jump into things, especially relationships.

His mother said he had trust issues and maybe he did. He'd been burned enough times by people who acted like they were interested in him when all they really wanted was to be close to the Hollywood life he'd been forced to live.

"You should get dressed so that we can talk," Summer said.

He realized then that she'd been waiting for him to say something. To deny her accusations. But what could he say now that she would believe? "It wasn't like that. I was needed there."

"Just get dressed," Summer said, turning her face away from him, as if she couldn't stand the sight of him.

"It's a little late to be worried about my state of undress, don't you think?" Alex said, though he made sure the towel covered him as he stood. They both needed to be at their best for the rest of this conversation. Life had suddenly done a one-eighty and his brain needed to catch up fast. "I'll be back in a few minutes. Don't leave."

His mind raced as he grabbed the first shirt and pair of jeans he found in his closet. He couldn't get past the moment that he'd seen Summer standing there, so beautiful, and so pregnant. Did she have any idea how that had hit him? She seemed so different, so detached from him. So unlike the Summer he'd known.

Going to the kitchen, he studied his fridge and decided on a bottle of water for each of them, though it was tempting to get himself something stronger.

"I think we should have the wedding soon. Something small, if you'd like. Just our friends," he said as he stepped back onto the patio, then handed her the water.

"You think? Excuse me, did I ask you what you thought?" Summer said as she straightened in her chair, her face taut with an anger that should have come with its own warning sign. He'd taken a step in the wrong direction, and he'd better find his way back soon.

"I'm sorry, I just assumed you'd want a smaller affair, but we can do whatever you'd like," Alex said as he sat beside her. He would have to contact his mother. The woman had been hounding him for grandchildren for years.

"It's so nice of you to let me determine how I will change my whole life for you, but I can see we have a terrible misunderstanding. There isn't going to be a wedding," Summer said, her words clipped.

The fact that history was repeating itself was not lost on him. His mother and father had once been in this situation, only then there had been a whole country to think of, something that had made the decision for them both.

But that wasn't the case here. He had no such responsibilities. He only had himself and Summer and their child to think of. And he would do the right thing for his child.

"I understand that this might not have been our plan, but—"

"Not our plan? Of course, this wasn't our plan. Do you think I did this on purpose?" Summer stood and moved away from him, her hand going protectively over her stomach.

"I never thought you did. This is just all a surprise." Alex got up and walked to her. He was messing this up, making things worse, and he didn't know how to stop. Every word he said seemed to be wrong. Why couldn't they just go back to the way things had been between them before he'd left? There had been none of this awkwardness then. They'd been able to talk out everything together.

"Oh, there's a bigger surprise," Summer said. "A lot more. As in a whole-other-baby more."

His eyes went to the prominent baby bump. Another baby? As in two?

"Twins?" Alex asked. Was that squeaky cartoon voice his?

"Yes. Twins. One boy, one girl," Summer said.

Alex noticed the way she smiled, all anger gone, as she rubbed the spot where her—their—babies were. It was the first time she'd smiled since she'd arrived. And this wasn't just a normal Summer smile, though he'd always thought of those as magical. This smile was filled with love and pride.

"None of this would have been a surprise if you hadn't just up and left," Summer said, "and stop staring at my stomach."

"Sorry," he said. He forced his eyes away from the evidence that their lives were about to change, but it wasn't easy. It was just so fascinating to think that there were two lives inside her that the two of them had made.

And it was scary at the same time. What did he know about being a father? He'd never truly had one. But it wasn't going to be that way for his children. He'd be ever-present in their lives.

"I tried to explain I had no choice." He knew his frustration was spilling out. He'd wanted to tell Summer about his family, his secret family, but he'd wanted to wait until he'd returned home. Or so he'd told himself. Hiding who he was had been ingrained so deep inside him, he wasn't sure if he would have told her then. At least not until a time had come when he'd had no choice.

"And I tried to tell you about the pregnancy, but you were in too much of a hurry," she said.

"You knew then and didn't tell me?"

"I tried. You were too busy rushing off to help your friend to stop and listen to me."

It hit him like a punch in the stomach. If he'd known, if he'd taken a few moments to find out what was so important, everything could have been different. "I'm sorry. I didn't realize."

"It doesn't really matter now, does it?" Summer said, turning away from him.

But it was plain to see that it did. He'd hurt her and though that hadn't been his intention, he knew now he'd been wrong. He should have taken the time to tell her what was really happening the moment he'd received the call from his father. But he'd been totally consumed with getting to his brother and he hadn't had the time he needed to deal with it.

But would he have told her the truth if he'd had the time? He didn't know, not for sure, but he was certain he had to tell her now, before she walked away from him.

"Can we both just sit and talk while I try to explain why I had to leave the way I did?" Alex asked.

He released the breath he hadn't known he'd been holding as she took a seat.

It had been hammered into his head as a young child that he couldn't tell this secret to anyone. When he was young, it had seemed like an adventure to have this big secret that he only shared with his mother and father, and later, his younger brother.

But as he'd gotten older, reality had set in, and he'd realized he wasn't sharing the secret. He was the secret.

The secret illegitimate son of a king that would not—or, until recently, could not—claim him.

But this was Summer. And she was going to be the mother of his children. She had more than a right to know. This wasn't just about him anymore. His children's lives, and Summer's, would be changed if the world found out about his parentage. He'd hidden out in Key West without any of the attention he would have received in New York and California from the media. If it came out who his father was, all of their privacy would be gone. He had to trust that Summer would understand that.

He sat down beside her again, then began, "I'm sorry that I didn't explain to you why I had to leave. It wasn't because I was hiding something—there are just some things in my life that I've never been free to discuss with anyone." He stopped and took a swallow of water, then picked up his phone from the side table, where he had left it. "You might know my mother was born in Tuscany, but what most people don't know is that her family moved when her father was assigned to the Italian embassy in Soura."

"Soura? The country where Prince Nicholas is from?" Summer asked.

"We'll get to him later, but yes. Nicholas is Prince of Soura," Alex answered. He should have known that she, like most of the women of the world, had heard of Soura's most eligible bachelor. His brother was always in the media. The attention was something that he seemed to thrive on, something that Alex would never understand.

"Soura's a small but powerful country due to its ports on the Mediterranean Sea. My mother says she fell in love with the country the day she arrived. A few years later, she met my father, the future King of Soura."

"Wait...what?" Summer asked. "I don't understand."

"It's a secret that's been hidden all my life. That's why I couldn't tell you where I was going. Summer, I'm the illegitimate son of King Christos, King of Soura, also known as Prince Nicholas's friend, Alexandro Michael Leonelli—" he handed her his phone "—and if the media ever gets wind of it, I will be hounded by the paparazzi for the rest of my life."

Summer stood up on shaky legs as she looked at the picture of two men standing together beside a large fireplace. She recognized the tall man standing on the left. He had a face that had graced the cover of many gossip magazines. It was the other man that she almost didn't recognize. Dressed in a tailored three-piece suit, the man stood ramrod-straight. His hair had been combed back in a sleek modern style and his face had been shaved meticulously, but none of it fooled Summer. She'd recognize those smoky brown eyes anywhere.

This was a joke. It had to be. Alex couldn't be the son of a king and have never told her. It didn't make sense.

But did it? He'd been only too happy to rush out the door without sharing where he was going with her. Why wouldn't she believe he'd hidden who he was from her, too?

"You're a prince," Summer said as she studied the picture.

It was such a handsome face. An honest face. Or so she had thought. She'd never imagined he was hiding such a big secret from her. But why? Why couldn't he have told her? If he'd planned for the two of them to have any future together, he would have. Wouldn't he? But if she was just a passing fling? No, he wouldn't have admitted anything then.

The fact that he hadn't been honest with her told her so much.

"I can see it. You and Prince Nicholas—you both have the same eyes. And the cheekbones, though his are a bit more angular," Summer said, staring at him for just a moment more before dropping her hand. She got up and quickly backed away from him. "And my babies? What does that mean for them, Alex?"

"This doesn't make a difference. They'll be our children. Both of ours. We'll protect them from all of this," Alex said. He stood now and approached her.

Her hands trembled when he took them into his. "I'm sorry I didn't tell you before. I should have. In a perfect world I would be able to tell everyone who my parents are and then go on with my life, but this isn't a perfect world."

"The news said Prince Nicholas, your brother, had a skiing accident." It made sense now. "That's why you left."

"My father wanted me to oversee Nicki's care," Alex said. "His injuries were worse than what was released to the media."

"This is all too crazy to believe," Summer said, her voice strained. She'd begun to believe that her rural Texas upbringing, when compared to Alex's Hollywood lifestyle as the son of a movie star, didn't matter. But now, to learn he was a prince?

No wonder he had never shared this information with her. She was so out of her depth that he didn't think it was necessary. Her importance in his world of wealth and power was very small, something he had proven when he'd left.

But what if Alex, or this king, wanted to fight her for custody of her babies? Between the two of them, they had more money than she would earn in a lifetime. Maybe she should get a lawyer now. But that took money, and she was going to be on a tight budget with two babies to take care of.

"I can see that it might take some time to process..." Alex began.

"You can't even imagine." She took another step back. "I'm still trying to process the fact that I'm going to be a mother. To twins. And then you tell me that you're this king's son. Oh, but not before you ask me if they are even yours, like I'm some woman that just jumps from man to man." She wouldn't let him see how much that question had hurt her. "And don't forget about your great proclamation that we are to get married as soon as possible."

She could hear the panic in her voice. She needed to leave before she lost it in front of Alex. She wouldn't let him see how much he'd hurt her.

She turned her back to him and started across the yard, but then she whipped back around. "Let's get something straight right now. I'm carrying these babies and for now I will be making all the decisions that concern them. Not you. Not some king. The three of us were doing just fine before you came back.

"No," she said as he opened his mouth to speak. "I've heard enough. I need some time to think."

With her head up, she turned and headed back to her car. She wasn't running away, she was just making a fast retreat so that she could shore up all her defenses in order to protect not only her children, but also her heart. Because though she'd never admit it to Alex, the idea of him asking her to marry him had once been all she had ever dreamed of. It was too bad it had come a few months too late and for all the wrong reasons.

CHAPTER THREE

A FLOCK OF seagulls circled over Summer's head, much like the crazy questions that were turning over and over in her mind.

She'd thought she'd known Alex. His likes, his dislikes. His favorite foods, his favorite sports. He loved a good steak, rare with butter, but he didn't care for roast. He didn't care for hockey, but he watched golf as if it was a religion. He said his favorite color was the blue that matched her eyes. She'd known he was joking, but it had been sweet of him to say it.

Alex had always been sweet, almost perfect; the perfect boss, friend, boyfriend. Until he'd left without telling her the truth, or at least not all of it. She'd known he was holding something back by the way he'd packed so recklessly. Been so unfocused. If only he'd told her the truth. If only he'd shared with her his secret past. And why hadn't he? Because he had never had a reason to. He never would have told her if it wasn't for the babies she was carrying.

And that hurt more than she wanted to admit.

She'd grown up in a town where she'd never been good enough. She'd been the poor kid, the troubled kid. Not good enough to be invited to the party the other kids went to. Not good enough for the other parents to want their kids to hang around her.

And now she knew she had never been good enough for a man who was a prince to share his real life with her. Because while she had been dreaming of their happily-ever-after, she'd just been another happily-for-now to him.

She opened a leftover bag of bread and broke off a piece, then threw it up, and watched as a bold seagull dived down to catch it. She threw another piece up as high as she could and watched as more birds dived toward her. She'd made it a habit to come feed them on her morning walks on the beach ever since she'd moved to the Keys.

She liked to watch the silly birds as they flew away into the sky with a freedom she had envied most of her life. The freedom to fly far away from all the bullying at school. The freedom to fly far away from a life where she'd had no future. She'd found that freedom when she'd become a flight nurse. She loved the rush of excitement she felt every time the helicopter skids left the ground. Being a flight nurse had been the most important thing in her life, until now. Now she had two little ones she was responsible for, so they would be the most important thing in her life.

Telling Alex about the babies was the right thing to do. She would never keep him out of their lives. But having him question if they were his? Having him insist that they needed to get married just because of the pregnancy? It brought back all her insecurities from her childhood and that was something she couldn't deal with right now.

Because one thing Alex had made clear was that he planned to be involved in their babies' lives. *Their* lives, not just hers, and she was going to have to find a way for the two of them to get along for their babies' sake. But how could she do that when every time she saw him her chest squeezed tight into a knot of regret? And how could she trust her babies' future to this man when everything she thought she had known about him was a lie?

Alex watched as the waves crashed against the shore. After a sleepless night, he'd arrived at the beach early enough to enjoy the last of the sunrise and the calming rhythmic motion of the waves before the crowds showed up. Summer loved her early morning walks on the beach, and in the past, he'd joined her whenever he could. He was hoping he'd have a chance to run in to her today.

He'd messed up. It was just that simple. He, a seasoned trauma doc, had panicked the moment he'd heard the naked fear in his father's voice five months ago. He'd always thought the man was made of steel, not flesh and bone, like everyone else. Something had to have been very wrong if his father, the king, was afraid.

"Come home, Alex. You need to see your brother. He's… It's not good. The doctors aren't sure…" His father's voice had trailed off.

The memory sent cold dread running through Alex's body and he was suddenly back in his bedroom, consumed by fear for his brother, a feeling that he had never known. The doctors weren't sure of what? That his brother would survive? What had his brother done now?

"How bad is it, Father? I need to know…" Alex's voice had trailed off as Summer came into the room. What had she heard? If she'd heard him call the king "Father" he'd have a lot of explaining to do—explaining that he hadn't had time for.

"The doctors are taking him to surgery now. There's

some internal bleeding they say needs to be stopped. Both of his legs are broken, but they say it is best to wait until he is more stable to operate on those. This is right, yes?"

It wasn't the broken bones that worried Alex. It was the internal bleeding. He'd seen more than one trauma patient bleed out.

"Alex, I need you here," his father said. "You need to come. Now."

It wasn't the demanding tone of a king that Alex heard in his father's voice. It was the fear of a father. His brother's condition had to be bad.

He headed to his closet and pulled down the first suitcase he found. His room at the palace contained most of the clothes he would need. "I'll take the first flight I can get."

"Michael has taken care of all the arrangements. There's a private jet headed from Miami now and a car is headed to your home," his father said. "I'll see you at the hospital."

Alex hung up and headed back into his room, where Summer was sitting on his bed.

"What's up?" she asked as he threw the suitcase on top of the bed.

"I've got to go." He didn't know whom to call first? His boss? Dylan?

"What do you mean you have to go?"

He sent a short text to Dylan. He'd email his boss as soon as he was on the plane. His boss could wait.

"Alex, what do you mean you have to go? What's going on?" Summer asked.

"I have to go out of town." He'd told Dylan that a friend needed him, and it was vital that he'd known it was important that he stuck to the same story. Besides, as far as everyone knew, Nicholas was just a friend. Just a friend of the family.

"A friend of mine needs me. I have to go," Alex said.

"Who is it? Someone from California?" she asked.

"No. No one you know," Alex answered as he headed to the door.

"How long are you going to be gone?" she asked as she followed him.

Alex didn't have the answer. Days? A week? "I don't know. I'll call and let you know as soon as I can."

"Alex, wait..." Her voice rose, and now he knew it was from panic. He'd been leaving her when she'd needed him the most. "I don't understand any of this. Who is this friend? What aren't you telling me?"

Stopping, he set his suitcase next to the door. He could remember now how she'd looked. Her eyes round, her face pale. He'd known he wasn't being fair to her then. He needed to tell her about his brother. He needed to tell her about his whole family. He should have done it sooner, but everything had been so perfect between them without the weight of his secret life and the complications that came along with it.

"It's going to be okay. I'll be back as soon as I can and I'll tell you all about it then, okay?" He hoped he was right. His brother had to be okay. He reached out for Summer, needing the warmth of her body to drive away the cold that had consumed him since his father's call.

"No, it's not okay," she said as she pushed away from him. "I need to talk to you. It's important."

His phone pinged with a text, and he pulled it out of his pocket. He hit the button next to the door to open the front gates.

"My ride to the airport is here. I've got to go." He bent down to kiss her, but she turned her face away from his, startling him. He should have stopped then. He should have known something was wrong. Instead of pushing her aside, he should have taken a moment and listened to her. But instead, he'd grabbed his suitcase and walked out the door.

His last memory was of Summer standing at the door. There'd been no smile, no wave, just a pale Summer leaning against the doorframe looking at him as if he was someone she didn't know.

He lowered his sunglasses and studied the crowd. Unless she'd changed her routine over the last few months, Summer was here.

He had to find a way to make things right between them. He'd been the little boy without a father. He couldn't let that happen to his own children.

Oh, he'd had a father, of course, but that man had lived across the ocean. He wasn't at any of his T-ball games or at any of the other sport events that he'd taken part in as a kid. He wasn't there when he'd won the fourth-grade science fair, or even when he'd been valedictorian of his high school's graduating class.

And when he did get to visit his father, Alex had spent all of his time with his younger brother while pretending to be just a family friend's son that was there for a summer visit. It was no wonder he had ended up confused about who he was. Only when he'd finally settled on a college major in medicine had he felt like he could be someone other than the pampered son of a Hollywood star, or the bastard son of a king.

He would claim his own children, never give them a reason to think that they weren't loved and wanted. And he wanted to do it as soon as possible. He wanted to be there to help them with every science project. He wanted to be there to show them how to throw their first pitch, though he had to admit his mother had tried with that one. If the tabloids had gotten a picture of the beautiful Melanie Leonelli dressed in cut-off jeans and a Dodgers T-shirt trying to throw a baseball, they would have put it on their front page.

He'd never told his mother how much he'd missed having a regular father. He would have never hurt her by admitting that he had needed more than what she was able to give him. She'd done her best to try to make up for his father not being there. But that hadn't been fair to her.

And it wouldn't be fair to their children to not give them the security of both a mother and a father. He just had to find a way to get Summer to accept him back into her life.

It had finally come to him in the middle of the night, that while his first instinct had been to take care of Summer and the babies, it had been unreasonable to think she would agree. He needed to start small. Let her get used to him being back. Remind her of what they'd had together before he'd left. Then he'd propose an equal partnership. While she went through the pregnancy, he'd be there every step. He would help out with chores, go with her to her obstetric appointments and, of course, he would help out financially. It was a simple plan that was beneficial to them both.

Only Summer wasn't a simple woman. And things between them were…complicated. There were still feelings there, no matter how much Summer wanted to deny it. The attraction between the two of them was strong. He'd felt it the moment he'd seen her again. An instant wave of attraction that had run up his spine, then curled deep inside of him, ready to explode at the slightest touch. They'd both felt that once, but it wasn't the same now.

Summer had made it clear that she didn't need him anymore. And it was his fault. Now it was up to him to find a way to make her see that she did need him. They needed each other. Because no matter how complicated things were between the two of them, the most important thing would be their children.

It was a familiar laugh that had him turning to see Summer coming up behind him. With her head thrown back as she threw bread crumbs up in the air for the seagulls to catch, it was almost as if the woman was just one of the carefree tourists here for a fun week in the sun. She had a guileless beauty, with her bright blue eyes and sweet, honest smile. That girl-next-door beauty that was so different than the cover-girl models his brother dated. They'd always seemed too perfect-looking to be real. Summer looked real.

"How many times have I told you that you're contributing to the delinquency of these poor birds?" he asked as he approached her, not sure how she was going to take his seeking her out.

"But they're hungry," Summer said as she threw another handful of bread crumbs into the air.

She put her whole body into it, her arms shooting up and her feet almost leaving the ground. Her pale blond hair flew in the wind and her eyes lit up with happiness as the seagulls dived down, catching their bounty and then hovering above her with anticipation. It was such a simple thing, feeding the obnoxious birds, but she found so much pleasure in it. But it wouldn't be much longer before she wouldn't be able to move so freely. Not with her carrying twins.

Twins. He'd stopped trying to wrap his mind around that one somewhere around midnight.

"Sorry, guys, I'm all out," Summer said as she folded an empty bag and stuck it in her beach bag. The seagulls circled a few seconds longer and then flew off to hunt for someone else willing to share a meal. "I told you I needed some time."

"It seems I'm running a few months late already. I need to catch up fast," Alex said.

Summer stopped and studied him, her eyes narrowed and her lips pursed. This was not the same woman who'd been laughing just minutes before. "Just because you're a prince doesn't mean you can set your own rules. You need to respect my wishes."

"You're right. I'm sorry. I should have given you some time. It's just like I said—I'm running behind. I haven't been here for you, and I want to change that."

"And like I said, I was doing just fine before you came back," Summer said. She continued walking down the beach, where the high tide was beginning to crash against the shore.

When she raised a leg to remove one of her sandals, Alex's hand instinctively reached out to steady her. With his hand resting on her hip, his fingers tingled with the need to circle around her and stroke her rounded belly. What would it be like to feel his babies moving inside of her?

What if his arms wrapped all the way around her? Would she lean into him the way she used to? Arch her back and lean her head back on his shoulder?

"I've got it," Summer said as she pushed away his hand from where it had tightened.

"Sorry," Alex said, reminding his body that he was on a mission to get Summer to talk to him, not go to bed with him. Alex wasn't really surprised that she'd shied away from his touch. What did surprise him was how much it hurt. It had been a long time since he'd let anyone get close enough to hurt him. But having her shrink from his touch just reminded him more of what he'd taken for granted.

And what did that say about him? That he'd been so wrapped up in the drama at the palace that he had put what he and Summer had on hold, and assumed that she would be there waiting for him? Maybe he was the spoiled rich kid his classmates had always said he was.

"How long have you been living two lives?" she asked, turning to him, her eyes studying him with an intensity that made him want to squirm.

"What do you mean?" he asked. When he'd shared his secret life with her, he'd known there would be questions. Questions like this that were uncomfortable. How could he make clear his need to separate the two parts of his life, the way he had?

"Don't avoid the question. I saw the picture and you even referred to yourself by another name. You called yourself 'Alexandro' instead of Alex. It's like you're trying to live two different lives. Alexandro and Alex couldn't be more different."

"It just makes things easier," he said. How did he explain the complicated life he'd created?

"For whom? You can't be happy living that way."

He wasn't. He hadn't been for a long time. But what could he do? It was his life.

"I just don't get it. Your mother is this famous actress living in Los Angeles. No one there would be shocked if she came out and acknowledged that your father was some European king. If anything, it would just make her appear even more glamorous."

"My mother wasn't always a movie star. When she came to Hollywood, she was twenty-two and fresh from drama school. I was only a baby. Unlike most of the people who run away to California to become a star, she got lucky. She found an agent that believed in her and within a year she was going on a callback that ended with her starring in the next year's Academy-Award-winning film."

"But what about your father? He is a king. Lots of kings have children by women that aren't their wives," Summer said, her statement such an innocent one.

"Members of royalty play games just like politicians. They have to consider how their actions will affect their popularity. And when I was born, my father was the crown prince, not the king."

They strolled down the beach, each deep in their own thoughts. Once they'd walked this beach hand in hand. Now there seemed to be miles between them. Miles he'd put between them when he'd left.

If he had just trusted her with his secret, they could be walking with hands entwined right now, making plans for the future of their children. Why couldn't he just learn to trust people? Was he so busy protecting his secret life from others that he couldn't take a chance at having a life of his own?

"When my parents met in college, they'd both known that there was no future for them. My father was a crown prince and was expected to marry for the greater good of his country. My mother had her eyes set on Hollywood. Their romance was meant to be a college fling without any complications. And then I came along."

The ocean breeze sent golden tendrils of her hair dancing around her face. She looked so young and innocent.

"Your mother must have been scared," Summer said,

her eyes glued to the ocean, where the gulls had been joined by egrets and the occasional pelican as they flew over the crashing waves.

Was she telling him she had been scared?

"I'm sure she was, but she'd never admit it," Alex said. "My mom's tough. You have to be to survive the movie industry."

"But your father was a future king. He could have fought to take custody of you. I checked. You were born eighteen months before Prince Nicholas. You're the true heir to the throne."

"No, I'm not." It was thoughts like this that scared him the most. "I'm considered a royal bastard. Illegitimate. I have no claim to the throne of Soura, nor do I want one. And my father would never have taken me away from my mother. Just like I would never take our children away from you. Never."

"And I would never let you. Not you. Not your father. Not anyone." Summer's harsh voice and fisted hands left him with no doubt that she would do anything to protect their babies.

"You're not on your own here." How did he tell her he wanted to share every part of his children's lives, including her pregnancy, without scaring her off? Maybe he should start with the apology he owed her. "I'm sorry I wasn't here for you. And I'm sorry I didn't tell you about my family."

"I thought..." she said, then shook her head. "Never mind. It's not important. Yes. You should have told me."

Every man knew that when a woman said that it didn't matter, it really, really mattered. "Still, I'm sorry I let my own...issues come between us."

"And when you came back without an explanation,

what did you think would happen? I'd forgive you and fall back into your arms?"

Because that was exactly what he had thought, he kept his mouth shut. He was a bastard in more than one way. He'd truly thought the two of them had all the time in the world until he'd found out their clocks weren't ticking at the same rate. Summer's clock was more than five months ahead of his.

"Well, that's not going to happen. I trusted you and I thought you trusted me, too. It's not like we just jumped into bed one night. We were friends. At least I thought we were."

"We were—are—friends. I'm sorry I hurt you. I was wrong. I shouldn't have left without telling you the whole story."

"You should have told me about your parents a long time before you left," Summer said. "If you had thought we had any type of future together, you should have told me."

"But I want to make things right now. I want to be there for you and the babies. Our babies. We can do this together a lot easier than we can do it separately, don't you think?" Alex asked.

"What I think is that I'm perfectly capable of doing everything by myself, as I have been for the last five months," Summer said.

"I'm not saying that you aren't—" The sound of a woman's scream cut through his words and his body went on high alert. He knew the sound of fear when he heard it. There was no doubt that someone was in trouble.

CHAPTER FOUR

"WHERE?" HE ASKED as he scanned the beach for the woman. Where had that scream come from?

"She's there," Summer said as she started sprinting toward the woman, her steps slowed by the thick sand.

Alex scanned the area where the woman was standing in water up to her chest and then turned his attention to the place where she was staring in horror.

"I see him," he shouted as he rushed into the water and began to swim. The teenage boy was still above the water, but Alex could see he was struggling. He poured more power into his breaststroke. If Alex didn't make it to the kid before he went down, his chances of saving him were slim.

Just ten yards to go. The boy's eyes, wide with fear, met Alex's as he closed in on him.

Alex pushed his arms and legs to maximum speed, but his limbs began to protest. Just five more yards. Just a couple more strokes. He would make it. He just needed the boy to hang on for a few more seconds. Alex reached out and grabbed for his hand, but his fingers met only water as the boy's body went under.

No. He wouldn't lose this kid. Alec dived down with powerful kicks even as his muscles began to cramp. He grabbed what he hoped was the boy's arm and headed for the surface. He broke through the water and took a badly needed breath, then looked around, quickly locating the beach. A crowd had gathered, and he headed toward land. The limp body in his arms told him he needed to get the boy to the shore fast.

As his muscles strained and cramped, he pushed himself harder, dragging the kid with him as he kept his arm tight across the boy's chest and worked his free arm and his legs until he reached the shallow water, where a man took the boy from Alex's shaking arms.

"Get him onto his back," he said to the man as soon as they made their way onto the sand, as Alex worked to catch his own breath. The fight for this boy's life was not over.

"Emergency services are on their way," Summer said as she went down on her knees beside Alex. Her own heart had seemed like it had stopped when she'd seen Alex go under the water, only restarting with a quick gallop when he'd broken through the surface, hauling the boy up with him.

She'd felt so helpless watching as Alex had risked his own life fighting through the waves to get to the boy. She considered herself a strong swimmer, but she would never have been able to do what Alex had done, even if she wasn't pregnant.

Seeing the boy was nonresponsive when the bystander placed him onto his back, she turned the boy's head to the side to help any water drain out as she watched his chest. After ten seconds with no respirations, she bent over the boy. The kid wasn't breathing, and his pale blue lips told her all she needed to know. There wasn't time to wait for the ambulance.

Pinching his nose, she positioned the young man's

head back and placed her lips against his cold lips, then breathed into him. The first breath went in easily, as did the next three. Her hope took a dive when she took another breath and saw that Alex had begun compressions on the boy's bare chest. Total arrest. The kid was barely into puberty. He had too much of life ahead of him.

She gave him another breath and another. They would get him back. Alex had risked his own life for him. They wouldn't give up.

It seemed like hours; though she knew it had likely been less than fifteen minutes since this nightmare had begun, when she heard the siren and then the welcome pounding of feet as a pair of EMTs joined them.

"I can take over," a young woman said to Summer as she pulled out an Ambu bag from her bag.

Summer had just lifted her head and started to pull away when she saw the boy's chest heave and his stomach muscles clench. As she turned the boy's head, both the EMT and Alex helped roll him onto his side.

Looking over at Alex, Summer grinned as the boy coughed up the water that had almost taken his life, then took his first breath on his own. They'd done it. The kid was still not out of the woods. The complications from nearly drowning could be serious. He'd have to be watched in an intensive-care setting for signs of respiratory complications such as pneumonia, but he was young. His chances of a full recovery were good.

Alex stood and offered her a hand as the EMTs moved in and took over. Looking up at the smile on his face, she took his hand.

And for a moment, as her body warmed and her heart raced, with her chest pressed against his, it was as if time had turned back. Back to before she'd told him he was to be a father to her twins. Before he had left her. Back to when things between them hadn't been complicated. It was as if they were a team again, working together, playing together and, yes, loving together.

Just two people that enjoyed being together. Carefree with no worries about the future, as both of them were willing to enjoy each day as it came. They'd been falling in love—at least, she had been—but there had been no commitments. They had plenty of time for that. Or so they had thought.

But that was their old life and she needed to put it into the past. She had her babies. They had to be her priority. It was time to move on. And standing here in Alex's arms was not making things any easier.

She pushed back from him, unwilling to admit to even herself how much strength it took when all she wanted to do was lay her head against his strong shoulder and let him take care of her.

And that was exactly what her mother would have done. Let someone take care of her. And she was not her mother. She could take care of herself. She always had.

She took another step back and was suddenly aware that the two of them had become the center of attention, as some of the crowd around them broke out into applause while others had their phones glued not on the EMTs and their patient, but on her and Alex.

"Thank you, thank you," said the woman, whom Summer assumed was the boy's mother, as she threw herself between the two of them, hugging Summer and then Alex.

"You saved my son," the woman said, breaking down in Alex's arms. Alex held her as she cried out her relief. He was always so good with people, dealing with the grief and worry of his patients' families. His empathy for his patients was one of the things that made him a favorite in the local hospital's emergency room.

"How about we drive you to the hospital?" Alex said, as the EMTs transferred her son, still coughing and looking dazed. "We'll follow the ambulance, and you can talk to the doctor."

Summer reached over and put an arm around the woman as the two of them guided her behind the EMTs. "Is there anyone you want us to call for you?"

The dazed woman looked down at her empty hands. "I need to call my husband—he's in a conference meeting at our hotel, but I left my phone in the car. Can we stop and get it?"

After picking up the woman's phone, Summer helped to explain to the boy's father what had happened and where to meet them at the hospital, while Alex kept up a dialogue of questions meant to keep the woman as calm as possible. The woman's name was Maggie and they'd arrived for her husband's business conference just the day before. She and her son had been amazed at the clear blue color of the water surrounding Key West when they'd flown in the night before, and had made plans to hit the beach early this morning. She couldn't imagine what had happened that her son had been pulled out in the water so quickly. Summer didn't think it was the time to explain the dangerous undercurrents that caught so many visitors off guard, or the fact that there were red flags out warning people of the danger.

As soon as they arrived at the hospital, Summer led the woman to a nearby waiting room while Alex went to find the doctor who would be taking care of the woman's son, Scottie.

"It's good news," Alex said as he rushed into the

waiting room. He'd changed into a pair of green hospital scrubs and looked every bit the doctor that he was. "Your son is doing well. He's not requiring any ventilation at this time. He's only on the minimum of oxygen, though you need to be prepared that could change. Because his lungs filled up with water, he could develop aspiration pneumonia, so he'll have to stay in the hospital a few days. But for now, he's stable and he's asking to see you. The nurses said they'll come and get you in as soon as they get him settled."

A man with graying hair hurried into the waiting room, an emergency-room nurse following behind him and offering to take them to see their son. The woman hugged them both once more before leaving the room.

Summer watched the couple leave arm in arm. This could have turned out a different way, Summer thought. They could have been going to say goodbye to their child if it hadn't been for Alex. "You saved that boy's life."

"We save people's lives every day," Alex said.

"But this time was different. You put your own life on the line." And she hadn't liked it one bit. She might have been angry, and hurt by Alex's actions, but she still cared. She cared a lot, and it didn't have anything to do with the children that she was carrying.

She stood, too quickly it seemed, because the room began to spin, and she felt light-headed. Instinct had her reaching for Alex and his arms went around her.

"What's wrong?" he said, his hand cupping her chin. "You're as pale as a sheet."

She closed her eyes and took a deep breath as she felt the blood rush back into her head. "I just got up too fast. My blood pressure dropped. I'll be fine in a couple of minutes."

She bit her bottom lip as she fought against the nausea that was soon to follow and continued to breathe deeply.

"Have you talked to your doctor? I can call them and we can check you into the emergency room," Alex said, his voice pitched higher than it had been just moments earlier.

The man had just saved a drowning victim and he was panicking over a little case of hypotension?

"No, I do not need to call my doctor. I'm fine. I'm just behind on my fluid intake for the day. We've been a bit busy this morning."

She stood perfectly still as Alex studied her eyes—he was checking her pupils, she was sure. He stood so close to her that she could smell the seawater that still dampened his skin, causing her heart rate to increase to a number that would have Alex admitting her to the hospital if he took her pulse. "I'm telling you I'm fine."

Unable to stand being close to him a second longer, she turned her chin away from him and stepped back. "We need to get back to the beach. I have some water and a granola bar in my car."

Alex didn't say a word as they made their way to the car, and she was glad. It was taking all the energy she had just to get back to the parking lot. After climbing into his truck, she found herself unable to keep her eyes open as he pulled out into traffic. The sleepless night and the excitement from the rescue had caught up with her. She closed her eyes and let the needed sleep take her.

Alex looked over to where Summer was now dozing in his passenger seat. She'd scared him when she'd turned that sickly color between slime-green and ghost-white. And he hadn't even known whom to call. He didn't know the name of the doctor who was taking care of her. What was wrong with him? That should have been one of the first things he'd asked. He needed to know that he was leaving the health of Summer and the babies in good hands. He hadn't even had the sense to ask if there were any complications with her pregnancy. A twin pregnancy could be dangerous. What if she had preeclampsia?

No, she'd said she was hypotensive and with her experience as a nurse he had no reason to doubt that she was aware of what was going on in her own body. Still… he couldn't help but worry.

He parked the truck a couple of blocks from the beach and turned to where Summer was sleeping. Her head leaned against the truck door window, and her long lashes swept down onto cheeks that still looked pale under her golden tan. All her anger at him seemed to be gone for this moment. She looked so innocent and sweet, as she had looked earlier on the beach, but he wasn't fooled. The woman was going to give him the fight of his life before she accepted any help from him. He just had to be ready for it. He could be as stubborn as she was when it came to the lives of his children. His plan had been to take small steps and that was what he would do.

Her eyes fluttered, and then opened. Baby blues stared up at him and his heart turned over in his chest. He loved that look. The one she had when she awoke to find him watching her sleep. The look she'd give him right before she lit up with a mischievous smile and rolled on top of him. With lips and tongues, hands and fingers, she'd given him the best mornings that he had ever had.

"Why are we here?" she asked. There was no smile directed at him now.

"We've had a busy morning. I thought we could both

use some food." It would do no good to point out the fact that she was still pale.

Her lips pursed and he waited for her protest. Summer had always been very independent, and he'd admired that. But now it seemed she was even more determined to prove, at least to him, that she didn't need anyone's help.

She turned away from him and climbed out of the truck, leaving him behind as she headed into the open French café.

"Hey, Summer," Kevin, one of the waiters called as he pulled out two menus. "Alex, it's been a while."

"I had to leave town for a few months," Alex said, looking over to Summer, "but I'm back now."

"That's good. We missed you around here," Kevin said. They followed him to a small table set beneath a tree covered in white blossoms. "What can I get you to drink?"

"A small iced coffee would be wonderful," Summer said.

"Make that two and we'll both have a glass of orange juice, too," Alex said, ignoring the deadly pointed stare Summer gave him.

"If I had wanted juice, I would have ordered it. And I'm allowed one coffee a day," Summer said as soon as the waiter walked away.

"I'm feeling a bit drained after this morning. I thought you might be, too," Alex said. The look of concern she gave him increased his guilt at lying to her, but if the juice helped put some color back into her face, it would be worth it.

"Can I take your picture?" a voice asked from behind him.

Turning, he saw a young girl who couldn't have been

over eleven or twelve. Beside her a stood a younger boy. Dread seeped into every pore of his body. It had happened. His father had finally called his bluff and outed him.

"Uh…sure, I guess," Summer said.

Before he could stop her, the young girl pointed her phone at them and clicked the picture before running back over to a table, where two women smiled and waved at him. After waving back with a smile as stiff as a porcupine quill, he quickly turned back to Summer. "We need to get out of here."

He had to make some calls and the first one would be to his traitor brother, who hadn't had the decency to warn him. Because he had to know. Nicholas always knew what social media was saying about the royals of Soura thanks to some app he'd set up to scan the internet. The man would have made quite the IT guy if it wasn't for that pesky royal title.

"What was that about?" she asked.

"My father might have—" Alex stopped as the waiter approached their table.

"How does it feel to be a hero?" Kevin asked as he put their drinks in front of them. "I just saw the video in the kitchen."

"What video?" Summer asked, then took a drink of her coffee.

"Someone posted it to the city's social-media accounts. It looks like the two of you had a busy morning. Jacques says your meal is on us today," Kevin said as he pulled out his order pad. "What will it be?"

As soon as their orders were taken, Alex reached for his phone only to realize it was in the wet shorts he'd thrown into the back seat of his truck when they'd left the hospital. He'd be lucky if it could be saved after the swim he'd taken, even though it was supposed to be waterproof.

"Here," Summer said as she pulled her phone out of her beach bag, "I've got mine."

He waited while she searched. After finding what she was looking for, she moved her chair next to his and started the video playing.

Whoever had taken the video had some major skills with their phone camera as they had zoomed in and captured the moment Alex had dived under the water to save the kid and then resurfaced. Then they'd zoomed out and caught the reaction of the crowd as he'd fought the waves back to shore. But instead of stopping at the rescue, they'd continued filming as he and Summer had worked together to resuscitate the boy, even filming when the poor kid had puked up half the ocean and finally taken a breath. They'd even videoed the moment when he'd helped Summer up and held her until she'd regained her footing.

"Are you feeling uncomfortable with this, or is it just me?" Summer asked. "I mean I'm used to being surrounded by a crowd. But it's just weird watching from the other side."

Alex felt more than uncomfortable. He'd been the subject of too many cameras growing up in Hollywood. It was never as simple as someone taking a picture or filming you. There were always those people that felt they had the right to make comments about your looks, what you were wearing or where you were going. Why couldn't people just mind their own business?

But this wasn't filmed by the paparazzi trying to make a quick buck; this had been done by someone who was just been caught up in the moment. He'd need to remind himself of that as this video made the local rounds.

"Go back a few seconds," Alex said, as he realized the cause of his concern.

Summer tapped the screen, taking the recording back thirty seconds. "Here?"

"Yeah," Alex said as he bent down closer to the phone screen. "Now stop it."

She tapped the screen again, pausing the recording. "What is it?"

The screen showed the two of them working on the patient, but that wasn't what had gotten his attention. "See that man in the back, the one with the black baseball hat?"

"Do you know him?" she asked.

"I think so. If he's who I think he is, he had no business being in Key West." No, the man on the screen should be far away from Key West. He should be in Soura, writing for the local tabloids and causing trouble for Nicholas.

"Who is he?" Summer asked, putting her phone away as their food was delivered.

"He's a journalist who makes his living by searching for smut on all the local royalty and celebrities in my father's country."

Alex dug in to the plate of eggs and ham while keeping a watchful eye on Summer, making sure that she was eating enough for three. Three. It was crazy to imagine, let alone accept, that the woman sitting next to him was carrying two tiny beings. How was that small body of hers supposed to support all of them?

"But what is he doing here?" Summer asked, before her eyes went wide. "He's here because of you?"

"I'm assuming so, though I don't know what he thinks he's going to find here. No one here knows anything about my relationship to Soura."

"No one but me," Summer said. "Should I be worried?"

"I don't know," Alex said, before going back to his eggs. What could the man want from him? Or was he following some lead that had landed him here? And how long had he been following? He'd been spotted at the palace the day before Alex had left. Had Alex been followed home? If so, the man might have seen Summer enter the grounds of his home. He'd have to call his brother and find out more about the man. Then he'd have to figure out how to handle him. There were times it was nice to have his father's backing. This might be one of those.

"My obstetrician is Dr. Wade. She came very well recommended," Summer said, surprising him.

It was such a small thing to know—the doctor who would be taking care of her and their twins—but it was the first step in finding his way to take part in Summer's life. "I know her from working in the emergency room. She's very good."

"I'd like to go to the next doctor's visit with you, if that's okay with you." He wouldn't push. Not yet. This would be one of those small steps. Things would go a lot more smoothly if Summer agreed to let him be involved with the pregnancy.

"I'll see," Summer said.

Her noncommittal response was disappointing, but it was a start. Seeking her out today had worked, though he would never have imagined that it would end up with the two of them working together to save a life. But that had been good, too. After all, that was where their relationship had started. But there was one thing that he didn't understand.

"Can I ask you something?" he said.

"You can ask," Summer said, her eyes narrowing with suspicion.

"I just want to know how in the world you managed to keep the whole helicopter crew, *my* crew, quiet about the fact that you were pregnant. That group can't keep quiet about anything," he said.

"I didn't have to do anything. Jo took care of it," Summer said as her lips turned up in a conspiratorial smile. "She claims to know where to hide the bodies."

"I see," he said. Jo could be a bit scary when she wanted to be. And with a six-foot Viking, Casey, as her best friend, it was easy to understand why the rest of the crew might have been intimidated. That and the fact that they respected Summer's privacy.

Summer's phone dinged once, followed quickly by two more alerts. She picked it up and laughed. "Speaking of the crew, it looks like they just saw the video."

She held out the phone to show him a screenshot of their faces on the local news station as she said, "It looks like the two of us are going to be famous for a few hours."

"I better give Corporate a call just in case they see it. Those risk-management people don't like being blindsided," he said.

A half hour later, he dropped off Summer at her car with orders to get some rest, because he knew she only had the one day off before she would be back on duty for a twenty-four-hour shift. When she grumbled back at him, he smiled and waved, pretending he didn't see her stick her tongue out at him.

Did she know how cute she looked with one hip cocked to the side, her hand across her new curvy abdomen? Or was she just trying to goad him?

If so, it was a dangerous game she was playing, because it was taking everything he had not to turn his truck around.

CHAPTER FIVE

ALEX HAD JUST turned onto US Highway 1, heading to Marathon, when his phone rang. He'd already made his dutiful call to Heli-Care's risk-management department. He'd been forwarded to Marketing to go through the whole story again of his and Summer's morning at the beach. The last thing he wanted to do was go over it once more with his boss. He could ignore the call. But after taking so much time off for his brother, he needed to play nice.

"You're a genius," his boss said immediately.

"That's nice to hear," Alex said, "but since I've been out of the office and Dylan was managing the crews, I think he's probably due the compliment."

"I'm talking about the video of you saving the boy. I've already heard from the marketing department that the news channels in Miami are picking up the story. You've been recognized as being the medical chief for the local Heli-Care by someone, and one of the stations has asked to interview you and your crewmate for the news."

The man had no idea what a can of worms an interview could open for him. The last thing he and Summer needed right now was to be put in the spotlight. Not that it sounded like his boss would care.

"I'm not sure that would be a good idea. Neither one of us really want the attention. We were just doing our jobs."

"But you weren't on the job. That's what makes this so appealing to the public. You went beyond what is expected when you dove into the surf to save that kid."

"We'll have to talk about it. Summer is pregnant with twins. This might be too much for her," Alex said as he searched for any way to get out of his boss's plans. Since the video had only been broadcast locally, he'd seen no real threat in it. But to be put on a Miami television stage, where thousands of people could recognize him?

All he wanted was to work in peace while convincing Summer that together they could make a family for their babies. Was that too much to ask for? It must be, because it seemed he'd spent his whole life searching for somewhere he could live in privacy, and he still hadn't found it.

"It will be great coverage to show that Heli-Care is a vital part of the community." As the man went on and on about negotiations with the Monroe County board of commissioners, Alex lost all hope of getting out of the interview. All he could do was hope that Summer was up for it. At least it was just Miami, which was a long way from both Hollywood and Soura.

Summer sat rigidly beside Alex as she waited to be called to the studio stage to be interviewed by the *Good Morning, Miami* hosts. She'd done her best, including threatening to puke on the audience, to get out of this pony show. It hadn't worked. And after attending Alex's staff meeting concerning the possible loss of Heli-Care's contract, she'd understood why. Her crew needed her to step up and represent them this morning. Unfortunately, she was afraid her threat of puking on the audience might come true.

"It's going to be okay," Alex told her, then patted her hand like she was some little old lady in need of comfort.

She pulled her hand away from him. The last thing she needed was for him to touch her. Between nerves and hormones, she didn't require any more stimulation.

And if he mentioned one more time how pale she looked, he'd be sporting a black eye for the whole television-viewing audience. "I'm fine. Me and Max got called out to help the Marathon crew at that pileup yesterday on Highway One. Five cars. Six injured. One fatality. This is nothing."

She rolled her shoulders and raised her chin. She could do this.

"It's time, guys," a perky redhead with her eyes glued to the tablet in her hand said as she rushed into the room. "Let's go."

The woman herded them onto a stage where Debbie Duncan, Miami's favorite TV host, or so the billboard Summer had passed on the way to the studio stated, was waiting for them.

"Now get comfortable." The platinum blonde with lips painted redder than a crime scene motioned for her to take the outer seat before she turned to Alex.

Dressed in a gray tailored suit that probably cost more than Summer's rent that month, he looked every bit the successful doctor, while it had been requested by Heli-Care's marketing department that Summer wear her flight suit. She felt like some dowdy Cinderella sitting next to His Highness. Summer watched the woman's eyes check out Alex's fingers before she patted the chair next to her. "Dr. Leonelli, you take the chair by me."

Could the woman be any more obvious? Now Summer knew she was going to puke. Except, no. Her queasy stomach had settled down for the moment. Her only problem now was the fireball of anger that wanted to explode outward when their lovely host leaned over, rubbing her chest against Alex's shoulder, and whispered something into his ear.

If that woman thought she was going to get Alex's attention, she was wrong. She wasn't his type.

And Summer knew this how? Her stomach dropped. Just because this woman was as far from Summer as possible didn't mean Alex wouldn't be interested in her. Maybe the doctor had been attracted to her, but it was possible that the prince would want someone from more acceptable circles.

And now her mind was turning to mush. It had to be the pregnancy playing with her normally sensible thoughts. Alex hadn't suddenly changed just because he had admitted to her that he was born of royal blood.

Well, Alex hadn't changed, but what did she really know about this Alexandro he pretended to be?

A man said something to Debbie and seconds later Summer was hit with a bright light as the studio audience began to clap on cue at the video starring Alex and Summer.

"Let's welcome Dr. Alex Leonelli and Summer Madison, our two local heroes," Debbie Duncan said as she turned her smile toward Alex and the audience clapped again. "Dr. Leonelli, can you tell us exactly what went through your head when you saw that young boy out in the water in trouble?"

"Well, Debbie, I think I thought the same thing anyone here would have thought. The kid needed help. Fortunately, I'm a good swimmer," Alex said, his voice strong.

"And you, Summer? What did you think when you saw your boss diving into the water?"

Summer froze. She couldn't tell them the truth. That for a moment her heart had stopped, and her brain had refused to function. She'd watched him go under and prayed that he would come back to her. But she couldn't tell them that. "Like Alex, I thought what anyone else would have. They needed help so I called 911."

She released the breath she'd been holding as Debbie turned her attention back to Alex. "I know the two of you work together in the medical field and are used to performing heroic measures, but what did you think when you discovered that someone had not only videoed the rescue, but also that the video had gone viral?"

Alex gave Debbie a smile so bright that Summer wondered if the glare from his white teeth would blind the people watching the show.

"I have to say that we were both surprised. Drowning victims are rescued every day. We just happened to be in the right place that morning," Alex said.

"Well, I have to tell you I had my own surprise after the video went viral and I did some digging and discovered that this wasn't the first time you've been videoed," Debbie Duncan said, her smile just as bright and blinding as Alex's. "And I'm sure our audience will also be surprised to discover that you're the son of one famously gorgeous and talented movie star."

Summer blinked. This had not been on the list of things that they had gone over that might be asked. Her attention went to Alex. If someone didn't know him, all they would be seeing was the same relaxed man that had entered the studio. But Summer knew him. Those brown eyes were guarded now, and his body had become rigid.

He had flown under the radar in Key West and now some snoopy reporter was going to change everything.

"My mother would appreciate the compliments, Debbie," he said, his smile never faltering.

Summer waited for the woman to continue to question him about his mother and was surprised when she turned to her instead.

"Summer, we also understand that you have a bit of exciting news. Would you like to share it with our audience today?" Debbie asked, her smile as sweet as Summer's grandma's tea.

"I'm not sure..." Summer's brain raced.

"It seems there was a lot of speculation in the viral-video world that you might be expecting a little one, and when I spoke to Scottie's mother, she let me in on the news that you are expecting not one, but two little ones later this year. She, as we all are, was impressed at the way you worked so hard to save her son. We just wanted to congratulate you." Debbie looked out into the audience as they all began to clap.

Summer remembered now the boy's mom had asked if she was okay as they'd made their way to the car from the beach that day. She'd been surprised at the woman's concern at first, until she'd realized that the T-shirt she'd been wearing had become damp from helping with the drowned boy's resuscitation and was outlining what clearly was her baby bump. As far as any comments on her condition after the video had come out, she hadn't even bothered to read them. It seemed now that had been a mistake.

"Yes, I am expecting twins," Summer said, keeping her answer short in the hope that the show's host would turn her attention back to Alex. Besides, there wasn't any reason for her to deny it and maybe now that this overbearing TV host had spilled everyone's secrets they could end this interview.

"And still, as we all saw in the video, you worked so hard to help save this young man. The father of those babies must be very proud of you," Debbie said, her smile still in place, though her eyes had narrowed into a beam of interest that Summer didn't like.

Summer had agreed to be interviewed for the good of Heli-Care, not to be hunted by a rabid journalist that smelled a story where there shouldn't have been one. But there was a story. A big juicy one that would shoot this woman's career up a notch if she ever learned about Alex being of royal blood. Or, more importantly, of Summer's twins being of royal blood.

Summer opened her mouth to respond, but nothing came out. She needed to say something. Something noncommittal that would stop Debbie's questions.

"Of course, I am," Alex said as his warm fingers covered hers where they rested on her chair.

Her eyes darted up to his in shock. Though there was no doubt their close friends knew that Alex was the father of her babies, there had been no conversation about how they would announce this.

And now, Alex basically had announced it to the world. Their local world, but still, this should have been something that they discussed first.

As the crowd once more gave them a round of applause, Summer looked back at the host. There was still something in the woman's eyes that made her uncomfortable. This woman wasn't done. For some reason, she had taken a professional, or personal, interest. Maybe it was just the glamour of Alex's Hollywood upbringing that had caught the woman's attention. Or maybe it was just the woman's physical attraction to the hot-doc image of Alex that Summer had seen over the years.

But whatever it was, Summer knew they hadn't seen the last of Debbie Duncan.

How she had made it through the rest of the show without losing it, Summer didn't know. But the moment the two of them stepped into the studio parking lot, she exploded. "Why did you do that?"

"What?" Alex asked, as if he didn't know what she could be upset about.

"Don't play dumb. You knew from the moment you opened your mouth that what you were doing was wrong." It was more likely that he had done it on purpose. "You should never have announced something like that to anyone, let alone the entire Miami population, without talking to me first. And what about that man that was following you? Did you stop and think about him? What if he saw the show?"

Alex scrubbed his hand over his face before he looked back at her. "I'm sorry. It just seemed as if that woman had you cornered."

It was true. Debbie had cornered her with the question. The woman must have suspected that there was something between the two of them. "Maybe she did, but you should have given me the opportunity to answer. I thought we had an understanding, but I guess I was wrong."

"They're my children, too, Summer. I couldn't sit there and not claim them."

And just that quickly, she realized what had happened. Alex had truly done what his father had never done. He'd claimed his children and had thousands of witnesses to the act. Not that it made what he had done okay.

She reluctantly climbed into Alex's car when he opened the door for her. For a man who could be so empathetic, he showed no signs of appreciating her feelings at being robbed of the decisions concerning her life and those of her children. If they were going to make co-parenting work, she had to find a way to make him understand.

She waited until he'd buckled himself into the car before turning toward him. "And if I had decided that since they are my children I should announce their royal heritage, that their father was really a prince in hiding, would that have been okay with you?"

His hands on the steering wheel stilled, but he didn't turn toward her. She'd known she was cutting open a wound that he denied existed, but she had to make a stand. It was better to do it now, rather than after the babies were born.

"Okay, I get it. I won't do or say anything about the babies before I get your permission," Alex said, though he still seemed a little too proud of himself. The man might deny that he was royalty, but he sure did act like it.

"Let's be clear. If you ever do anything like that again, make any decisions concerning these babies without talking to me first, I swear I'll get a lawyer involved. That's not what I want, but I'll do it."

Finally, he looked at her, the shock on his face telling her that she had hit her target right in the heart. Guilt flooded her, but she pushed it away. It hadn't been her goal to hurt him. All she had wanted was for him to understand how she felt about her own feelings not being considered.

The ride back to the Keys was long and uncomfortably silent. She rubbed her belly as one of the infants did a somersault with all four limbs jabbing her belly while she fumed about what Alex had done. She had thrown up a wall between them and she didn't know if she should leave it, or try to break through. Right now, leaving it between them seemed to be the best option.

She was sure Alex had grown up getting everything he had ever wanted. It was time for him to learn that it didn't always work that way. If he wanted to work with her, fine. But if he thought he was going to be in charge of their children's lives, she would have to show him just how wrong he was. And if that meant bringing in a third party, she would do it. She didn't want to, but she would. Because no one, not even the Prince of Soura, was going to be making decisions about these babies without her.

CHAPTER SIX

"I JUST TURNED my back for a moment," the young mother said as she ran her hand across her little girl's hair. "It happened so fast."

"It looks like she took a pretty good whack to the head," Alex said as he looked at the cut across the three-year-old's forehead, "but the CAT scan doesn't show a fracture. I'm just going to use a special glue to close this up. She's going to have a nasty-looking bruise, but just keep the cut clean and dry and she'll be fine."

"And you, Miss Valeria—swings are made to be sat in, not to get hit by." Unable to help himself, Alex brushed away the little girl's tears, then started to apply the bandage glue to the cut. "I bet as soon as we get your boo-boo taken care of, I can find you a lollipop. Do you have a favorite color you want?"

The little girl's wiggling stopped as Alex's offer got her attention. "I like red lollipops. Bubba likes red, too."

"In that case, we'll make it two lollipops," Alex said as he finished checking the cut and making sure the sides were approximated.

A few minutes later, after delivering on his promise of two lollipops, Alex left the room feeling like a real doctor for the first time in a long time.

He loved his work with Heli-Care, but he needed to

spend this time working with the everyday injuries and complaints of the patients that came in for treatment when they had nowhere else to go, especially after-hours, when the physician offices were closed for the night.

"Just got a call from the Heli-Care crew. They're bringing in a chest-pain patient. ETA, three minutes."

"Thanks," he told the unit coordinator before taking a seat at his desk. Summer was flying tonight with Jo, so he knew the patient was in the best of hands.

It had been two days since he had seen Summer. Two days of waiting for her to get over being mad at him for, quote "proclaiming to the world that you're the father of these babies." And, yes, it had brought him a lot of pleasure to make that announcement. Why shouldn't it have? He was going to be a father of two little babies that had already won his heart even though he had never even seen them.

But her threat of getting a lawyer? That had cut deep. How had things between them suddenly gone so wrong?

Oh, yeah, he'd gone rogue and not taken into account what Summer would think about his announcement. And now he had to fix things between them once again.

One of Heli-Care's gold-and-blue stretchers rolled by, accompanied by Jo and Summer, and he followed them to the small hospital's only trauma room.

"Mr. Martin is a sixty-three-year-old male who began having chest pain tonight while on a tour of Fort Jefferson," Jo said, which explained the reason why the man had to be flown instead of coming by land with the local emergency services. The Dry Tortugas, where the fort was located, could only be reached by water or air.

As she rattled off the man's vital signs, including an elevated blood pressure, Alex took in the man's color, which was still pink, though his skin did have a sheen of sweat.

"Here's a copy of the EKG," Summer said as she handed over the paper copy that had been printed off their monitors.

"It looks like an NSTEMI," Alex said as he studied the twelve-lead printout. "Let's get labs and some morphine."

"Mr. Martin, I'm Dr. Leonelli. Can you tell me about the pain you're having?"

"I know you. We watched that interview they did on the TV in our hotel room," the man said.

"Did you now?" Alex said before placing his stethoscope to the man's chest. The man's lungs were clear, but his heart did have an irregular beat. "We need to draw some blood and we are also going to get you something for the pain. If we determine that you need to have a heart catheterization tonight, we'll have to transfer you to Miami so that you can be treated by a cardiac intensivist."

After reassuring the man that his wife would be able to see him as soon as she arrived back from their island tour, Alex went in search of Summer as his team started the workup.

"Hey, boss," Jo said as he entered the room that was set up for the first responders who needed to take a break.

"Hey," Alex said. He watched as Jo pulled out a juice from the fridge and pushed it into Summer's trembling hands.

"What's wrong? Have you eaten?" Alex asked as he bent down to study Summer's color. He took her hand into his and began to take her pulse. "Jo, go get me a glucose monitor."

"No, Jo," Summer said, as color began coming back into her face. "Don't. It's not my glucose. I just bent down to get a drink out of the fridge. I'll be fine in just a moment."

Alex moved into the chair next to her, but he didn't let go of her arm, though her pulse was regular and strong now. "Usually after twenty-four weeks gestation, your blood pressure stabilizes."

"Been reading your obstetric medical books, Doc?" Summer asked before taking a long drink from the juice bottle.

"Maybe," he said. "There's nothing wrong with being prepared."

"Oh, yeah, I forgot. Congratulations," Jo said, her mouth curling up into a smile now that her friend was returning to normal. "Nice job with the announcement, too. I like your style. Most people just go for those little cards they send out in the mail."

"Thanks, it seemed the perfect time," Alex said as Summer removed her arm from his hand while shooting him a look that showed no amusement.

"How many times has this happened?" Alex asked.

"I don't know. I haven't been sitting around counting them," Summer said before finishing off her juice.

Alex looked up at Jo.

"Oh, no. I'm not getting between the two of you." Jo said.

Alex watched as she exited the room. "Look. We're on the same side here. We both want what is best for these babies. Right now, I'm more concerned about what could happen if you have one of these spells while you're at home alone. It's not safe."

"If we were on the same side, maybe we should get our stories straight so that the next time we go on television, we don't end up spilling all our secrets and making announcements without talking about them first."

"What secret? Everyone had to know that these were my babies. We hadn't made a secret that we were dating." His phone rang and he pulled it out to see that it was his brother. He sent the call to voice mail.

"I'm sorry that I didn't talk to you before I made the announcement. I shouldn't have done it before clearing it with you," Alex said, though in truth he wasn't really sorry for anything except for the fact that it had upset Summer. "Can't we put it in the past now? The interview is over, and everyone's attention has probably turned toward some other poor unlucky fools, thank goodness."

"But what if it hasn't?" Summer asked as she sat up in her chair. Leaning toward him, her cheeks now flushed with a rosy glow, her eyes turned serious. "Debbie Duncan seemed very determined to dig up some dirt on the two of us."

"She's just a local television celebrity looking for the latest human-interest story," Alex said, though he had noticed that the woman seemed to have spent more time than necessary with their story. The show had been pitched to Heli-Care's marketing department as good publicity for the company, but instead it had been more about their personal lives.

"About these dizzy spells, I want you to see the doctor as soon as they can get you in and I want you to consider moving in with me," Alex said, and then continued as she started to interrupt him, "What would happen if you passed out and fell? You know well and good that as a nurse you'd recommend that a patient with the same symptoms not be left alone."

"It's perfectly normal for a pregnant woman to get dizzy," Summer insisted, then shrugged her shoulders, "but I'll call in the morning. And if they think I need to be seen in the office, I'll go in."

"If I promise not to hound you or the doctor, would you consider letting me go with you?" Alex asked, and then waited as she studied him.

"Don't lie. You know that you're going to ask Dr. Wade a million questions. She's already been complaining about nurses making terrible patients," Summer said as she stood. The color had finally returned to her face. "But I'll agree to you coming if you agree to stop insisting that I need to move in with you when she tells you that there's nothing wrong with me."

His phone rang and he was surprised to see the number of the Soura palace on the display.

"Hold on a moment," he said to Summer, then answered the call.

"What? You are screening my calls now?" his brother asked from the other side of the world.

"I'm working. Couldn't you have left a message like a normal person?" He didn't have time to listen to his brother and his insistence that Alex make a decision concerning making a royal announcement about the circumstances of his birth, which now seemed very ironic considering how he'd handled the announcement of his own future children.

"This wasn't something that I could leave until you decided to return my call. It seems our friend from the tabloids has been busier than we thought. There's a picture of a pregnant young woman who he claims is a member of your helicopter crew. He also claims that you, Dr. Alex Leonelli, also known as Alexandro Leonelli, longtime friend of Crown Prince Nicholas, announced on a television show that you are the father.

Did you not think this was something you should share with your family?"

Alex swore, getting a surprised look from Summer. While he'd shared his news with his mother, he'd put off notifying his brother and father. He was getting enough pressure from the two of them. Once his father had decided that it would be best to admit to the affair he'd had with Alex's mother, he'd agreed to let Alex make the decision of when to share the information concerning his birth. But that had been before the reality of grandchildren had existed. He wasn't sure how his father would take this news, or how he would respond.

"Sorry, I've been busy. Can you send me the article with the picture?" he asked. "I'll get right back to you."

"Hey, Dr. Leonelli," the unit coordinator said from the break-room doorway, "Dr. Patel is on the phone and Robin said to tell you we have the lab results back on the patient in the trauma room."

"Are you okay to fly if I need to transfer Mr. Martin?" Alex asked, rising from the chair. He wouldn't let this new crisis make him forget what was really important right now.

"I'm fine. I just needed a moment," Summer said as she got up slowly. "What was that phone call about?"

This wasn't the time or place to discuss things, but how could he expect her to trust him if he didn't share this part of himself with her? "It looks like you were right. The journalist from Soura somehow found out about our television interview. My brother wanted me to know that there's been a new article published and they included you and my announcement."

"You hadn't told your father about the babies?"

"Not yet. I was afraid he'd do something crazy like announce that he was going to be a grandfather." The look Summer gave him told him exactly what she thought. Yes, he was living a double standard and, yes, he needed to get his act together.

"I just don't understand why this guy is so interested in us. You said you've spent time with your brother since you were children, and no one seemed to suspect anything about your relationship then. What has changed? Why would he be so interested in you now, if it wasn't because he suspects that you are the king's son?"

"I don't know, but I'm going to find out. As soon as I get the article I'll forward it to you," Alex said. He wanted to protect her from all the media, but he couldn't do that and leave her in the dark at the same time.

"Thanks. And I'll text you with a time if I get an appointment," she said as they walked back into the emergency room.

As Alex watched her join Jo, who was talking to one of the local EMTs, he realized that for just a moment the two of them had acted like a couple working together instead of two individuals with their own agendas. Maybe this was the beginning of a new path for their relationship.

"So that was interesting," Jo said the moment Summer climbed back into the helicopter after it was determined that the patient's condition was stable, and he would be admitted to the local hospital.

"What?" Summer asked. No matter how much she might deny it to Alex, she could still feel the residual effects from the earlier drop in her blood pressure. Or maybe it was the anxiety that she felt every time her name was coupled with Alex's in the media. While he was concerned about losing their privacy, she was more worried about the possibility that someone would eventually start wondering about her. It wouldn't take much for someone to dig up her past. A past that would destroy everyone's opinion of her. All she could do was wait for Alex to send her the article that had been published and hope that would be the end of it.

"The way Alex was all concerned about you. It didn't look like a man that didn't care about his girlfriend to me," Jo said. They both worked together to clean and store their monitor cords and supplies, so that they would be ready to respond to the next call.

"Ex-girlfriend. Besides, it's not me he's worried about. It's the babies I'm carrying that concern him." Summer wouldn't tell her friend that he wanted her to move in with him. Jo was too much of a romantic. She'd never believe that it was only an interest in his children that had caused Alex to worry about her being alone.

"There was nothing fatherly about the look Alex was giving you. I'm not going to tell you what you should do," Jo said, "but if I was you, I wouldn't accept that everything between the two of you is over. Because that man isn't giving up on you."

"You're wrong. If he'd had any real interest in more than just a friendly fling, he wouldn't have left like he did." Summer knew her friend was trying to be helpful. But there was nothing that Jo or Alex could say that could change the past. The only thing her ex was interested in was the two babies that she was carrying. He had made it plain by his actions that he had never meant for them to be more than two friends who became lovers. Whether he had expected them to fall back into that relationship when he'd returned, she didn't know. What she did know was her being pregnant had changed everything. He'd do whatever he had to do to be part of their babies' lives, including marrying her.

And what kind of mother was she that she was jealous of the love Alex felt for her own children? One like her own mother?

Well, that wasn't going to happen. She wouldn't let it. It was time for her to start acting like the responsible mother she wanted to be, and that meant no more wondering about what it would be like to have Alex direct some of the same love and pride he had for their children toward her.

Because no matter what Jo thought, there was no chance of a future for her and Alex. Knowing what she knew about Alex's family now, there never had been. She would never have fitted in. It would take a fairy godmother to convince her that she belonged in his world, and she hadn't seen any of those flying around Key West.

The next afternoon, Summer found herself staring at two little bodies displayed on the ultrasound screen. She counted arms and legs, then hands and feet. They were perfect. Just perfect.

"Their growth is right on target, though baby *A* is a little bigger than baby *B*," the ultrasound tech said to Alex as he studied the screen. The man hadn't said a word since the woman had first applied the probe, with its thick cold gel, to her abdomen.

"Baby *A* is the boy," Summer said, realizing that he hadn't been there for the ultrasound where she had discovered the sex of the twins. Nor had he been there when she had found out that she was carrying twins. He'd missed so much while he'd been off playing doctor to royalty. Not that she had needed him. She'd attended each visit by herself and listened carefully to all the advice of her doctor.

But it would have been nice not to have been alone. Not that it was all Alex's fault. She'd been stubborn, swearing her best friend and then the rest of the crew to secrecy concerning her pregnancy. Because she hadn't wanted to have Alex rush back to her just because she was expecting.

No. She'd wanted him to come back to her because he'd missed her. She'd wanted him to tell her where he'd been and what was so important, more important than her, that he couldn't share it with her. She'd wanted him to reassure her that she was more than just a casual fling that he had left behind.

And what she had gotten instead was a man so entranced by the two babies that they'd made that he had forgotten what it was they used to have together. It was her parents' history repeating itself. She could only hope for her babies' sake that Alex never turned his back on their children, like her father had turned his back on her.

She felt a kick and a thump against her abdomen, and her attention went back to the ultrasound screen.

"Did you see that? That little rascal just kicked his sister," Alex said, his smile big and infectious.

"Dr. Leonelli, that was your daughter kicking her brother," the ultrasound tech said as she removed the ultrasound probe and gave Summer a towel to clean off the gel. "Dr. Wade will be in soon."

"Really?" Alex said as he turned and stared at Summer's abdomen while she mopped at the sticky gel. "It's amazing, isn't it? The two of them in there already bonding together."

"And a little bit scary," Summer said as the technician left the room. "Can you imagine the trouble that the two of them could get into?"

"Me and my brother certainly got into more than our

share, though I can blame most of that on Nicholas, because he knew no matter what, none of the royal staff would go tattling to his father."

Summer found it hard to imagine a life like the two of them had shared. She'd been an only child and spent most of her time alone. "It's nice to know that they'll have each other to play with as they grow up."

"If that ultrasound is any sign of things to come, the two of them will spend as much time fighting as they will playing," Alex said.

The door opened and Dr. Wade came in. "Well, good morning, you two. It isn't every day I have two local heroes in my office."

"It's nice to see you, Dr. Wade," Alex said as he stood and shook the woman's hand.

"So tell me about these dizzy spells that you've been having," the doctor said to Summer.

As she explained the dizziness and weakness she was experiencing, she kept an eye on Alex. He'd agreed not to interfere today, but the set of his clenched jaw told her it was killing the physician in him to not share his own observations.

"Well, you're right. It does sound like hypotension, as it's mainly when you are getting up or moving too fast," Dr. Wade said. Summer shot Alex a grin. She'd been right. "And I looked over your labs today. Your hemoglobin is on the low side of normal, not surprising, but I think we should increase your iron."

"Is there anything else we can do to decrease these spells?" Alex asked, apparently unable to stay quiet any longer. She had to give him credit, though. He'd lasted a lot longer than she had expected. "She lives alone, and I'm concerned that she's going to get dizzy and fall, and there won't be anyone around to help her."

It was plain to see where this was going. The man had been insisting ever since he'd found out about the babies that she move in with him.

"Continue fluids and watch for signs of dehydration. You both know how hot it is right now and how fast you can deplete your intake. And just be mindful of the situation. The biggest risk with hypotension in pregnancy is the possibility of falling and hurting not only yourself, but also the pregnancy."

"I told you so," they both said together.

"And you are right, Alex. It would be best if Summer wasn't left alone for now. Maybe a friend could stay with you," the doctor said when Summer protested. "I'm going to order some more tests just to make sure your electrolytes are all good and I want to see you back in two weeks."

The moment the doctor walked out of the room, Summer exploded. "I can't believe you're trying to use a little case of hypotension to make me move in with you."

"I don't know what you are talking about. I just voiced my concerns with your doctor. She's the one who said that you didn't need to be staying alone."

"You've seen my work schedule. I'm only home a few nights a week." She was being manipulated and she didn't like it.

"And that's another thing—I don't think you should be working so much. It's not good for you or the babies," Alex said as he offered her a hand to get off the exam table. She wanted to ignore him, but it wouldn't help her case if she got dizzy and fell in front of him.

"Just take a moment," Alex told her as she stood, his hands going to her sides to support her.

She wondered what he would say if she told him the

warm skin of his hand against her waist was doing more to unsteady her than getting up had done.

"I'm just worried you might be overdoing it."

"What do you mean? Dr. Wade just said I was fine." She moved away from him before she did something stupid, like step into his arms. This was why it wasn't a good idea for her to move in with him. Who knew what stupid thing she might be tempted to do?

"She said that there was a risk of you falling if you became too hypotensive. And she said you needed more iron," Alex said as he held the door open for Summer. It had been good news to hear that the lab work looked good, and seeing their babies had been amazing. More than amazing.

He patted his shirt pocket, where he had put a picture he'd been given by the ultrasound technician. He'd have to scan it and email it to his mother. The woman was beside herself with the news that she was going to be a *nonna*. She was already making plans for a visit as soon as the movie she was shooting wrapped up.

"I'm not going to argue with you. I agreed for you to come so that you could see for yourself that I'm fine," Summer said as they made their way out the office.

"I just want you to be careful. And don't give me that look," Alex said when she stopped and stared up at him. "I know you were doing fine before I returned. But I'm back now and I'm going to look out for you. Get used to it."

Alex waited while she let out a deep sigh. Yes, he was being a bit obsessive, but he'd just seen their babies for the first time. Who wouldn't be filled with a sense of responsibility looking at those tiny little arms and legs kicking around in their safe little home? He just wanted to make sure they stayed where they were for as long as was needed.

But that wasn't the only thing. Seeing Summer weak and dizzy scared him. He had to make sure she was safe, too. Because no matter how much she denied it, they needed each other as much as the two little babies growing in her stomach needed them. Maybe more. And then there was the article his brother had sent him.

"We need to talk about the article," Alex said as they both climbed into the car and buckled their seat belts. "You were right about me causing more problems. I'm sorry that I got you involved in all of this."

"I still don't understand why this reporter in Soura is so interested in someone who, as far as the world knows, is just a friend of the crown prince. He knows something, or thinks he does."

"My brother's looking into it, but he suspects the man is being backed by someone who doesn't support the king," Alex said. "Unfortunately, he hasn't been able to locate the reporter. Which means he could be in Soura or he could be in Key West. I can't help but worry that he might show up at your apartment."

"If he does, I'll tell him to go away," Summer said.

How did you explain to someone who hadn't grown up in the world of the paparazzi how much of a threat these tabloid reporters could be? "It's just not that easy. My brother thinks this guy could be a real threat. He has a reputation for being manipulative and demanding. It would make me feel a lot better if you would come stay with me, at least until this all dies down."

"Why are you so determined for me to move in with you?" Summer asked. Her eyes, so serious, caught his and held. They were such beautiful eyes. So intelligent. So inquisitive. He found them fascinating. They were a true mirror to her soul. A mirror that reflected a yearning for something that he wasn't sure he knew how to give. He reached over and brushed a strand of golden hair away from her face.

Did he tell her the truth? That he had developed this unexplainable need to have her near him? That he didn't understand it all himself, but that he wanted them to figure it out, together? Or would that be the very thing that would make her run from him? She didn't trust him, not anymore. She wouldn't give him another chance to hurt her. He had to earn back her trust before they could possibly have a future together.

He made himself pull away and busied himself starting the car and turning the air conditioner on high.

"It just makes sense, doesn't it? What are your plans when you get ready to bring the babies home from the hospital?"

"What do you mean? They'll come home with me, of course." Summer's chin tilted up. She had a look of determination he was very familiar with. "If you're talking about parental rights, you can talk to my lawyer. I'm not going to agree to one of those split-custody cases, like that movie about the twin girls whose parents split apart."

"*The Parent Trap*? No one with any sense or humanity could do that. I'm talking about where you are going to live. Your apartment is going to be crowded with not only two babies, but two of everything that it takes to care for them." He didn't think right now was the time to tell her that he considered both a mother and a father to be the two things that were necessary to take care of their twins.

"I've already cleared a space where I can fit two bassinets, which will take care of them for the first few months," Summer said. She'd moved across the seat until she was leaning against the car door.

"That's good, but what about your neighbors? Two crying babies are going to be awful loud at night while everyone's trying to sleep. And you're always complaining about the guy next door that likes to play his clarinet at six in the morning. I can't imagine the babies are going to sleep through that."

"Well, what kind of grown man gets up in the morning and starts playing a clarinet? I'll just tell him to stop," Summer said, and then sighed. "I know I need to start looking for somewhere else to live. I just haven't had the time to fight through the rental wars. As soon as something is listed, someone grabs it."

He pulled into her apartment's parking lot and put the car in Park. For a moment, he just stared ahead. It wasn't that her apartment complex wasn't nice, but besides being too small, it lacked security. He needed to find a way for her to agree to this plan for all their sakes. "I have an idea that I need you to consider. I think if you look at it closely, you'll see that it could work for all of us."

He wasn't surprised by the suspicion that filled her eyes. She seemed suspicious of everything he did where their babies were concerned, something that he hoped she'd get over soon. He didn't like that she continued to think of him as the villain in this situation.

No, he wanted to be the brave prince who rescued her by slaying all her dragons, even though he knew she could slay them herself.

"Go ahead. Tell me this plan of yours. Just be aware that I intend on making all my own decisions."

"I understand. I just need you to promise to hear me out and consider what's best for our children." It was all that he could hope for. He wouldn't force her to do anything she didn't want to do.

"Okay. Spill it," Summer said, her eyes showing him no sign of weakness.

"Things are going to be complicated with two newborn babies to care for. You know I want to be involved, which means I will be spending a lot of time with both you and the babies when you come home from the hospital. It just seems that you staying at my place makes more sense. There's plenty of room at my home. There's a whole wing that could be just for you and the babies. And there's security. I'm sorry I've dragged you into all this, but the truth is that our children are going to need security. And right now, with this tabloid reporter running around trying to find a story, you need to be someplace safe. You would still have your independence to come and go as you please."

He waited for her to explode. He waited for her to throw it in his face once more that she had done everything until now by herself and didn't need him to help her. But she didn't. Instead of taking offence and telling him what he could do with his offer, she just stared at him. Seconds ticked by. Her eyes left his and she looked down at her hands, where they were placed across her belly. He began to fear he had pushed for too much, too soon.

"I know you mean well, and I know right now you want to be a part of these babies' lives, but you need to understand that you can't just commit to take care of them while they're little. If you plan to be a parent, a father to them, it needs to be a lifelong commitment. If you plan to be there for the beginning, you need to be there forever. You can't just go in and out of their lives or, worse, just walk out one day when you get a new job offer or you decide that you want a new family. And don't think that I've lost my mind. Parents abandon their children every day and that's not what I want for my babies. Consider that and I'll consider your offer." She opened the car door, then turned back toward him. "Because I'm more scared of what it would do to my children if you walked away from them after they'd learned to count on you than what danger I'm in from some reporter."

She started to stand, but he reached for her, resting his hand against her back until she turned back to him. "I'm not going anywhere, and I would never leave my children behind. That, I promise you."

He felt the heat of her stare all the way to his soul. This woman was normally easygoing and lighthearted, but pregnancy had changed her into a momma bear who would not take any chances with her cubs.

Finally, she spoke. "Okay, we'll try it."

He sat there in the parking lot, staring at her apartment long after she had shut the door. There was more here than just a woman who was mad because he hadn't been there for her when she'd found out she was pregnant, though he knew that was part of it. But there was more.

Through all the time he had known Summer, she'd spoken very little about her childhood. He'd not thought that much of it, as he was in a habit of not sharing a lot of his own childhood memories. He hadn't lived the typical lifestyle and always had to be on guard, not sharing anything that would lead back to his father. But now, he knew someone had abandoned Summer, not unlike what he'd done for the five months he'd been gone. Whether it had been her mother or her father, he didn't know. Right now, the only thing that mattered was how he was going to make that hurt go away. And how he was going to make her believe that he would never abandon her or their babies again.

CHAPTER SEVEN

SUMMER WATCHED AS everyone around her worked. Everyone except her. It seemed every time she started to do something, someone appeared at her side to take over. She eyed the man standing at the grill. It was his fault, she was sure.

She'd recently realized that even though the man denied any interest in becoming a recognized member of Soura's royal family, he gave orders and commands like he was sitting on a throne. Like the order that she was to sit and *enjoy* herself while everyone else worked to get this party together.

Yet still, she'd arrived at Alex's with two suitcases, agreeing to give living here with him a try. What had she been thinking?

"I'd be careful with that look. You don't want to set our leader on fire while he's cooking our steaks," Jo said as she came to join her on the oversize lounging chair, where Summer had been basically confined since she'd walked into Alex's home earlier.

"If only that was my superpower," Summer said as she leaned back into the overstuffed cushion.

"He's actually looking hot without your laser-beam eyes toasting him alive," Jo said. "Doesn't his chest look a little more golden since he returned? Maybe he just left us to go work on his tan."

Summer raised her sunglasses and looked back over to the man. She knew Jo was just goading her. Her friend had been trying to get information about where Alex had gone off to ever since he'd returned. But Jo was right. Alex did look good tonight. With his swimsuit trunks—thank goodness, the man had opted not to swim in the buff tonight—and white shirt open against an impressively muscled chest, he looked like just another islander here in the Keys.

Only she knew that was far from the truth, but she wouldn't be sharing that information, or where Alex had disappeared to, with anyone, not even one of her best friends.

She lowered her glasses and leaned farther into the seat. She also wouldn't share how her heart was now pounding and with more than a little interest in the man who had fathered her babies. It was just those hormones again. Those stupid hormones that wouldn't let her forget just how good he'd looked rising from the water in all his sexy bareness.

"You okay? You look flushed. Is it too hot out here?" Jo asked, worry in her voice.

Oh, yes. It was definitely too hot out here while those images of Alex played over and over on some masochistic loop in her brain.

"No, I'm fine," Summer said. Or at least she would be if her pregnancy hormones would give her a break. She did not need to think of Alex that way. Things were complicated enough with a set of twins in their future. Sex with Alex would add a whole new level of complications.

But it was so tempting.

"Moving in with Alex is a good move," Jo said,

thankfully changing the subject. “I can think of a lot of places that would be worse living in than here.”

Summer didn’t have to think of those places. She’d lived in one most of her life. She scanned the yard and pool. Her gaze paused at the outside kitchen, and yep, there was Alex still looking as sexy as he had just moments earlier. She forced her eyes to move on to the back patio and the big sliding glass doors that had been opened so that people could enjoy both the inside and outside at the same time. It was so…perfect. It was everything that the home she’d grown up in hadn’t been.

But she wasn’t in Texas anymore. She wasn’t in the tiny, rusted trailer, or in the small-town high school, where everyone had known that she came from the trailer park. It had been all her mother could afford on her salary from the grocery store after Summer’s father had left them. Now she understood she should have been more appreciative, but when she’d been a teenager being bullied by her peers, it didn’t matter. She’d just wanted to run away.

Summer knew her children would never be in that situation. She’d worked hard to be independent, with a career that could support her. But was it fair to her children for her to turn down this life for them? Was it fair for Summer to not give her babies a chance to bond with their father? But what then? They wouldn’t be able to live in some limbo relationship forever. What happened when he fell for another woman, a woman that could fit in his life better than she ever could? Would he leave their children for that woman?

She looked back over to where he was standing, legs planted securely on the ground, one hand raised in a greeting to one of the local EMTs that had just arrived, while his other hand worked to move the sausages and steaks around on the grill.

A part of her knew that though Alex had let her down by leaving her, he'd never do that to his own children. A part of her was still hurt that he'd left her. That he couldn't have been honest with her and let her into his real life. She knew that part was the little girl in her that had been abandoned by her father, but she still couldn't seem to work through that memory without becoming angry that she'd been stupid enough to repeat her parents' history. And because of that, she couldn't trust her decision-making where her children were concerned.

"You still with me?" Jo said, concern in her voice.

"Sorry, just trying to think things through," Summer said, suddenly very tired. "I guess it's good I'm giving it a try before the babies arrive. It gives us some time to figure out if we can make things work."

"You only have three more months, and you know twins usually come early. But you're right. You have time. If I were you, I'd drag your decision out a bit. Make him work for it," Jo said.

"This is about the babies. Not about me getting some type of revenge. It's not personal." She loved her friends, but right now she wished every one of them would disappear and give her some peace and quiet.

"The look he's been giving you is definitely personal. I know you think things between you were finished after he left, but I don't think he thinks they're finished at all."

"You've read one too many romance books, my friend. Now go join the fun while I close my eyes for a moment. I only got a short nap after I got off this morning. Me and these babies need a minute of shut-eye before this party takes off."

As Jo moved away after making sure the umbrella

over the couch was positioned just right, Summer closed her eyes. Her friend was ever the romantic, something that was surprising after the way her marriage had ended, but she was wrong this time. Summer had spent enough time in the last three weeks around Alex to know that he wasn't interested in anything but the babies she was carrying.

She'd told herself over and over that it was okay. Both of their priorities needed to be on the babies right now. But that surely wasn't helping with these determined hormones that didn't seem to understand that their time had passed. There would be no more sexy times between her and Alex, no matter how much they protested.

Alex watched Summer as he piled the next piece of meat on the already full platter. He knew she'd only gotten off a twenty-four-hour shift a few hours earlier and the dark circles under her cloudy blue eyes were proof that she hadn't had enough rest. How much longer did she intend to push herself? He knew he didn't have the right to order her to decrease the amount of shifts she was working. She was an independent woman who was not going to put up with anyone telling her what to do. Especially not him.

So instead, he'd done the only thing he could do by sending out a message that Summer was not to help with the preparations for the party at all. Now, as she was lying stretched out under an umbrella with her eyes closed, he was glad he had done it, though he knew he'd hear about it later. And he was glad that she'd finally agreed to move in with him. No matter what Summer thought, someone needed to keep an eye on her, and the only person he trusted to do that was himself.

The speakers set around the pool screeched with a

sound worse than fingernails against a chalkboard, and the voice of Max, the grumpiest man on the Heli-Care crew, came over loud and clear.

Looking back over at the lounge chair, Alex saw that the noise had awakened Summer, along with probably half his neighborhood. He headed over to adjust the stereo system before Max could damage the ears of everyone attending the party.

"I just thought we should welcome back our boss, who we're all glad has been returned to us—" Max paused while some of the guests clapped "—and also to thank him for this party to celebrate the renewal of Heli-Care's contract here in the Keys."

The crowd, including all the first responders and the scattering of hospital staff that had come to celebrate, broke out in whistles and cheering.

"While I know it was all of our hard work and reputations in our community, we also need to acknowledge both Alex and Summer's heroic efforts that, rumor has it, helped the county board with their decision to continue our contract." Max paused again as the crowd broke out in more cheers.

Alex moved to take the microphone, but the tall Viking of a man, Casey, beat him to it. "Just one more thing, boss. We all wanted to do something for both you and Summer. Not because of the contract, but because you're both part of our family."

Casey turned toward the house, where Alex could now see Jo and other members of both the Key West crew and the Marathon crew bringing out stacks of pink and blue wrapped presents. Somehow all their friends had managed to surprise the two of them with a baby shower.

Turning to Summer, he saw that she was standing.

Her eyes were wide with the same surprise. For a moment, he felt self-conscious and a bit uncomfortable that everyone had gone to so much trouble. But then he realized that this was just their way of welcoming what they would consider new members into their family of friends.

He walked over to Summer and took her hand in his. They were in this together. She needed to start getting used to it.

"I didn't know," she said as they approached the tables that were now covered with presents.

"Well, the two of you were acting like you had all day to get ready for these babies," Dylan said as he held Katie's hand.

"Two babies mean two times the stuff," his daughter, Violet, said. "I'm hoping my dad and Katie have twins, too."

"I think it would be best if we take it one at a time," Katie said. "How are you, Alex?"

Alex let go of Summer's hand and gave his old friend a hug. "I'm doing fine. I'm glad the three of you got back in town in time for the party."

When he moved back to Summer, he took her hand again and knew it was just the surprise that kept her from pulling away from him as she had every other time he'd touched her.

As the crowd moved back to the tables where the food had been placed and the stereo speakers vibrated with music, the two of them continued to stare at the presents. It wasn't as if this was the first time Alex had been surprised with a party. His mother had loved to throw him parties as a child, and as everything in Hollywood, she'd always gone over the top.

But this was different. This was for their babies. His

and Summer's babies. His coworkers had included him in this celebration, though how Summer felt about that he wasn't sure.

"What am I supposed to do with all of this stuff? They can't really need it all, right?" Summer asked as she picked up one present, then placed it back reverently before picking up another one. It was easy to see that she was overwhelmed by the crew's generosity.

"I've heard that they take a lot of stuff. Let me show you something," he said as he reluctantly pulled her away.

They walked through the living room, then turned down a hallway in the opposite direction of his own suite. This wasn't the arrangement he wanted. He'd much prefer to have both Summer and the babies close to him, but he knew she wasn't going to accept that proposal. At least not yet.

Opening a door, he led her into the biggest room on the west wing of the house, where he had placed her suitcases when she'd arrived. He'd had a decorator come in the day after he had asked Summer to consider moving in with him. While the floors were still the light natural wood of the rest of his home, a big colorful rug now covered a large portion of the room, where there was a new queen bed and nightstands. The other side of the room had been cleared and only a rocker sat in the space.

"I thought that you might want to keep the babies here in the room with you at first, but there's the other room across the hall, which has plenty of room for cribs and all the stuff the babies will need." At least he hoped it was big enough. From the mountain of presents outside, he was afraid he might have to build an addition onto the house.

"It's so pretty," Summer said as she walked to the bed and fingered the pale green duvet that covered the bed.

"You can change anything that you don't like," Alex quickly assured her. He'd requested the pale green color as she had once told her it was one of her favorites.

"No, it's perfect," she said as she moved over to the rocker. "You don't play fair, do you?"

"Not when it's something important to me. And you and the babies are important to me."

"You sure it's that and not the fact that you're a spoiled rich kid who is used to getting his way?" she asked.

He knew she was teasing him, but the question did hurt. He'd worked hard not to have the reputation of being that kid who had everything given to him. He couldn't deny, though, that he'd been one of the lucky few who hadn't graduated from medical school with a load of tuition debt. His father had insisted on paying for all of his schooling.

"You know I'm joking," Summer said as she placed her hand against his cheek, her eyes anxious. "I didn't mean it."

His eyes met hers and something from the past passed between them. Something that he hadn't seen in the weeks since he had returned. Was it possible that even though she denied it, she still cared for him? Before she could move back and once more raise the walls she had insisted on putting between them, he lowered his head.

His lips met hers with only the lightest of touches. If she pulled away from him, he'd let her go no matter how much it hurt him. When her eyes closed, and her hand slid down to rest on his chest, he increased the pressure with first his lips and then his tongue until he was sliding it inside her mouth. He captured her moan and released one of his own as his hands swept down her sides and circled her. She leaned into him, her swollen belly pressing against the hard length of him. There was no way to deny his arousal, but neither could she when his hands skimmed over the hardened peaks of her nipples.

"Hey, boss, the girls are outside waiting with some baby-looking cake," Casey called from the living room.

"Please remind me why I put up with that Neanderthal?" he asked as Summer pushed away from him.

"Because despite his size and boorish manners, he's one of the best crew members we've ever had on the team," Summer said, turning her back to him. "It's a beautiful room."

"I'm glad you like it," he said. "We can decide what to do with the other room later," Alex said as he buttoned and tucked in the cotton shirt he'd been wearing earlier.

When she didn't say anything, he followed her out of the room. She might pretend that nothing had happened between them, but Alex knew better. She'd been just as aroused as he'd been. Something had changed between the two of them for those few moments he had held Summer in his arms. She might not trust him yet, but she still wanted him.

He'd accomplished his first goal of having her move in with him. Now he had to win back her trust and show her that they could make things between them work. That kiss had been a sure sign that there was still hope for the two of them. He just hoped that Summer wouldn't let her mistrust of him blind her to that hope.

Summer unwrapped the last present and placed the dainty newborn dress with the stack of other clothes that would need to be washed and hung up in the enormous closet in the room that would be hers and the babies.

"There you are," Alex said as he stuck his head into the doorway. "The last of the crew just left."

"Sorry, I should have helped with the cleanup. The girls helped bring all the presents inside and I just couldn't wait to open them. It kind of makes things more real seeing all the clothes they'll wear and the toys they'll play with," Summer said. Realizing the mess she had made of the room, she stood and bent down to pick up the discarded wrapping paper. "I'll get this cleaned up…"

Her head spun and she felt her body go limp as the blood rushed down to her toes. As her legs began to fold, she gripped the armrest of the rocker and began to lower herself, only to find that she was being swept up into Alex's arms.

"Hold on, let me look at you," he said as he sat down in the chair and held her in his lap. He examined her face and eyes, then took her hand and examined her nail beds.

"I'm okay. Let me up," she said, though she wasn't sure she had the energy to get up if he let her. After the kiss they'd shared earlier, this wasn't a good idea. Even her blood-deprived brain knew that.

"Just wait a minute, and quit wiggling," Alex said, his voice a snarl.

It didn't take but a moment for her to discover why he was being so sharp with her. Her wiggling was causing a problem. A big problem.

"Relax and close your eyes, and it will pass," Alex said.

She was pretty sure he was talking about her bout of dizziness and not his…problem. Still, she couldn't help but enjoy his moment of being uncomfortable. It only seemed right after the last few months she'd spent with morning sickness and now this awful dizziness. It was the first spell she'd had since she'd seen her doctor and she'd falsely hoped they were over.

She laid her head against his shoulder and closed her eyes as the doctor had ordered her to. She was tired. So tired. She just needed to rest for a few moments. It seemed she was always tired. She drifted off to sleep with the feel of Alex's arms tight around her, the feel of his hard body surrounding her. She loved this new protective side of him, though she would never admit that to him. She just wished she knew that it was for her instead of their babies.

When she opened her eyes again, the room was dark, and she was in the bed. An arm, Alex's arm, was lying across her, and his hand was resting against her stomach as if to protect the little ones inside her. Carefully, she lifted his arm and eased from the bed. She needed to find a bathroom. Opening the only door that didn't lead to the hall or the closet, she found a four-piece bathroom. She stared at the large soaker tub longingly. Her apartment only had a shower. The last time she'd soaked in a tub had been the last night she'd spent in the house with Alex. With Alex lying in the bed outside the bathroom door, it was best she didn't remember that night.

She'd already been pregnant then, but she didn't know it. Their life had seemed perfect. Their loving spectacular. And then it had all suddenly ended.

After washing up, she eased open the door and stared at the man sprawled facedown on the bed. He was still wearing the swim shorts he'd worn to the party, but that was all.

She should wake him and send him off to his own room. It was the smart thing to do. The safe thing to do. And she always played it safe.

One of the babies gave her a kick, reminding her that

maybe she hadn't played it as safe as she could have. But she didn't care. No matter how much trouble the two little ones got into, she would never have any regrets about them.

She just hoped neither she nor Alex had any regrets for what she was about to do. Because no matter how much she told herself she should run as fast as possible for a woman six months pregnant with twins, she couldn't do it. He was just too tempting. And after the kiss they'd shared, she knew that part of their old life, the attraction and desire, was still there.

She climbed back into the bed, then rolled over to where she could see Alex's face. Oh, there were other things she hoped to see—she had every intention of opening up that dam she'd built around those pesky hormones of hers—but right now she'd just enjoy watching him sleep.

He was such a handsome man, so strong and courageous. He'd never considered his own life when he'd jumped into the ocean to save the young boy, Scottie. He'd given up his own life here in Florida to go help his brother when he was injured, even though he had never been recognized by his family.

His eyes fluttered and he turned over onto his back, displaying his flat abdomen. A line of dark hair ran down his chest and her hand followed it, skimming across his chest, until the soft hair disappeared below the swim trunks. She'd touched him this way many times while he'd slept, patiently waiting for him to wake and take her into his arms. Tonight she was impatient. Her breasts were heavy and a warm tingling heat was gathering between her legs. He hadn't even touched her, and her body was already aroused. She'd read that a pregnant women's libido could increase. Hers seemed ready to set a record.

Her hand had started its path up his chest again when his own hand covered hers. She'd known he was awake by the way the muscles of his stomach had gone rigid as her fingertips had trailed across them.

"Is there something you want?" he asked, his hand holding hers tight over the spot where his heart was now hammering against it.

"Oh, yes. Most definitely." She licked her lips at the thought of all the things she wanted.

His hand cupped her chin, turning her face until his eyes met hers. "Are you sure?"

Sure that this wasn't a mistake? No. Sure that she wanted this, anyway?

"Yes," she said before her head could tell her what her heart was refusing to admit. Whether this was a mistake or not, she wasn't going to turn back now. They'd always been good in bed together. What would it hurt if she just let herself enjoy the moment?

He let go of her chin and shifted to his side until their bodies were perfectly in line. His eyes searched hers. For what? Misgivings? Yes, she had a truckload of those. Even before he'd left—before she'd learned she was pregnant—she'd begun to worry that what she felt for Alex was more than he wanted. She hadn't let it stop her then and she wasn't going to let it stop her now. She'd take what she wanted with no promises of anything but tonight.

She ran her hand up his chest until she cupped his chin, which was coarse with a day's worth of growth. She was filled with memories of the sweet sting of pleasure as the rough bristles had skimmed over the most sensitive places on her body.

Her core tightened. She wanted to feel that sting again. She wanted to wake in the morning with her body marked pink from his attention. She wanted him to get busy. What was he waiting for? For her to make the first move?

She placed her lips against his, much as he'd done earlier in the evening. His lips opened and he jerked away what little control she thought she'd had. He claimed her mouth, her tongue, her breath. She'd opened a geyser of pent-up sexual frustration that matched her own and she loved it.

He rolled her onto her back as one hand clasped the back of her head, then molded their mouths together while his other hand found one aching nipple. He teased its peak through her shirt, setting loose a jolt of heat that headed straight to her core.

She lost all her control. The control that had protected her from all of the dangerous emotions that she'd kept locked away from him. The joy she'd felt the moment she'd discovered he'd returned. The anger she'd felt when he'd ordered her to marry him for all the wrong reasons. The lust she'd felt every time his skin had brushed against hers.

She wanted to hug him, slap him and make love to him, all at the same time. But most of all she just wanted to feel him inside of her again. To feel, just for a few moments, that connection between them when there was no tomorrow to worry over. There was just that one moment in time when they both came together to give and receive pleasure. To share their bodies and their…love?

She pulled away from him and searched his eyes. Was that love or lust she saw there? Surely, it was only lust. She didn't need love.

Her hands followed the path down his chest, over

his stomach, until she felt the hard length of him in her hand. This was all she needed right now. Just the passion. Just the fire.

His mouth found her breast as he removed the rest of her clothes.

And then he was inside her, his body hot against hers. There were no words. No soft caresses. There was only the two of them racing for something that had been forgotten and lost. It was there, just outside her reach, but there. His body thrust against her, over and over. She spread her legs to take more. She wanted more. She wanted everything he could give her.

His hand touched that sweet spot between her legs as his mouth latched on to one overly sensitive nipple. She reached one more time for that final peak, her body straining against his, her core tightening around him. Her scream cut through the silent house as she flew apart as bolts of pleasure shot through her, and Alex joined her with a climax of his own.

They collapsed together into a pile of weak limbs and trembling muscles. Her body sated, her mind free of worries of the future, she let herself drift off to sleep, wrapped inside his arms. Tomorrow, she might call herself a fool, but tonight she would sleep without any regrets.

CHAPTER EIGHT

IT WAS THE smell of lilacs that awakened him. He was fond of the flowers that reminded him of a childhood full of hugs and laughter. But this wasn't the scent of flowers. This was the perfume that his mother had once made famous. Which could only mean one thing.

He opened his eyes to find his mother, dressed as if she was going for lunch in downtown New York, standing above him.

"That better be the mother of my grandchildren," his mother said, staring at the two of them with not one sign of self-consciousness.

"What are you doing here?" he whispered. Either Summer was still sleeping, or she was playing possum.

"I told you I was coming for a visit," his mother said. "Is this a bad time?"

Yes, it was a bad time. The worst of times. After last night, he knew there was some hope of him and Summer building back their relationship together. Having his mother drop in was a variable he didn't know if Summer was prepared for. No one was ever prepared for his mother.

But he couldn't tell his mother that. "No, it's fine. Could you give us a few moments, though?"

"Of course, my bambino, I'll make myself at home in the living room."

Not for the first time in his life, he wondered why he couldn't have been born to normal parents. Normal? He didn't even know what that looked like, but it was something he was hoping to give his own children.

He waited until his mother had shut the door behind her. "You can open your eyes now."

Summer's blue eyes popped open, all traces of sleep gone as she flung back the sheets. "Was that your mother? It was, wasn't it? Melanie Leonelli just caught me in bed with her son."

"Since she knows you are pregnant with my children, I'm sure she suspects we have slept together," Alex said as he wrapped an arm around her before she could sprint from the bed. "Stop for a moment."

"But I have to get out of here. I'm not dressed to meet your mother. I don't want her thinking any worse of me than she already does."

He pulled her back into the bed, then tucked her into his shoulder. Summer had made comments like this before. It was as if deep down there was some type of residual shame someone had instilled in her. He didn't think it was about the pregnancy, but there was definitely something that haunted her.

"Stay still for just a moment. You know the doctor said that you needed to get up slowly. You don't want another spell like you had last night." It was probably unprofessional for him to take advantage of the situation, but he needed a few more minutes alone with her before they had to deal with his mother.

Because he knew his mother. When she showed up things always got interesting.

"Right now, I'm more likely to pass out from embarrassment, rather than my blood pressure dropping," Summer said, though her body was relaxing deliciously against him now. If his mother wasn't here…

"You two need to get in here," his mother said from just outside the door. "There's a picture of you two on the television and Debbie Duncan just announced that she has an update on her story with two local heroes after the commercial break."

Summer stiffened against him, and he let her go after his mother disappeared back down the hall.

"It's probably nothing. Maybe it's an update on Scottie," Alex said. He'd checked on the boy himself and had shared with Summer that the kid was doing great, and his family had returned home.

"Maybe," Summer said. "But I told you that woman wasn't going to leave us alone. She's like a viper. One whiff of blood and she's determined to finish you off."

"There's nothing she can do to us. The only secret we have to worry about is who my father is, and there's no way she's good enough to dig that out," Alex said.

Summer took a moment to look over to where Alex was dressing as she pulled on her own shorts and top. Maybe Alex's only secret was that his father was a king, and, yes, that was a big one, but there were things in her own life that she didn't want discovered. Her juvenile record might be sealed, but it wouldn't take her record being open for Debbie Duncan to find out Summer's dirty secrets.

And then there was the bigger-than-life movie star that was waiting in the living room. It was only logical that Alex would have told his mother that he and Summer weren't a couple anymore. Finding the two of them in bed together had to be surprising. What must the woman think about Summer? That she was fickle?

What did Summer even think about herself? She'd promised herself that she would keep at least an emotional and physical distance between her and Alex, but the first time her hormones started a riot she'd given in.

And it had been worth every bit of the self-incrimination that she was throwing at herself this morning.

"You two slowpokes need to hurry, the story's coming on now," Alex's mom called from the other room. Not yelled, not screamed. No, the woman's voice just seemed to float into the room.

After hurrying down the hallway into the open living room, Summer stopped when she saw the oversize television screen filled with a picture of not only Alex, but also Prince Nicholas. Both men were looking straight at the camera, their matching brown eyes scowling at the cameraman, their imperious noses lifted in a sign of irritation. To anyone with anything close to twenty-twenty vision, it was easy to tell that these two men were somehow connected by blood.

Alex came up behind her, his body going rigid when he saw the screen. He bit out a mild curse but then quieted when his mother shot him a glare as she turned up the volume.

"Well, don't we have some fun news for our audience today? It seems that local hero Dr. Alex Leonelli has been living a second life, my friends. Not only has he been working tirelessly in our community, but it seems that he's also been taking care of one of the world's most recognized royal members, Prince Nicholas, the Crown Prince of Soura," Debbie Duncan said, speaking to her adoring audience. It was enough to make Summer sick.

This woman was about to ruin someone's life and everyone in the audience couldn't wait.

"As many of you may know if you follow the royal community, Prince Nicholas was injured earlier this year in a skiing accident. Exactly how Dr. Leonelli was brought into the picture, we are not sure. It seems possible that the two of them could have met somewhere, as the doctor's mother, Melanie Leonelli, is one of Hollywood's favorites, but no one seems to know for sure. Stay tuned this week as we hope to have more on this story."

The three of them stared silently at the television set as a commercial began to play, then Alex walked over to his mother and took the remote.

"She's just fishing. If she had more, she would have spilled it," Alex said as he turned his back on the television, which was now showing a commercial advertising a local pest cleaning service.

She couldn't help but wonder if she could hire their services to spray the offices of their local television station, because right now, she'd put Debbie Duncan in the category of their biggest pest.

"I don't know this woman," Alex's mother began, "but I don't like the way she is handling this story. The two of you were heralded as two local heroes just a week ago and now you are being dissected for any bit of publicity the woman can get from you."

Summer wanted to high-five the famous actress on her expert appraisal of the situation, but the regal woman would probably think she was crazy. They were already starting on the wrong foot after she'd been caught in bed with her son. She didn't want the woman to think that she wasn't a suitable mother for her grandchildren. She'd have to do better.

"I warned Alex that Debbie was out for more of a story than just the two of us saving a young boy, especially after she learned that we were expecting twins together," Summer said, then held out her hand. "I'm Summer."

"Of course you are. And I have to say that you are every bit as lovely as Alex said you were. I'm sure the two of you have made the most beautiful of babies." Melanie ignored Summer's hand and instead wrapped her in a tight hug.

Summer stared over the woman's shoulder at Alex, who was busy starting a pot of coffee. He gave her a smile and shrugged his shoulders. "Mom, Summer needs to take a breath. She's breathing for three now."

"Yes, she is. And please, call me Melanie. I can't believe Alex has kept you hidden from me for so long. I don't know what he was thinking. There's so much to do to get ready for these two." The woman placed her hand on Summer's abdomen.

The face that had been plastered on hundreds of billboards glowed with a beauty that hadn't been touched by time. Summer waited for her body to withdraw from Alex's mother's touch, as it usually did when someone other than her closest of friends touched her, but it didn't. Instead, both women laughed when one of the twins kicked against Melanie's hand. Who would have thought that two little babies who hadn't even been born could bring together two women from such different backgrounds?

"Well, I'm going to go put my luggage away and then I'm going to call your father, Alex. He'll know how to handle this. He always does."

Summer watched as Melanie swept out of the room. The woman was so beautiful and kind, but still she was a bit much for this early in the morning. What Summer needed was a cup of coffee.

Alex handed her a glass of juice and she sighed. She really needed coffee.

"I'm sorry my mother interrupted us this morning," Alex said as he moved closer.

"It was probably for the best," Summer said. A flush of heat crept up her face. She'd ignored all her rules last night and now she had to deal with the consequences. Which meant she had to figure out where it was safe for her relationship with Alex to go. She'd seen how unhealthy her mom's pattern of going back and forth with her many boyfriends was, and she didn't want that for her and Alex. Or for her babies, who would be even more confused by their parents' relationship.

"I better go. You need to spend some time with your mother," Summer said. She needed to leave before she let the look in Alex's eyes seduce her back into bed while his mother waited for him.

"Aren't you forgetting something?" he asked, his eyes bright with laughter as if he knew her thoughts.

"What?" she asked. It had to be some residual sex hormones that were making her mind all foggy.

"You live here now. You don't need to go anywhere."

She blinked and fought through the fog. How could she have forgotten that she'd moved in the night before?

"I have to go back to the apartment. To pack. To finish packing, I mean." Once more she was making a fool of herself. Today was just one of those days that she needed to go back in bed and burrow under the covers. "I'm just going to go to my room to get dressed first."

"Can you join us tonight for dinner? There's an Italian restaurant in Old Town that my mother loves to visit when she is here," Alex said. "We need to discuss what we learn from my father today."

"I'm sure your mother would like to spend some time alone with you." And Summer needed some time alone, too.

"If Debbie Duncan has discovered who my father is, the media will go crazy," Alex said, then took a sip of coffee. "We both need to be ready for that."

"But I'm not—" she began.

"You are the mother to my father's grandchildren. They'll go after any story they can get concerning the two of us. You need to be prepared. Besides, my mother will be disappointed if you don't come."

Summer knew when she had been expertly maneuvered. If she refused now, Melanie could take offence. "Fine, I'll only be a few hours. I don't have a lot left to go through."

"I know it will make my mother very happy." Alex's mischievous smile told her he was going to be using his mother as an excuse for as long as possible. She could only imagine the ways he had used that smile while growing up.

"I need to make it an early night. I'm working a shift for Dylan tomorrow," she said before leaving the room.

Happy to find Alex on the phone when she returned, she hurried out the door before he could stop her.

After last night and then everything that had happened this morning, she needed some time alone. She kept thinking about Debbie Duncan's announcement that had warned of more to come in *their* story. Alex and his mother had assumed that the woman was talking about something concerning Alex. But what if it wasn't about Alex at all? What if the woman had been talking about something she'd found in Summer's background? What would Alex think about her if he learned about her past? How would he feel about her then? She could only imagine, and it what she imagined wasn't good.

Summer thought she knew how the wealthy lived. Her mother had always loved the glitz and glamour of her soap operas, and as a little girl Summer had been fascinated to find that somewhere out there were people who didn't wear clothes from the thrift stores, or eat leftover beans and franks every other night.

But this restaurant and the way they were treating Melanie and, subsequently, her, was so unlike anything Summer had ever experienced.

She'd settled on wearing the one and only maternity sundress she owned. This was Key West after all. A sundress would be considered formal wear in most of the city. Fortunately, Alex's mother had dressed with comfort in mind also, though the flowing dress Melanie had on would probably cost more than two of Summer's paychecks.

"Christos is looking into Debbie Duncan," Melanie said as soon as the waitress walked away. "He told me about the journalist in Soura that has been asking questions of the staff concerning you and Nicholas, and that you saw him here. Neither one of us like that."

"Are we sure that he isn't the one that been encouraging these questions?" Alex asked. "He's been pushing for me to come forward and acknowledge him."

"I thought he was the one that didn't want to acknowledge you," Summer said, sure that she hadn't misunderstood what Alex had told him about his birth.

"Times have changed. When I first met Christos, we knew that his country would not accept me, an outsider, as their queen consort even if his father hadn't already become involved in looking for his son's wife. Now things are different," Melanie said with not one hint of bitterness.

"And with all the social media and all the journalists looking for the next big story, like our friend Debbie, my father thinks it would be best if we controlled when my existence is released to the public."

"I think you both worry too much. If it comes out that you are Christos's son, so what? His father and wife have both left this world. His country loves him and will stand behind him no matter if he had hidden three or four children," Melanie said.

"He hasn't, has he?" Alex asked.

"No, my bambino. Your father was always true to his wife, until her death."

Summer wondered how the woman could be so sure. Was it possible that Alex's mother and father had more than just a past relationship? It did seem that the two of them had remained close. Maybe that was a sign that there was a glimmer of hope for Summer and Alex to remain friends.

The waitress delivered their first course, a creamy Italian soup covered with Parmesan cheese.

"Excuse me," a woman asked as she approached them. "I just wanted to tell you, Miss Leonelli, how much I enjoy your work."

Summer watched the rest of the night as Alex's mother graciously signed autographs and talked to other patrons.

"Was this what you had expected when you decided to go into acting?" Summer asked as the last fan left their table.

"It was a long time ago, but I don't think I really considered it much. I had been in theater since I was very young. After college, it just made sense that I would go to California. I worked hard, became the star I had always dreamed of being and raised my son. The fans and paparazzi are just a small part of my life."

Later, as she prepared for bed, Summer thought about the difference in how Melanie accepted her fame and the attention that she dealt with daily, while Alex was fighting against having to accept his father's world and the attention that would come along with it. From the outside, it was easy for Summer to see that while the paparazzi were part of the job for her, Alex had never wanted that fame.

She thought about how quiet Alex had been during their meal. It would be easy to blame it on the stress of worrying about what the Miami morning-show host would broadcast next, but he'd shown no signs of being unhappy on the way to the restaurant. It had only been when his mother had become the center of attention, pulling Summer and Alex into the other restaurant patrons' focus with her, that he had become quiet and withdrawn from their conversations. It was plain for her to see that Alex preferred to be left in the background, which was the real reason he was still fighting to keep his connections to the royal house of Soura buried. It wasn't that he didn't want to have a normal relationship with his father and brother. He just didn't want the attention that would come with it.

She didn't think either his father or mother understood their son in that way. He wanted to be the person in the background that helped the man who was experiencing an MI or the child that had a fever.

He'd chosen a job a world apart from his mother's. He'd chosen to help people through medicine. There was no fanfare. No applause. There was just the satisfaction that you had made a difference in someone's life.

He wanted to live his life without having to worry about phones recording him as he tried to revive a young man on the beach. And that was what he wanted for their children.

Unable to sleep, Summer headed to the kitchen for a glass of milk. Seeing the light from the television was on, she hesitated. She didn't think running into Alex right now was a good idea, since every time she looked at her bed, her face heated with memories of the night before. She was glad to see that it was his mother instead.

Dressed in a long sleep shirt and boxer shorts, Melanie looked almost normal, making Summer feel comfortable dressed in her maternity pajamas that were covered with pink flamingos.

"Sorry, I don't mean to disturb you," Summer said. There had been a time when Alex's home had felt like her own, but now she felt out of place, like a visitor that had overstayed her welcome.

"I'm still stuck on another time zone. I just thought I would watch some television before I headed to bed. Come sit beside me for a minute and tell me what's bothering you."

"Why do you think something is bothering me?" Summer asked as she opened the fridge. After pouring herself a glass of milk, she joined Alex's mom on the couch.

"Why do you think there's something wrong?"

"As an actress, I study people's expressions. I can see the worry on your face. Is it that Debbie woman?"

This was an opportunity for her to learn more about

Alex. All she had to do was stop thinking of Melanie as a movie star and instead think of her as a mother.

"No, not really. I mean she's part of it. She does seem to be focusing on us and I can't figure out why."

"She's a journalist, so she smells a story, though she might not know what it is yet," Melanie said.

"Maybe, but her I understand. It's her job to look for stories, to find something about us that no one else knows. I still don't like it, but I know it's not personal." Summer pulled her legs up on the couch and looked at the woman next to her. The lights were down low and shadows played off the older woman's face.

It was now or never. "Alex has explained why he grew up unable to tell anyone about his father. I know you didn't have a choice, not then, but it must have been hard for you to raise him on your own."

"I never felt that I was on my own, not with Christos calling every day checking on the two of us. I always knew he would be there if I needed him. Are you worried that Alex won't be there to help? Because I can tell you he will be. My son is a very responsible man."

"Oh, I know Alex is responsible," she said, then took a sip of milk. Summer just didn't want to be another responsibility to the man.

"But why did you let his father even be involved with Alex if he couldn't be a real father to him?"

"I never blamed Christos. He was as much a victim of the situation as Alex. I knew that if he could, he would have done things differently, but his father was old-fashioned, and he never would have accepted Alex. In his way, Christos protected Alex from a life where he would have been shunned."

"But it had to have confused Alex when he was young." Summer suspected that it still confused the man that Alex had become. He was so determined to live quietly out of the spotlight, but he'd been quick to drop everything and rush to his father's side when his brother had been injured.

Melanie pulled her feet onto the couch, then turned toward her. For a moment, Summer thought she might have pushed too hard. She didn't want Melanie to think she was judging her. If anything, Summer was amazed at how well-adjusted Alex was, considering it had been a childhood spent dodging cameras and playing the part of a fatherless boy.

"I'm sure he was at times, though I tried to make his life as normal as possible," Melanie said, a bittersweet smile following her words.

"I didn't mean to imply you did anything wrong," Summer responded, than drank a little more milk.

"I know, dear," Melanie said before moving closer to Summer and covering her hand. "If you could have seen the look on his face when I'd tell him he was going to visit his father, you'd understand. He loves his father, and his father loves him. The fact that they've had to hide that has been hard on them both, but it would have been harder if Christos hadn't been there at all."

"But he seems so determined to keep his relationship with his father a secret," Summer said, wondering, not for the first time, if Alex was wrong to hide himself from the world. Maybe if he admitted to the everyone who he really was, he could finally have the open relationship any child would want to have with their parent. "It's almost like he's ashamed of who he is, which doesn't make sense."

"You forget, Alex grew up in a Hollywood spotlight. From the time he could crawl, he was the subject of the media's curiosity about the identity of his father. By the time he was a teenager, he couldn't leave the house without a bodyguard. Living in my world is hard for any kid. Alex spent his school years trying to blend in with the other kids as much as possible, but that's difficult when your picture is plastered on the tabloids at the grocery store. It seemed everyone was either jealous of him, or they wanted to be his friend just to enjoy some of the attention he was getting."

Summer had been bullied enough in school to understand Alex wanting to blend into the background. It was a lonely place, but it was bctter than the pain.

She tried to cover a yawn as she stood. The milk had done its job and she knew she needed to call it a night. She had a long shift ahead of her the next day. It seemed the further along she got in her pregnancy, the longer the shifts were.

"Thank you for answering my questions. I don't mean to be nosy. I just..." How could she explain her feelings for her son to this woman, when she didn't understand them herself?

"It's okay. You're carrying his babies. It's only natural that you would want to know more about his life before you met him."

"His life has been so different from mine." And Summer was beginning to understand that her children's lives would vastly different from what her life as a child had been.

But wasn't that what she had always wanted? Only now, it didn't seem enough that they would never have to miss a meal or do without the simple things a child needed. She had always wanted to give her kids the one thing she'd lost when her father had left—a family.

"I don't know what happened between the two of you, but I can tell you Alex has shared information about his family that he has never shared with anyone before. That tells me that he trusts you, and it takes a lot for Alex to trust. He's been burned too many times by people who said they were his friend, but only cared what his friendship could do for them."

"I won't do that to him. I won't use him." No matter how tempting it might be to accept the security he was offering her.

"I know that. So does Alex. He trusts you. Now you just need to decide if you are ready to trust him," Melanie said. Rising from the couch, the woman moved to Summer and pressed a motherly kiss against her cheek. Summer's hand went to her cheek and her eyes filled with tears as Melanie left the room. This woman who barely knew her had shown her more affection than her own mother had in years. But was it an act? Or, like Alex, was she willing to do whatever was needed to be a part of Summer's babies' lives?

Was this what it had been like for Alex when he was growing up? Never knowing who cared for him and who wanted to use him? If so, she could only feel sorry for the little boy. No one deserved to feel the pain of wanting someone to care for you while being afraid it wasn't you they really wanted.

CHAPTER NINE

ALEX TRIED TO read the latest corporate email for the third time. When his boss had informed him they had been able to retain the county contract, he hadn't bothered to mention that they had promised the county a price cut. A cut that was being passed on to their local budget. Now it was up to him to find where he could make those cuts.

With the size of the population, the Keys were unable to maintain a large hospital, so the service of a medevac helicopter was a necessity. In the five years he had been been there, they had added a second helicopter located in Marathon and their service stayed busy throughout the year, between transfers from the local hospital to Miami and transport from the beach or accident scenes. It didn't make any sense that they were being asked to cut back to cover costs.

Standing, he stretched out his back. He was tired and cranky after a sleepless night and an early shift in the emergency room. Unfortunately, he already knew he wouldn't be sleeping any better tonight than he had the night before, because the woman he wanted to be sharing his bed would be sleeping here at headquarters tonight.

After their night together, he'd hoped she would join him in his room, but she'd continued to remain on her side of the house, and he couldn't understand why. The desire between them had been just as strong as it had been before he'd left. Didn't that prove there was still something that connected the two of them? He just needed to find a way to get her back into his bed. Then he'd work on keeping her there.

The sound of the helicopter landing on the helipad beside their headquarters filled the building and he relaxed. It always made him feel good when his crew returned safely from a call. Having Summer out on the calls this far into her pregnancy was especially stressful.

He met them in the kitchen. From the look of the crew, it hadn't been an easy call. All three of them clearly needed some rest. Hopefully, the remainder of their shift would be quiet. "Everything go okay?"

"Winds were a little rough," Roy, their pilot, said before moving past him with a bottle of his favorite soda product.

"The transport went fine, but our patient wasn't looking so good when we left. Septic shock from an infected knee. We had maxed out her IV pressure support before we landed. I'm not sure she's going to make it," Summer said.

Was that worry that was shadowing her eyes, or was she just tired? This was the second extra twenty-four-hour shift she'd picked up this week. It needed to stop.

"She should have come in earlier. Her husband said he tried to get her to cancel their trip after she had knee surgery, but she was determined that they were going to spend their anniversary in the Keys. I just hope it isn't their last anniversary," Max said, then moved past him.

"Is it possible that he's even grumpier than usual today?" Alex asked as he watched the man head into his sleep room.

"He might be. He's mainly been speaking in grunts and growls," Summer said.

As she took a chair at the kitchen table, he took the one opposite. He reached down and lifted her foot into his lap, then began to untie the laces of her boots. When she didn't pull her foot away from him, he moved to the next one. The moan she released when he began to massage her feet sent a spark of desire through his blood. The swelling he found when he got to her ankles doused it.

"You have to stop working these extra shifts," he said as he kneaded the pads of her feet. She closed her eyes and stretched back. When she didn't answer, he thought she might have fallen asleep.

"Are you speaking as my boss or as these babies' daddy?" she asked as she rubbed her hand over her stomach, as if trying to soothe them.

"What if I'm speaking as a friend?" Alex asked. And what if he was speaking as her lover? Would that allow him the right to be concerned for her?

"I need to work, Alex. I'm saving so that I can take a few months off after the babies are born," Summer said.

"You know that isn't necessary. You know I can take care of you." He couldn't understand why she was being so stubborn.

"Do you know me at all?" she asked. "I don't want or need anyone to take care of me. I left home the day I turned eighteen and I've paid my own way since then."

"If we were married… Wait a moment," Alex said as Summer began to pull her feet from his hands. "I just need you to listen to me for a moment before you explode. I just want you to consider what would have happened if things had been different. What if I had told you about my family before I had left? Or what if there'd never been a reason for me to leave at all? What if things between us were like they were before I left? We had something special. You know we did. What if you had discovered that you were pregnant then? Would you have married me?"

"But you did leave me. That's reality. Things changed. We can't just turn back time. We're not the same people we were then." There was no anger in Summer's voice as she said the words. And that scared him. She'd given up on them.

"It sure didn't feel like that when you were in my arms. How can there be nothing between us, yet we can still make love that way? You can deny it all you want, but I felt it. You still want me, and I still want you. Nothing there has changed." If she thought he was going to give up on them, she was very wrong. He'd glimpsed what he had lost, and he wasn't giving it up again.

"That was just sex. Just like all the times before was just sex," Summer said.

"You know that isn't true," Alex said, letting go of her feet as she pulled away from him and stood.

"You weren't honest with me," Summer said. She was looking down at him now, arms locked across her chest. She was as closed off from him as she had been the day she'd marched across his lawn and declared that they were having a baby. "Why, Alex? If I'd meant something to you, why did you leave without telling me? Why didn't you trust me with your secrets?"

As painful as it might be for her, he needed to break through to her if he had any hope of them getting back to where they had been before he'd left. Because he hadn't been just trying to persuade her when he'd said they had something special. It had been special. They'd been special together. And he wanted what they'd had back.

"I know you're angry at me for leaving. But that's not the entire problem, is it? Someone left you. They left you and they didn't come back. Who, Summer? Who hurt you?" Alex said, getting up and stepping toward her, then brushing her hair from her face.

A crash sounded down the hall and the two of them sprang apart. For a moment, he had forgotten where they were.

"What was that?" Roy asked as Alex passed him as he came out of his sleep room.

"It came from Max's room," Summer said as she joined Alex at the other man's door.

"You okay, Max?" Alex asked as he knocked on the door lightly. He didn't want to startle him. Maybe he'd simply knocked something off his bedside table.

When a deep moan came in answer to his question, Alex tried the doorknob. It was locked.

"Here," Roy said, handing him a privacy key that was kept above the doorframe.

After the door was unlocked, Alex pushed into the room, only then realizing that Max was lying on the floor, blocking the door.

"Get the pack from the helicopter," Alex said to Roy as he leaned down to Max and began an assessment. A lamp was lying broken by the side of the bed and the nightstand by the door had been turned over. It looked like Max had been trying to get to the door for help before he had fallen. Max's skin was clammy and his hand was clutching his left arm. Alex didn't have to ask if he was feeling pain. It was etched into every wrinkle on his face.

This had either come on fast, or his friend had been ignoring his body's cry for help. Lifting his arm, Alex checked Max's pulse. It was fast but strong. His respirations were fast and labored. The man needed an EKG as soon as possible.

"When did the pain start?" Summer asked as she rushed to his other side.

"Watch the glass," Alex warned her.

"It wasn't bad," Max said. "I thought…indigestion."

"You know this isn't indigestion," Summer said as she began her own assessment. "Are we flying local or are we headed to Miami?"

She didn't ask who would replace her partner on the flight. She knew Alex would be going with her.

Roy returned and handed Alex the EKG monitor. The pilot had been working as a medevac pilot long enough to know what they were looking at. Max was having a myocardial infarction. They just needed the EKG reading to confirm.

While Summer applied the electro patches for the monitor, Alex pulled a stethoscope from the go bag and listened to Max's heart and lungs. While his breathing was fast, Max's lungs were clear.

"Any allergies, Max?" Summer asked when she pulled a small container of medication from the bag.

"Just penicillin," Max stated, taking the chewable baby aspirin Summer handed him. "Can you call Stacey? She'll be worried if I'm late coming home in the morning."

Alex looked at the reading on the heart monitor. Max wouldn't be coming home in the morning, and they all knew it.

"You're having a STEMI. We could take you to the local emergency room, but that would just be a waste of time. You need to be in Miami, where they have an interventional cardiologist and a cath lab available," Alex said.

There was only a nod of his head from Max, but it was enough. “Roy, contact Dispatch and let them know we’re flying one of our own to the city.”

“I’ll get the stretcher,” Summer said, following Roy out to the copter.

“I can walk,” Max said, though he didn’t attempt to get up.

Alex would let the man have his pride. It was hard for someone used to being the caretaker to find themselves on the other side of the stretcher.

“We’ll get you on some oxygen and morphine as soon as we get you loaded.”

Max grunted an acceptance. Just more proof that the man was hurting.

Alex saw that Summer had her boots back on when she brought the flight stretcher. As they loaded Max, Alex noticed the difficulty she was having lifting the stretcher up. Whether the stubborn woman wanted to admit it or not, her hours of flying were about to end.

But that was a problem that would have to wait. Right now, he had to keep his concentration on Max.

They were in the air in record time. Alex contacted the Miami emergency room and sent the EKG strip to confirm what was wrong with Max. A cardiologist and their cath-lab team would be waiting for them as soon as they landed.

“What can I do?” Alex asked as he ended the call.

Summer might have had trouble with getting up and down with the stretcher, but she was running the flight single-handedly, as if she flew solo every flight. She’d already started an IV and hung fluids.

“His heart rate is in the one-thirties and his blood pressure is one hundred and eighty-eight over a hundred and two, both possibly elevated due to pain. I’ve given him five mg's of morphine. I'm going to repeat it in five minutes."

"Oxygen?" he asked. Max's normal ruddy-colored cheeks had turned ashen.

"He's on five liters with an oxygen saturation of ninety-five percent," Summer said.

"How's the pain, Max?" Alex asked.

The man opened his eyes and gave his boss a thumbs-up before closing them again.

"I'm giving him another five mg's of morphine now," Summer said as she pushed the IV medication.

It was so frustrating that they couldn't do more for him. If he was in an emergency room, he could be ordering tests and speaking with the cardiologist himself instead of depending on some doctor he had never met to pass on all the correct information.

"ETA, three minutes," Roy said into their earphones.

"We're almost there, Max. These guys are going to fix you up as good as new," Summer said as she patted Max's hand.

As the skids touched down, Alex could see the hospital crew waiting for them. In seconds, Max was unloaded and headed to the cath lab, where the team was waiting for him.

"What are we going to do?" Roy asked.

"I can fly back with Roy and call in someone to take the rest of the shift with me," Summer volunteered, though Alex could see that she didn't want to leave her coworker.

"Roy, if you can call Dispatch, I'll call the Marathon crew and let them know they're covering all the Keys until I can get a second crew together," Alex said. "Summer, if you can call Jo and get her to go to Max's and get Stacey, I'll start calling the rest of the crew."

With everyone assigned a duty, Alex and Summer headed into the emergency room while Roy lifted off to head back to headquarters.

"Did you find a crew?" Summer asked before taking a seat in the waiting room outside the cath lab, where they'd been told they could wait.

"Dylan and Casey are headed in now," Alex said. "You?"

"Jo's headed to Max's to get Stacey, but they're still hours out," Summer said, taking a seat on a waiting-room couch that didn't look like it had been bought for comfort. She'd been tired when she and Max had returned from their last flight together. With both her feet and her back aching, she couldn't have flown another call tonight.

Alex was right. She couldn't keep continuing working like this. A lot of women continued to fly while pregnant, but she'd never known one to do it carrying twins. She'd saved up her vacation time and she had her savings to help cover her time off. If she started picking up shifts in the emergency room, she would be able to cover most of her leave. Because no matter how much Alex insisted, she wasn't going to let him support her. Somehow, she would make it work.

Her eyes slipped closed, and her mind drifted off to a place where there were no worries about bills or work. She felt someone lift her legs onto the couch and undo her shoes. A blanket covered her, and she snuggled into it. Alex. He wasn't really a bad guy. She thought he might have a hero complex, though. Always wanting to take care of her.

It was as if he truly wanted to be that Prince Charming who saved poor Cinderella. She'd spent her own life taking care of others with no one ever taking care of her. What must it feel like to be rescued like that? Not that she would ever know. After all, she would never be princess material.

It was the sound of her name that brought her out of her dreams. And Alex's name. Someone, a woman, was talking about her and Alex. Was it his mother? No. Alex's mother didn't even know Max. There was no reason she would be here. It had to be Jo or Stacey. They were coming to the hospital. But if was them, she'd slept a lot longer than she should have. She needed to get up and check on Max. She just needed another moment to rest her eyes.

"When interviewed, Prince Nicholas, the Crown Prince of Soura, refused to comment," a woman said, her voice carrying across the room from the television.

Summer's eyes flashed open as she expected to see Debbie Duncan's morning show on, but this woman wasn't the blond host who'd been giving updates about Summer and Alex for the last week. This woman was older, her natural brown hair lacquered in a perfect dome around her face. Her plain black glasses gave her a look of authority.

No, this wasn't the Miami morning-show host. This was someone a lot more dangerous.

"Sorry, I left you. I had hoped you'd still be asleep," Alex said as he rushed back into the room. "I stepped out with the cardiologist to see Max. He's in recovery."

Summer ignored him as she searched the cushions for the remote. It had to be there. Where had it gone?

"What's wrong?" Alex said.

He was staring at her like she was a crazy woman. Maybe she was. Had she dreamed the whole thing?

Her hand touched something hard and plastic under the last cushion on the couch. Bingo.

"They were talking about us on the television," she said as she used the remote to back up the television until a picture of Prince Nicholas came on the screen. She went back farther until there was a picture of both her and Alex together—a picture she had never seen before.

"Someone was following us the night we went out with my mother," Alex said. He walked closer to the television, where a picture of Alex and Summer at the restaurant with his mother was frozen on the screen.

Summer hit Play and they listened to the news anchor relate the story of their rescue of the young boy, Scottie, and the information that had come from Debbie Duncan's morning show about the two of them expecting twins.

When the picture of Nicholas came on, Alex took the remote from her and turned up the volume. "Further investigation has led to some speculation that there is some connection between the royal family of the Mediterranean country of Soura and this doctor. Something that the small country's population has now taken an interest in. When questioned by a Soura journalist, Crown Prince Nicholas refused to make any comments, something seen as unusual for this outspoken member of the royal family."

The woman ended the segment and went on to what had to be more newsworthy than a story about a doctor and pregnant nurse.

"I need to make some phone calls," Alex said.

Summer watched him pull out his phone and begin to scroll through his contacts. "Max is okay?"

"Sorry, yes. Two stents to the blocked vessels and the prognosis is good. They'll take him to a room on the cardiac floor as soon as he's more awake and you can see him there," Alex said as he punched a number on his phone.

Expecting that he was calling either his father or his mother, she was surprised to hear him talking to a lawyer. Who had a lawyer's personal number? Who had the nerve to call a lawyer this early in the morning? Someone who had a Hollywood star as his mother and the king of a country as a father, it seemed. She and Alex came from such different worlds.

And that fact would be even clearer if Summer's own past came to light. What if someone got in touch with her mother? Their contact with each other had been minimal since Summer had left home. Her mother had never understood why Summer had needed to leave and had made it plain that she'd expected her daughter to stay to help with the bills. Summer sent her mother a check each month to help. It was all she could do for the woman who had raised her.

"I just spoke to Jo," Alex said as he walked over to where Summer was staring out the window, as the sun began to rise. "They should be here in another hour. She's going to stay with Stacey until Max's brother gets into town.

"As soon as they get here, we can take a car to the airport. My mother is having her pilot meet us there."

She couldn't help but be impressed that the man only had to ask to have a private jet at his beck and call.

"Look at you, acting all princely," she teased. Not that there was anything funny about the situation that both of them were in. "How did the two of us go from local heroes to international celebrities?"

"This is my fault. I should have refused to do the interview with Debbie no matter how much pressure I was under from the guys in marketing." Alex started to run his hands through his hair.

Before she could stop herself, her hands began to comb through the dark brown strands, smoothing the ends back down. "It's not your fault. Maybe the interview wasn't the smartest thing we did, but you saw that look in her eyes. Debbie was going to get a story from us no matter if we did the interview on not."

Alex shook his head—whether in agreement or denial, she wasn't sure. He had to be as surprised as she was that the local morning-show reporter was helping to break open a story that his parents had managed to keep hidden for over thirty years.

A half hour later, Jo and Stacey had been deposited in Max's room, so Summer and Alex headed to a small private airport. After arriving and embarking, the pilot requested they buckle their seat belts just as Alex was finishing his last call. Since it had been in a language she didn't understand, only the look on his face told her the discussion had not gone well.

"The story on the Miami news is correct. That journalist who followed me here has run several articles concerning my mother and father's friendship in college, and how I have spent time in the palace since I was young. While my brother and father have refused any comment at this time, there has been a meeting arranged with the prime minister."

"Which means?" Summer asked.

"Which means that my father is probably considering all his options. He could just let this blow over, or he could decide to send out a royal announcement concerning my birth."

"Would that be like those little baby-announcement

cards Jo was talking about?" Summer asked, not surprised when Alex didn't get the humor in the situation.

"You're not taking this seriously," Alex said. "If he announces I'm his illegitimate son, the sky will rain down reporters on us. They'll be everywhere."

Alex waited as an attendant brought in two trays and placed one on each of the tables in front of their seats. "Is there anything else I can get you?" he asked.

Summer lifted the tray and found a full breakfast of eggs and bacon, along with potatoes and fruit. One of the phone calls Alex had made must have been to place an order for their meals.

"This looks amazing, thank you," she said to the man.

"Is this what your life was like before you moved to Key West?" She couldn't imagine it. Alex had always been so self-dependent.

"Sometimes, when I traveled with my mother, but most of the time I was at home," Alex said.

"Where you had a private cook and a nanny, I'm sure," she said. When Alex just shrugged his shoulders, she let it go. How could she ask someone who lived like this to understand the way she had lived? He'd never appreciate the things that living in poverty had driven her to do when she was young. "Maybe it won't be that bad. They're a world away. Your father could be right and it's just time to let everything out in the open. Maybe you're just fighting the inevitable."

"If it means keeping my privacy and protecting you and my children, I'll fight it until the day I die."

And by the fury in Alex's eyes, she knew he intended to do just that. She could only hope he wouldn't regret it.

CHAPTER TEN

SUMMER PLACED THE last of her clothes in the huge walk-in closet as she listened to Jo's update on Max. The man was back to his grumpy self, which they both considered a good sign.

She'd taken a long nap only to find that Alex was still tied up in phone calls when she had awakened. It seemed his mother had suggested a reputable personal publicist, who could handle any stories that broke concerning her and Alex.

"I need to tell Alex everything," she said, interrupting Jo as she was critiquing the care their coworker was getting in the big-city hospital.

"And that's a problem?" Jo asked.

"You know it is," Summer said. It was so hard not to tell her friend the truth about Alex. How had he lived with this secret for so long? Not that she didn't understand secrets. Her own secrets were not something she wanted to share. She didn't want to see that look of disappointment in his face. And what about his mother? If Summer's past came out, she'd never be able to face Melanie again.

"You were young, Summer. It's not as big a deal as you think it is," Jo said.

It would definitely be a big deal if it was splattered

all over the internet and TV screens that the mother of Prince Alexandro Leonelli's twins had once been a teenage shoplifter.

"Just get it over with. Does this mean that you've accepted his offer and are moving in with him for good?" Jo asked. "Because personally, I think it would be good for both of you. It will take some of the financial pressure off you. You can't keep working the way you are for much longer. I bet you can't even see your toes anymore, can you?"

Summer looked down over a rounded belly that seemed to have grown overnight.

"Yes, I can see my toes," she said as she wiggled her toes in a thick rug that covered the closet floor, happy that she could still see the tip of both of her big toes. "And, yes, I'm staying with Alex for now. But I'll be staying on my side of the house," Summer said before her friend could get any ideas.

"For now," Jo said, following with a laugh. "Want to make a bet on how long it takes for one of you to find your way to the other's side of the house?"

"No, I do not," Summer said. She didn't want to think about their sleeping arrangements. So far, she had managed to keep herself away from Alex's bed, though she'd been tempted. But the two of them had enough complications as it was. Alex had already turned their one night of sex into a sign that they had a future together, something she would deny no matter how her heart was arguing with her brain.

Besides, his mother was staying on his side of the house. There was no way she would take a chance at getting caught sneaking into the woman's son's room.

"Seriously, Summer, Alex isn't going to judge you for something that you did when you were a kid. He probably has his own secrets. We all have something we're not proud of."

Summer knew some of Jo's own secrets. Her friend was determined to feel responsible for her ex-husband's actions. Not the abuse—Jo knew that wasn't her fault. It was the fact that she'd waited too long before she had left that still haunted Jo.

And she couldn't tell her friend that there were a lot of people that might be judging her really soon if the story broke on Alex, and Summer got dragged into it.

Once more, she was reminded of the burden Alex had lived with all of his life. It made it a little easier to understand why he had been so reluctant to share things about his life with her. Like why he'd leave the country without sharing where he was going. He'd grown up hiding from the attention his mother lived with. All he'd ever known was that he needed to keep anything that had to do with his father a secret.

Maybe Melanie was right. The fact that Alex had shared his secret with her now had to have been difficult for him. It had been a true sign that he did trust her now.

She was still thinking about what Melanie said later that afternoon, when Alex appeared at her bedroom door.

"Would you like something to eat? My mother made up some sandwiches for us before she left," Alex said.

"She's gone?" Summer asked, not sure if that was a good thing or not. It had been nice to have a buffer between her and Alex in the evenings.

"You were sleeping and she didn't want to disturb you. It was decided that her presence here could add to the attention we receive. She'll be back soon, though. She's so excited about the babies. She'll take on all of the paparazzi if they get in her way when they're born."

Summer had no doubt the woman was up for the challenge. She'd managed to raise a son out of the limelight. She had to be very talented in avoiding the reporters.

"My father is just as happy, though I know he won't be able to come to the States anytime soon."

She didn't even want to think about what having a king for a grandfather meant for her children. Having her children keep the kind of secret Alex had lived with wasn't something that she could imagine.

"Sandwich?" Alex asked again. "I've been stuck on the phone all day. We can eat outside by the pool."

As they carried the food outside, Summer could see the lines and shadows under his eyes from his lack of sleep in the last twenty-four hours. She hated to be the person to add to his worries.

"Did it go well with the publicist?" she asked.

"As well as it could. My mother assures me that the woman has been trusted with secrets much bigger than ours," Alex said.

She had to tell him now. "I was arrested when I was seventeen for shoplifting," she said, the words pouring out of her mouth without a filter to lessen the awfulness of the truth.

She waited for Alex to react. She waited to see the shock, the disappointment she expected. But none of it came. After laying down his sandwich, he turned his eyes to her. But it wasn't disgust or disappointment she saw. Was it sympathy? She didn't need his sympathy. She'd had enough of that growing up. Sympathy from the teachers when she didn't have half the supplies from the school each year. Sympathy from the food-service workers who snuck in extra servings of food that weren't covered by the free-lunch program. Sympathy from the few friends that weren't too embarrassed to be seen with her in her hand-me-down clothes purchased at the thrift store.

"It was a long time ago, but I thought you should know. You should probably tell the publicist, too." Unable to sit there a moment longer, she stood and left the table. She wondered if his mother would suggest he count the silverware now.

Alex waited a moment before following her inside. She needed a moment to deal with whatever this whole media mess had dragged up in her past. Whatever had happened in her childhood was causing her a lot of pain. They'd never finished the conversation they'd had before Max had collapsed and he knew that they were tied together.

"I'm sorry," Summer said when he stepped in the room. She was sitting on a rug, where various baby clothes had been separated into stacks. She looked so young, so innocent.

"I don't understand why you are apologizing. You have nothing to be sorry about," he said as he took a seat beside her. He picked up a tiny aqua-and-orange football jersey. He laid it down, then picked up a pink dress with ruffles around the edges. It was hard to comprehend that in just a number of weeks there would be a baby boy and a baby girl wearing these. They were so tiny.

"How did I get here?" Summer asked.

Knowing it wasn't meant as a question for him, he didn't respond. He suspected that she had taken a path much different than the one he'd taken that had brought him to the Florida Keys.

"It was only through scholarships and student loans that I managed to even finish nursing school. These babies will be in college by the time I get those loans paid off," she said, rubbing her abdomen.

She'd never mentioned the loans before. Probably because she knew he'd offer to pay them for her.

"And this..." She spread her arms and looked around the room. "I never imagined anything like this for me."

"What did you imagine?" he asked. Knowing where Summer came from and where she had planned to go might answer a lot of the unanswered questions he had about who had hurt her.

"Freedom. Escape. A life far away from my hometown. Independence," Summer said. She leaned back and stretched out on the carpet. Staring up at the ceiling, she smiled. "What do you call all this fancy woodwork on the ceiling?"

Stretching out beside her, he studied the wooden framed panels that covered the ceiling.

"It's a coffered ceiling," he said. "It's just an architecture feature. If you don't like it, we can have it removed."

Her laugh wasn't one of humor. "See. You don't like something you just have it removed. I looked up at the same water stain over my bed for my whole childhood. My whole bedroom would fit inside of your closet. Twice. I can't relate to your life. It's too foreign. Just like my life growing up would be foreign to you."

"It didn't seem that we were that different before I went away, did it?" he asked. "Am I so different now?"

She turned her head toward him; her lips were barely a breath from his. Her hair smelled of sunshine and honeysuckle. Had he moved closer? Or had she?

"No, you didn't. It seems I had done a good job of putting that time of my life in the past. But the past is always there. Your past. Your parents' past. My past. My parents' past. It's always there," she said.

"Tell me about it. The part of your past that's bothering you now," he said. Leaning over her, he brushed his hand across her cheek. "I've shared my secrets. Trust me with yours."

"There's certainly no king hidden in my ancestry. That, I'm sure. My parents grew up in the same little town in Texas as I did. The paper mill was the biggest employer there. Something you'd know if you ever drove through the town. There's no mistaking the smell of a paper mill." She turned her face back to the ceiling. "It probably wasn't as bad as I imagine it. I think I just saw the worst of the place. Not that there's really any good place to grow up poor. To say I grew up on the wrong side of the railroad tracks would not be wrong, except we were almost on top of the tracks, since they ran right beside our trailer."

"I'm sorry your childhood was so hard," Alex said.

"It wasn't always bad. For the first few years I think I was happy. We had food and clothes. I don't remember thinking I was any different than my friends then."

"What changed? Who left you, Summer?" he asked.

"My daddy left when I was around five. Or maybe six. I should know that, shouldn't I? But it doesn't really matter. He married my mother when she got pregnant. The marriage lasted a few years. More than a lot of marriages in those circumstances. End of story. Not much different than a lot of people's story."

So that was why she'd gotten mad when he'd suggested they marry. At least that was part of it. There was sure to be something deeper than her parents' failed marriage.

"So things were hard for you and your mom when your father left," Alex said.

"Hard? We lived on my mother's grocery-store

paychecks. I helped when I got old enough to work. I babysat, cleaned houses. I even worked at one of those automatic car washes, where you get paid by the day. But it was never enough. So when things were a little short at the end of the month, I learned how to pick up a few things at the store without getting caught."

"Do you think I'm going to judge you because you got caught shoplifting at the grocery store when you were hungry?" he asked. Her body was so tense. He wanted to take her in his arms. He wanted to feel her relax against his body. He wanted her to trust him to take care of her.

"No. I don't think anyone would condemn a kid for stealing some food when they were hungry. I'm pretty sure the people at the market knew what I was doing."

"But you can't forgive yourself?" he asked.

"If I'd stopped there. Sure. That's not what I'm worried about the media getting a hold of. It's the four-hundred-dollar dress I stole for senior prom. How do you think it's going to look if it comes out that the mother of King Christos's grandchildren went to jail for stealing a stupid dress?"

"Was it at least a pretty dress?" Alex asked.

"What?" she asked as she turned toward him. "What difference does that make?"

"I just think our publicist should know what she's dealing with. It would be a lot better if she knew that you at least had good taste."

"You're joking, right?" she asked.

"It's okay, Summer. Do you really think my father, after raising my brother, Nicholas, is going to be shocked because a teenage girl wanted a pretty dress for her senior prom?"

"But the media..." she said.

He pulled her against him, then rested his forehead

against hers. He reached between the two of them and rubbed his hand in circles over her abdomen. "Let me take care of the media. You have enough to take care of with these two."

She leaned her head on his shoulder and for that moment things were all right with Alex's world. Tomorrow the paparazzi might be chasing the two of them down. Tonight, they were together.

"You really don't care, do you?" she asked, her voice breathy and sweet.

"Do you believe that this one thing in your past defines you? You're an excellent nurse, a great friend and you are going to be a great mother to our babies. That's who you are, who you've become. It might not be what you imagined for your life, but you can be proud of the person you are."

His hand brushed back her hair and he kissed her forehead, then continued a path down to her temple and her cheek. He pressed a kiss behind her ear to that secret spot that brought a gasp from her lips. Her body arched into his. His hand went to another hidden spot behind her knee before running it up her bare legs until it met the fabric of her shorts.

"Don't stop," she said as she began to unbutton his shirt.

"Never," he said, before continuing his dual paths, his lips trailing down to her lips while his hand traveled up to the juncture between her legs.

He kept his kisses gentle, teasing her lips until she opened hers in a sweet smile.

"You're tired, let me..." Her voice broke on a gasp as his hand dipped under her shorts.

"I'm fine. Better than fine," he said as his fingers touched her soft folds. She was so wet. For him. She wanted him and there was nothing he wanted more than her.

She moved against his fingers and his own body strained against the bonds of his clothing. He wanted to pleasure her, to fill her. To make love to her, taste her and excite her until she couldn't imagine a life without him touching her. Adrenaline shot through him with that thought and his heart sped up to a dangerous rate. Holding himself back might kill him, but he wouldn't rush this for her.

He rolled her onto her back while she still fought against the buttons of his shirt. He ripped it from her hands, scattering buttons across the room as he flung it to the side.

"Now you?" he asked, knowing this woman didn't like demands. The cotton T-shirt landed beside his shirt. Her bra followed. "Your shorts?"

She arched her back to push down her shorts and he ran one finger between her folds before plunging it into her. She gasped and her legs tightened around his hand as his finger continued to pump inside her. He could enter her now, end this torture for both of them, but she refused to take anything from him. He could give her this first.

His mouth kissed the top of each of her pretty breasts. Her skin smelled of the same honeysuckle as her hair.

Her breath caught as his lips continued down until his mouth took one tight nipple into his mouth. He sucked hard and her core clenched his finger. She was so tight and needy.

He ran his thumb between her slick folds as his finger pumped inside her until the sound of her labored panting filled the room. He took another deep suck as her body arched up against his hand.

"Mine," he growled before his lips took hers, swallowing her gasp with a kiss that held none of the gentleness he'd shown her before. His tongue tangled with hers as her core throbbed against his hand, her legs tightening around his hand as she rode out her climax.

His body was on fire with the need to take her. Such a primal need. Such a humbling weakness. His life's breath seemed to depend on this one moment.

His shorts disappeared. Had he removed them or had she? When her hand clenched the length of him in her tight fist, that mystery was solved. She guided him into her, her breath coming as fast as his.

"More," she demanded.

He answered her demand with one thrust straight to the deepest part of her. She answered him back, taking him deeper, faster, with each stroke. There was nothing left in their world as this frenzied need to mate engulfed them.

Her body exploded around him as a new orgasm gripped her, taking him with her as his own orgasm tore through him.

A weakness like he had never known filled Alex's limbs. He rolled to his back, taking Summer with him. Her hair tickled the inside of his arm, where her head rested on his shoulder.

The axis of his world had been changed forever. He had turned into some primal male who had just marked his female as his own. Did she know? Had she felt that desperate need that had driven him? This woman was his now. He'd fight for her and their children with every breath of their body. He could never leave her.

And he would prove it to her if it took every moment of the rest of his lifetime.

CHAPTER ELEVEN

"YOU KNOW HOW much I hate these things," Summer said. Being part of the crew that got stuck having to take part in the show-and-tell day at the local elementary school wasn't her idea of a fun outing, no matter how much her boss tried to sell it to them. Over a hundred kids running back and forth between a helicopter, an ambulance and a police car had disaster written all over it.

She was going to use the pregnancy card, but Alex was already making some noise about grounding her. After she'd weighed in that morning, Alex had made their new pilot, Sam, confirm that she was not over the weight limit with the fuel they were carrying.

He'd been joking, mostly. And she really couldn't complain. For the last week, the man had been totally undemanding.

Except in her bed, which he had somehow taken over. Her hormones had never been so happy. And if she was honest, neither had she. She was playing a dangerous game with her emotions, but she was willing to risk it.

He'd even listened to her thoughts about when she would need to stop flying altogether. She'd made it to thirty weeks. She knew her days of flying were numbered, but he'd finally agreed, as her boss, to allow her to fly as long as her physician said it was safe and she could still do her job. He'd argued that as the father of her babies he deserved an extra vote in the matter. He'd lost that argument. She'd agreed that she would continue to stay with him for the rest of the pregnancy and at least the first few weeks after the babies were born. She refused to tell him that her happy hormones had helped him with the vote on that one.

"I would love to go with you, but I've got an afternoon shift at the hospital, and I still have to deal with implementing some of Corporate's new policy changes," Alex said.

"Maybe we'll get lucky and there'll be a pileup on the highway," Jo said, her perky but sadistic smile making Summer wonder if she was serious.

"It's not that bad. It's only for an hour," Alex said as his phone rang. The sharp look he gave her said it was one of two people, his father or his publicist. A call from either of them could contain bad news.

"Let's go," Summer said to Jo. "We're not going to talk him out of it."

"I think we should ask for hazard pay," Jo said.

Summer pulled the door to Alex's office closed behind them. Her friend looked back at the door and her eyes narrowed.

"When are you going to tell me what's going on? Every time I turn around Alex is on some hush-hush phone call. I know it has something to do with all those rumors hitting the internet. The ones about him being tied up with some royal family. That's where he went, isn't it?"

Summer wanted to tell her friend everything. She wanted to spill her guts. She'd even discussed it with Alex. Their crew could be trusted. They'd been nothing but protective when some of them had been contacted by the press. No one had commented when they'd been asked about their boss's disappearance.

But no matter how much she thought it would be better to just tell all of Alex's secrets so that they could move on, it wasn't her place. He'd trusted her and she wouldn't let him down. For now, they would just wait out the rumors.

"You know how much he's got on him right now. Debbie Duncan and all the things she's saying will die down soon," Summer said, not believing her own words. If she'd learned anything since she and Alex had been dragged into this mess, it was that the more someone learned about them, the more they wanted. No matter what Alex said, the local reporters smelled blood and they weren't going to stop hounding them until they got the last drop.

The hour flew by as one child followed another in an organized line, as much as you could organize a field full of kids, up to the helicopter. Each one took their turn sitting in the passenger seat while Sam talked about the basic parts of the helicopter and Jo explained the medical equipment they used. Summer had set up an impromptu safety-education post using their stretcher as a table, along with some of the supplies donated by the ambulance crew stationed beside them. She needed to have Alex talk to the corporate office about providing some give-away items for the kids.

"How about a chair?" one of the teachers said. It was a nice offer, considering the woman looked like she was dead on her feet herself.

"I'm Kathy. That's my class by the police car. I just wanted to tell you how much we appreciate you taking your time with the kids."

Summer winced. She shouldn't have complained about having to take time out for these kids. This poor woman managed to handle them every day. And one day it would be Summer's own kids running and playing on this field. Maybe Kathy would even be their teacher.

"We appreciate you, too. I have to admit I would be more comfortable scraping up some poor accident victim off the road and loading them into the copter for a ride to the nearest emergency room." The look the woman gave Summer told her she'd been a little too honest. Not everyone understood the humor of first responders.

"You're that woman on the beach from the video, aren't you? The one that helped save that kid from drowning?"

It seemed she would be known as "that woman on the beach" forever now. "If you are talking about the video where the real hot guy risked his life to save a young boy, yes, I am."

The teacher laughed as her cheeks turned rosy. "I'm being rude. I'm sorry."

"It's okay. It's been an interesting experience going viral." Summer could only hope it would be her last. But with her children having a Hollywood star for a grandmother, she was doubtful. Was it too much to ask to spend a quiet life in the islands? She was beginning to understand why Alex was fighting so hard to keep his identity a secret. How would she ever know if someone wanted a play date with her kids or if they just wanted to say they knew the grandchildren of Melanie Leonelli?

Another group of kids descended on her and she went through some safety rules that she hoped would keep these kids out of her helicopter, then she handed out some cartoon bandages.

Even with sitting in the chair, her back was aching

by the time the last group of children headed back to their class.

"Next year we're sending Max and Casey," Jo said as she climbed back into her seat in the helicopter.

Summer had no idea what next year looked like for her. She'd have two babies to consider then. Finding childcare for twenty-four-hour coverage for one child would be hard. She had to find someone willing to do it for two babies.

She didn't want to admit it, but staying with Alex would at least take some pressure off of her finances. And if things continued as they were, maybe the two of them could work together on the childcare problem. Alex had said he wanted to be a hands-on dad. She just hoped he realized how many hands he was going to need with twins.

The voice of a dispatcher came over their headphones. Summer and Jo groaned in unison.

Their pilot laughed as she changed their course. "Three-vehicle MVA on the Highway One bridge. It looks like your wish was just running a little behind schedule, Jo."

By the time they had returned to headquarters, the pain in Summer's back was throbbing. She carefully sat down into the first recliner she came to. "I can't go another step."

"I thought they'd never get that guy out of the car. How he managed to escape with only a broken femur and a few crushed ribs, I don't know," Jo said as she passed by on her way to the kitchen.

"Can you bring me a water?" Summer asked. She knew she was behind on her fluid intake. Constantly chugging on a water bottle wasn't an option when you were ten thousand feet in the air.

Closing her eyes, she laid her hands across her belly and took deep breaths. Something wasn't right. Instead of the pain in her back subsiding, as it usually did when she put her feet up, it was getting worse.

Her eyes opened when she felt the cold of a bottle pressed into her hands.

"Are you okay?" Jo asked. Her friend's eyes went into nurse mode.

But it wasn't what Summer saw in her friend's eyes that alarmed her. It was the picture of a woman on the television screen across from her.

"I need to turn up the sound," Summer said as she pushed the bottle back into Jo's hands and started to stand.

"I'll get it. You sit down," Jo said, grabbing the remote and turning up the volume on the local news channel.

"Summer's mother states that she has been estranged from her daughter since Summer left home at eighteen and has not been back. Her mother blames the fact that Summer turned her back on her family on the fact that Summer had a problem with always wanting more than what she had, claiming that her daughter had been caught shoplifting and had spent time in jail."

"Yeah, I wanted more. I wanted to have food in the cabinets when I was hungry and clothes that weren't worn out and stained when I got them. What kid doesn't want more when they're made fun of because of the way they dress or where they live?" All of a sudden, her body became cold and clammy. She was glad she was sitting because she knew her weak legs wouldn't have been able to support her. "Jo, call Alex. I need Alex."

"It's okay. No one's going to listen to those reporters.

We all have things we wished we hadn't done as kids. And you had every right to want more than what you had as a kid. No kid should ever go hungry."

"I don't care what they say. Not now. Right now, all I need is for you to call Alex and tell him we're on the way to the hospital. I'm pretty sure my water just broke."

Jo's face turned white as her eyes locked on the puddle of water between Summer's legs. They were both experts in the smell of bodily fluids.

"Maybe it's just a leak," Jo said, always the optimist. Not even a plumber would call the size of the puddle that Summer was sitting in a leak.

"Contractions?" Jo asked as she laid her hand across Summer's abdomen.

"Maybe. I've been having some back pain all day. I didn't think anything of it. I'm only thirty weeks. I'm not supposed to have contractions yet," Summer said. There was panic in her voice, and she fought to control it. She needed to stay calm for her babies.

Insisting that flying would cut down on the drive time to the hospital, Jo went to find Sam while she called Dispatch, leaving Summer alone with her fears. She should have known something was wrong when the back pain didn't go away. She should have listened to her body more. She should have listened when Alex told her to cut back on working, even though she knew she needed the money to provide for the babies.

What if something happened to the babies because she had been too proud to let Alex help her? How would she be able to live with the knowledge that she'd let her pride come before them?

She looked up at the television screen, which had shown a picture of her mother just seconds before. Her own mother had spilled all of Summer's secrets.

No matter what happened, Summer would take care of these babies. She would protect them with her life. She would not lose them.

CHAPTER TWELVE

ALEX WAS FURIOUS the moment his publicist called to tell him about Summer's mother being interviewed. How could a woman say things like that about her daughter? It made him wonder if Summer's home life as a child had been even worse than she had admitted.

"Dr. Leonelli, there's a call coming in on the radio for you. It's from the flight crew," said Anna, the charge nurse.

"Go ahead," Alex said into the radio, his voice sharp and clipped. He reminded himself that no matter what was going on in his personal life, he needed to remain professional. It wasn't unusual for him to receive calls from the crew for instructions when they had any medical-care questions. It was part of his job as medical chief of the crew.

"Alex, this is Jo. We're bringing in a patient for OB triage. Thirty weeks gestation, premature rupture of membranes."

Jo knew the process for caring for the pregnant woman in flight. They had specific procedures in place, including transferring any preterm pregnancy to a Miami hospital unless the delivery seemed imminent. They were seldom involved until they received a call from the hospital for transport because most preterm patients arrived by car or ambulance. Why was this woman even being flown?

An uneasy feeling settled in his stomach. Summer was primary nurse today. Why was Jo calling instead of her? "Jo, let me talk to Summer."

"Now is not a good time," Jo said.

"When?" he asked. PROM at thirty weeks was not common and Summer hadn't had any signs of preterm labor. At least none she'd shared with him.

"Just a few minutes ago," Jo said. "I've only palpated one contraction and it was mild. She says she feels the babies moving. All she wants is for you to call Dr. Wade for her. We have an ETA of three minutes."

Alex's fingers were already speeding through his contacts on his phone.

"Give me her vitals. How's her blood pressure?" He knew that her problem wasn't her hypotension. This was something entirely different. Something unexpected. Thirty-week babies had a good survival rate. But there could be complications. There always could be complications with twins.

"She's okay, Alex, I promise," Jo said.

He was waiting at the emergency-room doors as Jo and Sam rushed through with the stretcher carrying Summer. "I told them I could walk, but they refused to let me. It's like I'm talking to two strangers."

Just the sound of her voice calmed his fears. His heartbeat settled into a steady rhythm and his breathing became easier. She was okay for now. They would tackle the rest after the obstetrician examined her, though he had already begun to make inquiries about which hospitals had the best NICU unit in the Miami area.

"I told her to shut up and enjoy the ride," Jo said, as she pushed the stretcher through the emergency room.

"The labor and delivery nurses are expecting you. I'll be up there as soon as my relief gets here. She agreed to come in early for me so it won't be very long." Alex couldn't leave the emergency room uncovered though he wanted nothing more than to be with Summer.

"Text me if you need me," he called after them as they headed down the hall that led to the elevator to the L&D unit. He stood and watched them until they disappeared into the elevator. He didn't want to be one of those overbearing fathers. He'd give them fifteen minutes to get Summer to her room and the monitors applied before he called and started hounding the nurses.

As he went back to his desk to finish up discharge orders on a patient, he remembered the call he'd received from the publicist. The last thing Summer needed was to hear about her mother's interview on the television while she was lying in a hospital bed. Who knew what that would do to her? He needed to protect her. He pulled out his phone and began to type.

Jo, try to keep Summer from watching any television.

Seconds later her reply came over his phone.

Too late, boss. She's already seen it.

When?

Right before her water broke. She's handling it. She's stronger than you think.

Stronger? His publicist had told him that her mother had made hard, cold comments that were sure to damage Summer's reputation. He didn't care about Summer's reputation, or his own. All he cared about was her and the babies. Was watching her mother's interview what had caused this? Had the stress been too much, sending her into labor?

This would never have happened if it wasn't for him and the rumors coming from Soura. He'd tried to protect her, but it seemed he had only made things worse.

The first beat of Baby A's heart started a trickle of Summer's tears. When the beat of Baby B's heartbeat joined in, the trickle became a waterfall. She would never in her life hear such a beautiful sound. The sound of both heartbeats, with each beating its own rhythm while still blending together into a beautiful ballad. She'd managed to keep a calm facade, never letting Alex or Jo see just how scared she was, but she couldn't hold it in any longer.

"Dr. Wade called and is only five minutes out. I did inform her that you were still leaking fluid and that it had tested positive for ROM ruptured membranes.Besides monitoring, she's ordered an ultrasound for dating the babies' gestation age and estimating weight, and also for measuring amniotic fluid. Do you have any questions for me?" the nurse asked.

"I don't think so. Not now." She was sure she would have a hundred questions before this was over with.

Summer had never felt so much out of her element. Labor and delivery was one of the few areas she hadn't worked as a nurse. Give her a severed limb or a cardiac emergency and she was fine. Give her a patient in labor and the most she knew was how to catch the baby, resuscitate it if necessary and keep the mother from bleeding out. All the testing and monitoring that she knew she was in for now was just foreign. What she did know was that it was too early for these two to be born.

"You just need to stay in there a little bit longer, guys," she whispered to her little ones. She placed her hands against her belly and laughed when one of them kicked against her hand. They were strong and active babies. Everything was going to be okay.

"Would you like me to turn the television on for you?" the nurse asked.

"No," Summer said. Her voice seemed to bounce around the oversize room, startling both her and the nurse. Even the babies responded with a flurry of movement. She couldn't stand the thought of these nurses hearing the interview that her mother had given. At least not while she was a patient here. After what her mother had said to the press, everyone would think that she was some gold digger.

"Sorry, but no. I don't want it on." She might not even want to turn on a television again after seeing how the truth could be twisted so easily. She'd done the crime and she'd paid the price. Shaming her now only had one purpose and that was to raise ratings. Why would someone like Debbie Duncan or any of the other people who called themselves reporters ever be interested in little old her? Oh, yeah. Because she was carrying his babies. She suddenly remembered that she had forgotten to warn Alex. "Can my friends come in, though?"

"Sure, I'll get them. And Dr. Leonelli called to say he'd be here in just a few minutes."

Once the nurse was gone, Summer tried to relax in the bed. Her back still ached and occasionally she felt a tightening spread over her abdomen that might be a contraction. Fortunately, they were very far apart.

She watched the labor monitor for a few minutes, remembering enough from nursing school to understand what all the squiggly lines stood for. She assumed since no one was rushing in the door that none of the lines showed anything ominous.

But soon she was bored and began taking in the rest of the room. It was a pretty room, decorated with a floral wallpaper of bright pinks and greens against a white background. The whole place had a happy vibe, though she wasn't sure what was up with the fluffy couches that were so big that they could seat up to seven or eight people. What was it people did here that they needed that size of an audience?

Still, the place was so different than the emergency room that was just one floor down that it was fascinating. They could have been different realms. Happiness was not something you found in the emergency room. If you were happy you didn't go to the ER. Except maybe Max, if he was going around feeling happy someone might want to rush him into the hospital. They'd heard from his wife that he was being a horrible patient. It wasn't a surprise.

Her stomach tightened and she took in a deep breath the way she'd coached pregnant patients to do when they'd had to fly out of Key West.

A coach? She didn't have a coach. She hadn't even taken any classes for labor. She and Dr. Wade had planned a C-section because of the twin factor. What if they couldn't stop her labor? Would they do a C-section today?

They didn't have even have car seats ready. The cribs that Alex had helped her pick out were still in their boxes. They weren't ready for any of this.

Before she could panic, a new nurse came into the room carrying a tray of supplies and a large bag of fluid, along with another, smaller bag. Summer recognized the med as soon as she read the label. They were going to start her on IV magnesium sulfate in order to stop her labor? So she was in labor and they were going to try to stop it? What if they couldn't? It was much too soon for these babies to come into the world. She'd assumed that she'd just be on bed rest for a few weeks until the babies were old enough to deliver.

She should know better. She was a nurse. She looked at the clock on the wall. Where was Alex? She needed him to be here.

And when had she gotten dependent on Alex? Since he'd come back and inserted himself in every part of her life? No, in their babies' lives. Not hers. Just the fact that she wanted him right by her side was scary, though. They were getting too involved. She was getting too dependent on him. Because she was too in love with him? So in love that she was forgetting all the reasons why she couldn't trust him? Forgetting that he might someday disappear like he had before? Like her father had disappeared?

She tried not to flinch when the nurse stuck the large bore IV needle in her arm at the same time that another contraction had started. Were they getting closer together? Looking at the monitor, she tried to measure out the minutes.

The door opened and the man she had been thinking about too much entered the room, followed by her obstetrician. She wasn't sure which one she was the most glad to see. And that was a big problem. One that she would have to deal with later because the serious look in her doctor's eyes said she wasn't going to like what she had to say.

"How are you feeling?" the doctor asked as she

looked over to where the nurse was busy taping up Summer's IV.

"I've had a couple contractions, but they weren't bad. More like cramps," Summer said, trying to stay positive, no matter that the nurse was programming an IV medication that would make her feel flushed and lethargic. She remembered that from nursing school, too. Not that it would make any difference.

"I'll do whatever it is to keep these babies inside of me," she blurted out as her nerves finally got the best of her. She really didn't like to be on this side of the bed. She wanted to be the one making the decisions. Not waiting for others to make them for her.

"I know you will. That's what we need to talk about. The ultrasound tech should be here soon, and I need to perform a pelvic exam. Then we'll talk about our next move. We definitely want to get some steroids on board for the babies, so the nurses will give you your first injection here."

"You mean the next move as in to transfer me to another hospital?" Summer asked, though she knew the answer. She'd always known she couldn't deliver preterm babies here.

"I'm afraid so and probably soon. I just want to confirm that you're not dilated and are safe enough to fly first. Your contractions are not regular, so that's a good sign, and the mag will slow them down if not stop them altogether."

From then on things seemed to move faster than she could keep up with, partly because the magnesium drip had her light-headed and nauseated. She felt like she'd partied too hard the night before, not a feeling she was fond of.

And Alex sat beside her bed the whole time. He'd

held her hand while Dr. Wade had examined her. He'd held her hair when she'd been sick from the medicine. And when Dr. Wade had declared her safe to fly, he'd been on the phone making arrangements for her transport while giving Katie the access code to his gate and house so that she could pack bags for the two of them.

She remembered about needing to tell Alex about her mother, but then realized his publicist had probably already contacted him. It was what he was paying the woman for. He wouldn't have mentioned it to her because he didn't want to upset her. Right now, with the worry for the babies, nothing her mother could have said would have bothered her. But he didn't know that.

He was so determined to take care of her and the babies—babies he'd only known about for a month, but whom she knew he already loved as much as she did. How had that happened so fast? The same way she had begun to realize she was in love with him? Had always been in love with him?

"You don't have to fly over with me. For that matter, I don't see why I'm not going by ground. Dr. Wade says I'm barely dilated, and the babies are doing great. The mag is doing its job. I'm stable." It was the second time Summer had gone over this with him, but he wasn't hearing her.

So, less than two hours from when her water had broken, Summer found herself once more on the wrong side of the helicopter. She wasn't a fan. It was a lot more fun sitting up in the seat watching monitors and landscape instead of being stuck staring up at the ceiling on an aircraft. Still, it was better than lying helpless in a bed while people scurried all around her. Fortunately for all of them, the hum of the rotors put her right to sleep.

CHAPTER THIRTEEN

ALEX KNEW IT wasn't a good idea the moment they turned on the TV to the television-and-film award show. He was trying to keep Summer insulated from all the Hollywood gossip that they had suddenly become a part of. While he'd been approached multiple times now by reporters wanting information about him and his connection to Soura, Summer had been protected inside the hospital, where no type of press was allowed. Knowing that had made it a lot easier for him to work the last week, though he returned to Miami every other day.

It was the nights when he couldn't return to the hospital that were hard to endure. He'd found he preferred sleeping in a chair at Summer's side, the sound of the babies' heartbeats in the background, to returning home to a house that was quiet and empty. How had his life changed so much?

"I feel like we should have popcorn or something," Summer said, sitting up with her legs crossed in the bed. Now that the mag had been discontinued, her face once more had a healthy glow and she had returned to her happy self. It had been hard to watch her suffer through the side effects of the medicine.

"I can see if the nurses have some, though I think this is more a champagne type of event," Alex said.

"If I had popcorn I'd throw it at you right now," Summer said as she acted out throwing imaginary popcorn at him.

"I can see I'm going to have to take you to the Oscars next year," he said, brushing the pretend popcorn from his shoulder.

"What? You can do that?" she asked. "You're joking, right?"

"No, I'm not joking. I'm sure my mother could get us in if you want to go."

She seemed to think about it a moment before she shook her head, her happy mood now gone. "No, I don't think that's something I should do."

Alex could understand her reluctance to put herself out there after all the publicity they had recently gotten. Instead of the media's interest dying down, it had increased when news of Summer's preterm labor had broken. It seemed the public had taken an unusual interest in the two of them. His brother had called earlier that day with the news that the television stations in Soura were showing clips of Alex that had been recorded over the years. With so much focus on their lives, his brother had encouraged him to speak with their father. Alex sometimes felt like he was on a train heading straight into a dead-end tunnel with no way to stop the collision ahead of him.

"It's your mom, there," Summer squealed, and the rustle of sudden baby movement came over the monitors. She rubbed at her belly. "Sorry, guys."

There was more movement over the monitor and then the steady sound of two heartbeats returned.

"She sent me a picture of the dress. Isn't it amazing? Look, the host is going to speak to her. Turn the sound up," Summer said, clapping her hands. "I have to admit, this is a lot more exciting when you actually know someone that's been nominated."

"You are looking beautiful tonight, Melanie. We're so glad that you were able to attend," said the bald man dressed in the three-piece suit. Was the man's collar too tight or did he always have that condescending look on his face?

"You know, John, that I'd never miss the chance to support my colleagues," his mother said as she turned and waved to another star before turning back.

"Well, we know that you have a lot going on right now. You've just finished filming and we understand that your son's girlfriend is in the hospital. I know that you have to be so proud of the two of them after that video of them helping to save that young boy came out," said the man.

"I can turn it off," Alex offered. Summer's excitement at seeing his mother in all her Hollywood glory had dimmed.

"I'm always very proud of Alex and Summer. They both are hardworking health-care workers. They make a difference in people's lives every day." Melanie smiled at the man and started to move on.

"Running away isn't going to help. Your mother can handle that weasel," Summer said, and then giggled. "He kind of does look like a weasel in that suit. Maybe you should give him the name of your publicist."

But this man, who from now on would be known as the weasel, had apparently forgotten about the other celebrities that were arriving. Instead, he'd chosen to follow his mother down the red carpet, his microphone still stuck in front of her. "There have been rumors lately of your son somehow being involved with the royal family of Soura. It seems that you were friends with members of the royal family before you moved to the States. Do you have any comments concerning these rumors?"

"Of course, there are rumors. There are always rumors. Isn't that how you make a living?" With no signs of hurrying, his mother waved a bejeweled hand at someone and with the flirty smile she had made famous, continued down the carpet.

Both he and Summe inhaled deep breaths as the camera followed Alex's mother until she disappeared inside the theater.

"It could have been worse," Summer said.

"I think you spoke too soon," Alex said as a photo of Summer and Alex taken from the viral video was suddenly displayed on the screen followed by a picture of Summer on the beach that had to have been taken only days before she had been admitted to the hospital.

"Where did that come from?" Summer asked. "Why would someone want a picture of me just walking on the beach?"

Something in Alex broke. The beach had always been her happy place. Her place of escape.

He'd tried to be nice. He'd given the interview he'd been asked to give. He'd ignored the reporter that had tried to ruin Summer's reputation instead of hunting him down. But still he hadn't been able to protect Summer from some stalker on the beach.

"Why me, Alex? I'm a nobody. According to one reporter I'm basically a gold digger. What is so interesting about me?"

He didn't need to tell her it was all because of him. She knew that. They both did. He turned the television channel until he found one of Summer's favorite shows.

"It will get better." But he wasn't sure anymore. No

matter how many times his publicist assured him that it would.

"We can't keep trying to hide from them. All of this," Summer said as she raised her hands toward the television. "It's not our life. I won't have these babies raised in all of this."

Did that mean she wouldn't let their babies be raised around him? Could he even blame her for being worried after finding out someone had secretly been taking pictures of her? Because she was partly right. This wasn't her life, but it was his. It had always been his life; he had just chosen to ignore it.

"What do they want, Alex?" Summer asked, her eyes focused so intently on him, as if he had the answer to make all of this go away.

And maybe he did. Maybe it was time to give the world what they wanted.

Summer thought she was ready. The doctors had managed to hold off her labor for three weeks. Each week the babies had stayed inside her had decreased their chances of complications, but it also increased the chance of infection from the ruptured membranes. While she'd been treated with antibiotics, the neonatologist and the perinatologist both agreed it was time for delivery.

Summer's only regret was that they'd have to go to the NICU as soon as they were born so they could be watched for any respiratory issues and to ensure they were able to maintain their body temperature. It made her sad and it wasn't the way she had imagined their birth to be, but she understood why the doctors were being cautious. Right now, all she wanted was her babies to be healthy.

Alex stood beside her as they draped her and began

the procedure. Even with two NICU teams in the operating room, the room was extremely quiet. Alex held her hand and she squeezed his when she felt a tug at her abdomen.

"Are you hurting?" the anesthesiologist asked.

She shook her head as she watched Alex's face. A smile spread across it only a second before a cry filled the room. The doctor held the tiny, screaming baby girl over the drape for her to see before handing it to the waiting NICU nurse.

"And here's the second one," the doctor said as she once more felt a tug inside her.

When she didn't hear the answering cry, she looked up at Alex. He was concentrating so hard on something that Summer wanted to reach up and tear down the drape. Once more, a smile lit Alex's face, though she still couldn't hear the cry she wanted to hear.

"Here he is," the doctor said, holding up her son for her to see. Dark eyes blinked down at her. Eyes that she knew would someday match his father's.

"He's a serious one, isn't he?" the doctor asked before he handed him over to the waiting nurse.

"They're beautiful," Summer said to Alex as he strained over the operating table to see the nurses and their babies. "Go on. I'm okay. Go watch over our babies."

Pulling his eyes away from the babies, he gave her a quick kiss and a fast "I love you," then headed across the room.

Summer knew it had been only a spontaneous sentiment. A flash of emotion with all the excitement of the day. How could he not feel emotional after such an experience as watching your babies be born? He didn't really mean it as he loved her like he was in love with her, no matter how much she wished it to be so.

Alex stood beside the wheelchair he'd used to transfer Summer to the NICU. While their daughter continued to expand her lungs with a cry that refused to be ignore, their son was being was sleeping quietly under the warming unit, where the nurses were continuing to monitor him.

"She's going to be a princess," Summer said.

"I know she is," Alex agreed.

"I didn't mean an actual princess. I meant she was going to be spoiled. You know, an everyday princess," Summer said. "Isn't it time for you to go?"

"Let them wait. It serves them right," Alex said.

"It's going to be okay," Summer assured him.

He straightened his tie and smoothed his hands down his suit. "But what if it makes things worse?"

"Does it feel like a mistake?" his father asked as a heavy hand came to rest on Alex's shoulder. "I knew the moment that your mother and I agreed to keep your birth a secret that it was a mistake. At the time, with the way the country was struggling, it seemed the only thing to do. But I can tell you I have always dreamed of this day."

Alex straightened his shoulders. "Well, let's go do this then."

"Where's your mother?" his father asked. "She needs to be there by your side. We will show these fools that there is no weakness to be found here."

"We're not declaring war, Your Majesty," Summer said. Alex could see that she was holding back a laugh.

"As you say," his father agreed. "Let's get this over with. I want to spend some time with my grandchildren before I have to fly home."

"They're not letting—" Summer began before Alex cut her off.

"I'm sure we can arrange something," Alex said. Summer had a lot to learn if she thought that something as insignificant as hospital protocol was going to stop his father from seeing his grandchildren.

Alex wasn't surprised to find his mother entertaining the reporters that had been invited to the press conference. They'd been allowed to use the hospital auditorium only because it was separated from the main hospital, where patient privacy dictated a hospital policy of not allowing press on the premises.

As soon as he and his father entered the room, the hated cameras flashed until all Alex could see were yellow spots that clouded out the faces that shouted out questions in a rapid fire from all directions.

He could have had his father take the lead, but this needed to come from him. He would answer as many questions as possible and hope that once they had their answers, the reporters would leave with a sense that there was no longer a story here.

"Good afternoon. I want to thank you for coming today. I have some things to say and then I will take questions." He looked over at his father and his mother sitting next to him. No matter how this went today, he knew he had their support. He'd dreamed of being able to acknowledge who he was for as long as he could remember. Not the Prince of Soura, or son of the king and a movie star. He wanted to acknowledge that he was Christos and Melanie's son. How the media handled that was their problem. He only hoped that once this was out there would be no more reason for Summer and their children to hide from who they were: his family.

"Today is a special day for our family as we have just welcomed my daughter and son into this world." He waited as a smattering of clapping broke out in the audience.

"With these precious additions to my and Summer's life comes the responsibility of giving them the best life possible. Because of this..." He paused and looked to both sides. It was important for everyone to realize that they were a strong unit. There would be no stories going out that there was any discord between the three of them.

"We have decided that it would be the best of times to acknowledge that not only do I have the pleasure of being the son of the most talented star in the movie industry..." He paused again and waited for the blinding cameras to flash and another round of clapping to end until a silence settled over the room. It was like everyone in the room had inhaled a breath but was now afraid to exhale because they were too scared they might miss something. He'd never understand what drove these people.

"But I am also proud to be the son of His Royal Highness, King Christos Konstantinos of the House of Rothinburg." Alex took in a deep breath and let it out. It was done. There would be no more secrets about who he was. No more reason for these people to haunt his family. Or so he hoped.

He'd watched his mom deal with the media for years and one thing he had noticed was the way she worked to get them on her side of a story. He was counting on this working for him as well. He and his parents ignored the shouted questions that had immediately erupted from the crowd and waited for them to finally settle down so that he could continue.

"If you will all remember this all started because

Summer and I were fortunately at the right place at the right time, and using our training, we saved the life of a young boy whom we both hope will go on to have a long and miraculous life. Even though the results of this act have interrupted our lives, we would never do anything different than what we did that day. It is what we do. It is who we are. We work each day in the hope to make our community, where we will now raise our children, a safe place for all. At no point have I or Summer ever desired to have our lives put into the spotlight that we now find ourselves in. It seems we have somehow gone from local heroes to a target for hurtful stories with no basis of truth and we can't help but wonder how this has happened."

His eyes searched through the faces of the reporters. Did any of them even understand the lines they crossed when they ran stories that could destroy other people's lives? Did they care? He had to believe that they did. There were reporters that were ethical in their reporting.

"Therefore, going forward, we request that you respect our privacy." Alex stopped and took a much-needed breath. This had to be the longest speech he had ever given. It would be the most important in his life. Now was the time to use one of the tricks his mother used.

"Look, guys, I understand the need for a good story. My parents will be answering your questions in a few moments and I'm sure what they have to say will be a lot more interesting than anything I'll say today. I'm a simple small-island doctor who has the privilege to be born to two wonderful people. Summer is a nurse who worked hard to get an education so that she could help others. Her job is to save lives and she's good at it. Let us do our jobs."

He started to leave, ready to end this, when he heard one question rise over the rest. "You refer to you and Summer as a family. Does that mean there will be a royal wedding in your future?"

Alex turned toward the man and smiled. Now this was a question that he didn't mind answering. "My greatest desire is to marry the love of my life and the mother of my children. Unfortunately, it seems not every woman is eager to marry a prince, so I have some work to do."

With that, he turned his back on the cameras and reporters, leaving his parents to handle them. He'd said what he had come to say. His parents would answer the rest of their questions, as well as inform the media that if there were any other attempts to interrupt Alex and Summer's lives, there would be legal consequences. They had decided that the threat would be taken more seriously if it came from two people who had the power to back it up. They weren't playing any more games. The media attacks had to stop.

Summer sat and stared at the television with Jo sitting beside her. Summer had informed, not asked, Alex that she would be telling her friend about his announcement before the press conference. She felt bad enough that she hadn't been able to share everything with her before now. She wasn't about to let her be blindsided by the news.

"Just, wow," Jo said. "This is too much. And that was so romantic."

Summer just stared at the television, unable to follow the questions as Alex's last statement had taken her breath away. Had he meant what he'd said? Did he really want to marry her, for her, or was this still just about wanting his children to have a father? Since the moment her water had broken, she'd shared every decision that had to be made about the babies with him. They didn't have to be married for him to be present in his children's lives.

But he'd called her the love of his life. The *love* of his life. And he'd declared it to the world, sharing something personal with a group of reporters that he didn't even trust. She'd never had someone love her that way.

"I'm going to go get another look at those beautiful babies," Jo said as the door opened, and Alex walked into the room.

"Are they still going at it?" Alex asked when he saw that his mother and father were still live on the local news channel.

How could he be so calm, when he'd just announced to the world that he loved her? That he wanted to marry her.

"You're wrong," she said, her thoughts pouring from her mouth before she could think better of it. "It's not that you're a prince. Where you came from has nothing to do with who you are now. I'm much prouder to have Dr. Alex as the father of my children then I ever would be to have any old prince."

"As where you came from has nothing to do with who you are," Alex said. He took a seat at the end of the hospital bed and took her hands into his.

"I know you don't care about that, but others..."

"I think I pretty much just told the whole world that I don't care what they think about anything. I love you and I want you to marry me. If not now, then a year from now. Or six years from now. I don't care how long I have to wait."

"But how do I know that it's me that you love? How

do I know that you won't someday walk away from me?" Her heart wanted to believe him, but her head kept throwing up objections. Which did she trust?

Taking her hands in his, he placed them over his heart. "My heart beats for you and our children. That is not a love I can separate. But the way my heart races when I see you, the way your smile sends a jolt of joy through my soul, the way my whole body feels empty when I'm not near you, that is a love I have only for you, and it will never fade. I will always be there to take care of you no matter if you ever agree to be my wife."

The man slayed her with his words, words that mirrored her own feelings for him. Feelings that she had never been able to put into words. She knew so little about love that she didn't know how to describe it.

Suddenly a hidden part of herself, a part deep inside her heart that she had protected since the day she'd realized her father would never return, opened, letting loose a flood of joy and relief that she had never felt. If Alex had the same feelings for her that she felt for him, surely that meant that she could trust that he would never leave her. And she knew if she had a choice, she would never leave him. Oh, he might have to leave her for a week or a day, or even a month, but she would never doubt that he would return to her again.

"Yes," Summer said.

"Yes? As in 'yes, I'll marry you,' yes?" Alex asked.

"Yes, I'll marry you. Because I do love you, all of you. I love the doctor in you that risked your life to save another's. I love the man that holds me in his arms at night while we share our dreams for our children. I even love the prince in you who works so hard to make my dreams come true. I'll live beside you and work with you to give our children all the love possible. Because not only are you the doctor, the lover and the prince, but you will always be more than that."

"And what will that be?" Alex said before he pressed her hands against his lips.

"You will always be mine."

EPILOGUE

THE SOUND OF her heels echoed against the marble floors in the empty hallway. Holding up the front hem of her dress made from yards of white silk and lace, she could only walk so fast without tripping. It would never do for her to show up for her wedding in a dress with a tear, not after all the work Melanie and King Christos had gone through.

She glanced up at the white domed ceiling that was etched with gold vines. Was that real gold? It wouldn't surprise her if it was. She was so far from the little rusted trailer with the water-stained ceiling where she had lived as a child. At this point, pinching herself would do no good. It would take a full-on slap across her face to wake her from this dream.

Because it wasn't a dream. This was her new reality, for better or worse, or so the vows she was about to say said.

Finally reaching the door she sought, she entered to find a room full of nannies along with a head nurse that the king had insisted on, even though Summer and Alex had assured him that his grandchildren were perfectly healthy and in no need of a nurse. They'd made it to three months old without any complications from their premature births.

"Is there something we can do for you?" the head nurse asked.

From the looks she was receiving, it was plain to see that they all thought her crazy. She was supposed to be downstairs in the grand ballroom marrying their new prince.

"I just need to see them," she said as she picked up the bottom of her dress again as she stepped over to the two matching cribs the palace had provided.

Each dressed in the white and gold colors of Soura, they looked like little angels as they slept. Or the little prince and little princess, as they now were.

"I thought this was where I might find you," King Christos said, entering the room. She tried to curtsy as the other women in the room did. As usual, she only felt foolish and awkward. Royal etiquette did not come easy to her even with the training she had received from her future mother-in-law.

"I'm sorry. I didn't mean to put you out," Summer said as the king took her hand, rested it on his arm and led her out of the room. Was the man afraid she was about to bolt?

"It's not that I don't want to marry Alex," she said. "I just can't help wondering how I got here."

"Well, that's simple enough. You fell in love with my son," the king said as they approached the double doors that led to the ballroom where Alex was waiting for her. He patted her hand and for the first time she felt that maybe the man understood her. She was just a simple woman with simple needs. "Are you ready, now?"

"Yes," she said as the doors opened and the crowd who had gathered to observe the marriage of Prince Alexandro and his bride rose from their seats. "I'm ready now."

* * *

The doors to the balcony opened. Alex, holding his son, Jacob Alexander Leonelli, and Summer holding their daughter, Margaret Marie Leonelli, stepped out into the sunshine and were greeted with cheers as his father presented the four of them as official members of the royal house.

A year ago, he would not have thought this was possible. Not the acceptance of his father's people, now his own people, or more importantly, the wife and two babies that made up his own family. Because all this pomp and ceremony was a wonderful change from hiding in the shadows of his brother and father. He no longer had to pretend that Nicholas was just a friend. They could be the brothers they were when no one was looking.

Most importantly, there were no more secrets between him and the rest of the world. His friends had taken the news with nothing but happiness for him. There had been no hard feelings because he had held back part of himself from people who had worked side by side with him.

"There is only one thing I want in this world," he said to Summer, who stood beside him waving to the crowd.

"And what is that, my prince?" she asked, her smile turned toward him now.

"To live out the rest of my life with you and our children," he said before bending down to kiss her lips.

"Of course, Your Highness," Summer said, "because everyone knows that a prince and princess deserve nothing less than to live happily ever after."

* * * * *

MILLS & BOON®

Coming next month

SINGLE DAD FOR THE HEART DOCTOR
Karin Baine

'Is this really necessary?' Lily batted away the heart-shaped helium balloons lining her path but managed to walk straight into the red and pink streamers hanging from the ceiling.

'I think they're keen to reiterate the purpose of this scheme. That it's for heart patients only and shouldn't be abused by those hoping for a lift to hospital appointments or who want us to pop round with a takeaway. Plus it's Valentine's Day so, you know...' Finn's soft voice in her ear caused the hairs on the back of her neck to stand to attention when he was so close she could feel his breath on her skin.

'Oh, I know. Let's bring in all the clichés we can to hammer the point home.' She rolled her eyes. Being deceived by the idea of love and romance wasn't an affliction she suffered from. She left it to naïve young couples who had forever to fool themselves into thinking it could solve everything. Life, and death, had taught her it only complicated things and made life so much harder. All the people she had ever loved had died and, as for romance, it had brought nothing but heartache when she couldn't give her partners what they needed—children and time.

'Something tells me you didn't get any cards in the post.'

'And I suppose you did?'

'Two, actually.'

More eye-rolling. Not only was he handsome but he knew it. One of the worst traits a man could have.

'Let me guess, one came from a grateful young woman who found herself locked out of her house in nothing but a towel and you came to the rescue? And the other…some impressionable schoolgirl whose class had a tour of the fire station?' Boasting about how many cards he'd received was juvenile, and clearly mentioned to get a rise out of her. He had, of course, succeeded.

Finn laughed so hard she actually felt the vibration through to her very bones. 'Actually, they were from my daughters, but it's good to know what you really think about me. You'll have to take my word for it that I'm not a ladies' man who would take advantage of vulnerable females.'

Continue reading
SINGLE DAD FOR THE HEART DOCTOR
Karin Baine

Available next month
www.millsandboon.co.uk

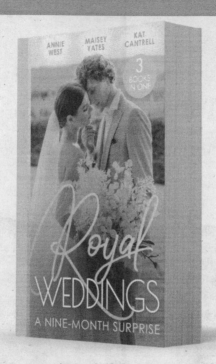